W9-ABE-771

CHALK'S WOMAN

CHALK'S WOMAN

DAVID BALLANTINE

A TOM DOHERTY ASSOCIATES BOOK

NEW YORK

CHALK'S WOMAN

Copyright © 2000 by David Ballantine

This book is printed on acid-free paper.

A Forge Book
Published by Tom Doherty Associates, LLC
175 Fifth Avenue
New York, NY 10010

www.tor.com

DEC   7   00

Forge® is a registered trademark of Tom Doherty Associates, LLC.

Library of Congress Cataloging-in-Publication Data

Ballantine, David.
    Chalk's woman / David Ballantine.
        p. cm
    "A Tom Doherty Associates book."
    ISBN 0-312-87348-4
        1. Orphans—Fiction.   2. Women pioneers—Fiction.   3. Santa Fe Trail—
    Fiction.   I. Title.

    PS3552.A4634 C48 2000
    813'.54—dc21

                                                    00-031695

First Edition: December 2000

Printed in the United States of America

0   9   8   7   6   5   4   3   2   1

To all of this world's Anns
Past, present, and future

1

Large wars have small, important corners, where the damage that they do can sometimes be repaired. A flat wash of blackness lay underneath the bluffs down by the river. It was a part of the same night that filled the streets of the town, growing deeper beyond the entrenchments where forest stretched away forever. The dim horizon line throbbed as faint red flames flickered. This might have been summer lightning someplace far. Except, like shooting stars, the tracks of burning fuses flew, and when mortar bombs struck there was no distance left. Falling shells brought death into the town. Pemberton was trapped in Vicksburg, and so were all his men.

At first Ulysses S. Grant tried to wash over Pemberton's butternut boys, but the rebels stuck. The Union dead lay in windrows facing trenches they couldn't storm. The attacks would have to stop. New York and Ohio boys spoke hopefully, telling each other no general could keep on forever killing his own men. In this they were correct. Instead of attack it was siege, a sensible improvement. While digging was harder than dying, it was a thing men could complain about.

Now at last the Union troops were readied, the guns drawn

close so as to throw harsh iron against the fragile town. Porter's fleet of tin clads increased the devastation as they bombarded from the river. Burning fuses through the night gracefully arched the sky. Where they hit, houses, mules, and people died or got so broken it was an ugly shame. Staying was bad. Leaving was worse. Federals tightly ringed the town.

The dreary days of siege had turned from weeks into months of misery, and the invested city sensed its dying, hammered to death by Union guns.

A Vicksburg lady paused to watch a horse's agony—one slight wound in his sleek black side and at first the blood was only a dribble. The horse was tied to a tree. When he could not reach to gnaw his hurt he turned. The whole body arched to rake the tree's bark with his teeth. Such a little wound, yet so much pain.

Death came in so many different ways. The soldiers claimed they could hear from various whistles, shrieks, and screams which guns were turned against them. It didn't seem to matter much. A churning explosion destroyed a house or made a tiny gout of blood. There were so many ways to die.

On life's side, the woman thought, her clothes were clean and she had—she hefted them—two fine-formed apples in a parchment envelope. An officer had been kind to her. It was a gentleman's gesture amid these ruins. Suffering and death could be intolerable if men should lose their honor.

The owner of the wounded horse argued with three other men. It was only a little wound. Perhaps he would recover. One of his comrades had his pistol drawn, holding it without the hammer pulled so as to fire. The woman watched closely and noticed other soldiers, the tattered infantry, who were gathering one by one.

Once, when bands played, the horses were all sleek and fed and these men marched in proud straight ranks. How her heart had lifted to hear the battle hymns and see the companies stride by in springing step. Now, these men walked, one by one or two at a time. She sensed an aimlessness about them. It was because the siege was tight. There was no place to go. She looked for what those gray, empty faces might say. They were starving and had no expression as they waited for the horse to die.

The horse's blood was now flowing faster, but its agony remained the same. He did not fight the halter that held him to the tree. He fought at what had come to lodge inside him. Corded muscles whipped his body into huge arcs and arabesques. He could no longer find the tree to bite, so now the horse could only scream. These were screams a woman knew, the sounds of an infant's agony grown huge. The horse's owner was crying now, and the man with the revolver holstered it. An artillery man had his short sword drawn. He used it like an axe. The heavy blade flashed above his head. He had both hands to the scaled grip. The woman looked away to see ragged soldiers moving in on the kill. The horse's screaming stopped.

She walked along the broken street toward her undamaged home. There were no shells falling now. How long ago, or was it just last month, this war had been such gallant pageantry.

Then there had been Vesuvius fountains of fire in the night. At first alarm empty houses along the river, soaked with turpentine, had been turned into torches. Everyone—women, soldiers, and children—had come to see the huge black waterbugs of Porter's fleet spit sheets of flame as those Union gunboats ran the river down, past Vicksburg's protective batteries.

She had been at the grand ball. When the gun thunder started, her partner and all other men ran to be with their troops. Suddenly in that bright-lit hall only women in their ball gowns stood. She still kept that dance card with young officers' names inked beside dances never danced.

Everywhere men ran through the light-filled streets. The flares and flaming barns lit the river brightly until it was hard to see the winking flashes of the guns. The billowing smoke reflected muzzle flashes and a glare from the houses and ships that burned. One gunboat, like a child's toy in a roadside rivulet, was caught in the current and then whirled just beneath the batteries. Somehow its armor held, or the crew had the luck, for the ship floated free and fled down the river from her sight.

With clash and clatter, horse artillery arrived to set their guns up in the street. The roar was continuous. The guns would never sound so loud again.

She came back from her memories into the daytime street. The dead horse was hidden by a crowd of quietly struggling men. Two months ago the city had fought back against the gunboats in the river. Today it sat to suffer siege. Those silent men were frightening.

Her eyes returned to memories of the river. Then sparks shot skyward like a comet trail erupting from the ground. The gunners worked in a frenzy but one by one the armored boats fought through. As they did the city had one last, long breath to catch. Fires in the houses died and the river blackened to empty night. When sleep finally came to Vicksburg's people, they knew with sureness, defeat had started. Federal gunboats had run past their batteries.

The town's deeper caves were safe havens against huge mortars in the siege train of the Federals. Frightened people who had lost their homes cowered deep within them, and the army's main hospital had moved into the deepest one. Even the shallow caves were safe unless there, was what people, called a "lucky" hit. It was hard to remember which was which. As she hurried home from the death of the horse, the woman thought, lucky or unlucky for who or whom. The whos did the shooting and the whoms got hit. Once the cannon was discharged— This thought was interrupted. She stopped to stare at a neighbor's house. It had once been so like her own. Now there was just smoke-blackened shambles. Walking by she noticed broken, hanging beams. Three chimneys stood as though expectant, with thick rubble piled around their bases. She had always wondered how houses were made that they could hold together. What a complication of boards and beams. So long a time to build them up and how quickly blown and burnt to hell. She looked around to see if anyone had heard her think so coarse a word.

Inside her own house, all roughness of board and beam still hid behind smooth panelings and plaster. Her clean-scrubbed window-panes winked back the light. She was sure to always have them polished clean. The chimney pots were like little hats and the chimney bodies were comfortably clothed by this building's walls. There was no need for a hearth fire now. The June day was already hot. She called for Ann. Then she saw some movement. It was merely the black girl. "Where's Ann? I mean to say, where is Miss Ann?"

"She be still up the stairs and lying in her room."

Mrs. Baxter's feet were quiet on the carpet-covered stairs. Ann's door was open and she was reading, stretched out on her bed. "You are late abed, Ann, my dear, but certainly with the shades drawn down this room is cool."

Ann wondered if she'd heard a statement, a question, or an order.

"With no food for the belly, Mother, I thought to feed my mind."

"The word most proper, Ann, is stomach." Mrs. Baxter now looked at the book, holding its pages to where a sun's ray had escaped the lowered shades. "Ann, dear, there is fine kilted romance where the Highlands run. I wonder what Mister Scott would have to say of here. For later I have," Mrs. Baxter held up the parchment envelope, "something very pleasant for both of us to eat."

"A package of flour for johnnycake, or have you found a piece of meat?"

"Neither. Apples, two apples. One for each of us."

"Apples, Mother," the girl answered slowly. "What a strange thing to eat when one is starving."

*   *   *

Within the Federal siege line soldiers stuffed brush and logs to corduroy across a sea of mud. Mosquitoes there hungered more for blood than soldiers did for beans. Railroad tracks had been laid to almost everywhere. Without the tracks and the puffing engines that ran along them they could not have ever brought the huge mortars to position. At the emplacements, bombs were piled all around, some empty and the filled ones off by themselves, all readied for their firing.

A bearded sergeant from Vermont cautioned his crew. "Now you swab down good when that gun's had its shot. There's many dead in the artillery whose only sin was pouring powder on a spark."

Boys from Ohio looked around. They'd never seen a mess like this.

"It seems the shame to plow that place so harshly with our guns."

"Shame for what? We didn't start the war."

"That's my words too," a third man said. "The shame is, this siege will be over soon. Then there'll be work enough for everyone." He pointed to the piled shells. "Why in the hell carry them back to the riverboats again? If you have an ass for breaking, just you go ahead, but you do it by yourself. I say let's shoot off every last son-of-a-bitching one. And don't feel bad. I do have doubts if out there," he pointed across the mortar's muzzle to the town, "anything is still alive to kill."

In the late afternoon orders came and the batteries all started up at once. They flung those shells so fast as shucked corn in a barn. The piled pyramids seemed to melt away. With nightfall, the bombardment slackened. Fresh shells would doubtless come up on the train. Firing only occasional shots, the mortar men could load and wait. In their exhaustion they wondered if and when they would be resupplied. If they'd shot through the afternoon this hard, what would they do next week, for Independence Day?

*   *   *

All day long clusters of oil lamps and flickering candles burned to
illuminate the far recess of a bomb-proof cave where time had
stopped. Every twinkle of light was needed where the surgeon
worked. In some cases ambulances came quickly and then raced
away again. But most of the horses, weakened and half starved,
pulled their conveyances at a walk. One slave who still wore his
master's tattered livery held back his lively team. He thought it
lacked dignity to ride dead and dying men at a gallop.

Women bearing candles walked with care through the close
crowd of wounded that spread across the floor. There were no beds.
Some were on litters, which were just canvas stretched on sticks.
Even these were in short supply and most of the wounded lay on
piled straw. A candle was held close to see a man who'd died in his
island of silence. Right next to him, another screamed out in hopeless agony. The walls dripped moisture to mix with the greased
mud on the floor, and blood seeped or flowed from under paper
bandages. In a feeble network, rivulets of running water washed
some of this slime away.

There was only one long table to put broken bodies on. Some
were so far gone they could not live past the knife's first cutting
shock. The doctor motioned others away as soon as he touched their
faces or saw wounds beyond repair. There was little he could do.
The bloody bubbling of a punctured lung or the purple sheen of
handheld guts was a sure sign that a man would die. Fellow soldiers
set and splinted simple breaks, arms and legs, out in the field. Only
when an arm was shattered or a leg was crushed into oozing pulp,
then, at long last there was something to bring to a doctor's skill.
A good one could cut and saw and get it done so quickly that the
patient didn't die from shock.

This doctor had been in this cave forever. It was cut, saw, fold, and stitch, cut, saw, fold, and stitch, over and over again. Then there would come a pause. The doctor motioned another hopeless hurt away to die, a body violated by the steel splinters from the guns. As he cut, the doctor thought. There was only one good thing about this goddamned war: The further west it got, the less the wounded died from tetanus.

"Frazier!"

The doctor looked up from his cruelly wounded patient. For only a second he studied his own upturned blood-soaked palms. The hands were his own, but at the same time they were strangers. He wanted them to save everyone brought to him, but even his hands knew that so many of them would die.

His own name sounded oddly to him. Was he still here? Of a certainty he was, and the fatigue such as few men ever experience engulfed him once again.

Nearby, an army surgeon asked him, "How's it going?" This friendly shred of ebullience was a product of the man's recent arrival.

Frazier wondered and then said, "Not so well. I'd do much better if so many of my patients didn't die."

In the midst of all this slaughter, to be human was to be a foreigner and in this instant he didn't think he would ever be able to doctor anyone again.

A colonel, the front of whose uniform remained a splendor, approached this ring of activity and light. He didn't seem aware of the vomit and the blood cascading down his back. Slung partially over his shoulder, the wounded man he carried spread stains where his lolling head gained some support across the colonel's shoulder. As he made his way, the colonel had trouble seeing the wounded scattered on the floor. He stepped heavily on one man's arm, but the man was safely dead.

The doctor's needle still moved even as he briefly glanced at the colonel's face, which was radiant, like a child come to Christmas morning. "This is a hero, Doctor. I want you to give him your best. He's not my son, yet I'd be a proud man if he was."

As he spoke the colonel looked for a place to set this living body down. Orderlies carried off the amputee as the last stitch was sewn. The colonel's boy was fortunate. A shattered foot to come off—spent cannon ball or caisson wheel, what did it matter now? The doctor picked up his scalpel. It was coated and bloody so he wiped it carefully on his sleeve. The doctor could see this officer didn't want to know what death was really like.

"Every once in a while," the colonel said, "you see something that's so slam-bang gutsy it raises your blood up in your veins like, well, like the maple sap in spring."

The doctor made the first incision. The blood was new and freshly red against the surrounding mud and filth. The colonel turned away. Wasn't that typical? They could shoot and be shot in windrows and in ranks. They could ride mindlessly across a field made from a thousand butcher shops. But damn it! When someone did something to clean up the mess, some little step away from death, that turned their guts to water. The doctor could sew stitches in his sleep, so he repeated the colonel's words to himself. Gutsy and blood rising up like maple sap, and that's the key word, sap. The darling, darling boy, a hero personally delivered by his colonel. The sap, which runs like blood, blood caught up by paper sponges he'd had to use throughout the day. The more daring there is, the surer you have some boy looking in your eyes to wonder for a short time where his arm or leg is gone. Then like as not he'll bleed to death so as not to bother you. All that takes the fun from glory. The words in the doctor's mind were paced evenly like the feeble pulse beats coming from his patient.

God damn it, he, of all people, should know better. Yet from the bluffs, he'd seen the Federal ironclad *Arkansas* make its run. He'd jumped up and down in excitement along with everyone else. That was then. Now he was cured. Weeks later, a Northern newspaper had passed through the lines. Some imbecile writing for it had thought the war was "delightfully, refreshingly daring." The words gushed out, pulsing, like blood from an untieable artery. Those were the words. The son of a bitch's eyes must have been shining to watch that ironclad come down the stream, but then so had his. It seemed long ago, and now he loudly said, "Large balls of horse shit to you, good fellow."

An orderly looked up. The doctor shook his head. Even if that journalist were here and I could say it to him, it would do no good. The son of a bitch would be stupid enough so as not to hear me. The doctor bit off a fresh piece of silk and deftly moistened it to rethread his needle. If there was not too much infection, this boy'd be nearly sure to live.

White faces surrounded him, and naked arms held lanterns and lamps so he might see to work. He dropped a severed arm into the large tub at his side. Before releasing his grasp the doctor held onto the wrist. The fingers were stilled and no longer twisted in agony. All the feeling and all the pain remained buried in the body underneath the bloody stump. For the arm, as he now held it, the war was over. Its owner was being carted away to a straw pallet and a small chance for life again. Before disposing of this relic he looked closely at the hand. He always looked at the hands, powder stained and farmer calloused. It wasn't often you cut away a gambler's clean soft hand, or for that matter any gentleman's.

The arms and legs kept coming off inside this stifling cave. The light from the lanterns swayed and the hot oil smell and the smoke mixed with the smell of blood and pain. Time had stopped long ago and his dripping sleeve was sodden as he mopped his brow for the thousandth time. Suddenly this one operation seemed easier. Had someone finally found a sharpened bone saw, or was this his second wind? As he folded the flaps of skin back over the stump he looked to see. It was neither. He had just cut the left arm from a very young adolescent girl.

*   *   *

A horse had been butchered. Its hooves and hide still rested beside a shambled tree. The shells and bombs of the afternoon had pounded homes into a ruin. Men had come to dig. They found the broken body of a girl. There had been soft moans to guide them to her. As an ambulance drove away the rescuers wondered, in the midst of all those wounded soldiers what would become of her? Some went to dig in other places, or to fall, finally with exhaustion, into sleep. A few had the luck to find whisky in unbroken bottles and used it to soften the night.

There was one small joy in Vicksburg as darkness filled the streets. No one could see or hear it. Deep in the cellar ruins, thin and starved himself, a rare surviving rat, untrapped and uneaten through all the siege, came upon the freshly broken body of a woman beside two perfect apples in a shattered parchment envelope.

2

Ann had gone to wash where she could be alone. She wouldn't care a bit should Indians come to kill her. She would wash and she would stretch and she would have some time, maybe even minutes, to be by herself in privacy. She ran through cottonwooded bottoms. The stream was near. Where it was shallow she could skip through the water, throwing wings of spray that soaked her dress. Her dress was so poor and a thin cotton thing, its wetness made for immodesty. In a still, unruffled pool she looked down. Instead of its actual brown-pink the wet dress made her skin almost look as if it was a faded gingham blue. No harm. It was warm out in the sun, and the dress would soon dry. Here it was cool and the air was soft. Riding in the wagons, that sun beat down so hard as to make a burning oven of each and every day. The trail dust roiled in choking clouds and all of a sudden you couldn't see anything except the nearspan's ox's tails waving. It was a torture to ride across these sunbaked plains.

For the last five years she'd lived from place to place. She wouldn't ever tell what it had been like in a Southern orphanage in those years just after the war had been lost. They called it an asylum, but Ann always wondered if an insane asylum would have been better because she couldn't imagine anything that could have been worse then that place they kept for orphans.

She knew better than to bitch, even to herself, either then or now. She'd learned early to look for any slivers of happiness that could be found. There'd been damn-all food and little heat in winter, but there were islands of human decency and she knew enough to cling to each one when it floated by.

Ann clearly remembered an old woman, who was nearly blind. She'd been a slave and now she worked in the kitchen at the orphanage for not much more than her board and keep. The war and all that killing hadn't changed things much for that small old person with a wrinkled face. One day she told Ann, "Having less arms than most you'll have to get the strength you need from someplace that's deep inside you. Keep your eyes open for a way of getting through and don't waste your time breeding tears." Ann remembered and had obeyed both pieces of advice.

Now, it was the kind Mrs. Eleve she was traveling with. She'd lived with them back in St. Joe, and she'd live with them, she guessed, in Oregon. She'd been with them since the orphanage. They'd taken her out as a pious Christian act, but then Mrs. Eleve had fired her hired girl on that same day she'd brought Ann home. There was a Mr. Eleve too. He came to mind most always as an afterthought, a decent man who'd gotten overshadowed by his wife. Now she was living with the Eleves in the wagon, except for these few minutes when she did not have to be with anyone except herself.

As usual Mrs. Eleve would bitch, but for now that could not matter. This was the place where she needed to be. She'd surely get told about charity and about good nature, and that she was taking advantage of both. She'd been taken in. Saved from starvation and various other unspecified difficulties, and all she did was take. What did she take? She took advantage. Ann felt she did her share fine. She couldn't see that Mrs. Eleve ever did all that much. Often Mrs.

Eleve would say, "One mouth to eat usually comes with two hands to work." And while she wouldn't look exactly pleased, she would always stop and stare when Ann had to puzzle through a double-handed chore. Sometimes, it seemed Mrs. Eleve didn't want it to get done.

There were birds flying here and maybe even nests were close by. A big fox squirrel had seen her. It took fright, and she watched it run along a branch until at the last moment it made its jump. She held her mouth open. Then she shook her head and smiled. Every time, at the last possible moment and sixty feet above the ground, it grabbed itself back to life to head down the branch that had been caught. Where it joined the trunk the squirrel would start its climb in this new tree, to where the branches vanished into air. Then it was time to make the jump again.

Watching the squirrel as she walked, Ann didn't see the Conestoga until she was upon it. This place was nearly hidden from the breaks beside the river. What was a single wagon doing here and why was it separate from the train? Past the wagon Ann could see the small place for graze where six oxen chomped away. Grass was thick where the meadow came up from the stream. Ann looked around carefully. No one was watching after the animals.

She walked over to the wagon to tell them hello. She didn't recognize the painted color nor the lines—it was a fine, trim wagon. It didn't seem right to not see a single person where this wagon was parked. But then a little boy appeared. She had not seen him before, and he didn't speak even after she smiled. He was probably around seven or maybe even eight years old. To know how small a child can be, she thought, see him when he stands beside a Conestoga's rear wheel. Later she would look at this child and he would shrink down even more. He was joined by a boy maybe just starting up his teens. He held a baby clumsily cradled in his left arm. Ann always looked at arms. As he turned toward her she could see his

right one too. It ended in a hand that held a revolver pointed
straight at her. Ann stood very still.

"You by yourself?" The boy was talking over the muzzle of his
gun, and he looked around from here to there as though he were
afraid.

Ann nodded her head. It was true. Right now she was by herself
and that is what she told him.

"Well, how in the hell do you eat if you are by yourself?"

"First, there's no need to swear. Second, to answer your question, what I can't find or beg off people, I steal."

The boy kept his revolver on her. "Well, you ain't going to
steal from us, I do not believe."

"No, I don't believe I will steal from you." Ann looked around
and then asked, "Where are your folks?"

"Dead."

"Well, if your folks is dead, what are you doing here?" These
were orphans like herself and maybe she from out of long experience
might be able to be of help.

"Oh." The boy paused. "Here is where our folks is dead. They're
dead in the wagon. So far as I can tell they've been dead for two
days now." As he spoke the boy threw the revolver to the ground
and he thrust the baby toward Ann with both his hands, adding,
"And I don't think this baby'll make it through on just a sugar tit."

Ann had always wondered how she would ever hold a baby.
She did it easily, but the baby stank of shit and she would need
help to wash it clean.

From where the oxen grazed, another child walked toward
them. She was small, yet older than the little boy. It had been her
job to watch after the stock.

Ann could see that a cow grazed with the oxen. "Won't she
drink the cow's milk?" she asked. "Or don't you know how to
milk it?"

"That's just nonsense talk," the little eight-year-old boy said. His sister nodded in agreement. "Everybody knows how to milk a cow, but she's just gone and dried up on us."

Breasts were in proximity and the baby was hardly in Ann's arm when it tried to find its way through her dress. With only one hand to hold the child there was no easy way for Ann to fend it off. So she moved it up until its head was at her shoulder's height. The baby's sense of loss was immediate. A rage howl started.

"Good God, I do wish that there was some milk for the baby." The teenage boy looked frankly at the drying top of Ann's dress. Beneath it her young breasts showed, high-formed and perky. She colored, but the boy couldn't be shy. He was thinking about keeping the baby alive.

"Don't you know nothing?" Ann paused. She wanted to say his name.

"Jim."

"Jim, human being women are just like animals. They don't come into milk until they have their children born. Having milk all the time would be like swinging an axe when there wasn't any trees."

"Having milk now would feed the baby." Jim answered her back with a hint of apology. He'd seen the blush start. "But if we don't get it, then we have to puzzle something else. For now let's try another piece of dried beef for her to gum."

The baby wasn't content, but was quiet. She held the sliver of meat, sucking on it avidly. "Darn, if we had a goat in milk," Jim observed, "we could put the baby on the tit."

The small girl answered him. "Well, we don't. And if you're going to wish for things that we don't have, you might better wish Mother alive again. We need her more than some dumb old nanny goat."

"I'm sorry, Margaret." Jim turned to Ann. "I guess we kids

were near played out. We've just been sitting here sad for two days now. Miss . . ."

"My name is Ann."

"Ann, maybe we'd better get ourselves yoked up and come back to your wagon train with you. Or maybe we'd just better walk back and get some of the men to come . . ."

"I've just got a feeling," Ann said, "that you had better do as much for yourself as you can. If you or we are going to that wagon train, let's get there on your own. Can you yoke up the team?"

"With all of us I think we'll get it done." They brought in the oxen, which were merely taking half bites in the deepest grass. It took some time to puzzle out the traces. The children had just let them fall when they'd freed their team out to pasture.

The cow was tied behind. The brake was off. The little boy came from behind the wagon just as they began to move. He'd take his place and, with his little whip, he'd walk beside the team. Ann, peering around the canvas, now saw how small that child was. It wasn't only the size of the wagon she thought. Parents newly dead flood their children with littleness. Ann reminded Jim to fetch the pistol he had thrown. It was something that they might be needing.

The six oxen moved the wagon easily, and where they crossed the meadow the wheels left two crushed tracks of green behind. They forded the stream where it ran shallow over a pebbled bar. Then, from out of the lacework of shadows, the wagon lurched into the burning sun.

The wagon train was circled even for this midday stop. The oxen grazed under guard. Tripods and cooking fires were scattered in the enclosure. The river bottom would have been a pleasant change, but the wagon boss had said they'd water when they passed. He didn't want to halt where there wasn't clear view all around. So from the encampment and from the herd, all could see a single wagon approach.

The Eleves watched together. There had been no question of them waiting for Ann's return. The wagons moved and theirs moved with them. If Ann didn't find her own way back, so much the worse for her. Mr. Eleve gestured with his thumb. "Looks like they's going back the other way. Maybe they got Pike's Peak busted."

"If they really are going back, they'll sure be able to pick up a wagon load or two of fine furniture on the way. There is a trail of things across this continent."

"Maybe they got broken down, although them oxen is bringing her along quite smart. Maybe they got broken down and left behind."

Mrs. Eleve shook her head. "People wouldn't leave a wagon like that. I see people mostly being helpful to each other."

"When they can, Martha, when they can. A lot of times in the war people came to the aid of others. I saw and I heard of many a sick man that was brought to his own regiment and saved from going into hospital. Back then our uniforms were a fellowship. I talked to men so poorly then, that they wondered who the man that saved them was. Many told that they wouldn't know if they sat beside him the next day. No, they'd be back safe and they'd come awake only knowing they'd been helped by someone. But all that was in the war, and that war is over now." Mr. Eleve removed his slouch hat to hold it against the sun. "That's our Ann riding up on the seat."

"I was wondering where she'd got off to or at. She's not 'our Ann.' She's naught but a broken girl who eats our food two times faster than she works."

The wagon halted outside the circle in front of the Eleves. Both of them stepped forward. Jim tied down the brake. They were joined by several others, and a small gathering stood looking at the children on the seat. The wagon boss rode over from the herd.

"What you doing up there, Ann?"

Before Ann could answer him, and although Ann held the baby ·
in her arm, Mrs. Eleve added, "Get down off that seat right now
and come back to your work. Having you I don't need to wait for
moving out to get new water hauled."

Ann handed the baby to Jim, and then she climbed from the
seat to the wheel and then to the ground. The men watched each
one of her movements and no one offered to help. As the wagon
boss saw her, she was somewhat big. But she easily missed being
a big woman. Looked like a strong one, a hard puller with a long
waist. Held high everywhere, and legs, as she landed, that pushed
hard against the ground. Mr. Eleve watched her too, but from a
corner of his eye.

The wagon boss noted that there were only children on the
wagon. He naturally addressed the oldest male. "What you doing
here, boy?"

"Did you forget and leave your schoolbooks back there in St.
Joe?" a man named Thompson asked. There was half a laugh around
for that. Jim shook his head just once. With his one free hand he
fiddled on the brake lever stay.

"I ask you where's your other wagons, boy?" The wagon boss
was properly disturbed to see anything out here that didn't fit.

"Four days on ahead, sir," Jim answered crisply.

"And where's your dad and momma?"

Jim motioned toward the back of the wagon with his thumb.

"They's maybe sleepin' through the middle of the day?" Both
Mr. Eleve and the wagon boss looked hard at the questioner, but
there were others who gave Thompson his second laugh.

"I've heard that said, sir." Jim was speaking to the wagon boss,
but he looked at the men, whose laughter stopped.

"They sick?" Mrs. Eleve demanded. Several of the crowd
stepped back and away from the wagon's front. The boy shook his
head.

"Indians?" the wagon boss asked.

Again Jim shook his head.

"Then what, boy?"

"From what little I know I believe they was choleraed . . . to death." The last two words were mumbled and they went unheard.

The wagon boss back-stepped his horse. "Now, get that brake off, get that wagon away from here. You be downwind from us. Then we'll think over all of this." He knew about cholera. There was no need to ask about it further. Cholera was just another name for death. Like most sickness it seemed to come from nowhere, and no one knew why it killed some and spared others. The ones it killed, it killed quick, and while the reason of it wasn't known the symptoms surely were. The victims' eyes got sunken and their hands were dried out like stale prunes. It was as if a person's moisture was gone from them and then in a little while they were dead.

The smaller children, Margaret and Bill, stood undecidedly at the head of the team. They had been watching the adults and hoping that one of them would come forward, preferably one of the thicker women in a long wool skirt and sunbonnet, just like every woman wore. Then they could rush into the folds of that skirt to hide. Once there they'd feel a woman's sheltering arms reaching down around them. No one came forward, so they just stood until the one-armed girl, Ann, came to put her hand to the lead ox's halter. Jim threw off the brake. The wagon moved again. Bill heard only one woman call. She wasn't one of the thick ones who held people. She was one of the scraggly ones who yelled at them.

"Ann, you come back here this minute. I tell you. Are you fixing to die?"

Mrs. Eleve called. Ann ignored her. It was the first time that she had been able to do so, though she was still civil enough to shake her head from side to side.

The wagon boss was already bringing men with spades. The yoked oxen were standing, and the cow found a little grass off at the far end of her tie. "Burial comes pretty sudden," Ann said, looking up at Jim on the wagon seat.

"I was hoping for something else. That's why we were waiting. But I'm past knowing what I was waiting for."

A hundred yards downwind from the wagons, spades cut into the prairie sod. Thompson opinioned that one hole would be enough. He was overruled. One man walked over with his spade to dig. He didn't speak but started a second grave beside the first. "I said that we could do them both in one." Thompson was going to make a point of this. He wiped his forehead to show how hard it was to dig.

The new man didn't stop, and he spoke in rhythm with the shoveled earth. "Thompson, it is no more work for you to do if I dig here." Looking at one particular shovelful before dumping it, he paused, spilled the dirt, and then continued, slowly. "But with all of us here maybe not an hour from our own ends, I think it right to plant these folks with as much dignity as we can manage here." He paused again. There was no answer and Thompson went back to his spade. Other men joined and very soon, through the grass they had two brown, oblong openings.

Jim called down. "Thank you, mister, for that second grave."

The man touched his fingertips to his brow. Then he walked to stand beside the isolated wagon. The two small children were at the head of the team, and it was their pleasure now to pet the right lead ox's face.

The wagon boss called, "Hey, Ann. Or . . ." He was looking at Jim.

"Jim's my name, sir."

"Jim, we are going to have a funeral. There's no glass-sided wagon with waving plumes so as men can slide the coffin slowly out on rails from the back. There's none to touch the bodies but yourself or Ann here. Someone just stand in the back of the wagon and a man will sling you a rope. Put the loop under the arms and draw it tight because the other end of that rope'll be around a saddle horn. It's the only way to move bodies without touching them.

"There's no pain in dead bodies, Jim, though it does look hellishly mean. So maybe, for a while, take the little ones away on a walk across the prairie."

Thompson complained, but he'd do things too. He came riding up to the back of the wagon fast. He put a small loop right in under the canvas. Ann had stayed behind. It was sad and sick in the wagon. She tried to only half look at the body of the man as she struggled to stretch the loop and secure it under the arms of his wife. The horseman kept at a distance now. His horse was moving its feet up and down in its own nervous manner. Ann called out, but low enough so the children couldn't hear. "Take it easy at first because I'll have to help her over the gate."

It wouldn't do for the body to catch against something in the wagon. It slid as the rope tightened. Ann guided as the dead woman moved. Then she lifted. This was straining. She didn't know if she'd be able to manage the man. The stiff body tilted and then hit down on the ground with a thump that seemed to shake the world. Even remembering that dead people didn't hurt, that thump made a hard fist at the bottom of Ann's gut. Thompson spurred his horse and the stiffened corpse bounced along behind. Ann turned away. She didn't want to see how quick and neat he was to snake the body to its grave. All the men who had been waiting at both sides of the opening rushed up with spades. Cascading soil poured upon the final resting place as one man carefully used his shovel to cut the throwing rope. A fresh running noose was tied and Thompson was back and waiting. There was a blanket under the man and that made pulling easier. He wasn't huge, but when his body caught halfway out of the wagon, Ann could lift no further. She got her back against a crate and used her feet to push him on his final way. The thump was just as loud, and then again the bouncing race.

Ann didn't watch that or the final frenzy of earth and flashing spades.

She went out to bring the children back. The men were forming two even mounds. The cleansing earth covered, and everyone came to stand around.

Jim held the baby. The two smaller children were in front of him, going nowhere.

"It was best that you walked off," Ann said. "I don't think the baby would understand putting people in the ground."

The baby fed contentedly from a bottle. There were fresh cows with the wagon train, and women had come forward to give many cans of milk.

"I don't think it's big enough to understand," Jim said, although he'd not yet found his own time to cry.

Ann shrugged. "I don't know how old a child needs to be before it understands or doesn't, but it was a risk we didn't have to take."

The two smaller children turned with them and walked back in the quiet careless way they had come from the wagon, so as to join the gathering. No one came forward to say much and people moved to avoid touching them. Finally it was the wagon boss who said, "If somebody has a Bible."

"There's one in our wagon," Margaret said. "I'll run and get it."

"Hold on. I don't want no cholera Bible. I don't want nothing that's been so long close to sickness. I'll just say what I can remember." The wagon boss stood silently for a moment. People quieted. He cleared his throat. Once he started he went on without hesitation.

"We have walked into the valley of the shadow of death and we have been unafraid, because we have walked out the other side."

"Well, there's two here that didn't make it out. I'm sorry there was so little we could do for them. It is naught but a Christian burial and these few words." He paused and, looking up, continued.

"To God up there, please look after them. I do not know them so I do not know their needs. All I can ask is, please God, do your best. Amen."

Ann's brow wrinkled. Somehow it wasn't a satisfactory service, but it had been arranged and performed in a hurry and was better than no words at all. Jim agreed with her. It was quiet, and they looked around to find the children gone. Margaret and Bill were walking back to the wagon hand in hand.

Ann wondered about them. It was so hard to know what little children believed death to be. Come to think, she had no easy thoughts of it. Some time later when she wandered back to the graves, Ann saw the monuments that Jim, or maybe the small ones, had made. At the head of each grave a short pole had been set. The mother's bonnet was tied to one, not lashed but tied as though it were being worn. As the sun began to set, shadows came to fill its hood.

Earlier, inside the emptied wagon, Margaret had held the bonnet by its ribbons. Bill had picked up his father's heavy boots. He thought to put them on the grave as if taken off at the end of the day. Margaret said that they needed to be saved. Jim would grow into them soon enough. The little boy did not insist. After looking at the bonnet, he'd gone to get his father's bummer hat. His father had worn it sometimes when he told the family about the war. It was faded blue and shabby now. When Bill placed the hat on its post he said, "That'll help Pa remember all the places that he's been." It was balanced precariously on the stake, and as the boy withdrew his hand it slued around. The late sun reflected only from the visor. The brass ornament of the hundred and twentieth New York had tarnished dull. The boy set the cap back, wadding up a ball of dry grass to hold it properly in place. Now both hats faced back toward the East. When the sun came again tomorrow those two hats would be waiting to welcome it.

Jim saw how people looked at the wagon as though it was lost and ownerless. He didn't like their looks much, so he went and found his dad's revolver holstered beside the seat. After checking the chambers for loads and the nipples for caps, he stuffed the gun inside his belt. He'd cooked up some mush sweetened with molasses. That was a treat for the little ones. Now they were fast asleep. The baby was milk filled and sleeping too, at least for this little while. He'd put her in the cradle that hung from the wagon bows but snubbed it so as not to swing too far.

Mrs. Eleve had it all planned. The children, just like Ann, needed decent people's charity. She'd take them in and see them through to wherever the settlement was to be. Then she and Mr. Eleve would have all this extra gear. That ox team was very nearly the best in the train. When they got to the West Coast there might be a good home for orphan children there. No, that was foolish thinking. Nothing formal would have happened yet. She couldn't suppose they had proper homes already to place orphaned children in. God knows they should. Mrs. Eleve knew that homes were the best places for children who didn't have any parents nor kin keeping track of them.

The wagon boss kept the animals a couple of extra hours on graze. After that it almost wasn't worth the trouble moving wagons in the late afternoon. The burial had taken time. It seemed too harsh not to give the dug ground at least a few watched hours for settling. The kids had tied up their parents' hats for tombstones out here. Back home there was marble and granite for those who could pay and there was bluestone for the poor. Even that lasted well. The wagon boss couldn't remember seeing a tombstone that had worn out. But daylight held on well, and they still had time to move out for the night's encampment he had chosen. The animals were brought in and hitched. The circle of wagons became a line, and in passing they watered lightly at the stream. If his guidebook was to be believed, they'd come to it again a few miles further on. There were no trees growing there and they would camp beside the water.

The book was true. There were hardly any trees. The river was wide and shallow between low-falling banks. As always, the wagons circled and the night camp formed. The six new oxen from the children's wagon were turned into the herd. Oxen by themselves were safe. They didn't sicken from the cholera.

In the dusk a vague shape of white canvas was off by itself. For the wagon boss's job to be done right, he shouldn't let them kids spend the night out there. They could have their hair lifted and be stiff and fly-crawled by the morning. Would it make too much difference to what their chances were alone? In particular the three little ones. There was no going back to St. Joe, and kids couldn't take a wagon west. He'd have tomorrow to find out who would or who could take the children in, of course after they'd been watched awhile to see if they had the cholera in them. Then he'd also have to see who'd bring the wagon along. If men were to take the job for hire, well, it would about come to the full value of the wagon and its traps. For these children it wouldn't matter either way. Hiring men would be the same as if they left their wagon standing where they'd come up with the train. If that was what was to be done, well then it would be a shame not to leave off one of the poorer rigs. One of those could end up delaying the entire train some far place along the line. If people took these kids in then they should get to keep the wagon too. That was the least the kids could do. It wasn't only that they would lose their wagon anyway.

Here he was, now a wagon boss and guide. He'd been a soldier. Well, that was true of nearly everyone. There wasn't much to guiding. The trail of wagon wreckage and animal bones led all the way to either California, or if you headed north, to Oregon. He did make sure all stood to just before the dawn. Some people didn't feature that. Too bad. He meant to get them to Sacramento or the

Willamette. That was the reason that he took their pay.

Before bedding down himself he'd ride the circle round. It wasn't a large train. There were only fifteen wagons, but they'd made a good late-May start. Water was down. Grass was up. The ground was firm. Soon people would be going West in the railroad cars, but how would they take their teams with them and what would they do for wagons once they got there?

There was all the animal noise, and people still moved around. He wished sometimes they wouldn't do it. There was time enough for wakefulness by day and when it was the time to go on guard. Some was young and they would bustle. He had no wagon of his own, so he spread his bedroll underneath the Eleves'. She was a loud woman in the day, yet a quiet one by night. Some of the other emigrants, little matter how many children they already had, it was an embarrassment to try and sleep beneath their wagons. Firelight flicker reached him, and he could see where the night's first pickets walked just on the outside of the circle.

Turning in his blankets, he could watch the flame glow on wagon spokes. He listened to the night guard's boots go marching back and forth. Hovering on the edge of sleep he thought about those kids. He'd shared them all out, yet to think on it, their wagon and them too had wallowed in that choleraed death. There was too many ways, all different, of dying on the trail. Again, how could he leave them here just to die alone out on these prairies? Before his thought could finish he had a need to listen. Now, what in the hell was that? There was a liquid rushing sound, and he hoped some son of a bitch wasn't pissing against a wagon wheel. He was hard put to keep the campgrounds clean, and it was surely a pain to try and be a one-man sanitary commission. No, it was a pulsing noise, yet strange, as if someone was milking a cow. By moving slightly he could see between the wheel spokes. It was the Eleves' hired girl. She was milking their old brindle cow with one hand into the bucket held between her knees. That was why the sound came through so strange. She rose and carefully put the milking stool back up in the wagon. Now she was walking right by him to go outside the circle. From here he could near reach out and touch her. He got up on one elbow and hissed so that she started slightly. Then, bending down, she looked at him. What a smile that girl could glow across her face. Her arm was through the bucket's hoop so she could put one finger to her lips to tell she wanted quiet. He nodded back at her because it was figured now. She was taking the milk out to the kids in the wagon. It was Mrs. Eleve's milk, and giving it to kids had probably not been one of Mrs. Eleve's thoughts.

A bird called just between night and morning. Everyone was up, and the men were grumbling to stand to arms. For a while yet, until it was light, there would be no fires. "This part of the morning is the best for sleeping," Mr. Eleve said as he stretched and yawned.

"And the best time for dying too. So stand your watch," the wagon boss replied, "and we'll keep both our eyes rubbed and bright."

In an hour people had fires lit and a cooked breakfast eaten. Then they hurriedly washed up and kicked their fires out. Horses were harnessed or oxen yoked. The wagon off by itself had been the first to have its team harnessed up. There was no fuss, and those children led their big oxen out just as if they were household pets. Ann helped them, and they'd been in and out so sharp no one had time to worry if or how their sickness could be caught.

The numerous children of the wagon train watched every move. Emotions ranged from awed interest to the blackest jealousy.

"Imagine to have a wagon all your own," the fourteen-year-old Miles boy said. "Why, a person could go to anywheres."

Mrs. Miles looked down at her boy. "Rather than own a

wagon," she said, "I am certain sure those children there would wish to have their parents back to life."

The boy knew better than to make a face and shrug. With harness leather in hand his father could whop from almost anywhere.

The wagon boss had nearly forgotten about the children, but seeing their wagon reminded him. Later, in council, everyone would have to figure what to do. Looking at his stem-winder gave the day an official start. It was just seven and a good time to be moving. Again the circle led off into line. There was a space and then the children's wagon tagged along behind.

As the wagons moved, Mrs. Eleve called down to her husband from the seat. "I've milked the cow this morning by myself."

He walked at the head of the team. "Well, I harnessed up by myself, so what's the matter?"

"If that girl's hiding out someplace to shirk chores, I'll peel the skin off her . . ." Mrs. Eleve stopped. Any reference to a woman's body was frightening to her, and particularly if it was this girl's. She stared down at her husband for a second time. She'd seen that snake, standing now beside the lead ox, look close enough on Ann, despite the fact of one arm gone. What would it take, she wondered, to make that old lecher turn his eyes away from any skirt-wrapped thing? Only blindness would really do the job, but no hope of that. He had the eyes of a lynx.

Ann led the final team. Sometimes she walked backward to look up to the wagon's seat. Jim had the baby with him, and some of last night's milk was in the bottle that he held. It was lucky they had the cow to sneak milk from, because Ann didn't know what else a small babe might eat. The canned milk they'd save for emergencies. Sometimes the little girl and boy, Margaret and Bill, would ride the wagon. More often they would walk beside her at the head of the team. Ann stepped out hard, striding long and proudly. There was no need for moving prim. The day's heat wasn't up yet, and there was grass here under the wheels. As yet no trail dust billowed over them.

They'd been quickly to the stream. The yoked oxen watered standing. Ann had the barrel on the wagon filled and she faintly heard screaming coming after her. Now, if those screams were faint it figured Mrs. Eleve was a fair distance away. She'd see her soon enough when the wagons stopped for noon. Maybe she'd suggest Jim help her with her chores. Then she'd have time to help Jim and the little ones with theirs. That wouldn't work out, although the first half would suit Mrs. Eleve fine. From past experience Ann knew a scream was building in that woman to blush a steamboat's whistle. Well, if there was no way to avoid it, she'd spend the morning nice and then she'd take it when it came.

The children seemed happy around her, and it was not as if they'd just left their parents dead behind them. There were few questions from the younger ones. Mostly she answered them with the pious hopes she'd been taught in Sunday school. Whether these were true she didn't know, but for now they'd have to do as comforting. Maybe the questions came later, because she'd left her own parents somewhere, and she always wondered where they were. She well remembered having a mother and a dad. It was along about the time she'd also had another arm. She'd never seen her mother dead but surely her mother would have come after her had she been able. Her dad had gone missing. Older folks told her that missing was an especial army word. It didn't mean lost or strayed. Mostly it meant, he's dead and we can't find the body. So as soon as those hats got blown away or stolen, those two people would be missing too. No, that wasn't true because so long as Jim and the children were alive they'd remember where they were buried, and she would always remember too.

There was a nice light breeze blowing and the sky was piled

high with clouds. She'd feel their fluffiness and just watch the way they glided. It would be noontime soon enough.

When the train stopped, one by one the wagons bunched. At this halt they didn't circle. Ann and Jim rushed to get the ox yokes off so Ann could run forward to her chores. Even fifteen wagons was a fair distance to go. But as things turned out there was no need for hurry. They had the first yoke off and were started on the second when they saw Mrs. Eleve approach. Ann thought she was mostly hopping as she came along down the line of wagons. Mrs. Eleve hopped when she was mad and she hopped when she was glad. When she was mad she just hopped a little higher. Ann turned to face her.

"Ungrateful little bitch," Mrs. Eleve said. She had to reach up slightly to slap Ann across the face. Ann wouldn't put her own hand up to touch the smart. She wouldn't speak either. This was something usual and something she could bear. She had taken worse. Ann could bear it. Bill could not. Standing beside her as a child, he was small. Springing like an unleashed dog, he appeared huge to Mrs. Eleve. The little boy got in his bite right through the heavy skirt and petticoats. It wasn't just a snap. He grabbed both arms around her leg and shut his eyes to gnaw on down. Mrs. Eleve had been yelling before. She was shrieking now. Men were running, and Jim knew not to mix with them. It would be dangerous. In addition there was the baby, awake and screaming too.

"Margaret, take your sister, please." Jim said this as he made his grab for Bill. Ann was helping him to pull the child clear and the noise from Mrs. Eleve was a horrible thing to hear. The woman didn't have a stick nor umbrella so she couldn't get at little Bill too well. He held, she screamed, and they pulled. It occurred to Jim that if Bill would open his mouth it might be easier to drag him away. At the same time Bill realized that if they were to pull much harder he'd leave some of his new grown-up teeth in this woman's leg, so he let go his bite.

Mrs. Eleve sputtered down. Jim held his brother and his brother spat. The material had been coarse and musty in his mouth, like an old feed sack filled with sticks. Ann, completely composed, stood facing Mrs. Eleve nearly nose to nose. For one second she wanted to punch her. She wanted to throw her clenched fist right out from the shoulder, and then roll every body muscle that she had in back of it. Slowly she unclenched the fist she'd held at her side.

Just about everybody was gathered now. The wagon boss was there and so was Mr. Eleve. He was on the outside of the crowd and couldn't seem to push a way through. However, when the screaming stopped, he was there soon enough.

"I'm bit."

"Where at, dear?"

"She held the back of her leg high up. "Where I am holding it of course."

"I can't help it if I can't see it."

Mrs. Eleve looked around at all the others. A wound like this could not be shown in public. Some faces showed concern. Others tried to hide the gladness found from a small hole in the boredom of the usual trailing day.

"And *you*, girl," Mrs. Eleve screamed. "Get back to your place. You are the cause of all of this."

Ann didn't know what "all of this" was, but "this" suddenly became a time for saying no. She shook her head.

Margaret held the baby. She was seated up on the box, and "all of this" was starting to look unpleasant. There were so many people gathered out in front of the wagon. Bill was little. Jim was bigger, but there was only one of him. If he got pressed maybe she could throw him down the Navy Colt. With one hand she reached back to feel the protruding butt where the open holster was tied handy to the wagon seat. She was too little to shoot a gun herself, and it would not be right anyway. This close the noise would be so fearful to the baby. If it was needed she'd just toss it down. For now the oil-smooth wood grip was comfort for her hand.

The wagon boss was the first to speak. "It's harsh, Son, but you kids can't manage. Even if you could, we'd get held back just out of worry over you. We'll divide you up with them that will take you. Then we'll get on to Oregon. I wish there was another way."

Jim had thought to sweet-talk the woman who'd been bit. But this came from a man, and the head one too. It was a whole lot more serious. All alone and when the wagon was down in the breaks he'd wondered how he'd keep himself and the kids alive. Then this wagon train had appeared and it looked like there would be adults to take them through. He'd felt that with them, the family wagon had a chance, but that wasn't what the wagon boss was saying.

"It's our wagon, sir, and our team. And I have a mind to keep it."

Thompson was standing close. "Every person keeps what he can, Son. But for keeping things, the first rule is that a person should be grown-up enough to do it."

Most of the men wanted to be easy on the boy. Several voices joined in. "If you can't handle it, you can't keep it. People that take you in have something coming." Many heads nodded and all the adults agreed.

"I had a mercy in my soul," Mrs. Eleve pointed as she spoke, "for that little boy who attacked me like some wild, vicious animal. I would have gladly looked to him and I would have taken in them all, his poor brother and his sisters too. But now, I will not nourish a viper at my breast."

"I guess that vipers don't get very thirsty, ma'am," Margaret called down from the seat. The baby was awake and hungry now.

Jim didn't hear his sister. He was thinking hard and he could only say, "Let us have some time and think all of this over, because . . . because I've got to talk to all the other kids."

"To what other kids?" the wagon boss inquired. He wasn't

being mean, just curious. All he could see was two children, around eight or ten years of age, and a babe in arms.

Goddamnit, kids was uppity now. The spans were restless. They hadn't been unyoked. Thompson wanted talk to be over with. "We aren't waiting and we aren't feeding. You do like you are told . . . or damn it, you'll just stay out here on these plains and rot."

"Rot," Mrs. Eleve seconded him. "Rot, hell, they'll die before they rot." She looked at Jim. Ann still stood before her. She also glanced quickly up to the wagon seat. "If you are talking about staying behind, then you are going to die. All you kids. Here on this prairie by yourselves, you are all going to die."

Her husband tried to shush her while Ann spoke. "Everyone's going to die, Mrs. Eleve. Even you. For now, and just this once, you may be right. If dying comes I know about it because part of me is gone already." Ann indicated where an arm should be. "I'd just rather do it here with these kids, and soon if need be, then die with you, no matter how long it took." Ann had finally said the words. The husband looked dumbfounded, but Mrs. Eleve knew what she was hearing. This wasn't any longer a broken little girl before her. Then Ann spoke so quietly and evenly that no one else could hear. "Your screaming's finished from hurting me now, and don't talk of all our troubles and of death so needless in front of ones so young. Even you haven't rotted enough so as to want fear put into them."

Mrs. Eleve left shaking her head. The crowd drifted apart. Nothing had been accomplished for now. Jim finished unyoking the team. He showed Bill where he wanted the animals to graze. It was off a ways and separated from the teams of the wagons up ahead.

While the stock was at its midday feed the kids gathered for a council of their own. They all waited for Jim to begin. He started suddenly. "Now, you look here, kids. There's nothing left, save us and our wagon. What I mean is, we have the wagon and the cow, and well, we're what's left of our family. Dad and Ma so much wanted to live in Oregon. The plan was to find a place for us, I guess to grow up on that land. So, first we owe them to stay in good health and alive. Second, we owe them to get on up that trail. We owe them at least to get this part of the family to where all of us were started for."

Ann whistled. "Jesus, and how are you going to take it all along and through to there?" She looked back and forth along the wagon and she didn't forget to note the presence of the baby.

"I wasn't so much just thinking of me all alone and by myself," Jim said. "Out there in front of those others I thought I heard you stand along with us."

"Well, if that's what I said, I'd best just do it. In fact I may have to, because that woman doubtless won't want to have me back."

Various groups came out from the gathered wagons. They had a way of looking that showed they thought to see something that was theirs, if only they could puzzle out the way. For privacy the children were inside the wagon now, and for an eye to the grazing oxen, Jim and Ann peeked through a slit where the canvas gathered.

One man, Jim thought his name was Tomkins, turned to a friend and said, "I guess she's gone into the wagon with the boy, though I'd say he's a might bit young for a girl that size even if she's got one of her arms that's gone." Both men laughed loudly and Jim wanted out of the wagon to run and bust them in their laughing mouths. He knew he couldn't manage it, and he wouldn't look at Ann until she tapped him on the shoulder once. There was a piece of charcoal in her hand and without saying anything she touched it lightly all around his face. She also rubbed some fatback over his cheeks and then splashed water over that. Only a few drops stayed behind like oily beads of sweat. When she finished she held his jaw to turn his face toward the light. After nodding her head for his attention, she spoke loudly for everyone to hear.

"You can't go out there now, Jim. Jim you just cannot." In a whisper she added, "Now, Jim, peer out over the tailgate. He did for a few seconds, then Ann dragged him back. Now it was her turn to look out. The men were puzzled and waiting for the next thing to happen.

"I'll need some help, please," Ann said. "It started about an hour ago and you saw for yourself how sick the boy has got."

All the smiles and all the laughs were gone. The men legged it for the wagons shouting, "The kids has got it now," and "I hain't ever seen a boy so close by to death."

The wagon boss rode up fast. To see Thompson on his feet and running too, usually said something was wrong. The wagon boss heard them describe the boy's face as they relayed the girl's request as a question of their own. Heads shook in unison. The wagon boss's spit-wet finger felt the air. "They's downwind, and we'll leave them there. I fear that wagon's choleraed all to hell. It may not be the kindest thing to do, but we are going to Oregon without them."

Mrs. Eleve walked over to the conversation. She agreed. "That ungrateful girl brought them to us, and if we can get away all right I'd be content to have her die."

That sounded hard, her husband thought, but what else was there to do?

As the wagon train made up, Ann went out to join Bill beside the oxen and the cow. Together they brought them in. Ann knew there were people who'd feel so cheated of the wagon that they would for fairness try to take the animals. To her relief no one came riding close. This midday halt was ended early. Men gathered their own stock. As they hurried they were careful not to look toward the Conestoga standing by itself. Ann, Jim, and the children watched. There was nothing to say and there were no words that would hold the wagon train. The people were silent over there. Harnessed up, they moved off without shouts or calls. The children watched the wagons off into the distance. It was a long, long time until the last speck of white canvas winked over the edge of their horizon. Ann faced around to Jim. Both had the same thought. He spoke it first. "I guess from now on it's up to us." Ann nodded and they smiled for the first time in a world that was all their own.

They decided to make their night camp. There was no other trail they knew of leading to Oregon. Then they would follow along as best they could, knowing they would never catch up with the wagon train.

Bill and Margaret were too young to stand watches in the night. In the morning, if the baby didn't waken them, Ann and Jim could both sleep a little later than the rest. Then the two small children were awake and on watch together.

The most pressing problem was the baby's food. There was the canned milk, but not nearly enough to get the baby to Oregon. Jim showed Ann how he tied the finger of a woman's leather glove over the neck of a bottle. He mixed molasses, canned milk, and hot water from before coffee was made. Ann asked him how he knew to do all this, and Jim told her it was something his mother showed him when first she knew she was dying.

The passage of a single wagon didn't frighten off the game. On the third day Jim was able to take a buffalo calf. His dad's old leather army cartridge box still hung inside the wagon. He showed Ann how he carefully cut the paper cartridge and measured off the powder charge in equal piles. "That wartime charge is heavy enough for a full grown man to stand to. I'm not so much a fool as to let myself be kicked into a jelly. The bang's less and the bullet doesn't hit as hard, but a person doesn't have to be big to shoot an animal through the head. He just has to know to draw his sights down fine."

"How are we going to cook it?" Ann asked.

"I didn't ask you how I'm going to shoot it. Now, you're the girl, don't ask me how it's going to be cooked."

This was not like shooting fox squirrels in a pecan grove. There wasn't any hunting to it. Margaret protested loudly, and Bill, although still young, just glowed and licked his chops in contemplation of fresh meat on the table.

Margaret called, "Jim, can't we wait and shoot a big old mean one? That calf over there is so, well, so cute and just a baby too."

Jim shushed her. The calf could still be frightened off. He called back softly, "Margaret, a big bull might just be over my edge. We need fresh meat now. We might just let that calf run free. Then without stuff to eat we'd be digging a hole to put the baby in when she got starved enough."

Jim didn't want to shoot the calf either, but there was no use to look around for someone else to do it. What little shakes he'd had were gone. He held right on and there wasn't even a bleat. The calf's mother ran off in a panic. She didn't even look to see if her calf followed her. This was a relief to Jim, yet it didn't make that calf's death the least bit easier.

The two young children watched while Ann and Jim worked together at the butchering. Ann had never done it before, and for a second it took her in the pit of the stomach. Here was all the smell of butchering. It was the gutsy smell of new blood and body heat. Now that she was grown it was on her too, about once every month. That was nothing bad or unhuman at all. Everything alive is filled right up with blood, she thought. Getting this animal cut up and cooked was part of being alive, just like the other was. If she'd gotten used to that there was no reason why she couldn't get used to this.

She wished there was some way to get milk for the baby from it. There wasn't. Milk came from things alive. The baby gladly drank the broth from boiled meat out of its bottle. In addition, if you cracked the bones, she licked the cooked marrow from your fingers. This put Jim to the idea of mashing up boiled pieces of the liver and that was something else the baby liked to eat just fine.

Progress was as slow as it was even. The weather held nicely into the week, and when the calf meat started to get ripe, it always seemed that they could take another animal. Against bad times they hung out thin strips of meat that waved like small stiff flags as the wagon went along.

Jim and Ann both realized that there was no way to fort up a single wagon. They made their camps, when possible, streamside and under cottonwoods, and each one of these camps was a hard place to leave. But leave them they did. There were no buts or can'ts available. The children knew their journey had to be finished long before the winter came. Everyone knew of the Donners and of what happened to emigrants who got trapped by snow. They did have mixed feelings about other wagon trains coming up behind them. If there were adults and people grown and a real trail boss, well, Jim thought, that would be the more proper way to get across the plains. Neither Ann nor Jim had decided how they would deal with ferrymen, soldiers, or any other adults they might meet.

Jim and Ann were walking at the head of the team. The two younger children and the baby slept back in the wagon. It was as drowsy an afternoon as one could find out on the plains. They'd been long silent. Jim spoke first. "Let's puzzle out both the forts and the soldiers that are in 'em."

"What's there to puzzle out?"

"If they see kids without folks they'll want to put us in a home."

"Well I'm not kids," Ann said, "but you're right. We have to think. And thinking tells me one nice thing. Out here they don't have homes to put kids in."

"No, I don't mean with families. I'm talking about homes for kids who some way get parted from their kin. Either through people dying like has happened just now, or by the kin never having been there in the first place at all."

"Well they don't have those kind of homes either. But you're talking silly, Jim. Everybody's got kin. Without kin there'd be no people."

"I'm grown enough to know that. What I mean is, some kin pulls out fast and leaves you standing as the only sign they ever been any place at all. Then you try to find them and you couldn't even if you were a Pinkerton detective grown. Mostly it's just the little kids that's looking."

"Jim, you're big enough to know where your parents are."

"Oh, sure. I was asking after yours."

As Ann looked over at him she didn't slow her pace. He was just into his teens and nearly as tall as she. There was little weight to his body anywhere. Tirelessly they walked together at the head of the team and the prairie was so wide it didn't ever seem to move. Clouds drifted and for once the sky was softened to patches of blue and the sun did not shine cruelly. Ann traced the horizon with her eyes to think before she said, "Where my parents are, I just don't know. They are off somewheres with my other arm."

The boy caught his breath and glanced at her. There was a pause, and then she had more to say. "No, Jim, that's all right you asked. I'm glad you thought to do it."

They knew that they were dropping behind the wagon train. The ashes of big camp fires had been two days warm. Now they were three days cold.

At one ford Jim was in a hurry to run on ahead to test for depth and the current's strength. Ann called him back, and Margaret with directions helped tie two little kegs behind his shoulders. Ann said, "Jim, it isn't that I think you small. I just want you to be safe. There's just too few of us for any to be daring."

Three times, the water got Jim's feet out from under him. It was on the fourth try he found a place where the wagon could cross easily with the water below the front wheel hubs. It was a fresh place with no tracks leading down. Once or twice after rains or where the prairie had been fired over, they'd lost the track of the wagons going on before them. Jim was quick to explain it as no problem. If they let the sun come up behind them and then let it set a little off in front and to their left, then that would tell them they were still headed truly. Jim was correct to claim a proper heading. However, the loss of the exact trail caused them to miss the checkpoint where the soldiers waited. The soldiers, in turn, could not conceive of one single wagon trying to get through, and only scouted to find and direct the massive wagon trains.

It was the Bozeman trail that had been closed. In a rare move the government was honoring a treaty it had signed with Sioux. The wagon train, now seven days ahead of them, was continuing on to Oregon. Ann and the children never saw it again, nor did they meet up with any soldiers. They plodded on and now, as the result of one wrong turning, they had this trail to themselves.

It was an empty world they drove the oxen through. Smoothly they moved up long valleys and sometimes through meadows ox-belly deep with grass. There was no fresh sign to be found and they wondered how much the other wagons could have gained. Sure there were tin cans to be found, although every time Jim picked one up, Ann could see the rust flakes covering it. It never occurred to them that they were totally alone.

The day they wanted to see the wagon train and a real wagon boss came when a hidden stone and a thoughtless turn collapsed their left front wheel. Spokes stuck into the ground like the broken fingers of a crumpled hand. The iron tire had snapped and there were four spokes and three felloes shattered. The oxen knew to stop. Jim kicked the rock so hard he hurt his foot. It had been all so smooth he'd forgotten fear. Now, he couldn't think of anything except that they didn't have a jack, and this wagon was the biggest thing there ever was in the world. Jim looked away to see a land filled with mountains, clouds, and trees. There was nothing man-made to be seen. In the train, when they were with everyone, he'd seen a bunch of men do things to make a broken wheel right. Damn it, he wasn't even a man yet. Now, just like that woman said, they'd just set here to rot or die, whichever it was came at them first.

Ann waited a long time before asking if a repair was possible.

Jim gave the wheel a kick. "Ann, we need a man who knows to get it done."

With the sudden stop, the younger children were peering out. Both climbed down from the seat. They regarded the broken wheel thoughtfully. Bill shot a single glance at his elder brother.

"Jim, what did you do to your foot? You hopping around like that."

"Never the hell you mind what I did to my foot."

Margaret was at the edge of tears. "We need a grown-us. We need a grown-us. Why did we ever leave all of the grown-uses behind?"

Ann asked the child to stop the grown-us talk. She told her that the job was here and it was to get the wagon fixed. She pointed to where freed oxen grazed and said that it was a happy time and place for them. This was a new direction for Jim's anger. "Happy time," he almost shouted. "See those sleek white bastards chewing as though nothing had happened at all."

"I'm not sure that it's right for you to use harsh language, Jim. I know it isn't right with little ones nearby. It's hardly yet time for you to learn to swear."

"I won't ever have a better time, and I've damn near learned everything else . . ."

"Now, that is enough. If you've learned so much let's hear how we're going to get that broken wheel fixed."

Jim's head shook. He was through with shouting. They had some money in the wagon. It was maybe enough to hire . . . to hire, hell. You have to have people before you can hire anyone. Well, they would have to find somebody for help. Jim looked at Ann until she frowned. With his head cocked off to one side he said,

"Maybe if you could attract a man. We've got some of Mama's nice dresses and there must be something that could happen to your hair. Then if your face was washed," he continued hopefully, "we might get somebody to fix this broken wheel."

Bill got into the conversation, but they had to listen especially well because the words came out so carefully. "The sort of man you'll get that way, well, he's not going to want a bunch of kids. He'll take Ann away and we'll be left here again just the same as we was down in the river by those breaks. That's unless he steals our stock and even maybe our wagon too."

Ann turned on young Bill. "You're saying I could only bring in a thieving man if you was to set me out like some kind of bait. Maybe I could bring in a man so nice he'd be able to have help enough for us all."

It was Margaret's turn to shake her head. "A man like that," she declared, "most generally has a woman and his family already made."

Ann was angry now. "You're after getting me to go out there and drag some man back so as to fix this wagon. You want the wagon fixed, but you don't care at all what happens to me. And I am but hardly eighteen years of age." She spoke directly toward Jim. He replied in an attempt to justify his plan.

"There's a great deal of women married by the time they are sixteen, and well, you are built as big as many women grown."

"Well we just better think of something else, because in the first place I wouldn't know what to do for a man that wanted me, and in the second there's not many men would much want a one-armed girl."

Jim wasn't ready to give up on the only idea he had. "Well, maybe attract an old one. I've heard they don't do much, so then you wouldn't have to know . . ." Jim's idea was going lame. "Anything to do."

Ann was crying for the first time ever. Jim put out his hand.

"Of all the people in the world," she said, "don't you touch me now."

He pulled back. "Please, don't, don't cry. It was the only idea that I had. We'll think of something else." All four were in tears. Only the youngest was still asleep and quiet in her cradle.

It was a grand place to make camp and there was nothing else to do. They had a fire burning from gathered wood mixed in with some buffalo chips.

Much later embers were glowing and Jim sat next to Ann, their backs against a rear wagon wheel. They didn't want to decide who was to stand the first watch of that night. Jim apologized in every way he knew. It was almost as if he'd actually let someone or something take Ann off to a place he couldn't think about. He realized by himself, one's closest friends were not a thing that could be traded away. She soothed him saying everything was fine. No matter what they'd thought to do with grown-uses. Ann mimicked Maggie's word. That at least was something for them both to smile with. No matter what, it didn't matter because there weren't any of them around. Jim had been fighting this idea down. He always thought that wagon trains were thick on all these westward trails. He was correct to assume this, but the rusty cans had been a hint that had escaped him and there was no way for him to know this trail had been closed.

Jim watched sparks fly up from the dying fire. He spoke to break the silence. "If you know to study up on things enough, well you can never tell just when those things will come in handy for you." Ann puzzled what to answer, but the boy hadn't finished speaking. "There ain't no end until you're dead, so the end's not what's important. The way you get there is what counts."

"That's a pretty smart-alecky sort of thing for just a boy to say." The last small shreds of Ann's anger weren't completely melted away. It wasn't really Jim's fault she'd chosen this family, and now she was without a glimmer of a way to leave. It was her way to stay with whatever choice she made. Once she'd thrown in with these kids she could never think of leaving them.

"I'll smart-mouth with the best," he preferred an alternative. "That doesn't mean I've forgotten how to cry. I want you to help me not to do it. So, please listen when I tell you about the trains.

"Well, you go right ahead, though it seems that often you don't talk about much else. You only talk or dream or think about those railroad trains. This here is just six old oxen, one cow, and some children stuck in the middle of no place at all, and you are talking trains to me." Jim was silent. Ann continued. "You are hardly past thirteen years of age and trains is all you have within your mind. Or should I say, not a whole day passes that you haven't told us ten things about one single train, or one thing about ten different ones."

"Make fun of me if you like, but I do wish that us five kids was right now riding in the cars."

"There's not 'five of us kids.' A kid is a young goat and I am near to being grown. You said that yourself. You are thirteen and doing more than most people could expect. Maggie's the kid. The others are the baby and Bill. As you say, he's eight years old."

"You're right. He's little, but he does his part. One of his jobs is to see that the oxen don't stray. When minding them, that child gets right in amongst those six huge animals. If they even think to wander, he's after them with his little switch. Or mostly he uses his hands to reach up and push against their faces. It seems they know what he wants them to do.

"When we are out walking at the lead, Maggie looks after the baby fine," Jim paused. He was counting up his team, and in doing it he brought himself away from the tearful sadness of the wagon being wrecked. "Now, Ann, you go to sleep and take the second watch."

She offered to take the first but he declined. He was fine. He wanted to be awake awhile so as to think. They'd start work in the morning. If she didn't want to hear about the trains, well, just for now, he wouldn't tell her how two grown-ups got a free tire to stick back on the wheel of the *C. R. Mason* and they were stranded too out in the pucker-brush. It had just been a tank engine on the Virginia Central. The crew made a forge using an old iron soap kettle to hold the charcoal. They'd hand-made shims to tighten up that tire fine. Well, if two grown-ups did that for a locomotive wheel, then four kids could surely get at one from off an old wagon.

When Jim was a boy, he would go down to the engine sheds. The forge fires glowed red again as he watched the sparks rise up in front of him. The last glow of the fire reflected off the brass bands and the patch-box cover of his father's old Zouave. The Remington people had made it, up in Ilion, New York. The fittings were brass, although they had tarnished dull. It was a sleepy way they caught the dimming fire's light.

For a moment Jim's eyes had almost closed. He snapped them open with a start. His dad had told him that in the war, if they caught a man asleep on picket he could be court-martialed and shot. His dad told him that it was said nearly every day: court-martialed and shot. It ended things so finally and so neat, and just for sleeping.

What would Ann or Maggie do if they found him asleep? No they were kin, or at least Mag was. They couldn't have him shot. Now he couldn't find any bottom to his blankets, and he woke to realize that there weren't any blankets. No, Bill and all the rest wouldn't have him shot if he were to go . . .

He sat upright again. If that were the case he really should be shot. He meant that they were kin and he shouldn't fall asleep on picket. If you fall asleep on picket you might well be shot. The thought didn't keep him awake. The fire had died down further, but he felt that he'd been mostly wakeful. It would be best to build it up. He did. It's hard to sleep before a rising fire. The flames found new wood and the new fire was a wakeful one. The night went on and there were no alarms. He checked the oxen where they lay. He looked into the wagon to see how the children slept. Finally it was time for him to wake Ann. She was quick to rise without wonderment for where they were and what she was meant to do. Before turning in, Jim handed her the rifle. They didn't talk about however she'd reload. She was strong enough to draw it to her shoulder, one armed as she was, and that old Zouave was not some English sportsman's toy. She'd stand with the butt tucked into her hip. A noise outside the fire light and she'd thumb the hammer back as the gun drew to her shoulder. It pointed so steadily as if there was another hand to hold it at the balance. He'd lain in his blankets and seen her do it. Other times he'd watched when she practiced until you would think a whole body would droop down with tiredness. As he drifted off to sleep he thought where in the hell would they all be if this girl hadn't come along. Tomorrow would be a brand new day and he'd be getting after that wheel. It took only minutes to be fast asleep and then it seemed no time was passed. Ann woke him for his second tour. She handed him his father's watch and then the musket to hold. They didn't even talk, and he crouched down beside the broken wagon wheel. The rifle was across his knees. For a fresh new two hours he would have to fight going off to sleep.

They spent the whole first day trying to get the broken wheel up and clear from the ground. They were fortunate to find a small cliff some distance from the wagon. At its base many flat rocks had fallen down.

Bill hefted the rock in front of his chest and carried it to their wagon. Ann expressed doubt. "I don't know about rocks to hold something up in the air."

Bill held his rock and it was quite a load. If he could hold and carry it then he could have a say back to Ann. "Well, I do. These rocks will hold up fine. If you hit 'em sharp they'll smash like

plates, but if you push 'em easy, well, they won't ever break. I
believe if rocks broke when they were under things, then we
couldn't have the world, because all that's underground, if you dig
down far enough, is rocks. Father told us that."

He placed the rock near the broken wheel and again he went
back and picked up another slab. Uneven rocks were thrust aside.
Finally the chosen ones were formed in two piles. One came up
snug under the axle. The other was about a foot away. This was
the fulcrum, and a small trimmed tree trunk was the lever. Jim,
Ann, and Margaret bore down heavily. Bill waited with a flat rock
so as to add it to the supporting pile. He was poised but nothing
happened. He put down the rock and and went to add his weight
to the strain, and still the wagon didn't move. Next they cut a
wooden wedge to maul between the axle and the stones. This lifted
the wagon hardly an inch, and it was evident a second wedge could
do nothing more, except maybe knock over the entire pile. A second
pile would be needed under the axle too, and then they could build
and wedge back and forth until the broken wheel cleared. The first
flush of industry slowed. Seldom was any gain noticeable, and on
several occasions height was clearly lost. Bill spat and shook his
head. Ann just kept working back and forth.

By way of encouragement Jim said, "If this is our best then
we'll just have to keep on doing it." Even with its broken spokes,
the wreckage of the wheel still kept the wagon off the ground. Had
it rested on the hub Jim didn't think they'd have had a chance.
Even now some worry started. Ann looked at how little they had
gained and then asked if they couldn't dig down until the wheel
cleared. When it was fixed they could make a ramplike trench.
Instead of lifting they would be digging the earth out from underneath. When the wheel was repaired and back on its axle then
the oxen could pull the wagon back up to the even surface of the
ground. The first part of her plan worked fine. Jim dug a hole deep
and wide so they could slide the wheel off.

There were spare planks and boards laid on the wagon's floor. It was clear that they had been brought along for just a time like this. The tools were in the big carpenter's chest. Jim had often watched his father work, but some of the tools were strange to him. With the chest lid open, the worn handles and the oiled blades looked cold and lonely for his father's hands. As Ann saw him hesitate she said, "If there's tools enough for your father to fix near everything, then there's enough for you. It will just take us longer because we have a bunch of puzzling to do."

The felloes were the hardest for the children to make. A whole day was over before they had one that curved right with properly positioned holes to hold its spokes. They didn't know how deeply wheelwrights talked about this job. Men that did it every day piled rules on top of theory when they told each other how hard this felloe forming was. Fortunately the children didn't know enough to be afraid to start.

They'd carefully traced each felloe that was broken on a plank of proper thickness. Then Jim had put the bow saw together. It had been stored in its parts. He was slow to turn up the windless stick because he had to remember just how taut the blade should be. When he'd finally got the first one cut, the others were not so slow at being sawed. The spokes were easier to do, and there was no need to shape them as nicely as a wagon builder did—they were working to move out and as soon as possible. Still, Jim would not be in a hurry and he made the spokes fit perfectly where they went into the hub.

It wasn't until the third day that the big round fire was laid. As it burnt down to a ring of glowing coals Jim worked on a piece of strap iron so that he might patch the broken tire. It would have to be on the outside, and it wouldn't be anything as good as a blacksmith's weld. He shrugged. If they were coming out of here this was the only way. The patch was put in the bed of coals until it came up red. With narrow tongs Jim touched and turned it this

way and that. The children with Ann stood watching him. Evening
was down and the red came up in the metal so that each time
it was out from the coals they could see the glow reflected on Jim's
face. He'd told Ann and each of the children where to stand and
what to do. They had all been aghast when Jim had gone to his
parents' small store of money. He had taken three whole silver
dollars. With a coal chisel he'd cut them into little slivers. He also
had a clean stick and a dish of paste he'd made from water and just
regular borax washing powder. He hadn't told them everything,
although with Ann, Margaret, and Bill he had rehearsed the way
he wanted the iron tire moved. There were three loops of wire
spaced evenly around. A wetted stick was held at the ready for each.
Several times they had practiced picking up the broken tire and
then lowering it down above the newly mended wheel.

Jim painted the white paste evenly on the red hot metal held
in his tongs. It changed to look like a sugar glaze. When the coating
was even and while the heat still held, he used a small pincers to
drop the scraps of silver on the patch. They melted and flowed out
to join each other as a dully shining silver coat.

If he'd been in the shops he could have riveted, but here there
was no clanking post drill to bite its way down through the iron
tire. He couldn't hire men to work for him, yet money could be
used to stick their wheel back together. He laid the patch aside.
As the heat went the silver frosted and turned dull. When his spit
didn't sizzle anymore he dunked the metal in the water bucket so
that it might be handled.

He'd filed the tire bright on both sides of the break. Now it
was painted thickly with the paste and the patch was wired neatly
in place. Under the wire Jim drove cut nails to serve him for
wedges. "You'll see," he said, "the wire will get up to red-hot too."

With the patch in place they lifted the tire and set it evenly
on four stones that were amongst the coals. The fire had burned
down just right. For now the tire reddened, and with his pincers

Jim dropped little scraps of silver to see them flow away beneath the patch. He also gently tapped his little wedges so as to hold the tie wires taut. He pulled the coals from beneath the patch and this was the first part to cool. It darkened, and a sliver of silver remained bright and angular when placed against it.

As planned, the wet wood sticks were passed through the wire loops. The tire lifted evenly from its bed of coals. They had brushed the ground and planned each step, and the three of them together carried it until they stood over the wheel. Now, carefully, they lowered the tire down until the ring of metal was even and level to the wood. Bill could see that the metal was larger than the wood. Just then, with the tire now at rest, Jim picked up the water bucket. In it was a dipper made from a big tin can. At its top was a bent wire handle, and with a hammer and nail Jim had punched numerous holes in its bottom. He took it from the bucket and slowly moved around the wheel. Hissing steam rose up in clouds, but Ann and the children held their sticks with breathless steadiness. Evenly, around and around, Jim sprinkled until they couldn't see each other for the steam. Finally the hissing stopped. Wisps of vapor remained.

Jim stepped back. He set the water bucket down. Ann asked, "Do we still have to hold the wires up?"

"You can let them be now." Jim was not yet sure that the tire was fixed. He wasn't even all together hopeful. He knew that you could never be sure. It had already broken once.

"Didn't you make that tire too big?" Bill asked. Jim didn't answer. He pointed to the completed wheel. The rough new spokes were drawn tight as the old. The shrunken iron tire was scaled and fire-blackened. The wire loops around it pressed into the wood. These would be easily cut away.

"She even looks pretty round," Jim said.

Bill and Maggie just jumped up and down with glee.

"How did you know to do it?" Ann asked.

"I knew to do it because I went around and watched them do it in the Chattanooga railroad shops when I was a little boy." Ann laughed and he told her not to. "It was three years ago and you weren't so grown up over me then. You still aren't now, even if you know a spate of things that I have never learned. Like who's got milk and when."

"What would have happened if something had slipped?" Ann asked.

"Then we would have just done it again," he held his hand up against her requestioning, "and then again, until we got it fixed."

"How did you know you'd remembered it just right?"

She still kept coming

"I didn't know," Jim replied. He was right at the edge of being angry. "And if I'd remembered wrong then it would have been just like what Mrs. Eleve said. We would rot here until we died, or we'd have died here until we rotted. But the thing of it is," Jim winked at the fire and at himself, "I remembered right."

Damn it, he thought, how like a girl to remind you to be fearful when all the danger's past. Well, at least she was steady enough so's not to tell him useless things when fear was standing right out in front of him.

When they left in the morning there was a slight thump each time the wheel turned. That was the patch. It complained, but it went, and the way they'd fixed it lasted further than they had to go.

Though Ann was nearly grown, they really were just four kids carrying a newborn baby with them. They'd been moving slowly, and wherever Oregon was they weren't getting to it. The snow on the wagon's canvas had also settled on the oxen's roughened coats. They were stopped and the only food they had was for the baby, and good God, Ann thought, didn't those last few cans of milk look as lonely as the white wilderness surrounding them.

When she had asked about the trail Jim only shrugged. There was no trail, nor any trace of anyone. They were lost, and there was no crying over that. They'd just gone along on their own and now it was too late. For a long time Jim hadn't seen anything to hunt. The meat had kept well in the cold but that was finished too. Even though there was good dry grass forage for the oxen and the cow, there was nothing for the people.

Jim and Ann went away from the kids to talk about how they would kill the cow. She'd come with them so far, and so willingly. On thinking that, they both discovered they weren't grown-up enough for killing a creature that had been their friend, even if they starved themselves. Jim said that he could starve and for a while even the younger kids could suffer. Yet the baby's first hunger would surely firm him up. When the canned milk was gone the cow would have to die.

Ann was on the seat with the shawl-wrapped baby in her arm. The little kids and Jim were curled up inside the wagon asleep. Moving through this falling snow would only succeed in getting them more lost. Let them sleep. It was the one thing to do when there wasn't any food.

Now, suddenly there was a sense of color mixed with the snow. Something moved behind and across the falling white, formlessly, just at the corner of her eye. It was the only the slightest movement, and then it was another. The colors changed and grew more bright. Then there were steaming nostrils and mounted men, gathered so close that the falling snow was a curtain behind them. A dozen blanketed Indians with rifles and bows gathered around the team. There was no way for Ann to make a fight. The Navy Colt was handy to the seat, but she had the baby to hold. There were so many of them here. She wouldn't cry out. If Jim moved suddenly it could all end right here. Well, maybe it had from the snow and these Indians wouldn't make any difference. Damn it though, they'd come so far so well.

Ann heard one Indian say, "Whow-haw." It was their word for both oxen and beef. He pointed hungrily to the team and from behind the wagon she heard "Whow-haw," called again. Still she didn't turn. It was surely some other Indian discovering the cow. There was no reason to wake the children or Jim, yet it was lonely on the seat, watching with the baby in her arm. Then there was a thump. A horseman struck the snow-covered canvas with his lance. From the seat Ann couldn't see it happen. The Indian hadn't tried to pierce the cover. It was merely a steadying movement. His horse had stumbled. Ann heard the soft thump of the snow blanket dropping. Then she watched as the Indians moved around to the wagon's side. Shouts and loud words came from this gathering.

Jim was awake and reaching for the rifle. All Ann could say was "Don't." Maggie and Bill were waking too. Margaret came from her blankets to stand beside the seat, offering to hold the baby. Ann shook her head. Bill stayed back inside with Jim. There was a further shout and a conversation outside. Ann knew these Indians had seen what, months before, another Indian had painted on the wagon's canvas cover. The children had never decided what they should do about the pictograph so it had been left. While the details were not clear to them, they knew it told about the Indian who had been killed. These Indians wanted their oxen and their cow. With the snow knocked away, they could see this wagon had once killed one of their kind. All Ann could say was, "Jim, please stay there quiet and wait. This is maybe as far as we all will get."

The large spiral pictograph covered almost one whole canvas side. Buffalo fat and ashes, both gray and black, outlined the lasting design. Dried blood and various ground earths supplied the extra colors. The gathered Indians could easily read the pictured narrative. It could not have been so quickly told in words.

*   *   *

The painting told of two Indians of high rank on a trip. They confront a single white man's wagon by itself. There are no horsemen or outriders. On the wagon's seat is a little girl, while a grown boy leads the oxen. The two Indians are shown galloping forward. Lightly they dodge their ponies aside. The boy quits the oxen. He is running toward the wagon. With his bow one Indian clubs the boy down from behind. A skidding horse slides to a stop as its rider jumps to the ground, a scalping knife in hand. He looks up. The picture continues and there is only a small girl child on the wagon seat. The second Indian gallops by. His readied arrow is released to find a solid hit in the flank of the cow. A second arrow is already drawn. Low in the saddle he rides back to the front of the wagon.

Now, high on the seat, the little girl is shown holding a pistol in both hands. The man with the knife is close, but he doesn't see her. The girls eyes are shut. Her hands tighten convulsively. Now her eyes are open. The Indian with the knife is gone. Behind her in its cradle a frightened baby starts to cry. As the pistol fires it falls to lie beside the man it killed. Margaret's eyes are closed again. She has started to sob. On the wagon's canvas the Indian had painted the symbol for tears all around her head.

As the painted account continued the second Indian and his pony dance away. His bow is drawn and he expects further shots, but sees only the little girl up on the wagon's seat. His horse skids nearly to its haunches and now he sees where his friend has fallen.

The pictograph ended there, but the confrontation continued.

Jim lay unconscious on the ground and Bill was waking in the wagon. At the sound of the shot Ann jumped from the tailgate. The cow was rearing against its rope and Ann saw the arrow sticking in her. Running to the front of the wagon, she surprised the Indian on his horse. Had it been her intention she could have shot him by snatching up the gun. It lay between them on the ground.

Margaret, pointing down to the corpse, said, "He hit Jim and then held a knife. I turned Pa's gun on him and that's what woke the baby."

Ann defiantly bestrode Jim's fallen body. It still hadn't occurred to her to take the gun. She just wouldn't let any more hurt come at Jim. The Indian was off his horse. His bow hung at his side.

He looked toward this strangely defiant and protecting girl. What kind of a woman was this? Indian braves find manhood in the sun dance, when little thorns are pushed beneath their skin. These thorns are attached to rawhide ties and for a man to pull away they must tear out through his flesh. How brave this woman's body must be to have pulled free from an entire arm. Or was that the magic of the white man's shamans? When death grabs a hand to pull one way she had pulled the other. Of course she'd had help. With little medicine knives the white shaman makes the cuts that tell the arm where it must separate.

The Indian heard the little girl's words and he realized how his companion had died. He walked over to shake his friend only to find life extinct as he turned the body over. He tapped his finger on the dead man's chest and, pointing to the wagon seat, he told the story through in sign language, laughing continually as he worked his hands. He needed to go over the story a second time, because he could not relish the situation enough with only a single telling. "Running Wolf, Sioux chief, brave in war. Little girl, holds revolver. One shot. Running Wolf, Sioux warrior chief, is dead."

Ann easily forbore to join his laughter. Billy was peeking out of the wagon beside his sister.

The Indian picked up the fallen gun. Holding it in both hands he half cocked the hammer so as to revolve the cylinder. With a fingernail he withdrew the unfired caps. He handed the gun toward Margaret, holding it by the barrel, the butt offered first. Ann nodded and the child took the weapon from him and placed it quickly on the seat. Jim had been saved and she was grown enough to know just what happened. A man was dead and she hated the noise of killing him. Then it had been so loud and fearful sudden, and now it was not yet a time to cry again.

The various skin-wrapped pots that held the paints were in a medicine bag on the dead man's horse. When they were properly arranged the Indian painted so that the wagon could tell how Running Wolf had died. Jim awoke. He had a moment of convulsive fright to see the Indian there beside him. Ann shushed and reassured and all of them watched the spiral of figures and signs appear. Many miles to the west this careful painting told other Indians that the people in the wagon had been brave, both in peace and in war. And over time the cow recovered from the arrow's wound.

Now, these painted horses stood in the silent snow. Every rider had to read the pictograph to assure himself that Running Wolf had been killed by a little girl. Months later she was still up there on the seat of this wagon. Looking from the painting to the child made them almost think there was no time, except of course for Running Wolf. He had been dead that long. He had died in the hunting moon and now the beaver moon was nearly done.

One of the mounted Indians, whom Ann took to be their war chief or leader motioned for the wagon to follow as they moved off at a walking pace. Ann didn't know if the sign was a command or a request. However it didn't matter much because there was no other place to go.

The team and wagon followed the mounted Indians through the falling snow. Ann led from the off side because it slowed the team for anyone to walk in front. As the snow lessened she could see they weren't far from a large village on a river. Near its center they were shown into an empty tepee. It was a soft-snow winter

and the oxen and the cow were able to graze down through the fall
of snow. Also, the Indians did not molest the cattle and that was
a double bounty because usually the whow-haws got killed, the
first thing off, for food. Good hunting through a mild winter was
the source of their salvation. There was no hungry moon that year.

Some of the Indians spoke English well enough, so Jim and
Ann learned the Bozeman trail had been closed. That was why they
hadn't seen another wagon. The soldiers were gone now, and the
Indians of this village looked ahead to full enjoyment of their lands.
Red Cloud had agreed not to attack the railroad trains in exchange
for a treaty that gave the Black Hills to the Sioux forever. It was a
happy winter, and in the very early spring they traveled on Indian
ponies to see where a huge fort had been abandoned and burned.

When grass was up far enough for the animals to travel, Ann
and the children continued their journey. Their Indian hosts gave
clear directions so that they would be able to find the nearest mining town. Even the baby was old enough now to wave good-by as
the wagon started on its way again.

3

The dim lit room was long and smelt of beer. It was the hotel's bar, easily accessible through an archway from the lobby or more directly by glass doors that opened onto the street. On an empty winter's night the inside lamps were turned down to barely a glow. Only three men were present and only the long thin man behind the bar was sober. He carefully polished a glass that was already clean, and then he shrugged his shoulders slightly. These customers of his were throwing their money away— it didn't seem that either of them could get any drunker—but that wasn't the bartender's problem. These two had slept here before, together and singly, with sawdust for a pillow and vomit for a rug. For now, the barkeep had to admit, with all the liquor stowed they both still stood strongly at the bar.

The man dressed like a cowboy was half hidden behind a growing forest of emptied beer bottles. Tides and oceans of beer flowed through this man. A wide and drowsy smile had crept across his face. Perhaps he was happy to feel the level of beer rising up inside of him. It sure was an awful lot, maybe like a canal lock filling, with the wet stone walls disappearing lower and lower until a whole new world appeared when the lock was fully filled. The cowboy mentioned his imagined view to the bartender, who nodded as he thought, some people didn't have experiences, because past performance indicated this particular boat was not going to sail anywhere. It usually sunk long before the lock was ever filled.

The cowboy opened another bottle of beer as though it were the first he'd ever handled. The smile grew easily, like when a child remembers Christmas.

The barkeep wished for more customers—he was standing around doing nothing. These two were content with their drunkenness, and he didn't think the cowboy had made any special plans. This evening had crept up on him. He was dressed casually and range rough, but he had not come in from working on a horse. No, his shoes were flat and he had no gun belt on. In fact his pants were gallused up. He didn't have a vest, yet the felt hat he wore had some vague traces of style left. It had been battered down and torn up long past sensible keeping, except maybe for sentiment or as a badge or both. His open canvas coat wasn't dusty, although it looked like it had never been taken off. All his clothing was very much a part of the man. It had no particular cut. His linen was clean, very white, and gathered at his throat by a patented bow. Half-filled with beer, he held himself with a constrained dignity. What conversation there had been was now lagged out.

Chalk's fellow drinker was not a gulper, nor was he the sort of drinker who could survive on beer. Cold beer was something that he took, like a medicine, in order to quench thirst. Whisky was what he drank. He drank the best. He drank it thoughtfully and in large amounts.

Somewhat older than Chalk, this other gentleman almost hid behind the somberness of his clothes. His coat was dark and cut to the style a quiet man could wear. A gold chain led to his watch, and the vest that held it filled like a well-pushed sail. This man was portly without being fat. His stiff hat lay on the bar before him. He turned his drink just once to see the change of light on it. He was not a person to sit there merely twirling. He took a carefully measured sip. Both customers, for now, liked the quiet place that surrounded them. The barkeep wouldn't disrupt it by suggesting conversation.

Frazier, the man in the somber suit, had once been a real doctor. He remembered that too well. A vague woman was poised in his imagination, and waiting for him at home. He imagined their conversation now. "Who was in the bar?" she'd ask.

"Chalk," he would reply. Would she identify him as that good-hearted helpful man who pays so much attention to the needs of others that he never seems to have the time to address his own? But she wouldn't think of him as a ne'er-do-well. He works hard enough to support a wife, and if there's any time left over then he should be free to spend it in any way he wishes. Maybe she'd want to know how he could be with Chalk's company, that was so quiet, so quiet as to be hardly there. Or might she be a woman—he never clearly pictured her—who knew that people were in different places in many different ways. Some people were just a gentle presence and shouldn't try to tell you any reasons for being where they were. It was something you had to know just for yourself. The ex-doctor thought this conversation with an imaginary wife was beginning to unravel. No harm. It could be abruptly ended and with no one's feelings hurt.

He smiled back to this other man, and it was a smile that didn't happen often. He motioned for the bartender to set out another beer, but raised his hand gently against an addition to his own drink. He nursed what he had, holding himself just in that one place in the bar with nothing being said, and all memories of other and outside places carefully put away.

Their quiet was not to last. The door to the bar opened and a pause was loudly followed by heavy stomping boots. There was noise enough to announce the entrance of several men, but a glance up at the mirror showed only three.

Now for Chalk the evening was ruined, or at least brought to a halt. When you planned to get carefully drunk, the whole process could become pointless and not worth doing if circumstances were spoiled with needless sounds and insistent voices shouting from a world outside your own.

These were real cowboys: spurs, hats, gun belts, doubtless even down to their underdrawers. It pained the ex-doctor to see them belly up at the bar. It wasn't only what they drank, it was how they drank it. Chalk's contented smile was gone even before the newcomers turned to greet him. He desperately wanted to disguise himself as one of the real full-time cowboys just in from the range. He smoothed down the front of his coat and tried to think of some way that his hat might be squared. He put one foot on the bar rail with a show of certainty. There was no proper way to roughly gulp a beer so he just went on sipping.

Without any pretence of enjoyment one of these new men thoughtlessly gulped down his drink. Then he went over to coin up the crystal, glassed-in music box. There were big tin disks inside that turned when a person put money in the slot. Sipping his beer, Chalk wished that he could fill this whole bar with the music of his own choice sounding out from his own coin. Even if he had been here alone there'd be no tune he'd enjoy playing. Someone else might come in while he was doing it and it could be a song they didn't like. The disk caught the light as it spun round and round to fill the bar with tinkle music. What a loud noise it seemed to make.

The man nearest Chalk turned, and his two companions looked past him. "Hi, there, Mr. Frazier." The ex-doctor saluted with one finger pleasantly. Next this man greeted the cowboy, "Hi, there Chalk."

Chalk put down his beer and nodded furtively. He wished these men hadn't come in. He knew pretty much what they were going to say and do. If they got under his skin, even just a little, well, hell, that was just his own fault. Damn it, though, he hoped they wouldn't ride him hard. He drew at his beer again. When they got to riding him, that was when he really hated other people being here. The middle man of the group knew the most about being mean. As he opened his mouth to start, the boss cowboy's elbow jabbed him in the ribs. Having silenced his companion he turned toward him with a great big smile. It took a little while for the other man to be able to smile back. Whatever had been about to be said would not have been pleasant. Yes, that ramrod there was a decent man in ways. He spoke to Chalk in a friendly manner, yet he was asking something he already knew. But in fairness most bar conversations start out just like that.

"How you doing with those cows, Chalk?" was the question that he asked.

Those cows were a herd that Chalk carefully planned someday to own. They calved, they grazed, and they fattened in a golden future that always seemed to elude the pains and problems of the present.

The center man of the trio could have said a hundred things, all true. Each would have been enough to drive Chalk from the bar. His companion's conversation was a ritual. It was friendly, interested, and in some ways more cruel.

"We saw some of those chunky new cows, not all horns and eye fire. More meat, and such you don't need half a pack of wolves to help you chew your steak. They are what's going to be."

"Those red Herefords?"

"That's them, Herefords. I'd think of them for myself if I had a ranch."

Chalk agreed. "Oh, I've thought of them. In fact, there's nothing else. I've had several chances to start up with wild cows, but that isn't the way I plan to ranch."

"Sensible." Turning to his companions, the foreman nodded. Even the man in the middle nodded his agreement back.

The most distant man called out. "Hey, Chalk."

"Yes, Cricket."

"You sell your six-gun, Chalk?"

Chalk put his hands down to feel where his gun belt wasn't.
"No, I didn't sell my gun belt, or even the gun that was in it." In
replying Chalk could feel the mistake of being friendly. It had been
coaxed from him by the talk of cows. Continuing, he asked, "What
made you think of that?"

The man pointed at the litter of empty beer bottles. "So as to
raise up some capital to buck that brewery. Don't you know a
brewery's not like a faro bank? There just ain't no way for one man
to break it."

Chalk could smile and nod to that one and things were becoming pleasanter. The three men laughed, and the ex-doctor motioned
that he would like his glass refilled. It was an extra drink he was
taking by himself.

Soon there would be rounds to buy. Chalk realized this even
though he was just drinking beer. Oh, Chalk had the money all
right. If he couldn't pay his way he knew enough to stay outside.
No matter how painful that was, it would be the lesser agony.
Afford was not the word. He had the money with him and he
needed it here even though temperance people would point out it
could be better spent at home.

He certainly hadn't sold his gun. It was in the shed behind the
house, hanging in its holster from a peg. If he was getting drunk
it was only sensible not to do it armed. If he should be drunk and
feeling mean then it was needful to keep clear from firearms. Tonight he was happy or had been until now. It wasn't always like
that. If the world pushed in too hard and fast there could be occasion to use a handy gun to push it out again. Then the barn door
would be wide open and just from anger at one thing there would
be no sane and restful places left to find his way back to.

He had something of his own house. It wasn't sod. It wasn't

bricks. It was somewhat in between. He guessed his wife was there. Damn it, he knew she was. He wondered about Doc's woman and where she was, if he'd ever had one. They were just the sort of friends who only saw each other in the bar here, or to pass by on the street. He did know not to call him Doc. He never answered to that. Now Chalk heard someone say, "Beer drinkers don't have to buy."

So he replied, "This one, however, is." He'd been figuring the cost of a round for the last five minutes and he placed the exact amount on the bar. The drinks were poured and everyone saluted him with upraised glasses. As custom had it he would not have to pay through the next four beers. It was almost like having money in the bank. He wouldn't want to chew those beers down fast. It should take as long a time as possible, getting back there to where he needed to pay again. Even people you didn't know well, it was sometimes fun just to be with them.

Frazier was an example. What in the hell do they ever talk about? Well, there were all the various wagons that would be needed on Chalk's ranch. That was something the doctor knew about. He seemed to know more about wagons than any person living. He knew how to tell if wheel spokes had been real oil-boiled and not just made pretty with some boat varnish coats. Frazier even knew about making an overland stage and could describe all the various carriages and coaches back in the East. There was vehicles that a person out here never even saw. For himself however, Frazier only kept a light spring wagon that was nearly beat to hell. It seemed like every day he was going to buy a new one, but . . . Chalk remembered what Frazier once had said: Actually owning one decent proper wagon could wipe out a dozen dreams of all the other wagons a man might plan to own.

Chalk picked up a bottle of beer. There were certain pleasures that a whisky drinker could not experience. The sign behind the bar said that iced beer was for sale. Well, that was nonsense. Still the bottle was pleasingly cool in his hand. The small noise that a loosened top made was friendly. No, he wouldn't start in again about the wagons, nor would he plague his friend about why he was no longer doctoring. Right now he was a doctor, just like Chalk was a rancher. With one difference, Chalk thought. Frazier had once really been a doctor, although he wouldn't talk about it anymore. It seemed there were a lot of things men wouldn't talk about.

The beer glowed warm. Chalk thought what a damned fine man that ramrod was standing over there. He was the sort that never worried over what would happen, and never had to know how things would be before even they were started. Jesus, what a big-assed man, and Jesus, what a hole Doc had to pour whisky into. Pieces of the bar kept going in and out of focus, and on occasion the whole place would just shake itself like a sleeping dog that dreams. He shook his head. One of the few good things about not having anything to do was that you didn't have to be in any sort of shape to do it. Chalk put a fresh cool bottle to his lips. He wasn't about to go through both the effort of pouring and then raising a glass up from the bar. A man could not gulp beer, but he could sure as hell drain it away. The bottle was empty and Chalk put it down hard. It was an assertive thonk and it was time for him to order up another round. This time he didn't have the money counted right. The bartender had to ask for more. Chalk passed him over some extra change to thank him for his trouble. While doing this he couldn't know if he would have to stop. With a full sense of accomplishment he sucked away a last few flecks of foam. He put down that bottle on the bar with a bang. The tone was just right, not angry loud nor pussyfoot-soft like a man who was ashamed to have a beer. Those three cattlemen were still there and they were either silent or talking quietly amongst themselves. The Doc, he was really drinking whisky. No, that wasn't right. He was breathing it in through all the pores of his skin. It wasn't swelling him up, and to see how steady he was standing up to that bar, you'd hardly think he'd been drinking at all. Chalk knew better. Frazier had been drinking. Not as much as he could, but much more than he should. Chalk smiled his thought to himself.

The ranch foreman raised up his glass just for an eyeball toast, and Chalk flourished his beer bottle in the air. It had been full and now it was empty. He had to exercise a little care to get it down so that it would stand by itself upright on the bar.

"Powder River and let 'er buck." Chalk followed this statement, which had been delivered suddenly and at the top of his voice, with a yell that overreached his first level of rowdiness. Then he was quiet. A big smile spread over his face. For a second the barkeep had jumped back. Then he relaxed. It had been as harmless as it was loud.

The ramrod said, now that it was quiet again, "What in hell kind of noise is that to make here in this bar where men are drinking. He indicated his companions and Frazier too.

The ex-doctor moved closer so as to speak quietly. It was nearly a whisper.

"That was just a little catchphrase that he said." The ex-doctor paused. "Let's see, it was 'Powder River and let her buck.' Of course it's foolish and maybe Chalk is a boor. But damn it, he's," Frazier indicated Chalk with an imperceptible nod of his head, "not all that much of a person. If yelling a little bit makes him feel good I'd be the first to say he should. He needs every little bit of cheering up that he can get, either from himself or from," Frazier paused again, "whatever in the hell others there happen to be."

The ramrod made an affirmative movement with his hand, directed down the bar. It was toward Chalk and it warmed him. One nice thing about bars, he thought, is that there are people, yes, there are people who don't matter a damn, but you can look at them and talk to them as though they really were your friends. The sort of friends—a tear came to the corner of Chalk's eye as he started up the thought again—the sort of friends people need so much and

so seldom have. This was the first time he'd thought sad thoughts
tonight and he knew he'd best stop doing it.

Frazier continued and it certainly wasn't his habit to, because
drunk or sober he seldom was a man who made explanations. He
addressed the ramrod quietly. "One reason I like my friend over
there is just because I've never met a man, doesn't matter how
stupid or thick-headed, who hasn't seen or thought just one thing
new and different from every other human being. If he or she had
not been born, that thought or thing might never have ever happened."

The ramrod wasn't about to be intimidated by the intensity of
someone else's drunkenness. "What in the hell different from everybody else has our friend Chalk discovered? You tell me that if you
can."

"Just one. Out of muddleheadedness, and sometimes a laziness
to melt the heart of God, from all his dead-assed shortcomings he
can get a happiness. If they could see it, the world's fortunate few
would wish they somehow knew to be half that much alive."

The ramrod's eyebrows raised, so the ex-doctor filled him in.
"Needless to say, if he could do it all the time, he wouldn't need
the drink nor would he be the person whom he is." Frazier almost
wanted to hear some sort of answer, and he kept his face open but
the ramrod turned silently back toward the bar.

Frazier thought about open eyes. He glanced at Chalk. When
the bar's dim light reached Chalk's eyes it stopped. The cords or
wires that ran back to his brain were closed down for the night.
There was a smile still on his lips, and he kept steadily to his post.
He could with seeming soberness acknowledge the nods from the
trio he now barely saw. They were distant, not in space but in
perception.

Of course, as a medical man, Frazier knew that there were no
wires inside a human head, but he walked the few steps back down

the bar to look again into Chalk's eyes. If those optic nerves were telegraph cables they now led to an open key.

By now Chalk had flowed over several of his edges. His beer-filled bladder drove him from the bar. He didn't find an outhouse until after a dozen tries. Then something strange and insistent started to happen from deep within. The green sickness that he hated came. He wished he knew some way to avoid it.

The evening was moist and cool. A thin wet snow was freshly fallen. It was dark inside the outhouse now that the door was closed. Chalk worried that he might fall forward and then down into the hole. In addition this outhouse wasn't sweet enough for his stomach to stand. With a big movement he turned and had the door flung wide. He pitched out to find instant sleep half on the trodden pathway and half on the cold comfort of the snow.

Frazier wondered for a few idle moments about what had become of Chalk. Well, he'd either gone home or he had anesthetized himself by the gradual and laborious addition of sufficient alcohol to blood and brain. The forest of bottles was impressive. The bartender must have guessed that Chalk was done. He started putting them away.

"Hey, Doc," the ramrod called. Frazier never answered to that form of address. "Hey, mister . . ." There was a pause.

"Mister is good enough."

"Where do you think your buddy's gone?"

"I have no idea. And does it really matter?"

"No, I don't guess so, even if he was your buddy." Now the ramrod pounded on the bar shouting that the bottle should be left out in front of him.

The street door opened quietly. Even though he was facing it the barkeep couldn't be certain he saw a small figure enter. Both the ramrod and the ex-doctor felt one breath of air yet neither turned to see who or what had come in through the door.

A child had come in. He stood inside. The place was at least achieved. As new minutes passed nothing happened to him. He remained inside. The man he was looking for stood alone nearby. There were three other men over there in a group and then the man behind the bar. Well, he knew him. It was just the hotel clerk here, made different now that it was night. The child moved to the bar. He looked up at the ex-doctor's back. He hadn't decided to find this man himself. All the children were looking everywhere, and this was one of the places he'd been assigned to. It was obvious that this huge grown-up was not taking notice. Now that he had found him, what was there to do? The child tried to make a wish that the man would turn around, but it seemed a long time passed and the wish wasn't working. He was afraid to talk. Somehow talking wouldn't work. The group of three men were looking down at him with smiles. He hadn't been sent to find them and the man he needed still wouldn't acknowledge him. It didn't matter how many wishes he was making. He was still afraid to speak because he'd never been inside the hotel and bar. All that was left would be to kick hard against this man's ankle, just above where his pants leg was stuffed into a low-top boot. This was something the boy knew how to do, and knowing it had to be done, he aimed carefully.

The man spun suddenly away from the bar. In an instant he had turned around and was facing nothing. Well, at least he hadn't spilt his drink. As he reached down to rub his ankle a child was there. It was a small child whose eyes looked unblinkingly into his. No words and no motion, just that one kick and now standing there. What in the hell had he done to have this boy seek him out in the middle of the night in order to perpetrate this brazen and courageous assault? In particular courageous because the little monster was just standing there as if Frazier, the man, was something that he owned. As always with children, there was the option of striking them and with more than the usual justification due to the fact that he had just been kicked. The three cowboys were smiling big while waiting to see what would happen. Was Chalk in trouble? Frazier had no worry or thought for what had happened to Chalk. It would have been impossible for him to drink with enjoyment if he had to give even the slightest concentration to what happened to people after they left the bar. This child was staring silently up into his eyes. It had been a mistake to look, but then how could he properly ignore a firmly planted kick against his ankle?

"What the hell is the meaning of all this?" The question was asked of the bartender, who held his empty palms upward to show that he didn't know. At the same time he made to move from behind the bar.

The child saw this as an immediate danger. He had more to do than just find this man. He finally forced himself to say, "Sick." Then he grimaced to mimic pain. He moaned and it was nearly a high-pitched wail. Then he moaned again.

The ex-doctor forgot himself just long enough to say, "You've got to describe the symptoms," words were just a little difficult, "with greater clarity."

Talking was wrong, the boy knew. He had not been sent to use the time for talking. He knew that there was pain. He didn't know how much time there was. The children had gathered around her bed. They couldn't know what adult assistance was available. Sometimes there had been very little, and sometimes there had been none. So, in the house they made the preparations they thought most suitable. Then they had run out to find this man. The boy, it was Bill, had seen drunken men before. They were both useless and frightening. This one wasn't. Right now the man was gently patting him on the head. The barkeep was out from behind the bar and moving toward him with an outstretched hand. There was no time left to talk.

At first he reached up to touch the man's coat and then he had it firmly grasped in both his hands. He pulled, no longer gently and as a request. He was demanding, like a heavy fish on a line's end making its first run to where the current flows across a pool.

If the doctor was fogged by what he'd drunk, he wasn't that fogged he couldn't recognize where both life and immediacy strove. The child's whole world trembled. This was the feeling of sudden and now. The pull against his coat was strong. He waved the bartender off.

Bill felt his wish becoming real, but he still kept pulling. He knew better than to try and talk. Success brought his courage back. He'd really known the bartender wouldn't try to kill him. He'd even known in his heart it was unlikely. A white person seldom killed a child colored the same as they.

To drink properly one had to concentrate. Before the advent of the child the ex-doctor had been making an inventory of the room. He had carefully looked along the level rows of bottles behind the bar, and then, cleverly husbanding his energies, he'd allowed his eyes to move up to the mirror. There he could see paneling and the tables behind his back that composed into straight lines he'd traced into new and comforting horizons. Now all were gone. He was being shaken, and bullied by a child. With his eyes cast downward at an angle, Frazier felt a slight shift to the room. He resisted it. With one hand he was still gently attempting to pat the child's head. The other, holding his drink, was raised as a quiet sign to the bartender that he would handle this annoyance on his own. If indeed it was an annoyance after all. The child's movements weren't large. He was indeed still only a boy who needed to use intensity for strength.

There was no way he could force this huge man to move. If only he could, or even carry him out of this bar and down along the street. The man in his grasp neatly emptied his glass. It was a problem to sip while being shaken, but with concentration it was accomplished. With the glass back on the bar, Frazier reached his hand into his pocket. He put down a coin as carefully as he'd set the glass. Then turning he gave his hand to the child whose deepest wish had been fulfilled.

He had the man moving toward the door and the night outside. Now there was no more shaking insistence. The child sought to lead as swiftly as possible. He must do it, now that the man was coming with him, without seeming to pull.

Outside a thin covering of new snow showed the emptiness of the town. There was only one set of tracks. The doctor could see where the child had gone looking and pulling at the shut doors which faced the street. Lastly he had come to peer into the empty lobby of the hotel. Then he'd stood on tiptoe to see through the partially frosted windows of the bar. There were only toe imprints, and then the widely spaced tracks to the door. The child had run in without waiting to get his courage up. Chalk's footprints weren't out in the street. He must have left through the back entrance. The doctor vaguely hoped that Chalk would be all right. Up until now, he always had been. Together the man and the boy walked beside the hurried set of tracks that had brought the child into town. Occasional oil lamps winked from scattered windows, but most houses in this deepening time of night were completely dark.

A young man on horseback was coming toward them. There was a dusting of snow flakes on him. The horse was warm and flakes melted as they touched his coat.

"You found him, Bill. You found him."

A light grew in the child's face. He grasped the hand he held for affirmation. Frazier sensed the child's heightened pulse. Whatever this was about, he thought, an adult is already here. Well, if that was the case it was time to get out of the snow and back into the shelter of the bar.

"I'm glad he found you, Mr. Frazier." The youngster on the horse looked familiar. Frazier was trying to disengage himself from the child's grasp, but he couldn't very well shake the child off as though he were a wetness. Now they were coming to the edge of town. Frazier looked around and could see no reason for being here. Then he noticed. Not far distant was one building brightly lit at several of its windows. A large space of yellow light spilled from an opening door and a voice called out, "Now's the time, Jim. Don't you stand there in the street." At this call the horse turned beneath the rider's knees, and the small child seemed to leap forward, bringing Frazier with him.

The open door led into a big kitchen room. The light inside was sudden, and now Frazier could see clearly. There was the child who still held his hand, and on their heels was the boy who'd just slid off his horse. This was Jim. The girl who'd called to him was about fourteen or nearing it. Behind her, unfearing and peering, was a baby of three or four. She came forward to see who had come here in between her brothers.

"Mr. Frazier," the girl in the doorway said as she stepped back, "I am so glad to see you here." The light inside was still very bright. Frazier nodded. The young boy had done his job, and his insistence had stopped as they'd crossed the threshold.

A new hand plucked at him from the near-grown girl at his side. Even before she could move him, he heard the long sound of a cry that came from muffled pain. For a second he wished the drinks inside him could silence it away. They didn't. He was being led into a bedroom lit by several candles and a lamp. There was a blanket-covered unevenness to the bed. A woman's face sweated above it. The girl beside him said, "Ann, I just had to go to the door. Mr. Frazier is with us now." With a cloth wrung out in cool water she wiped Ann's sweat away.

Frazier put his hand beneath the blankets. It was regular labor in a young woman, even pulsed and strong. Even distended there was a ripple to this woman's muscles. "Why didn't you go for a doctor?" he asked.

"Well, we thought it might be all right."

"Then why did you come for me?"

"Well, later we decided that there should be someone here, other than just us kids." The girl answered him and then by way of further explanation went on to say, "For when the baby was due."

There'd be plenty of time for a lot of things before the baby came, but another drink was not among them. First he'd get into the kitchen. At least the kids knew about boiling lots of water, and there were clean sheets laid out in handy piles. Frazier poured some of the hot water into a pan so that he might wash his hands. The young boy who'd brought him watched most carefully while looking slightly puzzled.

Frazier explained. "It's one of the things I have a feeling about. One thing for sure I know, it can't do any harm." While washing, Frazier sensed that something here was askew. The situation seemed quite simple to him, a woman in normal labor. It couldn't be the labor that puzzled him. It was the feeling he'd had in the bedroom.

His own two hands, as they washed each other, were hinting to him. A woman had to labor for each person born into the world. Had his doctoring been so long ago that he didn't know the message he was missing? That wasn't it. He looked back to his hands. As they rubbed together they were still a hint to him; a hint he couldn't touch. And what in the hell was he doing here anyway, doctoring again after so many years? However, with only kids around he'd probably better stay. As he stepped away from the sink the young boy took his place.

In the bedroom, Frazier found the woman composed between her pains. He'd never seen her before or if he had he'd never seen her closely. That was rather strange in a town so small as this, but Frazier kept schedules that were very much his own. She was about twenty, he thought, and her long blond hair was undone so as to almost hide the pillow. Her smile showed even teeth, and now that the girl had wiped her brow again, Frazier could see her skin still sunned to a honey color even with this much winter come. She held out her hand to take his. He held it on his left palm and patted it

with his right. The imbalance was now clear to him. She had lost
her other arm. It was gone at the shoulder. The sleeve of her gown
was pinned, and the haze of bourbon whisky was thinning like a
sun-shot morning's fog.

He'd heard there was a woman here in Comptonsville who had
only one arm. Now that he thought about it there could hardly be
two. It was Chalk's woman, and Frazier knew Chalk wouldn't find
his way home tonight.

4

On his way into town Ole Sorensen did not like seeing men like these. After one glance he looked back to stare ahead over his team. His wife never even turned to see who rode up behind them. The riders passed by bleakly and only for the slightest pause did the last horseman hesitate. Then he followed after the others. This happened on the road just as it entered Comptonsville. Up ahead the riders bunched to talk amongst themselves. Ole did not want to pass them again, so he turned and drove down the lane that led behind the school. He'd leave his team behind Brown's store where later there would be shade.

After watching carefully, the group of five riders unfolded as they rode into town. The last rider was the first to stop. He dismounted casually, and like someone who had the whole day to spare, he tied his horse to the nearby hitching rack. He was guarding the street at a distance from the bank. It had been agreed that his job was to keep a route open for their escape. If there was any trouble at the bank these men had carefully planned to revolver fight their way back through the town. His companions rode on without hesitation. The posted man looked up and down the street. At his back there was the blank windowless wall of some building.

The next building, on his left, was the general store. Next to that was a restaurant and then the bank. Now he looked back along the far side of the street. The hotel with bar faced the restaurant, and he could read that sign clear enough. The letters were big. COMP-TONSVILLE HOTEL AND SALOON. There was an empty-looking stage station next to it, and then coming back to just across the street there was a gunsmith's store still tightly closed. That part was planned. They'd found out he was never open this early in the morning. Beside the dismounted rider, a dusty lane ran back and forth. It had importance for the man standing there. This lane made two more roads that led away from the bank. If need arose he could keep them open too.

He was the oldest man in the group with a beard shot through with flecks of gray. He was slouched and sloppy and had more heft than size. Although he looked like a pile of old used rags, the inside of him was a steel trap. The face was tight as though the beardless parts were covered with a mummy's skin, and his nose was pointed. A big part of this job was to blend, like a gray lizard on a gray rock, into the weathered boards on the building just behind him.

As usually carried by normal men, a single gun was shown. A second big revolver was jammed underneath his loose hung coat. In its pockets were a couple of much smaller guns. The large hat he wore was a crumpled ruin. Anyone could clearly see, why he was called the Tramp. An observer would expect to see eyes rheumy and red, but on close examination these eyes were the only clean thing about the man, clear, ice-blue, and wide.

Robbing the bank had been the Tramp's idea. He'd formed it about twenty miles from town and high up on a mountain. There were ten of them holed up and hidden on that mountain in a cave. As unreconstructed rebels, they did their best to keep the war alive. Backbiting and bored, they lived together there. Lived, like hell they did. In that cave they were like animals, hardly ever clean and their grub either hunted or stole. It was a rotten place to be. The

Tramp, whose name was Kay Cee Smith, looked down at his clothes. They were rotting on him. That whole damned hideout was a mess. Yes, they did have safety there and could not be rooted out. Still, it was not a way to live—pretending to be waiting for something big to happen again. The war was long over and these men he was with had lost it with Johnson in the West. They lost again with those Frenchmen down in Mexico. Now there was this plan to go fighting up in Canada. The hell with that. If there was fighting to be done, Kay Cee Smith's plan was to do it here and for something he himself could use to buy out from that cave. With enough money he thought maybe to go and live an easeful life down in South America. He was finished with going out to steal little bits of food and lonely ranchers' horses. If a man was going to rob, a bank was the only place where there was any style to it.

The morning looked good and the street remained empty. Another man now lounged quietly on the steps of the bank. He was younger, but there was no way to guess his age because the sun on his face had changed his skin to leather. He was starved down to thinness. These two men had shared a thousand hidden camps and had no sense of excitement now. They knew exactly what was happening. The chance was taken. In half a dozen seconds they could die in a hundred ways. But if this bothered them they would be somewhere else. There wasn't even need for a reassuring glance. The man on the bank steps would be solid there. He watched the horses while the three others quickly went inside.

The five of them figured the morning as early. There'd be few people in the town and the ones there, well they'd be just awake and not set for any play. Sleepy and small like this, no one would expect trouble right down the main center street. This early in the day certainly should be a peaceful time. It was a robber's right to expect that quietly he would bag up the money and depart and there would be no injury to anyone, on a sensible Monday morning in a small-assed country town.

Sensibleness came apart in the beginning of the day. The teller who was setting up the money trays failed to properly notice the pistols pointed at his head. He threw the tray with coins and bills into the air. His city shoes were smooth and slid upon the polish of the oak-wood floor. His leap for the rear door sounded a first gunshot that went unheard, outside in the stirring street. There, movement was approaching fast with teamsters driving up at one end of the town, while, on the other side and still out of sight, a Concord coach was slowing opposite the first houses.

The teller was out the bank's rear door into an almost empty alley. Bubbled blood burst from his lips as he fell down the short flight of steps. He had a last strength that cried out, just once, for help. The only person to see him and know that he was dying there was the Sorensen boy, who'd just got into town. He'd gotten down from his parent's wagon the instant it had stopped, and even though unharnessing the horses was his job, his strict father wouldn't make him stay to help, because even a small empty town was vividly exciting to a boy who'd been so long out on the farm.

There was nothing this boy knew to say in English, though he could certainly see how it was this man was hurt. The boy started to scream. A skittish horse in the alley started back. Reins snapped and the horse left at a gallop when it found that it was free. A sleepy town was being wakened.

Inside the bank one of the robbers hissed, "For Jesus Christ's sake, don't pick up the silver coins." Money was spread all across the floor. Another robber was on his hands and knees while an older teller stood with arms raised above his head. Next to him the banker stood with his hands half upraised.

"Put your hands down at your sides," a second robber said, "because looking in from the street people will think that this is a robbery."

The two men obeyed.

"Now the safe."

The banker shook his head. The robber thumbed back the hammer of his second gun but the banker wouldn't wince or cringe. It was his bank and he'd be damned if he'd say anything. Words would only be the shadows of his fears. If the safe stayed shut, all they could do was kill him. But give into them once and there would be robbers in on you almost every day.

George Evans, who in his later years took the title of Major, was very close to being killed. The older clerk beside him said, "Take the goddamned money. Just for what it's worth the safe door isn't even locked."

Evans made his leap for the nearest gun. Slashing up, its barrel caught him underneath the jaw. A second downward blow bared his skull through an opened scalp. He was unconscious as he hit the floor. The pistol's loading lever hung stupidly down. The catch that held it remained firmly imbedded in George Evan's skull. Two of the robbers had feed sacks to the safe door and were filling them up with both paper and gold.

Marshal Kincade would not have wanted to see such trail-ready horses tied up in front of the bank. And if he'd seen the man who stood watch on the steps, he'd have liked him even less. The man stood with his fingertips stroking a rifle butt that stuck out from its scabbard.

The boy was around from the back of the bank. He was the Scandinavian farmer's son, and what crazy things was he yelling now? Two cowboys were inside Brown's general store. They'd come to town early, straight in from the range. They were here to get snuff and plug cut for the crew. It had been a fool thing for everyone to run out of every kind of tobacco all at once. They heard the kid yelling. The storekeeper heard him too.

"Son of a bitch, son of a bitch," the boy yelled at the top of his lungs. These were the only English words he knew.

"That's a hell of a goddamned thing to be saying right out in a public street," one of the cowboys said.

Brown, the storekeeper agreed.

"Well if it isn't right," the second cowboy said, "somebody ought to go out and tell him to damn well shut his rat-assed mouth."

Both cowboys were on the store's steps when the three men fled the bank. Real shooting was starting now. There was a twinkling of a second to decide, to maybe pretend that this wasn't to do with them. Behind them a window shattered and there was the storekeeper with a Cavalry Sharps. Its first shot was loud, and then, right in the middle of now, the cowboys found they were in a pistol fight.

In front of the bank a horse was down and dying in the street. The Sharps crashed loudly for a second time and then a third. The two cowboys were crouched in the doorway trying to reload their guns. They were tobacco buyers not revolver fighters, and the distance had been longer than their skill.

Chalk woke slowly. Doll-like his lids rolled up, wired to the little lead weights that he felt inside his brain. At least the air was clean and good to breathe. He was sleeping, or rather, he thought regretfully, he had slept, both comfortable and clean. But where in the hell was he at now? He tried to weave the various parts of last night together. That was much too hard. Something immediate and loud was happening here today.

He had slept between the bows, high up on a freight wagon's canvas covering. The wagon was parked between the hotel and the Wells Fargo station. No team was tied to it and that was luck. If this wagon moved he would find himself lying in the street. Chalk could see the whole street up and down. On the far side a man was standing. There was no noise from him. Chalk looked to his right where a cluster of people moved in front of the bank. What they were doing wasn't clear, and only one thing was sure: at least one horse was down and dead in the street. Chalk wondered about that. He felt exclusive and aloof up here as though he had been sleeping on a cloud.

He moved and his pistol nearly fled its holster so as to slide off the canvas to the ground. He hadn't been home, so where had he gotten it? He examined the pistol as he caught it. Yes, it certainly was his. Well, if he hadn't gone home he'd doubtless been over to the shed behind the house. That was where he kept his gun rig stashed, but what had he gone to get it for? He squinched down his eyes and opened them again. It could not be more true that he had gone there, yet he had no memory of it. No one had carried him there, and it was doubtful if anyone had carried him up here. He didn't like the height and he didn't like the noise.

It was a fair morning and there was a slight coat of snow on the wagon's covering. What had fallen on him had melted, leaving his clothes sticky and damp. He was like the road, from warmth of earth the snow there was mostly gone, and now he noticed that the snow remaining on the wagon's top was as slippery as hell. If he wasn't killed sliding down then he could just wait up here and freeze to death. He was shivering from both cold and thirst. Wouldn't it be warm and pleasant now to have a beer to drink.

The general store was up the street and it was Brown and two cowboys shooting. Chalk knew the storekeeper well, and it wasn't like Brown to try to kill a man. Chalk turned to look further up the street, and just this slight movement hurt his head. Again he could see the group in front of the bank. At least one of them had a feed bag or was it a pillow case in his hand. It then occurred to Chalk that only robbers needed bags when they made withdrawals from a bank. These men were desperately trying to catch frightened, plunging horses. As he looked around again, a man who had been in the background was starting to get into the fight. Those must be some gunmen at the bank and this man was joining in with Brown to shoot at them. It seemed that way to Chalk. Maybe

this was something he should be doing too. He had a weapon with
him. It was in his hand. Before being a hero too, he'd see what this
other man would do.

The Tramp looked carefully around with just one long sweeping glance and then he squeezed off a careful shot. One of the
cowboys on the stoop of Brown's store got spun and fell back across
the threshold. This held Chalk's attention. A second shot nearly
took the other cowboy off the stoop. His hat flew off into the road.
He realized that the shot hadn't come from in front of him, so he
yelled, "Watch out wherever in the hell you're shooting. Then he
put his hand up to his head. He'd hardly been welted, yet finding
blood across his palm caused him to leave the fight. He was being
prudent and wasn't panicked because he had the presence of mind
to drag along his buddy as he retreated to the inside of Brown's
store.

With all the action in the street, Chalk was the only one to
observe the Concord coach as it came into town. Either he'd slept
late or the coach was arriving early. It slowed down on the far side
of the bank. Seeing trouble, the driver whipped up his team so as
to drive on through. They swerved hard to miss the dead horse in
the street. The messenger leaned across the driver's lap. To shoot
down he had to poke underneath the driver's lines, and the double
boom of the long-barreled ten-gauge gun slapped one man dead
right on the steps. A second pitched back leaking badly.

One man, holding the money bag, was up on his horse. The
robbers were firing their revolvers, and window glass was crashing
everywhere. The mounted man drew up his buddy who'd been hit.
The lookout was on the remaining horse. He had his carbine now
and was putting shots up and down the street. The horses with the
men and money helter-skeltered right by Chalk. Both riders yelled,
"Kay Cee, come on!," but the man who'd shot the cowboys made
absolutely no reply. The wounded man riding double lost his hold
and fell into the street nearby. His buddy hesitated for one instant.

Then both horses were turned back and their riders thoroughly revolvered the street.

They could ignore where the stage coach had fallen. It was over on its side. One wheel had caught on the boardwalk's edge. The team was hopelessly harness-tangled and they couldn't move the fallen coach. Best of all it didn't block the road. The driver and the guard were sprawled there quietly, and like a jack-in-the-box the up side door flew open and passengers were jumping out to run in all directions. This was more confusion and noise. For seconds it helped the men attempting their escape.

Comptonsville's law officer had been inside the livery barn. Marshal Kincade was an older man, maybe nearing forty. Still, he had been in the war. He heard the first shots as he was getting ready to ride out to a section of the range so as to head off a useless fencing controversy. It was not official business. His plan had been to visit riled neighbors and get them gentled down before they came to lawyers, courts, and other outsider circumstances. There might still be time to save two men from becoming enemies.

Well, that would have to wait. Charlie Kincade wasn't new to this job. He had always discouraged the useless and high-spirited discharge of firearms, particularly right here in the settled part of town. Once in the air, a bullet couldn't tell if it had started from a drunken frolic or someone's set meanness to kill. The starting didn't matter, because when it hit, the bleeding and the dying was all the same. He had the Henry rifle from its scabbard before he stepped out into the street. He looked up and down carefully and slow. He didn't run out to see what was happening. He gave himself a few seconds' extra time so the bright sun didn't flash too sudden in his eyes. That was when the coach came by, trailing gunfire behind it. He had to jump back. He'd seen it swerve, and before he could wonder what the hell the driver had in mind, the coach crashed over on its side and galloping horses in the street were coming right at him.

The horsemen galloped by too fast. A real killer would have gotten at least one of them, but Kincade always hoped there'd be a decent way. In his mind he thought of them as resolutions without death. As a gunfighter this sometimes caused him to be a cat's whisker slow.

The horsemen disappeared behind parked wagons and Kincade didn't know who might be inside. He walked up the street toward the noise. The gunfight was hidden from him, though flashes of movement rippled up and down the road. It was that same damned insane gallantry of Meade's cavalry, or had it been A. P. Hill's? It caught your heart to watch those bastards fight. They fought so well it almost made a man forget he should be shooting them. This was something from the war. It was something they'd learned when young, some starting out as early as sixteen.

Brown had an empty cartridge in his hand as he saw the horsemen sweeping back. He dove inside the store, dropping his gun, because a man with an empty gun could easily be dead out there. Time was tight and shots remaining few. The robbers knew not to waste shots at men who were running from the fight.

However, from an upstairs window of the hotel a man was shooting nervously with an undersized pocket gun. One of the robbers danced his horse out into that street with a revolver in each hand. His horse was being signaled by its rider's knees, as this one man tried to keep a whole town down. His companion sought to lift the wounded man to ride behind him. Even as he pulled and as his companion's foot lifted to seek a stirrup they were both hit by shots from a new adversary. They turned. The wounded man sank to his knees and tried to shoot, but his gun no longer worked. Without its stud the rammer dropped to jamb the cylinder. Belatedly he held the lever up and cocked the gun. His world was fuzzing, and holding the lever in his left hand helped to steady him, if only momentarily. Now he would have to move it each time he wanted to shoot. He didn't have to, though, because he died right there, pitching slowly over, both his hands filled with an emptied gun.

Horsemen were coming down the street. Kincade saw a flash of movement and an upraised gun as he threw the Henry rifle to his shoulder. There was no consciousness of aim. He matched the swinging barrel of his rifle to the movement of the man as a waterfowler aiming at a crossing bird. There was even the slight second of hesitation just as the movements met. Another man was dead and his unencumbered horse galloped by.

Kincade wished he could get all these people quieted. There was certainly more shooting than there were things to shoot at. He knew that this could lead to people getting hurt or even killed.

The sound of every shot thwacked across some raw part of Chalk's throbbing head. He was spread out on the wagon top now and didn't have to worry about falling down. He'd seen there was no team harnessed to it.

That one man in the street who had fired into the store, he'd been called to by the mounted men. Why hadn't he gotten on his horse? Chalk had seen the stagecoach guard shoot and then the stage went over. The passengers had moved off like there was rattlesnakes in a chamber pot. The driver and guard were spilled behind the far side rear wheel, and they were not moving at all. Looking left he could see Marshal Kincade coming from the livery. Chalk had seen him make his shot and then whirled his head just in time to see a pistol fighter go down. Stood right up in his stirrups, pistol spinning off into the air and then thump into the street. The horse got clear and that made Chalk feel better. At least the man didn't have a foot caught to get dragged, though if he were dead, Chalk couldn't see how any further injury could be suffered.

The last horseman was leaving now. Doubtless he had ridden through worse than this. Atop the wagon's cover Chalk had his gun out. To steady it he held it with both hands. He was wishing

that he wasn't here. He wished he had something wet and cold
inside the dryness of his mouth. He also wished that he didn't have
to shoot the man there on that horse who was making his fight
alone out there in the street. Well Chalk could make that wish
come true. He'd just lay there atop the wagon and watch.

Someone new and serious had gotten to an upstairs window of
the hotel, because above the sound of all the little crackly fire something really blambed. Now the last horse was down and on top of
its rider. A huge final spasm shook the horse and the man was
freed. He rolled clear of being crushed, dragging the money sack
and a shattered leg. He took a shot at movement in the hotel. Glass
shattered. Another shot from the hotel's big rifle threw street dirt
and slush inches from the crawling man. Someone else was shooting. Maybe the guard had kicked clear of the stagecoach wreck.
The bandit was hit repeatedly.

Chalk saw the farm boy come racing around from behind the
bank. He was shouting something unintelligible. It was evident
that the boy wasn't paying any attention to the shooting. It was
something back there that had gotten this young hayseed mad as
hell.

The bank robbery had failed. Some were dead. Others might,
just might, in all this shooting, have gotten clear away. One had
not. The gravely wounded robber's pistol was pointed at the farm
boy who'd appeared from God knows where. Even from a distance
Chalk could see the man's leg was badly broken. It angled away
from his body in the strangest way. His horse was shot and one of
his hands still grasped the feed bag stuffed with bills and coin. The
kid with his hands waving in the air hadn't been the one to stop
him. Yet, for just this moment this kid could get the blame for a
robbery gone wrong. The pistol was pointed and the hammer back.
The man on the ground pressed the trigger. There was a click.
Then Chalk saw the robber toss the emptied gun away.

"You damn lucky, boy. I seem to be holding an empty wheel."

The robber with the money bag beside him smiled slightly with just the edges of his teeth.

The farm boy wore a long, heavy wool muffler that had trailed in the wet snow as he'd run. He undid it from around his neck in a single movement. Holding one end he used it to beat in a frenzy at the fallen man. The scarf lashed down like an endlessly whirling snake. The robber couldn't seem to grasp the muffler, and with one of his legs so badly broken neither could he get away from it.

"Damn, it. I give up."

The heavy scarf lashed down past counting.

The wounded bandit covered his face with his arms.

"I give up, you stupid little bastard."

The long muffler still laced back and forth.

The man curved his body like a grub. As clearly as he could he said, "I give up."

A boy's world had been violated. All the indignation and the injury this young boy felt was getting lashed into the man, and being beaten by a child was something the robber couldn't stand. The boy didn't realize he'd been nearly shot. Later he would. Just now he couldn't bear the pain he'd seen in the alley. He'd never seen so much hurt, or even someone dead. Before him was one of the men who had done that thing.

Every time the muffler fell, the boy would yell, "Son of a bitch." It was the only English swear word that he knew. Four times in cadence, once for every word, the scarf whipped down, over and over again. In addition this man had clicked his empty gun at him. He resented the hell out of a man who would have killed him without reason. He was one of those sullen men he'd seen from the wagon riding into town.

Clear of all the other movement, Chalk saw Kay Cee step out into the street. He walked to where the boy was whipping the fallen man.

Kay Cee's gun was in its holster now. From his wagon top

Chalk imagined he could reach out and touch those clustered people. He heard Kay Cee say, "Wilkenson, that's the goddamned kid
who saw us riding into town."

The man on the ground peered out from beneath his arms and
past the scarf. "Kay Cee, for Chrissakes stop the kid and get us the
hell out of here. Where's your horse?"

"Tied up back there." Kay Cee motioned with his thumb.

"The money's here." The wounded man held up the bag.

"That's the trouble, Wilkenson. I do wish there was another
way for you to leave."

The wounded robber spat at him, the kid wasn't noticing, and
Kay Cee's hand slowly reached toward his gun.

Chalk's first thought was that it didn't look good for the boy.
It wasn't too clear what the robbers would do, but one of them had
already tried to kill the kid. He'd seen enough of the wounded
robber so that he didn't, in any way, care about him. Chalk's gun
was already pointed at Kay Cee. His first thought was to try for a
head shot. That would be clean and quick, but there was always a
chance of missing, and Chalk had seen how Kay Cee could shoot.
So Chalk paid attention to old advice and aimed at the biggest part
of the man just so long as it was not his ass. The noise of his own
revolver going off was too much for a hungover person to bear.
Chalk winced and then kept shooting even though Kay Cee was
down with his fingertips still to his pistol butt. The boy had turned
and was looking up at him. The robber with the broken leg didn't
even seem to know where the shots were coming from.

Kincade's rifle was upraised. Then he saw it was Chalk.

Chalk wished now that he was using a bow and arrow. The
man was down and he'd try some fancier shots. Kincade shouted.
"Chalk, you stop that! You are killing that man."

"Well, good God, I know that. What in the hell did you think
I was shooting him for?" Chalk would have fired again. He couldn't.
Holding the front sight in the hammer notch he looked to see a

blasted cap. Pulling the trigger would only drop the hammer on an emptied chamber.

With the sound of the first shots, a clerk in the hotel had bolted up the stairs. From this front room he looked down into a chaotic street. Then he heard someone shooting from the room next door. By the sound it well might be a buffalo gun. The clerk had a Gallager carbine and a handful of shells. A repeater would raise more hell, but this would be hell enough, if only he could get the window open. It was stuck and glass was expensive. It seemed he struggled with it for an hour, but in the short time he took to open it the gunfight in the street was over. Chalk was stretched out on the new white canvas of a wagon top. Charlie Kincade had a gun on him, and all over, there were lots of dead men and horses too.

5

The doctor remained awake through the long night. Ann's baby was delivered, and it was a further exhilaration to be up and clearly awake as the dawn became early morning. His head was clear. He usually hid from these hours beneath a blanket cloud of the previous night's drinking, even knowing there was little daytime joy to be had from a night's boozing. But lately he'd stopped looking for joy in other places as well.

Now with the world awake again, Frazier felt a special elation from the morning after a good night's work had been done. He also felt a healthy tiredness. He turned the wicks down in the dawn-dimmed lamps and blew across their chimneys to fully extinguish them. Things had gone so smoothly. There'd been no need for any bottle as Ann would be a bountiful nurse. In other times he'd forceps-delivered babies plenty. This easy delivery saved him from having to remember the details of doctoring the difficult ones, and there'd been no need to hurry things.

How well the human body did for itself, if only you knew to let it find its own way. Jesus, he could devoutly love this one-armed girl as she'd brought her baby out. Fear of complications later? No,

he didn't think so. After one small ass-whomp the boy's first cry
had sounded. He'd cut and tied the cord and then wrapped the
baby carefully before giving him to his new young mother.

Children were sleeping here and there in chairs and on the floor.
They'd left the couch for him, and it would be a luxury to rest with
ankles crossed and fingers locked behind his head. Ann and the
baby must be sleeping. While Margaret stood at the bedroom's
doorway watching, he would take a few moments' rest.

By the time Frazier woke, the morning had fully formed. He heard
several distant popping noises. Then there was a steady back-and-
forth of guns being used in anger. Maybe it was a welcoming salute
for a baby newly in this world. No, that could not be true. As
Frazier sat up on the couch, Bill and Jim rushed into the street.
You'd think a circus had come to town. In their eagerness they left
the front door open. As they ran, he didn't call after them. The
baby was silent now and had a job to do. He was working to get
his mother's milk to flow.

The gunfire ceased, so the kids, he hoped, would be safe out
there. It hadn't been the sound of drunken cowboy fun. The timing
was far brisker. It certainly was a battle made up of thoughtfully
executed shots with several different guns involved.

The sound of heavy hoofbeats rattled against the clapboard
fronts of roadside houses. The two boys raced to dodge behind a
fence. Then they saw the horse was riderless. They half turned it
with their hats and Jim had one good grab at the reins. Fear-sweat
had lathered the animal, so they gentled it down with quiet words.
Its tracks showed that it had come from the center of the town.
The saddle was expensive and tied behind was a bedroll neatly
wrapped in oilskin. There was also a rifle in its scabbard and bulg-
ing saddle bags. The boys backtracked until they were around the

corner and on the main street. Jim tightly gripped the horse's halter
and to avoid questions he stayed way back from the crowd. This
was certainly the place where the excitement was.

Most obviously, the Concord was tipped over and several men
were trying to get its six-horse team untangled. Marshal Kincade
was holding his wartime Henry over one arm, and Chalk, awake
and seeming sober, was handing him his pistol belt.

In a combination of compassion and fear, big blond Mrs. Sorensen was carefully examining the body of her boy. She went over
him quickly like a dog searching for fleas. The father was looking
up and down the street, and the boy, nearly as big, was bawling
like a babe.

"Well, he's not hard hit," Jim said.

Bill nodded. "If he's been hit at all." He glanced past the boy
to where a crowd was gathering in front of the bank. From inside
there were shouts of "Give him air" and "Stop the bleeding if you
can." Someone else answered, "It's just his scalp that's cut." A reassuring voice disagreed. "It's one hell of a barrel cut, but he's
breathing fine."

From behind the building someone exclaimed, "God damn!"
loud and evenly. The bank clerk's body had been found.

Bill got underneath a wagon and then through the thin part
of a crowd that had backed against its side. He wriggled through
legs. People's attention was so drawn that no one thought to push
him away. In the center of this crowd was a short thick man ragged
dressed and crumpled small by death. Beside him another man
clutched a feed sack in one hand. He was looking up with live eyes
to the faces there. No one seemed to want to move, neither to pick
up the sack, nor to render assistance by plugging all the places this
man was bleeding from. Bill got back out through the crowd. There
wasn't anything he could do there, and watching a man that's hurt
is no help for anyone.

Jim still held the horse, and a dream, not yet even grown to hoping, came. No one had asked about the animal. As Bill came back to look up and down the street he wordlessly joined in this happy realization. Then, as an afterthought, he mentioned hearing of five dead men and another who might be dying.

Somebody brought the town's doctor around the corner at a run. Chubby and panting and already in a sweat, Dr. Taylor held his doctoring kit in one hand and his close-by specs in the other.

"Let the doctor through!" someone shouted, and the crowd made some room around the wounded robber. But Kincade called out loudly, "Doc," and pointed to the entrance of Brown's store. The doctor charged off in this new direction. He naturally wanted to know how all this had happened, but Kincade said that would have to wait until every last bit of doctoring was done.

The two wounded cowboys weren't badly hit and probably would have gotten better on their own. Both decided to be brave because this doctor's reputation had gotten out as far as the open range. Along with the people of the town, these two prospective patients were concerned about the doctor's competence.

Even as the doctor started to administer, another shout came from just outside the door. "That man across the street. He's hurt real bad. These is still up on their feet." The doctor hesitated until Kincade directed him.

"I certainly am aware of that," Kincade said, "but the law here says that the one who starts a mess is the one to get patched up last. That's fair and the way it will be. Start the mess and then wait your turn."

Returning to the street Kincade walked over to look closely at the man he'd shot. There was no help for him. Kincade said it to himself, "It was a damned poor and foolish thing for me to have to do." Looking again he thought of the waste. So recently there'd been a young cowboy's life on this earth with all its skills and competence. Then—and who knew why—he'd come into this town with the anger of violence in his heart. Again Kincade could almost see the running horse and feel the swing of his pointed rifle. But as always there was no memory of the gun's kick. That was something only felt when paper targets were being fired at.

The man with the Sharps buffalo gun poured out of the hotel. He ran right to where another dead man lay. Looking down he felt the flutter that comes to most people when they've gotten to the aftertaste of their excitement. "I got him right off with the first shot." No one was listening to him. They were concentrating on the wounded robber and how long it would be before he died.

Kincade could understand this man's excitement. Shooting a man didn't happen every day. As a public servant he thanked the man for showing active civic interest.

In reply and as a confirmation the big man who'd fired his Sharps rifle from the hotel went on to say, "If it was a train they'd robbed, the railroad's big enough to stand the fall. But you take this little bank we're getting started. Each dollar in that sack is one a man in this town has worked hard for and earned."

Later it turned out that the man with the buffalo gun had shot a horse but he had not killed its rider. This made Kincade wonder. If the man knew this fact, would it not in later years be a comfort to him?

Reminded of the robber's loot Kincade said, "Let's get that money back to where it belongs."

With authority to touch the sack, several men stepped forward and it was quickly up the steps and inside the bank.

If the town didn't get around to lynching him—which was unlikely because Kincade wouldn't stand for it—and if the wounded bandit didn't die, the mortal score was townspeople four, bandits one. The wounded tally went just about the other way. Both of the cowboys from the front of Brown's store were shot once each and in places unlikely to become infected. For one the bullet was like a pimple beneath the skin and the doctor could cut it out with hardly any pain. The other cowboy's bullet had just skipped around on the outside of his ribs, and was near as easily gotten out.

The banker, Charles Evans, got his head wound sewed up from end to end. Dr. Le Roy Taylor was prideful of his needlework, although he almost overlooked the loading-lever stud imbedded in the wound. His critics had to admit, however, that it was the smallest outside part of a prewar Navy Colt.

Jim held the horse, waiting, in growing expectation of not being noticed. He knew he'd have to ask it of someone, although for now everyone seemed to be so taken up and busy. He wouldn't interrupt. Maybe he would ask them later. One way to find out how people felt would be to inch away. He couldn't look back, but Bill's eyes swept the crowd of uninterested men. Once around the corner Bill said, "It's better we don't try to steal this horse. You know how people are."

"We aren't stealing, Bill. We are just looking after. We'll ask Mr. Frazier what he thinks is right for us to do." That sounded like a good idea, and Bill put a hand to the bridle to help lead the horse.

Chalk's head ached, and God his gut felt empty. He thought he must have thrown up his shoelaces, but looking down at his feet he saw they were still there. He'd handed Kincade his gun and holster just as he'd done so many times before without even being asked—coming out of a bar at the start of an evening and there would be Kincade with his hand outstretched. There was never anything they needed to say. Now it was bright morning, and people and words were everywhere.

"Whatever put you into mind to shoot that man? He was just standing there and didn't even have his weapon drawn." Kincade was looking down at Kay Cee's crumpled body. He was lying on his face, his left arm under him and his right stiff out at his side, its hand curled around the butt of his holstered gun.

The gathered crowd ebbed and whirled about as each new

person tried to inhale their full share of an excited atmosphere. One man approached Kincade. As he looked at the fallen man he said, "I guess they got him. I sure seen him shooting at those robbers. They tried to get him but he turned them back. He shot twice, as cool and easy as I've ever seen. Brave man, Charley. Do you know which one of the bandits got him?"

Kincade shrugged. "It wasn't one of the robbers shot him. It was Chalk. Unless he . . ."

Another witness asked, "How come Chalk was perched up there on that wagon top plumb in the middle of the robbery and just like he knew it was going to happen?"

In times when instants are being split most humans fail in their perception of reality. Their subsequent stories are authored by overwhelmed imaginations. And, in fairness, many events move so fast that human witnesses fail to view them clearly.

In addition there were townspeople who resented Chalk's apparent lightheartedness and the generosity he showed in helping others. If he were indeed a serious person like themselves he wouldn't have endless time to waste doing other people's work. Also, many deplored the fact that Chalk had shot a man who had not yet drawn his gun.

People make up rules to cover places and times that they are never at. Most all the talk about giving an opponent a fair chance was from people who had never faced someone who was homicidal either from insanity or the craziness of outlaw greed.

Finally, after listening to several of the townsmen give other versions of the fight, Kincade paused and then asked, "I mean, Chalk, if the man you shot had been with those bandits, how come he wasn't shooting back into the town?"

"How should I know why somebody wasn't doing something" was Chalk's only offered answer.

And at this time Kincade said, "Maybe, Chalk, you'd better come on over and sit inside our jail for a while."

Chalk turned to leave and Kincade asked, "Hey, where are you goin', Chalk?"

"To my usual cell, except this is the first time I've ever been in your jail sober."

Comptonsville wasn't a big town, however with the whole population in one place, it came to be quite a crowd. The blacksmith and his huge son were in the street now, and there were several of the girls from Laura's place. After a late night of work they had been woken early by the morning's excitement. Even Laura was out at the head of her team. Laura usually dressed gaudy like an advertisement for her place, yet for now she wore just an old hat and coat and no face paint at all. Everybody was telling his story to everybody else and Chalk felt left out and alone trudging off to jail long before the excitement settled.

The front door was unlocked and he walked into the office, but he'd be damned if he'd go straight back to that cell. He'd sit right here in the office so as to see into the street. It wasn't fair to leave him out of everything.

It occurred to Chalk that he'd better have a talk with that man whose life he'd saved and best with Kincade present. That time would come. For now he'd wait.

Mrs. Evans came running up the street. She always half listened for this kind of noise to come from her husband's bank and when the first shots sounded she'd put her mind to running there. Chalk was respectful toward the way this woman ran. Long skirts or not, she held them up. She wasn't making nervous little totters just to show concern. Covering ground was her intention and it was more a canter than a gallop. She disappeared inside the bank and the crowd around her husband opened. Still sewing, Dr. Taylor turned his head, "He'll be right as rain, Mrs. Evans." She smiled at him for thanks, and then she stood calm and quietly and didn't make a show of grabbing at her husband's hand, which would have only upset the doctor's small neat stitches.

The surviving teller had taken the bag of money back to the bank. He'd best count it carefully now that Mrs. Evans was safely here. His hands were shaking and that made it difficult for him to handle bills. He placed the sack in the safe and carefully closed the door. He should appear much more composed since customers were present, but he went white and had to sit when it occurred to him that he had told the robbers about the open safe. He'd been in the very midst of all of this and he was still alive. Those men had saved their shooting for where they would need it most and that was probably the only reason they hadn't put a shot in him. He was still alive. Being alive came over him in waves, and he wished right here in the bank he had something in the form of strong alcohol to drink. He stayed sitting at his desk. It would be pointless to go out into the alley just to see how he might have died.

As excitement waned, several people noticed the day still kept some of the last night's chill. A few went home for overcoats and wraps. Others stayed around to stomp and shiver. Several men carried the surviving bandit into the hotel. With two horse blankets under him the group slow-stepped out of the churned-up street and across the lobby to place their burden on an oblong table.

The man's lips were blue and he held tightly to his side where blood leaked between his clutching fingers. His face was unspoiled. The blankets were blood sodden from where buckshot had gotten to his body. As a misguided act of compassion someone rolled and lit a cigarette and it was offered to him. He looked through the cigarette and the man who'd made it. That was all right too. The man smoked it himself.

Inside Wilkenson's body, the slightest movement brought forth a symphony of pain. So long as he could lie still it only felt as though he was being beaten with logging chains.

If only, if. It wasn't or couldn't or didn't go that way. Just pass the money over. Then you do your peaceful business and we will do ours. That dead man in the alley, he would be still alive, and so would two of my brothers. Kay Cee, that bastard, he hung on out at the edge and had it played both ways. It was almost as if he was here more for the violence than for money. The plan had been his, and he was the first one to suggest they rob the bank. And then at the end he was going to pretend to have been on the side of the town, changing sides by shooting down one of his own men. It wasn't clear though how he could have explained the farm boy's death. Robbing the bank was a dumb gamble and they'd lost.

Wilkenson tried one of his little smiles. It was so small a movement that it didn't hurt. He let it broaden.

Kay Cee had lost it too. Who in the hell would think some son of a bitch'd be on the top of a wagon looking into the middle of your life? Well maybe not the middle of his life with one leg broken and all this lead in him. Broken though he was, it was still his life. Kay Cee wasn't in it anymore. Two brothers dead and there was also that young cowboy who'd joined them from fresh off the range. Hardly even knew his name. He'd said two things: "What in the hell's the difference" and "I'll try anything once." That too had been a piss-poor end to a life that might have amounted to something. Like anything that boy had done would have been better than being killed. A person can only get killed once, so there's no way to try different ways of doing it.

Come to think on it, they'd made a damned sorry fight. Just the townspeople around and there was four of them killed and maybe five if his life leaked away. If he got better would they hang him and how would you score that into the fight? In fairness to Kay Cee, he'd neatly put two men down. Then with everybody running and that stagecoach come and all the shots from the hotel, that was when, he guessed, old Kay Cee started to distance himself from the failure of the job they'd taken on.

Thirty was an old age to be if you were living on your luck.

He had a brother older and a brother younger and both of them were dead. If you went into this kind of a reckless life there was no need to worry about what was coming next. What was going to get you, got you. That clod up on the wagon; he thought he'd heard someone say his name was Chalk. He had handed his empty gun to the lawman and now he had something to worry about. Like as not, and under a complete mix-up in their minds, they might be planning to put him on trial.

There were several witnesses who couldn't see where the shots were going, or even coming from. They all swore Kay Cee was on the side of the law. That was funny enough to beat all hell. But why not let it run its course? O.K. If they wrongly hung that Chalk for murder, would that help to even up the score? Maybe some splinter of luck could be gotten from all of this. That stupid kid who'd been beating on him with his muffler. He'd had no thought but to kill him, and only an empty gun had made for one murder less.

Come to think on that they would doubtless hang him anyway. Though if they were after that, why have this doctor bandaging away? That proved naught. Sometimes they have a doctor fixing for hours on somebody they plan to hang that very day. People sure could do crazy things.

Though eager to test the legitimacy of their ownership, the two boys carefully put the still-saddled horse into the small barn behind Ann's house. Jim asked as he came inside the house, "Mr. Frazier?"

"Yes, Jim."

"If a man dies suddenly and he's got no relations . . ."

"Yes."

"Then who gets to keep his horse?" Frazier had seen the children go carefully around to the back. Little Bill had even picked up a broom and with a few deft sweeps obliterated the trail leading around and then behind the house.

"The man who has it safely in his barn. Any lawyer, Jim, will tell you that. Of course, he'll charge you the price of the horse for doing it." Frazier paused, "But don't you worry. I'll advocate for you if any questions do get raised because it's clear to me a man your age should have a decent horse."

"Now, you come here and see Ann's baby. While you were fooling with horses, gunfights, and other nonsense, he was at work getting her milk to flow."

Jim flushed a little bit and Bill half hid behind him. They'd never seen Ann's bared breasts before. And now there was that little baby smacking away just like he was Chalk on cold beer after three days of thirst. There was nothing so terrible about seeing them. Jim had always looked at her in clothes. He'd noticed those proud breasts with their nipples pressed against the tightness of her dress. A man could notice how fine his sister looked and there was nothing wrong with that, for Ann was just like a blood sister to them all.

"Jim, I'd be pleased if you would find Chalk home for his breakfast."

Jim sucked in his breath. In bringing home the horse he'd all but forgotten Chalk.

When he didn't immediately reply Ann asked, "Was Chalk in the shooting, Jim?" Ann didn't try to rise or half get up, nor would she leave the quiet world where her baby was first learning to eat. She just asked if Chalk was well.

"Chalk's fine, Ann. He wasn't shot, but Kincade has him."

"Jailed for drunkenness?" It was hardly a question and Ann asked it relieved.

"No, he's quite a good deal sober. Kincade sent him over to the jail. I believe they'll make some kind of a charge because Chalk has just killed a man."

Ann closed her eyes, and her face tightened in disbelief. "Oh, no, Chalk. I knew he could be stupid and I knew he could be drunken, though I'd have sworn he would not be so vicious so as to get drunked up and then kill a man."

"You did not hear me, Ann. He didn't do that. He was full sober when that man was killed."

A failed robbery mixed in with the stagecoach wreck was something that didn't happen every day. So the entire town was still out on its one main street. The gathering of course included Laura and her girls. She was proud to manage her own house, but she didn't sit idle in it flabbing herself up with good food and booze the way so many madams did. Laura maintained an active interest in the doings of the town. When her presence wasn't required by the house, she was almost always out and on the move.

It still being morning there was no business at hand, so the girls could stand around and gawk. Curiosity was fine if you could profit from it. But hanging around after the party was done didn't fit into Laura's style. Trying to keep a business up was tough enough work for one woman to handle. There was sufficient duds amidst the live men in this town to make Laura's interest slight for those who had gotten dead. There wasn't even copper money to be made from them.

Chalk had been taken, or rather he had been sent, over to the jail. Laura watched him trailing over there. If a man walked to jail on his own it just might do him some good. If he had to be carried there both you and him were wasting everybody's time. Unless, of course, he got locked away forever.

If Chalk was in jail, Laura felt she'd better go and talk with Ann. But first of all she'd look up and down the street. Now she could see her entire staff standing around in this early morning slush. Well and good. They weren't needed inside, and fresh air would do them fine. Except little Sophie there with a feather boa wrapped around a dress that was half of nothing.

"Sophie!" Laura roared like a train coming out of a tunnel. Then she pointed at the patched and partially melted snow and at the girl's flimsy slippers. "A coat or a shawl, and something on your feet. Us poor girls can never know what we may catch but we can damn well be careful it is not a cold. Have brains and don't wear your goddamned slippers in the snow."

Sophie made a little movement with her hands and then trotted toward the house. She'd either be in for the day or come out changed into something sensible. All the other girls looked snug and warm so Laura turned to go up the street. She better be the first to tell Ann the trouble Chalk was in. Laura didn't only just tell about problems. She also had a readiness to help out her friends.

Chalk was not the sort Laura had in mind for anyone. Before Ann he'd been in her place on several occasions, so drunken that to take his money would have been a crime. Another reason Laura had sent him away was because she would not put any of her girls underneath anything that had so much wobble to it. That was how he'd met Ann. He'd been in the house with a gut-shot brain, if a person could imagine that. Not shot dead. Just shot silly. It seemed a hurt to turn him into the night with all the big brags he'd made. Well, good little Ann had steered him home, and hell, if she'd been man hungry what a waste of time. That was not in it at all. Ann had her own reasons of compassion and caring. It might have to do with her bringing those kids and a wagon along across half a continent to safety. Whatever Ann wanted to do, Laura had not been one to stand in her way.

What in the world would the poor girl do, now that she was fully stuck with him? Laura realized she hadn't seen Ann for quite a while. She did know the girl was belly swollen, caught, and Ann, so like herself, took to it kindly. Good God, how little women knew of anything. She'd gotten that Chalk half-sobered. Then the next thing you knew she'd fallen half to hell in love with him. As a man, he'd been far from perfect but one halfway decent man out of jail was worth more than a dozen wonder boys inside. There were hoofprints in the streets on the way to where Ann lived. It was empty around her as Laura walked, everyone being gathered to the center of the town. On both sides of the muddied brown street some white snow still lay where the stalks of dead grass lingered.

Laura was a prim knocker. Frazier opened the door, and what was that man doing here? Laura knew that there was goodness in him, but he wasn't what a girl could use. If a man's been hurt too many times all he is good for is a friend. She then thought back and remembered that he'd once been a doctor and in an emergency he'd probably become one again.

Then Laura thought, as she went toward Ann's bedroom, goddamn it I will not blubber now. Suddenly on seeing the new baby she felt herself lighting up like all the candles on a Christmas tree she remembered from childhood.

"Ann, you never let me know the time had gotten so close. Now, you just let me see. Frazier told me, it's a boy. I've come without flowers, Ann, to tell you that Chalk—"

"Laura, he is in jail for shooting a man. I already know that. If it was done drunk I would be both disgusted and afraid. But if my Chalk shot somebody when he was sober, then there is, I am sure, some good reason for it."

"Well, dear, I hope so certainly. Things in town is stirred so it'll be a while before we discover . . . hopefully just what Chalk had in mind. One thing though I'd like to say . . ."

Ann held up her hand. "Don't. I already know. If he'd been here and so forth and so on. Laura, you know enough so as not to try to live by ifs and if onlys."

Laura looked at Ann. It was almost as if she was Laura's own child, and in a way she was. Laura had guided her and interfered in several places that she felt Ann didn't even have to know about.

Musingly she asked, "I always thought to find you a man who was more proud and more serious than Chalk will ever be."

"Proud men are unchanging," Ann said. "So give me a friendly one who's capable of improvement. I said capable of, not eager for. Eagerness would make a woman's life too easy. It takes less effort breeding reliability into friendliness, than, well the other way around. If I didn't have long-range hopes for Chalk I would never have brought him home. He wasn't just for me. Those children were entitled to a good-hearted father."

Laura touched the baby, then she bent over to kiss Ann on the cheek. "Pardon my flutter, girl. There's only three things to have in a town. A house, money, and friends. I have them all, so if you have a heart for keeping Chalk on—"

"Laura, I most certainly do. You are a woman who knows about the world. Before I just loved Chalk for the fun of it. But now," Ann indicated the baby, "Chalk is part of the family."

Laura put her specs on. They were just a gag with window glass for lenses. She looked hard at Frazier as she turned to leave, raising her eyebrows behind her transparent shield. He reassured her. "It couldn't have been a better birth, out of a more healthy body."

Laura gave his cheek a pat and promised to get custards and some other foods sent over. Then she thanked Frazier for being here. The visit had been brief. She left for her house, which shouldn't be too long unattended.

Out, even in a street that was empty, Laura looked both ways. There wasn't a single person back from the center of town.

It was a couple of years passed since Ann had rolled into town. Laura remembered seeing her then. A lot of girls she'd just have taken and put straight to work but Ann had been something different. She'd gotten here over a trail that was closed with four kids in tow, and one of them but a baby. If ever a day got really rotten, Laura needed only to think of those kids coming through and at least the edges of it brightened up. She sure owed Ann something

for that. She'd also known enough about this girl's pride so as not
to make her into a pet. There was cooking and cleaning for the
house, and Ann had got paid for that. Laura always tried to keep
good domestic help. Considering her girls' work, it would have
been cheap and mean to ask them to do the cleaning too.

Ann had gotten a little house of her own and thought it much
more than a shack but less than a mansion. Sometime after she'd
first moved in, she had also gotten Chalk. At first, her place was
one where he could be sobered up to usefulness, and although he
hadn't stopped he'd slowed his drinking down enough so as to grow
their two lives together. By now they'd been with each other more
than a year. Chalk wasn't a perfect man, but who ever was? At the
start of Ann's life in town the kids from the wagon had been scattered around in the homes of various helpful families. Ann had
kept the baby, but even with Laura's help she'd just not had enough
to supply the other three growing children's needs. There was no
sense of separation, because in that first year the kids found ways
to make a visit nearly every day. Now, with Chalk as a husband in
the house, there was a home and the children had come back to
stay, and once again there was a family.

Jim was growing fine and he would be a handsome man. Bill
still had the cuteness of a boy, and Margaret was ripening nicely.
The baby was three going near on four. If Ann didn't have time to
tend her, Laura helped. When she was too busy, she'd tell one of
the girls to do it, no matter how much money the house stood to
lose.

Laura always took pleasure in recalling Ann's triumphant journey. How they'd come across, just one wagon alone. From time to
time, Ann or Jim would tell a story about that trip. Certainly those
five kids would have died had they not wintered with hostile Indians. Laura thought about that. The Indians certainly hadn't been
hostile to the children. Hostile was just another one of the white
man's words that often meant "not on a reservation."

Ann and the children came into town in their wagon one day of the following summer. Then, and every day since, Laura thought about what she could do for those kids.

In that first year, other men than Chalk had looked at Ann. Jesus, now that Laura thought of it, the bastards wouldn't have been human if they hadn't. This didn't make Ann flighty, not one little bit. She'd passed some by, Laura helped others on their way. There had been one man who was traveling hard over long distances. He'd seen Ann and he'd known right off just how much woman was there.

He told Ann what he felt and Ann thanked him, but she said, "I'm not going with you, because one day no matter what was happening you'd want things to move much faster. I would know you were impatiently waiting for me and finding it hard to stand. You wouldn't have to say it. I'd read it in your eyes and then my heart would be broke or snapped like a summer garden bean. You go and find yourself a girl with all her parts, and that won't be enough because you are a man who's in a race with time. Happiness is something that's in a woman's soul and it will never be found with you."

He'd asked her back, "Don't you ever let anything just cozen by without thinking it inside out?"

"Cozen by," she said. "A lot of things cozen by and then you get an arm that's off. Something else comes skipping through and the children have parents to bury or you're wondering what there'll be for the baby to eat. No, sir, I am not sitting around waiting on whatever's going to hit me next."

To most women this man would be an apparent prize. He always remembered Ann. Someone in later years once asked if there'd ever been a girl.

"There sure once was," he said, describing Ann. He smiled still. "See a girl, if you can, that looks like a railroad locomotive made from sunbeams. Then there were other times when she'd just stand off somewhere, and in her privateness there was no way of knowing where she'd gone. But I believe she had her own places where she could go so as to rebuild her strength."

This was the man. Ann had known to send away.

There was another suitor, and it was Laura who spoke to him, straight and plain, after he'd told of all the wonderous things that he would do with Ann.

"Thanking you from all of us, but the prickliness of a man in heat is a damn small thing to bring to someone who's looking for an arm." She couldn't have made the message plainer and in fairness to him, he brought a double eagle's worth at the house. Then he drifted on.

6

There was no reason for Laura to walk back through the center of the town. Instead she chose a path that led between houses and then across several empty lots where the light accumulation was melting. Winter is mostly gray, she thought, when it gets uncovered. Deeper snows would come later on. Then there would be spring and gray again just before the growing started. Winter nights were good for business if you kept a whorehouse warm, both in the parlor and in the rooms. Laura had no desire to look again on the man whom Chalk had shot. She noticed how the seed pods still clustered on the stalks of frost-dead weeds.

The dead man's name was Kay Cee Smith. Here in this town she believed herself and that shot-to-pieces gunman were the only ones who knew it. Kay Cee Smith had been an idle curiosity hanging on the edges of her mind. Now, he had come back here to die, or to be killed? Except, if what she had heard was true, Chalk, of all people, had shot him where he was standing right out there in the middle of the street.

Having known Kay Cee, she'd thought killing him would be an effort a man like Chalk wouldn't be up for. As she walked, Laura tried to remember. She would or could only look at isolated scenes. She wouldn't recall why she'd finally left Kay Cee, or had he left her? Maybe he'd been dragged off by the police and then put in a jail. Again there were no pictures in her mind. Or did one day just come and then he wasn't there?

At the house there were newspaper clippings inside the safe. They were in a little japanned box, and if she really needed to remember she could get them out. When a weak or silly man goes bad, not too much happens, but Kay Cee was never weak or silly. She'd only met one man like that, good at doing so many things, but deep inside his heart was vicious mean.

Even with this much sun and snow, black shadows slipped past Laura. Why in the hell remember a man who was dead, if he'd been forgotten while alive? Now, suddenly, she remembered that one final incident.

She had run and she was not a fearful woman—any day she was with that man she easily could find herself dead. No, it wasn't even getting beaten up. A girl could survive that if it didn't happen too often, and now that she had her own house it didn't happen at all; no one's hand fell heavy on any girl in her employ. Laura looked up to the houses and the sky, and her glance swept around as though daring anyone to try.

What Laura had been fearful of had been the cloud of doom that wrapped around Kay Cee as if it were a cloak. The fearful ending that had made her run had finally happened here. It wasn't just him dead there in the street. It was all the others dead along side him. Laura knew that this wasn't the first place where Kay Cee'd brought men to die. He had to do with killings and he'd killed men himself. That could be any man, but there were other times when you almost knew that from a distance he'd caused other men to die. And he did it when there was no gain for him. That was why she'd been afraid.

She looked back into the sunshine and the day and there was

no need to tell anyone about him. She'd let those old clippings yellow and not look at them again. Why remind herself of a part of her life she remembered only as a darkness? A darkness like the inside of a covered bridge at night. Why get a lantern and go back to see what was lurking there? Just keep on going and leave it to forgetfulness. Laura decided she'd better get back to her house. Dead men didn't buy anything, yet in a way they brought the money in. Excitement and shootings got certain men all flustered up, and many of these seemed to be very slow starters during normal times.

Later, whenever the trial happened, people would be coming from all over and it wouldn't be just the extra crowd. They'd be special stirred up and tensed, in all kinds of ways. Any big excitement, for a whorehouse, was money in the bank. It was about the only place where excitement could be gotten rid of just by paying money down. Of course there were other games of chance involving pasteboard cards and whirling wheels.

One thing Laura could certainly do was send some decent food over to the jail. It would ease Ann's mind to know that Chalk was eating proper meals. She should have thought to tell Ann that this was already taken care of.

Dr. Le Roy Taylor elbowed through the hotel lobby to the table where the surviving robber lay. Even under sunbrown skin men got so white when they were to the edge of dying. This man had been one of those who started the mess and he was the one hurt hardest. Muscles like hard stretched ropes and rawhide was the best way to describe him. His clothing was saturated in blood, and he held a clasped hand to stanch his most grievous wound. He'd had to wait, but as Kincade said, that was only fair. He was awake, alive, and not even in shock, but he didn't greet the doctor, even with his eyes. They were level and unblinking. The man was silent, though you could almost hear the gushing blood, how rapidly it flowed from him. The doctor set down his bag so as to put on his specs. He'd take his own sweet time; Le Roy Taylor could work without talking too. Using a scalpel he ripped away cloth wherever blood was seeping. A couple of slugs were discovered near the surface. These were the easy ones to cut out. Mostly the work was plugging leaks. As the doctor sewed and bandaged he thought to tell this bandit, "I can plug the leaks, but if anything's gone inside, well, you know it's time to get ready for the end." But if this patient wasn't talking, why should he? He'd get on with his part of the job and leave this man to his.

As he worked, the doctor shook his head from side to side. This was the typical cowboy's build—lots of corded muscle with hardly any larding. These men were tough and sometimes got smashed beyond all belief, and then they'd live when they had every right to die. This one maybe had had too much. In the war they'd have that badly a broken leg off and thrown away by now. Le Roy didn't feel up to cutting and the bone wasn't through the skin. He set it the best he knew how, guessing it didn't matter much: gangrene or the gallows.

Finally, when the patient was all sewed up and patched, they carried him over to the jail and placed him in the cell next to Chalk's. Later in the day when Laura sent over food, it was so plentiful that Chalk shared easily with this man imprisoned with him. As he ate, the man kept to silence, not giving even one single slight nod of thanks. Chalk could take that fine. He hadn't fed the man out of any friendliness. He just didn't like seeing waste, and he didn't think there should be hunger anywhere. He knew hunger as an enemy. Ann and the kids had told him about real hunger, child and baby hunger. Hunger was one of the many things that nearly stopped Ann and the children from getting through.

Here in this jail was a place to remember things. Chalk didn't care for reading much, and for scenery there was nothing but the sky outside his high-barred window. The man in the next cell didn't speak a word. Of course today was important far much more than just being in jail. To think on it, they'd told him about his baby being born. That was in the here and now, so maybe he'd better not dream off into remembering all the things Ann had told him about the trip.

Chalk realized that Ann had every right to think poorly of him for not having been there with her when his son was born. Like most times, she was forgiving. Certainly if he'd been with Ann then both the immigrant boy and that Wilkins or Bilkensen would both be dead. It was hard to remember, out of the haze of that morning's awakening, just exactly what name the man he'd shot had called that wounded robber so shot to pieces in the street.

Again there was no reason for what-ifs. Neither he or Ann ever did them. No one ever said, either, "If I, or if you, had both arms then . . ." Accepting was a part of their love, and Chalk knew this world was the only one they had. Whatever had happened, had happened, and the world only turns in one direction. Things that hadn't happened yet could be changed, but the past was set in stone. Of course there was one control over past events, and that was the way one thought about them. Chalk knew that he would, if he could help it, never again be somewheres drunk when Ann and now his son had a need for him. After a second's pause he turned his thoughts around. The son was not his. It was theirs.

He and Ann surely had their own baby and it was a boy. Laura had told him that and so had Frazier. Frazier had brought over two cold beers to celebrate. He hadn't smuggled them in. Kincade had nothing against social drinking in the jail. If he wouldn't allow drunkenness, he was also careful not to be responsible for uselessly drying out any of his prisoners. Jail was bad enough, he felt, without it being turned into a beerless desert. Chalk smiled to think of his own baby just born, and of Ann, now a mother. It would be a very fine child. It was lucky for both of them to share in how

beautiful Ann knew how to be. If time was to be passed, Chalk
thought to do it with remembrance. With a bull team of six, Ann
and those kids had come on cross-country just like they was Nelson
Story. Chalk shook his head and felt a slight shiver as though someone had drawn a feather tip down between his shoulder blades. For
a while he daydreamed about that journey and then he fell asleep.

The surviving robber was an advantage because he was delicate
through having being shot so bad. They had to keep the jail nice
and warm for him, so it was in Chalk's best interest that the man
didn't die. To keep one cell warm, Kincade had to heat them all.
Of course, if the man was tried and hung, the old jail would be
back to freezing as usual.

Chalk worried maybe there was enough false or mistaken evidence to make Kincade believe Chalk had helped the robbers, and
if the law could prove that to itself, Chalk mightn't be around to
worry about the cold.

On occasion, the surviving robber would smile for a long time
at Chalk, making sure that Chalk's hands couldn't get at him
through the bars. The son of a bitch just wouldn't talk. He
wouldn't speak a word to anyone. Maybe twenty times and in
twenty ways Chalk begged him to tell Kincade that Kay Cee had
threatened death as he'd lain wounded in the street. Chalk had
heard it in Kay Cee's voice.

Wilkensen was the name he'd called this man, but now he
wouldn't answer to it. Kay Cee was going to kill the farm kid who
had been whipping him with a knitted muffler. Chalk had saved
both of their lives and please wouldn't Wilkenson just tell Kincade
that.

After a week Chalk wanted to be out of jail and back with his
family. But the robber's only response was an even-toothed and
silent grin.

In search of friendly witnesses Kincade had found the kid and his family and brought them back to town. They didn't speak English, and the jail and Kincade's badge frightened them so that all they could do was shake their heads and shyly look away. The father said a few words, but Chalk had no way of finding anyone who could speak whatever it was they meant.

After a week had passed, the robber decided that if he was well enough to stand trial, he was well enough to break jail on his own. This wasn't an adobe or a clapboard jail, where a lariat and a shock saddle were all your friends needed to bust you out. Being in jail was a time to plan for being free.

Kay Cee had broken jail once. Wilkenson remembered hearing the story. Some idiot had left a broom beside his cell. He'd gotten it in and he told how he'd unwound the wire from it, "Just like I was undressing a bride." He didn't want any kinks or bends because he needed it to make a noose. The story had been told around a campfire and the boy called Sonny asked if he'd planned to hang himself. Kay Cee didn't tell his story all at once, but at the boy's question he'd smiled, saying, "Never myself, Sonny. Always some-one else."

He'd spent three hours telling them every move, thought, and muscle twitch, both his and the guard's. As he talked his listeners couldn't know where Kay Cee's body left off and where the skin and muscles of the guard began. He was that skilled hunter who becomes the creature he seeks to kill. He was able to snatch the one perfect second from out of many months of waiting. In that one instant, he had the guard pulled back against the grilled door of his cell. The wire noose was cutting flesh just deep enough, and in his other hand he held the guard's pistol. "It was, after all those jailed months, like coming back to to life," he said.

"And then what happened?" Sonny'd asked.

The guard knew he would die not doing exactly what he was told. He might die anyway. Kay Cee's one word was "Keys." It had

been on the tip of his tongue ever since the guard's forgetfulness
had given him the broom. The straw had gone into his bed and in
the night the stick had been thrown from his window. Around the
campfire he'd told his companions that if they ever found a broom-
stick around a jail they should start guessing that someone was
planning to leave. "Most people will look at a common piece of
junk and not think about what its location means." He'd ended
with that.

Silently Wilkenson started to curse Kay Cee all over again for
maybe the hundredth time. Then he stopped. In a rough business
like this, the complaining man feeling sorry for himself had it so
much worse than most. Well there weren't any loose brooms in
Kincade's jail, and it didn't look like there would be time to wait
for one. The best he could do was pretend he was weaker than he
was. If it wasn't much of a plan, at least it was a place to start.

Around the final campfire the night before the robbery, Kay
Cee had told them what he remembered of the town. He'd drawn
the streets and alleyways, scratching out the picture in the roadway
with a stick. Here was the bank and this was how they were going
to leave the town. Kay Cee planned to stand off to one side, saying
that he wanted these boys to learn how to take a bank on their
own. He had each man empty his pockets. They burned every scrap
of personal identification all the way down to the photograph of a
lovely girl from a locket that Sonny wore around his neck. Kay Cee
had given out many pieces of advice. Here in jail only one might
be of use. "Forget you ever learned to talk." They'd burned a few
old letters and some papers from the army, but with four killed
and one taken what had been the use? The use was that with no
one knowing who they were, this town and marshal might convince
themselves that Chalk was a robber too. It wasn't much, but if
Chalk got hung the score would appear to be more even.

The doctor had warned him to be careful. Sudden movements
might start hemorrhages inside. Well, think of that. Sudden move-

ments would be caused by maybe riding a horse, or if he didn't
make those sudden movements, then one sudden movement would
be the ending of all others. The robber sniffed. This jail had a tarred
hemp stink to it. If people in a town have been killed, then it's
usual for their jail to have that new-rope smell. And damn all of
Kay Cee's advice. If he'd been so fast and smart down through all
the years, how come he didn't make it out to some foreign place
with one of those big stakes he'd stole, or claimed he had. Maybe
Kay Cee didn't rob for money. That dumb bastard Sonny had just
been along to party. He always talked about finding the excitement.
There was damn little excitement lying buckshot flattened in the
street, even if you had a big bag of cash grasped in your greedy
hand. He didn't miss the money much, though he didn't want to
hang for having stole it. Then, damn it, how was hanging different
from lying gut-shot in the street? If he hadn't wanted that, he'd
no business going into the town and hungering after the money in
its bank. Well, the difference was right there. Being shot was a
chance he'd taken, but being hung was as sure as waiting for the
judge to come. His only chance was not to wait, but no friends
showed and that old man Kincade was never careless even once.

Two weeks went by in jail. Chalk and the robber stayed. Laura's
place sent over food, and Ann was quickly up from childbed. Frazier
had been thanked and offered a fee, and of course he'd turned it
down. Certain evenings found him halfheartedly in the hotel bar.
Without Chalk present he'd somehow gotten off his drink. Most
of the other customers were loud-mouthed guzzlers. When Frazier
turned from the emptiness of the bar it was either to his own home
or to Laura's house. He went there just for conversation and the
piano's tinkle, not that he underrated the girls or their commodi-
ties. For now he was mostly inside himself and partially hidden in
a quiet corner of his life. He did always make it a point to pay

Laura or one of the girls at the going rate. Frazier wasn't schoolboy enough to think he could favor a whore with an evening of free talk.

During the day he'd see the kids around town and often he would visit Ann and the baby at their home. Each time his spirts lifted to see Ann's open face reflect a life that had overcome the places where others would have found only emptiness and sorrow. Instinctively she had used both her own hopes and acceptances as guideposts on her road to adulthood. Having experienced many desperate trials and vicissitudes, she didn't want to let them go to waste: That was one of the reasons she'd given Frazier for helping others find their way through life.

He also went to visit Chalk. Then afterward he'd try to think of how the town could be convinced Chalk knew what he was doing when he'd shot that man. The problem was several people believed Chalk's victim had been fighting the robbers in defense of the town.

Chalk was a pleasant someone to take a social drink with. And more important, with Chalk in jail, what would happen if Frazier really needed to get drunk? It was strange. This problem was not developing. He'd be reading a book or thinking, and before he knew what was happening he somehow neglected, through whole evenings, to reach for a nearby bottle. It wasn't forgetfulness and it wasn't laziness. He guessed other things just kept getting in the way.

Chalk's salvation was at the head of Frazier's list. Mixed in with Chalk's trouble there was an important gladness. Frazier saw Ann walking along the street, the baby cradled in her arm. Suddenly a clouded window opened back into his past. There is a way that something can be rolling endlessly in front of you with the answer right beside it. But for now he didn't want to or wasn't able to put all the pieces together.

The smoke of a remembered darkness covered Frazier as he stood in the full daylight of the street. Every one of Frazier's muscles ached. Six or was it seven years ago, he was saving or as often killing men in a cave under Vicksburg's bluffs. He held the pulped arm of a young woman in his hand. The turn of flap, the folds and stitches; an amputation was a surgeon's signature. At the delivery he'd not seen the stump. He didn't need to now, for with sudden certainty he knew who she was. He had a world that was coming back to him, right here in this street. His life would become more than just an empty house that wasn't home until he'd drunk so much he didn't have to see it. He had been hiding long enough.

At the end of a long silence Ann queried, "Doctor?"

He held up a single finger. Ann corrected herself. "Mr. Frazier." She couldn't move aside the baby's covering. He walked over to peek and carefully folded back the blanket. The baby was a sparkler, and he had been twice born in his hands, because if you've ever saved a woman's life you've saved the lives of all her children to be born. Oh, yes, it was a certainty: Ann had been Vicksburg's child. His excitement came from way back when his world was starting. Even as a boy he had dreamed of being a doctor and seeing wonder in the faces of all those he'd save. He had dreamed of the eyes that would wash him with gratitude. He'd been a kid then, and that was long before the war where he'd been broken by all the young men, dead and mutilated.

In this winter street and from this girl, hope was being re-awakened. He wanted to talk with her now and when he asked, there was a wonderful yes that he could see from the smile in her eyes. Together they walked up the street that led to Ann's house.

People who knew Ann were never exactly certain as to any details of her appearance. She wasn't a big woman nor was she slight. Even Frazier was at a loss to classify her. His medical school vocabulary of various classifications and types had long been forgotten, however he surmised that no medical school professor had an imagination vivid enough to contrive a classification system so extensive as to leave room in it for Ann. But then again Ann didn't need room. Room and space were something that she made for herself. Even when she'd left a room her presence stayed behind. It remained as a picture of gentle loveliness. It was almost as if she had been able to paint her own portrait in the air.

Ann was at home in this little cabin. Frazier held the door, and then he held the baby while she removed her coat. He passed the baby from arm to arm while Ann helped him off with his. She hung the coat on the rack beside the door and then took her child. The cradle basket was in the living room, and as Ann settled the baby in Frazier poked up the stove. None of the other children were there. Was he making a claim on Ann? With her discovered alive, would he tell her that he had saved her life so that now she could save his. He was asking her to bring him back to life. In a world of normal fairness that would not be too much to ask.

As Ann gestured him toward a chair there was the baby's sudden cry of wakening. She stood over the cradle loosening the buttoned front of her dress. She took the baby and sat facing Frazier.

"All he does is sleep and eat." Ann's arm supported the baby's body and her hand cradled his head to her breast. "You aren't shy to see a woman's bosom bared?" she asked, or maybe she explained.

Frazier shook his head. "I'm not frightened of human bodies." Nothing was coquettish or for show. It was a new baby at its sustenance. If only all human endeavor could be that competent. If no one stopped them or showed them wrong, the very young of most living things took to the world quite handily.

The windows were small and curtained with plain cotton cloth. Outside sunlight was glaring where it reflected off the snow, but in the room the warm rays glowed. This was a snug place to be sitting. Snug and unquestioning, like a lonesome man always hoped the next bar would be.

Doubts fled before him. This girl, or woman, Ann, would be Frazier's answer to everyone who ever raised questions about the reasons for anything that was decent and away from death. Frazier felt he had something here. In answer to all the questioning: why this and why that and what sense does it make? The answer was simple, and he said it to himself. "Someday we'll all be dead, you bastards. Everyone living will someday be dead. But remember there will be new people then that we don't even know about." It was time, Frazier thought, that he got back to where people were being born.

Without an effort, Ann had the baby turned around. Now its head lay inside her elbow. Her hand supported its bottom so it could be at her other breast.

"I can chop my wood, Mr. Frazier, and buck sawing is a cinch. If I don't have to wait too long I can shoot a musket fine. However, it is slow for me to load. Ever since I can remember, I have worried how I would do if a baby came. When you watch a mother it seems like such a two-handed thing. Mostly it's one hand for holding and the other for fussing. Well this baby isn't fussed much, but he gets held a lot. I was fearful. I'm not anymore. I saw you wanting to ask about how I am doing in general." She smiled at him but it was in part for herself. "A man that's nearly chopped to pieces comes through as a hero." Ann stopped for a moment. "Yes, a hero either of war or industry. He's obviously tried to accomplish something wonderful and against great odds, but no matter how slightly a woman's been injured people look at her like she was spoiled, and I do not mean in the sense of being ruined. With all the nonsense talk about a fate worse than death, I think I could handle a great deal of ruination if it left me with my offside arm."

"I guess I thought about it, Ann. That arm of yours. Mostly I see the onside one. I guess one arm shows very clearly when it's by itself."

In becoming a mother Ann clearly remembered her own. She could picture her clearly. In the time of her childhood Ann had lived in such a gentle world. Clothing either hung in heavy winter folds or were so light in summer that you almost had to remember that you had it on.

Then there were the smells. The faint waft of baking from the summer kitchen and the cleanliness of carefully laundered sheets that were never permitted to get even slightly soiled. She remembered cool breezes and of course the fact that as a child she had thought all this comfort was everywhere and the world was this luxurious, at least for all the white people whom she knew.

"I was reading a book," Ann said, "in a parlor bedroom filled with the most lovely furniture. Shutters had been closed and shades drawn down so as to hide us from that fearful siege. I remember reaching with my left hand to turn down a lamp. It had a round glass shade with flowers painted on or in someway baked. Then I must have been sick for so long. When I came conscious finally I never saw that hand or lamp again. I never saw my mother after that. She'd been alive, somewhere, outside the circle of that light. She was in that house, and the house was once in Vicksburg, Mississippi, when they had the siege. Were you ever there?"

Frazier just nodded and nodded again. It was too mean a thing that she couldn't remember or know where her arm had gone.

"Sometimes other kids would ask. Sometimes, hell. Your pardon, Mr. Frazier, they'd ask it all the time. I'd tell 'em it had been bitten off by a bear, or that a hog ate it when I was a little baby playing in the yard. Or I'd say that some people, and creatures also, get born without some of their parts. That's true, Mr. Frazier, isn't it?"

"Yes, Ann, that's true."

"I'd tell people anything rather than say I didn't know or remember where my arm had gone. Oh, I knew I'd had it once. You always remember fingertips and the things they've touched. You can nearly forget any other things. Even, I expect, some of the women you have loved."

"I do suppose so, Ann. I doubtless have forgotten the love of several women, but my memory has never set aside any circumstance connected to the taking of a trout exceeding two pounds in weight. And I have never been a womanizer. Yes, Ann, I've been to Vicksburg, and I believe that I cut off your arm," Frazier added in a near whisper of explanation, "so that I could save your life."

Frazier looked around him. This was Chalk's house too. It was very much so and he wondered what Chalk looked like when viewed through a woman's eyes. Would she be here if she hadn't lost an arm? For the moment she was silent, and Frazier asked if it had been decent of Chalk to take her in?

"To take me in!" Ann's response was nearly an explosion. Then she asked as an afterthought, "What the hell are you talking about?" There was always that old what-would-have-happened-if? She could read it in his mind. She glared back to him. "With both arms, Mr. Frazier, I might before times have been taken to, or by, some person other than he. Chalk was the person that was here. If I'd come with both arms and if the man was Chalk, then just like right now, I would have gone with him. There are decisions we don't make but that we get stuck with. Then there are the ones we do, and those are the ones we stick to." Ann moved her shoulder to let fall the loosened top of her dress. Frazier stood closer to look. Beside her breast, beside her skin where her hair fell, above there was that face and neck, the fold, the patch, the needlework, the red-and-white scars, they all were there to memorialize the carnage and the blood. Frazier's eyes could even see the pain. All of it was present. God damn everyone living in the world, except Ann and her baby. He pulled her dress protectively around her shoulder. The baby was finished with its food.

Each surgeon's work is particular. Skin is folded and the pattern of stitches is each time the same. Now there could be no doubt. For Frazier it was like finding his signature at the bottom of a forgotten letter about a world he had never known. Knowing it he'd tried not to remember. He would like to have been able to smile. "As I thought, Ann, it was your life I saved."

Ann had been silent. She hadn't noticed when he'd pulled up her dress. Now she could look away from her nursed-out baby.

"You didn't save my life. You just fixed my body so it wouldn't die in a mass of rot when it found out what had happened. You fooled the body by cutting the arm away. Then came the time, and it's coming still, when I, and I guess everybody, goes on living by themselves." Ann thought for words. She'd heard people say, "you've got to keep on going." She'd heard that often enough. This was something more. Keep-on-going people were already on their way. She and the kids had needed to figure out just getting started. There weren't many people to tell you how to get on with that.

"Yes, living by themselves," Ann's voice was heightened now, "and of course using any outside help that they can get."

"Such as?"

"Such as the kids and the wagon. They brought me along. In fact, they brought me here. That worked two ways because I doubt if they would have come through without me."

The baby was placed back in its cradle. Ann could now fully fasten up her dress. Frazier was strangely relieved. "Some people might come by," he said.

"And do what in the hell to me? I'm not harping on the subject of propriety, but this is the first time it's come up. If a dear person has cut off your arm with a saw, then no one's mean enough to cut me with their tongue." Then Ann smiled. "And also, Dr. or Mr. Frazier, I thank you very much." She then observed that the stove's fire was down and that there was wood outside.

There was already split and old whole-log wood out there. Frazier gathered up an armful of the split. He noticed that the chopping block had jaws. It was foot treadled like a harness maker's horse. He'd never seen that before. Putting the wood beside the stove he asked about it. Ann explained, "It's for split wood when

I want it. A log gets grabbed in those jaws and then I can bring an axe edge down one-handed and as true as any. Many a fire's been ruined by waiting too long for wood being split by the shiftless of men."

As Frazier started to indicate agreement Ann quickly corrected him. "I was talking about men in general."

To defend the opinion he had offered, Frazier went on to say, "But your husband, Chalk, is far from perfect."

Ann's reply was immediate. "Good God, I know that. But also consider, if there ever was a Mrs. Frazier I am certain this would be a piece of knowledge we could share.

"Out there in the yard you saw that chopping block.

"It's not just other people that Chalk thinks about. He also thinks of me and puzzles out all sorts of things to move my life along. The mechanical conveniences, body helpers he makes are very useful but Chalk's love is also about how, so much of the time, he thinks to make my life more . . ." Ann puzzled momentarily without the word and then said, "handy."

With fresh fuel and the draft cracked open, the fire was quick to freshen. Frazier stood with his back to the stove. Ann sat in a chair beside the cradle looking at her baby and finding time to think. She said, "It's caught fine now." Frazier turned to tighten down the draft.

For several minutes the room was silent and then Ann suddenly said, as though she had been thinking about it for a while.

"And another thing, now that I've got my own child, I'm going to get back the books I once had as a girl so I can read them to him like my mother did for me when I was little. One of the troubles with a hardscrabble life is that it doesn't give a person the time to sit down quietly alongside of their books." Then she went on to say "Chalk's been safe, comfortable, warm, and well fed. This first two weeks was for the baby. I didn't want naught else to think or do. There'll be people in jail again, I guess. But I'll never have the first week of my first baby, ever. I'm thankful for it. In the wagon I swore to a bunch of things. One was, if I ever had a baby of my own, I'd fill it with milk from me 'til it came near to bursting. I so looked forward to keeping something alive with something come from out of me.

"When we were traveling, there was buffalo marrow and buffalo broth. Then when the hunting pinched out I looked at those few cans of milk. One was gone and then another, and did I want to squish that baby to my breast."

"You and those kids got that baby through with cussedness, luck, and no milk of your own. You got it through on sugar water and leather tit. She did okay. In the bar, Chalk was always proud to tell me things about the trip you made."

"Well, sure, but for this baby, okay is not good enough for me. In the wagon I swore if ever I had one of my own it would come on through first class, and that's just what he's doing. Now, two weeks are up. A boy will need his father, so the next thing I want is my Chalk out of jail."

Frazier told Ann everything sensible. There was a charge and witnesses. In a week or two a judge was due to convene a real court. Kincade had assured him of that, and both of them had gone to visit Chalk. Frazier remembered everything that Chalk had said. The farmer's kid couldn't or wouldn't say a thing. He hadn't heard or understood any conversations. All he knew was that guns were being fired everywhere. He told that in his own crude sign language.

Other towns people asked, If Chalk had been on the citizens' side how come the robber on the ground was left alive? But all of this would be a matter for the law. There weren't as yet any lawyers living in the town. Until now there'd not been enough contention so as to keep and feed one, particularly through the long winter months. But when the judge came, people agreed, he'd feel the need of lawyers, and doubtless he would bring a couple of his own.

Ann was going to talk to everyone. She wasn't going to allow the court or count on the court to get her business done. When Chalk had told her about the farmer's boy he was content that he'd be brought in as a friendly witness. Chalk naturally assumed that it was the business of a court to supply itself with an interpreter. Ann was not so sure. She decided that when some special kind of a Scandinavian is wanted, it is always best to find one of your own.

Frazier had found out that Brown and the two cowboys at the store were not clear as to how they'd gotten shot. One thing might be well for Chalk. Why had the man he'd shot been so heavily engaged in fighting for the town? No one had ever seen him here before. Also, most men had something on them to tell you what or who they were. Like the silent man in the cell next to Chalk and the three robbers who'd been killed, the man didn't have even a scrap of identification on him. Jim had acquired the dead man's horse and Kincade had gone along with that. While looking over Jim's new horse, Ann and Frazier had carefully searched through the blanket roll and saddlebags. There was not a note, a label, or a word. There was a fine Henry rifle and lots and lots of boxed cartridges. There were far more than any peaceful man might need. The Henry was not an army gun marked by the government. Certainly, though, it had a number. Kincade made that point. It was a fine new store-bought rifle. This made Ann decide to write a letter. The company's name and address was on the barrel. The company should know whom it had sold the rifle to. Chalk and Frazier discouraged her. A gun could pass through so many hands. Ann did not discourage easily, nor would she be dissuaded. Her attitude was simple. People who'd cut a number on that hard iron barrel, right there on the top and for everyone to see—after taking all that trouble and working so neat, they weren't likely to forget what they'd done it for. When Frazier sought to discourage her for a second time, Ann told him Chalk had already given her every possible reason why writing would do no good.

"That," she said, with an old saying in mind, "was one of those days when I call myself cheese. Chalk knows why not to do most everything even before it gets started. I just keep trying out things to do, and, Mr. Frazier, it would surprise you how many of them work. Now, while I write would you please look over that gun for any other marks?"

Ann's letter was mostly questions. For one thing, she wished to know how so violent a man had been able to obtain one of Oliver Winchester's repeating rifles.

Looking further, Frazier could only find a small letter *w* and the number repeated on the butt plate's toe. Kincade had retained the dead man's revolver. Two shots were gone from it. The witnesses said that he'd shot at the bandits at least that many times. It was too good a gun not to hold as possible evidence. Whoever Chalk had killed had been a forward-thinking man, at least until he'd turned his back on Chalk. The gun's cylinder was bored out to take rifle cartridges just the same as for a Henry.

As things stood now, the letter was written and in the post. The serving robber kept his silence, and Chalk was still in jail. Kincade had half convinced himself Chalk was somehow a member or at least an accomplice to that gang. But then again Chalk was a person that he knew—a decent, friendly man. Kincade's hope was for someone to come forward and testify to his innocence. But then again so many different witnesses with "my very own eyes" had seen so many different things.

For the moment Ann rubbed her forehead with her hand. It seemed there wasn't much else to do. Except she knew not to slow herself down into the world of seeming.

7

With a woman's letter in his hand, The New Haven Arms Company's shipping clerk looked fondly through his ledger. The entry was in its proper place. He tapped the folded letter on his lips and wondered why a gun originally shipped to a Kansas railroad had gone to where, as yet, there were no trains. This seemed unusual to him. Of course he would promptly respond to this woman's inquiry and he'd do it this very day. In addition he would write the railroad's agent who'd seen fit to purchase rifles from Oliver Winchester's company. With all the surplus guns left over from the war it wasn't easy to sell the newly made. The man from the railroad was a good customer and familiar with the product. He obviously wanted to deal with a company that would be there firmly behind whatever it sold. Yes, the least that railroad man deserved was a prompt notice that possibly one of his guns had strayed. Letters cost time to write. Postage and paper did not come for free. As he dipped his pen, the clerk at his high desk smiled. Imagine, he thought, a future time when we might charge our customers for information about something purchased from us.

Both letters were signed and sanded. It would be twenty-four cents to get his reply to the woman. The post office department were robbers charging that much to carry a little letter from place to place. The clerk opened a box to root out a stamp for the proper amount. Many small stamps made one's correspondence untidy and undignified. He moistened the stamp on a sponge. It was neatly and squarely in place, and looking down at it he suddenly wondered. There were, he knew, various featherbrains in government. They had ears for a piper whom serious businessmen must never listen to. Until now he had believed there were limits. But in this stamp they had managed to combine carelessness with disrespect. The signing of the Declaration of Independence was the picture, and they had printed it upside down. Well, they who were so careless to print it doubtless wouldn't see it as improper when it came into their hands. If he was even slightly doubtful maybe he shouldn't send the letter out. That was nonsense. They'd better stand behind what they'd made, even if it was the government. Or he'd go down on his own time to the post office and raise the kind of hell most people were too slow to make. Now he called for a boy to take these letters for the post.

Here was time to catch up with the new shipping books. He wondered if the people with the Hartford post office knew how much of their business came right from this office here. The latest model rifle was off and selling like a barn afire. Even without a war it did appear that Oliver's business was a growing one.

Parlor cars, railroad, stagecoaches, horseback, and, in the end, afoot. How many damn ways did a man have to go? Cas shrugged in resignation. Certain places needed getting to, because it was very important that certain men be dead. If there was any doubt you just kept traveling until you knew for sure. Both Cas and his employer liked cases that were closed. Over a year ago as part of a train robbery and while blowing open the express car, some bandit gang had killed the messenger. Identities had been suspected but no suspects had been identified for sure. There was no way of stopping angry men from robbing trains. You only had to wait 'til it was done and then you never stopped looking for those who'd done it. That was the service Pinkerton's Detective Agency took the railroad's money for. Maybe, someday, if enough people got in jail or in graves, then others wouldn't think it larkish to go robbing banks and trains.

It had been a bloody mess, and the robbers hadn't even gotten into the through safe on that Kansas train. The express agent was killed in the blast. Two of the robbers were found shot nearby. This had been a puzzler, as there had been no one in pursuit of them. Cas had been there to look around. There were a million hoofprints, three bodies, and nothing else until now. At the time of the crime the railroad hadn't thought to tell his agency that one of their guns was gone. It had been the gun's maker all the way in Connecticut who'd written the railroad of the loss. And now, at last, the railroad had gotten on the key to the Pinkertons. For well over a year the trail had been a cold one. Now he was making this journey with no promise for success. That Henry might be something that had passed ownership ten faceless times in the darkness of an alley outside the back door of a bar.

Cas had fought the whole war through. At twenty-four he finished it, the oldest man in his troop. It wasn't so long ago he'd come off a cavalry horse from sword-waving and revolver-fighting back and forth across half the land. He didn't try to remember those times when each day had started and finished and was successful, just so long as he'd come out the far end alive. The war had painted harsh colors on him and they were only beginning to fade. If the war had bothered him so much, why in the hell was he carrying a gun for Allan Pinkerton? Maybe the war had trapped him and he could know naught else. Upon leaving the army he hadn't known where a job would be or where his feet would take him.

Clanging hammers driving spikes could wear a man's life away. At first he'd worked manual, as a laborer, on the railroad. Then he got the job of making sure that things of value belonging to the railroad were difficult to lose. A lot of times he'd told a bunch of men that *lose* too often was the word for *stole,* and further they would just have to stop losing things. He'd been bitten, scratched, gouged, and stomped on, and then he'd done it right back. Many a man left the job paid right up 'til he'd been knocked down for the final time.

His boss had been General Greenville M. Dodge, and very few people called him Greenville even once. He'd been a Union general and throughout the war he'd built railroads for the army. He was a very fair man to work for and said that a man fighting for his rights was entitled to be paid right up until he'd been knocked down for the final time. It was Dodge with the Casement brothers who brought the Union Pacific's rails westward to Utah's Promontory Point.

Before that happened it finally came to Cas that a man could have his looks and youthful vigor worn away merely by getting punched, so he left railroading and joined the business of a man who'd headed up the wartime secret service for the North. Now he was riding on a train to find who had carried that Henry rifle all the way from Kansas to the town of Comptonsville which was nearly to the country's northwest corner. There wasn't anything to do for now but sit and relax.

He was dressed, as he'd been told, like any quiet drummer on his day-to-day. His employer had been strong about this point. Allan Pinkerton had talked to him about seriousness. It was something you had to have but there was no need to show it all the time.

"If a man rides black," Pinkerton had said, "and I mean his horse, his habit, and his rig, well then, that shows he doesn't mind calling attention to himself. If you work for me, don't do it. Only when attention's wanted is when I want you to call for it." This was a subject that Allan could really go on about. Maybe that was how he'd gotten where he was. He had gone on. "Seriousness, Cas, is a form of presence, of being somewhere. After a while, if you want to get things done, you start looking for it. In a man or a woman it is a matter of attitude. I've known funny little squint-eyed men with pot bellies and they've had it fine. It's sort of a way of staying someplace until what you want to happen happens."

A thoughtful person riding in the cars, if he looked carefully at the relaxing drummer, would be quite certain that he wasn't one. Cas was newly broken to detective work. Looking out the window he thought, Take Kansas out and this country would seem only half as wide. Getting hungry now, he got up to look for the conductor. He wanted to know when they would stop. With the fares already paid the railroad didn't care who took the contract for poisoning its passengers.

Cas returned to his seat and looked out the window. Impatience was only a place to throw away your strength. A chaw of tobacco was an ugly messy thing, and what sort of a man would it be who'd smoke a cigarette. Presently he'd have a cigar if nobody nearby in the car would be offended. Damn it, to be inside the telegraph wire that was always drawn as a thin black line atop the flashing poles. He'd once been told how fast a message moved. He'd better wait 'til he was stagecoach borne before doing his wishing. Then this train and Kansas would seem just like riding outside time and on the inside of that wire.

8

If it had been summer they'd have held the trial at the livery barn. Much more room to sit around in there, but then, of course, people couldn't smoke. The lobby of the hotel, though tight for room, was warmable. The judge could sit up on a stool behind the registration desk. It was a good vantage point to oversee the jury in their chairs. Spectators jammed in as best they could. A way was kept clear to the bar so they could bring their drinks back to their seats. There would be no getting up and down, in and out, for refills. The judge made that very clear. There would be occasional pauses in the trial for freshening up, and that was to be it. Certain people present, some of them even members of the bar, felt this informality detracted from the dignity of the court. The judge contended that if courts used hotel facilities it would be improper to deprive the owner of his regular livelihood. Also, an extended trial that might go on for hours could make a desert of some men's insides.

For the trial the judge had brought two lawyers and a court clerk up to Comptonsville in a big box sled. The clerk was doubly useful because he could handle the team. A hired driver was the first needless expense that had been put aside.

The jury of twelve was quickly gathered. To preserve impartiality, bank employees and persons wounded during the robbery were excluded. Both lawyers agreed to this. In addition, one man, a drummer, was excused on the grounds of his not being a resident of the town, county, or even the territory itself. However he did seem to have some personal interest because he stayed on to watch the trial. He was a man who seemed large but slouchy. That made it hard to clearly see the size of the man he was.

With the jury impaneled and everyone settled, the judge banged his gavel sharply once. "We are going to run both trials at one time. I know they aren't for the same crimes, but I hope our jury's got brains enough to try two suspects both at once. Sometimes we've got to wriggle and move things through, for not one man is present who doesn't have his fullness of daily chores. We are all good citizens here. We want justice, yet we all want to get ourselves and our critters fed." The judge stood.

"This is no miner's court. If there was need to run a trial for the whole week, I'd run it for a week. I can assure you that the need is seldom. Now first off we are going to have the clerk of the court pass a hat around. If you want to witness this trial for free I cannot stop you. However, these two lawyers have been brought along without pay. The only remuneration they are likely to receive will come from your generous contributions. If you'll throw money on a concert hall stage just to see a lady dancing in her drawers, then you should be willing to shell something out to see the law's majesty unfold."

"Lynching's cheaper," someone shouted from the back.

"Not if I catch you at it," the judge replied. Then he remembered to ask for Kincade to bring the prisoners over. With the entrance of Chalk and the wounded gunman from the street their trial began. Chalk was first in the witness stand and the judge asked him what he had to say for himself. The defense lawyer objected, pointing out the prisoner's right to silence. The judge replied that the case of a man who could not speak for himself always appeared cloudy to him.

Chalk was freely open and eager to testify on his own behalf. His lawyer clamped shut his eyes. The prosecution's lawyer leaned eagerly forward in his seat. Neither had anything real to lose. However, the contest wasn't even. The prosecution's lawyer was only trying to get these two men hung. He wasn't even out of pocket if he failed. The man who'd taken the job of saving them could anticipate defeat with a greater sense of consternation. He would be losing possible future customers. However they were both in a courtroom where the finer points of the law did not stand much of a chance.

Yes, Chalk had heard the man called something. There'd been so much noise in the street he could not remember what. It sounded like the two letters Kay and Cee. No, he wasn't absolutely positive. He was, however, certain that the man he'd shot was going to kill the farm boy and the prisoner next to him in the dock. He was sure then and he was still sure now. Questions came foaming over Chalk. Why had he not called down to the man? How had he known for certain what the man was going to do? Hadn't he killed a man who had been shooting or attempting to shoot violent robbers in the street? So many of these questions made it quite clear that only Chalk thought he should do what had been done.

The court swarmed back over him again. The prisoner had shot a robber who was going to kill another robber, or that was what he claimed. And the man shot was about to do all this with a holstered gun. The prosecution had to smile slightly as that one went skipping by. After all, Chalk, safe atop the wagon, wasn't even being threatened. Now the prosecution addressed himself to Chalk directly. He phrased his statement as a question.

"You were going to be judge, jury, and executioner—all three and in about that many seconds?"

"That man's gun was in its holster," someone in the audience called out.

"And what are you telling me?" Chalk yelled back. "That shutting a timber rattler's mouth turns it into a garter snake? When it came his time to kill you, it wouldn't have mattered where his gun was at."

"That's what you say."

"That is what I say."

The judge's gavel came down once. The desk made a hollow booming sound that the judge found very pleasing. "We are agreed that the man's gun was holstered when he was shot. There's no way for this court to determine how quickly he could have drawed it if Chalk here hadn't denied him the opportunity."

No one was denying Chalk had shot this man, and Chalk the least of all. Five times at that. The hits, so close together as they were, held little hope for Chalk's lawyer to try as a defense that the gun had gone off as the result of some kind of an accident.

Ann was in the courtroom with the baby in her arm. Frazier sat beside her. He was doubtful of Chalk's chances. Ann was not. She had beaten down the trees until they'd found a Scandinavian of their own, one who, when speaking English, could be clearly understood. It wasn't merely that. Ann had insisted that he be taken around and tried out on the farm boy and his family. It wasn't her plan to arrive at the trial with the wrong kind of a Scandinavian. Most people would not have thought of that. Ann took the trouble to find out there were several kinds from different countries and each kind only spoke a language of his own.

The standoff came when the boy, clearly questioned and his answers translated, said that he hadn't understood anything those Americans had said to him. He only knew that he had been in the alley behind the bank. There he had seen a man get killed. This was clarified by closer questioning. He had seen the bank teller fall down some steps and die. The slow words of the boy effectively said that he had seen a horror happen. In panic he had run out into the main street of the town. That man—the boy pointed to the surviving bandit—had lain holding a money bag in the street. Did he know there was money in it? No, not at the time. It was just a bag and the man had pointed a gun at him. Here the boy's mother shrieked. Three men jumped up to grab her. She held a heavy chair firmly in her hands as she leapt toward the prisoner in the dock with Chalk.

The translator was still on the stand. As the yelling softened beneath his pounding gavel, the judge asked, "What does she say?"

The translator held placating hands in front of him. "Mrs. Sorensen realized afresh that this man would have killed her child. If he's not hung I'll tell him her words in private, as a punishment."

The judge would have been glad to let the trial end here. For him, there was a long cold sled ride coming up, but this wasn't to be, as many came forward to testify. Several waved upraised hands as though the court was an eager school. To be fair the judge called each in turn. The same message kept going to the jury. How could anyone know that Chalk had not been in with those men who'd robbed the bank?

The second prisoner didn't say a single word. Whatever questions were put to him, he smiled. His smile was more even than a row of piano keys. This didn't happen once. It happened over and over. The keys were slightly yellowed.

Finally Chalk got to his feet. As he sat, his fingers and palm had been wrapped around his mouth. He had been listening thoughtfully.

"Judge."

The judge responded with a nod.

It took Chalk some time to get his thoughts started. "I was sleeping on a wagon top between the bows. And before anyone asks

me, of course it wasn't a sensible place to be. That doesn't matter.
I was there.

"I was sleeping, and shots sounded all around me." Chalk
paused thoughtfully. "I was all sobered up and could see everything
that was happening. I saw Kincade's shot and the horseman put
down in death. I saw the horse get hit, a man down in the street
with his leg broke, and more shots into him from every side. I saw
the boy come running up and go to lashing that wounded man
with a piece of some kind of material. Later I found out it was his
muffler. That's something only an Indian would fully understand.
I mean, going after a man that holds a gun using a knitted woolen
muffler as a weapon, that takes a particular kind of courage. Well,
the time was right because all that was left in his gun," Chalk
pointed to the man beside him, "was clicks. That's why I want to
say this man here was going to kill that boy. And I'm saying, there's
no need to play around with witnesses and lies. That man I shot
was going to kill the boy and then kill the man who sits so silent
over there. The man I shot spoke words only I and him there could
hear." Chalk pointed again at the surviving bandit.

The prosecution stood. "Objection, your honor. The farm boy
heard the words."

"Without you know the language," Chalk replied, "you don't
hear the words."

"Objection overruled." The judge gestured for a pause as he
turned to the silent robber. "You want to say anything? Chalk is
claiming, among other things, that he saved your life."

The man merely exposed his teeth in his strange sort of smile.
He wasn't even going to move his head, either back and forth or
up and down.

"I'm just going to have to recess this trial right here for the
next couple of minutes." The judge rose as he spoke. He walked
from behind the hotel clerk's desk and up and down a few times

in front of the jury. He was looking at them carefully. Then he
turned slightly toward Chalk and the bandaged robber, who sat
immobile with his splinted leg resting on a stool in front of him.
The judge managed to get around and behind the prisoners. Chalk
turned and smiled. The other prisoner, as though unconcerned,
stared straight ahead.

With his right hand the judge drew a .32-caliber Smith and
Wesson No. 2 Army from the inside pocket of his coat. Smiling
back at Chalk he placed his left forefinger to his lips. No one else
in the court could see these movements. They were masked by the
prisoners in their makeshift dock. The judge waited for a pause and
when the room was silent he let the hammer spur slip from beneath
his thumb. The gun was carefully pointed at the floor. Chalk was
still smiling, although slightly puzzled. The man next to him
turned like a jump trap in his chair, splinted leg and all, his right
hand blurring to where his pistol butt had always been. All he saw
was gun smoke and the judge's smile. Repocketing the pistol the
judge returned to his makeshift bench. The room continued quiet.
The gavel slammed and the judge said, "Recess is over. The court
wished to determine if it was being heard, because it wouldn't be
fair to try a deaf man with only the sound of our voices.

"Now, George,—and that's what this court is going to call
you—you don't care to talk to us and that's your privilege. You
are of course protected by this court and by brave battles through
the centuries by men who loved the law. I mean really loved it.
There have been others who only thought they did. When it didn't
run smooth enough to suit them then they'd just heat up a running
iron and they'd decorate the accused like he was a page or two from
a stock detective's book of brands. In today's world this is known
as torture. If this failed to elicit a confession then they would give
their victim credit for having guts and then they would hang him
anyway. Well, I want you to know that we have developed away
from that. So, George, if you or your lawyer here don't have any

objections, we aren't going to have a witness or witnesses come forward to testify to something half this town has already seen. You were out in the street with a bag full of money that wasn't yours. I'm just holding on to that for one second.

"Now," the judge addressed the room at large, "is there anybody here who saw this man, George, kill another human being?" The judge looked to the banker with the bandaged head and his surviving clerk, who was beside him in the first row of the audience.

"No, your honor, but—" the banker, Evans, was getting to his feet.

"With your injuries, please, there is no need to rise."

Evans had been facing away when the shot was fired in the bank. The surviving teller also testified. He couldn't remember well but he had turned toward Evans at the sound of the shot. He thought, but couldn't be sure, some other man had fired the gun.

George remained silent. The judge did not ask for his statement twice. After a fair pause he turned to instruct the jury. "Well, enough people have been killed already. This man, George, is a person who would rob with violence. That's not the sign of a man who regards his own life highly. I am not making light of a robbery that has ended in several deaths. However, I will say it again. We have already had more than our fair share of corpses. So, if the jury agrees with me, I think that it would be best if the accused went off to jail for about the next twenty years. Any objections from anyone?"

The defense lawyer rose to be acknowledged by the judge.

"How do we know that he isn't, for example, your honor, a first offender?"

"Well, you have him say it. That's not for the court to prove, and besides I'm more interested in last offenders than in first ones. Anybody else?"

The room was silent and the judge continued. "The twenty years of thoughtfulness I suggested gives a man a second chance.

He can pretty soon start having good thoughts to get him out to
the far side of his time. Or he can have bad ones. Then you'd have
done him a favor to have hanged him. However, the decision is his,
and we still have the other part of this trial to get done. So, now
gentlemen of the jury, firstly, have I been leading you?"

As one the jury answered, "No."

"Then how about our prisoner here?" The jurymen didn't leave
the room. They all turned together for a brief whispered discussion.
It was soon over. The foreman rose to his feet.

"Guilty, of course, your honor. And if you think it would pain
the son of a bitch more thoroughly not to be hung, then by all
means let's just send him to the penitentiary."

The gavel came down. The judge announced that part one of
the trial was over. Formal sentencing would wait until the end.

Looking directly at Chalk, the judge said, "Well, part one's
over and part two needs finishing. Now, what have you got to say
for yourself?"

Before Chalk was on his feet, the prosecution's lawyer started.
"I did not press my case against the man whom the court calls
George. He is not a killer. He was riding through, perhaps misled
by bad companions."

"Who are no longer here to speak for themselves." An old miner
shouted this.

"But Chalk here," the lawyer continued, "sure did kill a man,
not once, but five times."

"Objection!" from the defense. It was sustained by a judicial
clarification.

"He shot the man five times. He only killed him once."

"And also," the prosecution's lawyer continued, "Chalk is a
resident of this town, and if he was a member of that gang, and if
he brought them here like wolves into a fold of sheep—"

There was another objection which was sustained. Wolves in a
fold of sheep don't usually get so badly chewed.

"If he brought them here, however or whichever way he did it, then he has everyone's blood upon his hands." No objections were voiced. Was there a conspiracy to rob the bank? That surely could have happened. The court just had to discover if Chalk had been a part of it.

The fact of Chalk's position on the wagon and the number of shots fired were established by testimony. The other prisoner remained silent, and the prosecution's lawyer suggested to him that cooperation might help lighten his final sentencing.

The gavel came down with a bang. "I never lie to a man in court, or for that matter anyplace else. There's not anything this man George is going to do in this court that will change whatever sentence he's going to get. He's been found guilty of holding a bag of money belonging to others with a dead horse fallen on top of his leg. I will tell him only one thing. If he has something decent to say, then it will maybe make the time he stays in prison easier to bear. But be a bastard now, and that's the sort of person he's going to be alone with for a long, long time."

George's jaw dropped down, but he remained silent.

Three witnesses clearly stated they'd seen Chalk's victim turn the mounted robbers back. Others came forward to say that they'd also seen him bravely mixing into the fight.

After listening to all the accusations, Chalk addressed the bench. Upon the judge's recognition he said, "Your honor, if I was part of that gang, how come I'm the only one that had my name writ on my coat collar and inside the sweat band of my hat. I didn't hide myself."

The prosecution's lawyer explained. "There was no need for you to hide yourself. You were known to all."

Chalk had to admit the lawyer's point, and this rattled him so that he forgot his plan to ask why the man he'd shot had no labels in his clothes.

A hand was raised. It was Cas, who'd declined doing jury duty.

"I do not know if at this time it is of importance to this court, but I can assure you that I know of at least one individual who, if you said, 'He's human,' as people on occasion do, it would be a lie."

"Hey, you there. If you wouldn't be part of the jury, how come you want to be part of the trial?" It was a new voice from the crowd. The drummer didn't turn to answer. He continued.

"As a private citizen I am asking that you be a little fair. Before murder's done you've got to know who it is that's getting killed. There's so many different kinds of people in the world, you can't rate them all the same. Oh, yes, I know the law extends its protection to almost everybody."

"Almost everybody!" Both lawyers spoke and rose together.

Cas looked around the room. "If there was an Indian here I'd—"

A man right next to him jumped up. "Don't you include Indians and other aberrations in with me."

The gavel banged. "That's talk we won't have in here. It's not the Indian's fault that the law does not reach out and shelter him. I of course speak of Indians who are lawful men themselves. Now, should you wish, continue, sir."

"There are certain men known to the law who have chosen to live outside it. To be without them would improve the town, the county, and in fact the entire nation. Two problems arise. First is finding them and second is the arrangements for having them either placed in jail or killed. I'm here as a concerned citizen. There's no officialness in my plea to this court. I think, however, we might do well to have a look at this person who has been killed. Then we'll see if murder has been done. I have hopes as to who he will prove out to be. If I was certain I'd tell it now."

Laura was relieved. She had taken a place discreetly back from the center of the room. Hopefully she could retain her silence. If it was to save Ann's Chalk she'd have to speak right out. Laura knew she had done many things that were salty and she'd have admitted to them gladly. This was no church picnic they were on. No, she wouldn't mind speaking out, but living with Kay Cee was the only thing she'd ever done shameful against herself. She could hardly tell her girls to be virtuous, but she would warn them that there was a sort of man whose touch left you feeling sticky ever afterward. Damn, didn't she know because she'd herded with the worst. Now, it was interesting to see the words that were being talked around the man Kay Cee had been.

Laura had held back from Ann's entreaties, all the while telling herself she'd make the move when the last moment came. Ann had kept asking, "Isn't there something we can do?"

Laura had half shrugged and mouthed out that Chalk was important only to Ann. "When you've made a man that important to you," she said, "then it's only natural to figure he's that way to everyone. You ask them to help you and the help you ask you call justice and bounden moral duty, but . . ." The end words were unspoken and stayed in Laura's mind. For some their privacy is more important than other people's justice. While Laura had her thoughts the court recessed for drinks. Chalk had looked so appealingly at the judge that he'd directed the lawyer for the defense to bring back . . .

Chalk answered readily, "Two beers. One is for nervousness and the other for enjoyment."

Before going to the bar the lawyer asked, "Your honor, are you sure it is all right for the accused to drink?"

The judge smiled in affirmation. "Certainly, if it is not done so extensively as to interfere with his defense. I have adjourned court when the accused was brought in too drunk to understand the nature of the charges brought against him. However, I have not heard of a mistrial caused by some defendant being so foolish as to allow himself to get drunk while court was in session. One way to find out if an accused is serious about his innocence is to see how much he drinks at his own trial."

With the recess over, Chalk nursed along his second beer.

Several additional witnesses came forward and further clouded the happening in the street. The judge knew it was difficult to get a clear picture of any circumstance. Solid facts got wispy and hard to see once they were brought to court. Now, they were trying to look at something that had happened to a whole town in maybe just a few minutes. The passage of time came clear when the hotel clerk testified. Once under oath and with leisure to think, he realized he hadn't seen anything except the jammed window's sash. When asked how long it usually took him to get that window free he thought for a pause and then said, "Never much more than a minute."

There were conversations going around in the audience now. In the warmth several people had fallen asleep. At least two of them were snoring. The judge heard the hotel clerk out and then brought his gavel down as a preamble to his pronouncement.

"A bag of money in a man's hand is one thing. But if the good citizen whom Chalk allegedly killed was facing a desperate robber on the ground after, as testimony has it, he had been gunfighting him and several others, why was that man's gun back in its holster? What's been clear to some has gotten unclear to me. You, sir."

Cas rose. The judge continued. "You, sir, have made intimations of special knowledge concerning the unidentified man that Chalk has shot. Hold. Strike that from the record, that is if we had one. What I mean is if you know who he is or was, it is important for the accused to have this information."

"If I could see the body, sir, and it would surprise many here to know how far I've come to see it—"

"It's gotten buried," Kincade said. "He's been buried and his grave is frosted over."

"Did no one in this entire town recognize the man?" Cas asked. The courtroom was silent. "Now, without knowing him," Cas pointed to several of the witnesses, "you are telling us what he intended to do. I don't even know which way some of my own best friends will jump."

One witness came to his feet and started with, "Most decent rational people—"

Cas interrupted. "Are on the other side of the Mississippi River. They never left Boston, Charleston, or New York. If nobody here knows who he was, I think it was damned careless of you to bury him. And I'd further like to suggest, your honor, that we dig him up and have a look. He's not been down so long as to ripen bad."

Before the judge could answer, a miner in the front row shouted, "Hydraulic the bastard out."

"How about that?" the judge asked.

A man stood up in the back. "It's not done here. It makes such a rotten mess that the town's never let them start it. Even so, if you hydrauliced him the whole cemetery might be ruined and you'd have to handle things pretty fine if you wanted any colors to show."

The judge was open to suggestions, and Cas, already on his feet, said, "I'd suggest we can afford to be a little patient. In the summertime further south, patience doesn't do well in this line of work. Here and now we'll get a shack put up over the grave with a good small stove inside. It'll need a door that a wheelbarrow can get easily through."

The judge realized that this would take some time, and he asked the jury how they felt. They excused themselves for a conference. Then the foreman ducked his head out to say that they agreed. If adjournment was just for more talk to be made they were willing to finish the case off right here and now. However, as it had been affirmed in open court that the shooting of a person depended upon who was shot, they, the jury, favored this sensible plan of getting Chalk's victim back up to the surface of this frozen ground. The court was adjourned for one week. There was no bail for Chalk, and the newly christened George, having been convicted, clanked around his cell constrained by manacles on both his arms and legs.

The town's carpenter worked one day and most of a night to build the little hut. It was on skids and a team dragged it up to a leveled site atop the grave.

There was a nice little stove inside, and the first day Cas went up to see how the work progressed. There was a pulley to the roof and a bucket down in the pit. He thought they must pay grave diggers here by the hour and not the hole because at the end of the second day the pit was only five feet deep. The old miner digging said that there wasn't even colors yet, let alone a sight of the mother lode. It turned out later that during this one burial a few pieces of likely looking quartz had appeared. So the grave diggers had dug right down to where the bedrock was. They'd been lucky to have gotten him in just before the ground froze hard. If he'd lingered any from his wounds they'd have had to keep him iced all through the winter while waiting for the spring. As he dug, the old miner thought, maybe they hadn't been so lucky after all. But then again they had made this wintertime job for him.

Kincade thought about the stranger who had bespoken himself at the trial. If he was a salesman, where were his things to sell? This same stranger was in the hotel bar at night and took his meals in the little restaurant that had just started up the street. Until now there hadn't been any decent place to eat. A lone girl could go to work for Laura or she could work for herself. The bachelors in the town were overjoyed when one girl opened her own clean-run eatery.

The frozen ground had been quickly penetrated, but as it had been explained, they were going to have to go deep to get that body back. Denver was the old miner's name. Winter work was rare and he kept at it slow and evenly. He wasn't about to embark on some crazy rush of activity and dig himself out of a job. The drummer was eager to have the body up, but the judge wouldn't be back for one whole week. That was another reason not to hurry. Denver was glad of the drummer's company. He came over at least once every day. Digging was lonely inside this little house, and some spookiness was starting as he dug closer to the corpse. The drummer wasn't much for conversation but it was appreciated that he'd roll up his own shirt sleeves to give a working man a pause for rest.

Kincade also made it a point to look in often. He wanted to be sure that whoever was found got brought back to see the judge.

Kincade was poking up the fire in the stove. The drummer was pulling the dirt-filled bucket up, and deep in the hole the old miner, waiting for the bucket, was resting on his shovel. His intention was never to move dug dirt more than once.

With the bucket back down, there was the sound of slow steady spadework for a while. Then Denver was up the ladder from the pit. "There's pay dirt down there, son. I just now turned up a hand. No, I was digging easy. There's nothing cut or spoiled. It's just, well, I was paid to dig. Now I've dug. Someone else is on for whatever assay work there is to be done."

Cas was down the ladder and into the pit. He dug with the spade where he could, and if the place was tight he used his hands. The dirt was loose. It had not had time to settle hard. Cas undid the bucket and passed the rope around the dead man's chest and then underneath his arms. When it was properly tied he climbed back up to pull. The wheel in the ceiling beam creaked and the lamp, left down in the hole, threw twisting shadows on the roof.

The corpse came slowly up, swinging half around and back and forth at the end of the line. At last there were four of them in this little house. The dead man hung with his toes just level to the surface of the ground. Pieces of earth and clay still stuck above his lip, and the hair of his head was thickly plastered down with clay. Denver looked directly in the corpse's face. "I doubt very much he was handsome when alive. Being dead has not helped his appearance. He's a mean-looking bastard now. I'd guess he was a mean-looking bastard then."

Cas reached out for the body, almost as though he were greeting a friend.

"I'll grab him," he said, "and then you two can slack off and untie that rope."

The body was stiff enough so that they could lean it against the wall. Cas's face was smiles now and he held a lantern close to study the dead man's face. With careful gestures he brushed the earth away. Death had drawn the features, but it had been a face that was tight in life.

"I could almost kiss that son of a bitch."

"Who could you almost kiss?" Denver wanted to know.

"Kay Cee Smith, right here in front of us." Even in the lamplight Cas's smile was sunshine pure. "Golly, if you knew all the places I've been just to kill this bastard. I am certainly glad we caught him in time, and Mr. Kincade, I hope this is a lesson to you. Just try to realize the kind of mischief that can come from burying a man you aren't acquainted with. Why, I might have spent my whole life looking to find someone who was peacefully resting in your little cemetery here."

"Mr. Whatever Your Name Is, I think by now—"

Cas raised his hand shaking it slightly. "No, Mr. Kincade, please wait. If you know what it's like to greet a long-lost friend alive, then you sure have some small idea how much pleasure there is for a decent person meeting up with this man dead. He was so much a bastard I've always halfway looked forward to killing him myself. That was something I didn't like in me. It wasn't good for the way I felt, and it was just another little piece of how old Kay Cee could cause whole worlds to rot."

"Would there be a reward for helping to find this man?" Denver asked as he held up a lantern. He stared closely at features from which Cas's fingers had brushed away the clinging earth. "He's looking mighty peaked, but he's sure kept good. I guess the touch of frost when they put him down was what turned the trick. If it was summer this little cabin wouldn't be a fitting place to take a smoke."

Denver had his pipe started and he held the stem toward the dead man's lips. "Care for a puff, old buddy?" Denver laughed at his little joke. It sounded like short muffled coughs. Then, serious again, he turned to the marshal and the salesman. "Life's the high grade, fellers. When it's gone there's no poorer trailing than a corpse. What would you say we get down to where there's something can be drunk?"

Cas shoveled the fire from the stove. Then he used the wheelbarrow to bring snow to carefully cover the body. He made a mound of the heavy snow, patting it down in a gentle way. He might have been tucking blankets around a child in its bed. They carefully latched the door behind them. Now they had Kay Cee. After all this trouble they didn't want critters to make their work for naught.

The three men walked down the hillside to the town. Snow crunched beneath the drummer's boots. Stars were sharp. In these mountains there was no winter haze. For Cas, Kay Cee's death was such a pleasure that the frost he walked on could have been soft sod and springtime's freshly sprouted flowers.

They'd have to wait for the judge to make the death official. But even before that, tomorrow morning a sometime drummer would come to the town's jail and tell Chalk all the good that he had done.

The hotel bar was lit and warm. Several men were seated at a game of cards. A scattering of others stood along the rail. Frazier was there, thoughtful, sober, and drinking just barely enough to support his system. He nodded as they came in. The miner was up to the bar with a loud hand slapping down. "Whisky for three gentlemen, and I'm not talking pilgrim whisky nor any of your forty-rod."

Pouring, the barkeep asked, "You get him up yet?"

The miner smacked his lips. "He surely is. Up like Lazarus. Not half so lively though. It sure is good to get out of a cold grave and into a nice warm bar."

The card players looked up from their game.

In a whisper the barkeep hesitantly asked, "How is he?"

"Real good," Denver replied, "for being shot five times and then buried for a month. Good but not perky is what I'd say. What would you say, Charlie?"

Kincade's drink was in his mouth so he had a pause to think. "I don't suppose he was handsome when alive. He's looking a bit green and cheesy now. That clay pomade did not improve his appearance much."

A hovering hand was drawn back from the free lunch spread. This selection of free, highly salted foods was carefully designed to effect an increase in the consumption of beer. A partially filled plate nearly dropped as a patron rushed outside with his ruined appetite.

"That's enough," the barkeeper said. "I'm sorry that I asked."

Denver turned to see the man leave. Tossing down his drink he wiped his hands once on the front of his flannel shirt. While piling his own sandwich together at the vacated place, he commented for the card players that there was nothing like digging to raise a miner's appetite.

"I'm glad for Chalk," the marshal said, "if it all comes out in his favor. Though I still say he had the drop and should have given that man a chance. I called out to Chalk, but of a certain I called too late."

"Mr. Kincade, you called just right," Cas said. "I'd have never tried to take Kay Cee from the front."

A range-dressed man, nearby at the bar, asked, "Was you afraid of him?" Then he laughed. "You were afraid of a man who was shot in the back by, of all people, Chalk."

"That boy knew what he was doing," was Cas's reply.

"He was a coward."

"I wouldn't know that. I only said, personally knowing the circumstances, he knew what he was doing."

Cas turned back to the bar.

"You weren't talking to me, mister."

The new voice was from behind Cas. He didn't want to think about it. It was doubtlessly from some towheaded hard-eyed idiot, one of thousands, who were always just a little angry no matter what was happening. Often they'd have a funny little hollow laugh, and their faces were just a little red from not knowing how to smile. Cas did not want even this faint reminder of Kay Cee's viciousness. The man behind him was just a flapping mouth without any serious bent for evil. Cas wanted to take his own thoughts back over those haunted years now past. He wished or rather hoped that the man behind him would not go squeaking on like the ungreased wheels of an old "Chihuahua" ore cart.

No matter how many other men had died, 'til now Kay Cee had always left alive. A man who doesn't amount to much when he goes wrong, Cas thought, it comes to something sad and small. A man like Kay Cee that has a power in him, have him go bad and all hell gets broken loose. It's usual for violence to come from anger, real anger and not the one-horse town, bad-assed, bar-talk kind. Everybody was sore at something. The nasty, small men got about as far as kicking dogs. The mean big ones bit back and then the whole world had to jump aside to escape their snapping teeth.

Like a damned wolverine. All fury, so as to scare an Indian who has never thought of showing fear. Steal and eat even when he isn't hungry. Then there's the mess he'll leave behind. Everything either sprayed or shat upon. Or maybe even both. A man remembers where a wolverine has been. That was Kay Cee's way. Through pure

clear ugliness he'd let the world know that he'd been in it. Mostly
he didn't even want the things he stole. He only was remembered
as the person who stole it. If it was something irreplaceable, he
would be remembered for as long as it was missed. If one person
could be the soul of rottenness, Kay Cee was certainly it.

Cas had tried to kill Kay Cee in the war. It was as long ago as
that. It was in May of 'Sixty-three when the springtime woods
caught fire after the battle of Chancelorsville had been fought.
There were all those helpless wounded men who got burned up
along with the dried out brush and trees. At first they'd heard
muskets being fired strangely, almost like a picket fight but without any back and forth. A sergeant returning from reconnoiter told
that the woods was burning. The shots had sounded as the fire came
to loaded muskets lying beside the wounded men. There was also
the louder sound as the fire burned to the cartridge boxes fastened
to their belts. The sergeant didn't need to ask for volunteers. Cas
went in behind him, even though he didn't have his horse.

A mix of men went into that fire to carry fellows out without
regard to which side they were on. They left their muskets stacked
back and away from the fire's edge. Shots from a distant rebel
company came down on them, but they didn't have the weapons
nor the time to spare for fighting back. They halted for only a
second to hear those scattered musket balls shred by, and then the
goddamn rebs had brains enough to see what they were doing. If
there was no way for the rebs to come and help, at least their
shooting stopped. All across the distance and over the crackling
flames the men could hear faint and scattered cheers.

It was against nature to see such small men scurry from the
smoke, bearing men of twice their size. If a horse had been hurt
inside those flames, it seemed these men would have found strength
to grab it in their arms.

Kay Cee had been a lieutenant. He'd ordered the rescuers to
keep their guns. Then when the rebels had got to firing, he'd or-

dered his men back from the woods. They'd put aside their muskets unordered and now they were turning from a fight. An officer's duty was to call them back. When that didn't work he was too quick to warn against the flames. He'd clutched at men who had the heart to go back again and again. They weren't crazed or suicides. When the burning fully got its strength they could only stand among the men they'd saved. When the screams of the tortured dying came through the smoke and fire the best men in the regiment flung down full length on the ground to cry. Kay Cee was walking by them without a tear or bead of sweat. Back and forth he paced, and then he made a smile. "Listen," he said, "how those rebel bastards die."

Cas had nothing in his hands to shoot him with. Minutes passed. One of the troubles with a war is that it interferes with a man's need to do important things. The moment was gone and Cas and Kay Cee went their separate ways out of this swirling agony of smoke and pain.

That was how Kay Cee had gotten inside Cas. Cas wasn't the sort to hold waves of hatred in his heart forever. It was possible he'd moved past Kay Cee other times before the war was done. Kay Cee was a man who knew when it was time just to hide and watch. He did know that to live he must keep certain men outside the world he wove around himself.

Once during the summer of 'Sixty-five, Cas had gotten news of Kay Cee from a man beside him in a bar. Cas made the one brag of his life. When it fuddled on him he never spoke of his intentions again.

If a man was half sober and in tears it never could hurt to hear his story out.

"One hundred and sixty acres," was how the man beside him started, "and every cent I ever had in my life. Cheated and lied out of it. That quarter was sure working nice. It was a place to remember me away from the war. If you ask me how or why I listened,

I've got no way of telling you. I don't even think he wanted my money or the land."

"It was your goddamned heart he was after," Cas knew enough to say. The description was pulling together out of a memory of smoke and screams. "He has more than just your spread. You'll ruin a whole life waiting to get up even with that man. Plotting, planning, and wondering what the bastard's up to next. Your trouble is he's gotten inside you and he's pushing your life out like a catbird chick in the middle of a soon-to-be emptied robin's nest.

Cas bought the man a drink. "There's no blame on you, but that same man has also slid into me. I can only hope he didn't get into me all the way. I don't think about him any more with the first morning light, and he's not any longer in my dreams. I just know I'll find him. When he's dead I'll stop hearing the screams from those dying wounded burning in the forest after Chancelorsville was fought."

Nodding thanks for the drink, the tearful man told Cas, "Oh, I know where he is. He keeps a bar now in Cairo where it's under the hill."

Cas turned to look carefully at the man. "You know where he's at, and you're eating your heart out for a whole lifetime? Sure it's dangerous and you might not come through it right, but kill that bastard and it will be a satisfaction for all the days of your life. Years and years spoiled and gone rotten because you had trouble with a man and then you wait for some outside justice to cure it?

"I had trouble with that same man, but as you know, he got away from me. I wasn't broken over it. The world's just so wide and I knew someday, I'd find him. You say he's in Cairo Under the Hill."

The man nodded.

"If he's going to die of old age he'll have to do it in the next three days."

"How's that?"

"Well, if I start riding now and treat my horse decent, it'll take three days to ride over there."

The man spilled his drink as he stood up. "You going to kill him?"

Cas looked and smiled.

"How you goin' to do it?"

"Sitting here, how should I know?"

"What's that mean? You got to know ahead to do something big like that."

"It means I don't know what's for tomorrow's breakfast. Might be eggs, and might just be grits. Could be grits with eggs and maybe even bacon. So, how can I know that man's to be killed, until the job gets done? If you plan things too far ahead you're liable for disappointment."

When Cas arrived, Kay Cee was gone. It wasn't like somebody'd warned him. He had no way of knowing Cas was on his way. It was just a sense he had. The time had come for him to find new, as yet unspoiled places.

The next time Cas came upon Kay Cee it was outside of Baxter, Kansas, in 'Sixty-six. That's where the quarantine was. You couldn't fault the real farmers. They had a tick fever fear. The Texas cattle were immune, but theirs were not. Kay Cee didn't have any endangered stock; he just had a nature to throw in with people who were stopping others. There were also many border ruffians leftover from the war who were using the quarantine as a mask for being cattle thieves. Kay Cee was naturally at home with them. The herds were moved off to follow the grass that seemed to grow on forever and right around there Cas lost Kay Cee again.

Then Cas had taken a regular full-time paying job. After the railroad he started as a cattle detective and then kept on with Allan Pinkerton's agency. As an operative he learned to deal with assignments as they came. More and more his work took him away from animals. Men were learning to rob trains.

In his job Cas always had to be ready to move at a moment's notice. Once he was riding a two-car special on a cleared track headed toward a siding by a water tower just outside some little town in Kansas. It was only a spot on the prairie underneath the burning sun.

As Cas and several other men stepped down, a wrecked express car waited on the siding. There was an older detective to show Cas around the damage. Buzzing flies were thick where blood had blown. The baggage man had never had a chance. Just about everyone blows an express car the same. Cas saw each detail but he had to be told that a single robber was implicated by the nature of this job. When Cas inquired after the robber's name he was told that it was Kay Cee Smith. The express car could have been opened without killing the messenger. Killing without need was one of Kay Cee's ways.

So right in the middle of being a Pinkerton, Cas was looking to find Kay Cee once again. The best sign of a really fine job, he thought, is when you get paid for something you'd be doing anyway. The years had been few but long, and now they were over.

Cas licked his lips and smiled. There was just no way for him to believe his pleasure from seeing Kay Cee at long last, dead. He voiced his satisfaction to the miner, Denver, who was drawn up at the bar beside him. Although they'd been ignoring loud adjacent conversations, Cas's joy and satisfaction had been overheard.

A probing finger tapped him on the back. Cas didn't move. This was something he'd never consider doing himself. An unseen person should never touch a grown man in a bar. In most places it was not a long-lived thing to do. The finger was there again. Cas turned around very slowly. He was experienced in barroom nastiness and was ever vigilant to head it off, but only when that could be accomplished in a proper manner.

The finger was attached to a towheaded young mouth who thought too much about his clothes and not enough about his Colt.

He'd had a fur holster made that matched his winter chaps. The boy stared angrily into Cas's eyes, saying, "That Chalk, he was a coward to—"

Cas touched his finger to his lips. Still thinking about Kay Cee he said, "And I say he was an angel to have shot that man."

The young man in his fur chaps didn't have any way to take these words in. He was unable even to think about what an angel was. He was a truculent young man whose intention was to get angry. Among the many things he didn't know was that this was the wrong place for doing it.

Before he could move it farther, Cas slapped him in the face. Cas slapped like a bullwhip's butt. He wasn't loose wristed like the old time Southern men who'd slap a man so as to start a duel. Without pause, it was as if this boy's face was being stuffed into a windmill's blades. Cas kept his mouth to himself. He wanted to drown this kid with the harshest words. It had been the kid's intention to tell Cas about anger. Cas had plenty of his own. He'd tried his best to get them all forgotten. With Kay Cee dead this could have been his nicest day and most quiet night, if just to spend it drinking in a bar. But someone had to put the edge of his mouth around something he didn't know anything about.

Every move the boy tried to make was wrong. He thought to pull his gun, and a hand struck his wrist to bury the gun's hammer spur in the flesh of his palm. The boy looked down to see what was happening there. A fist rang against his jaw. Then Cas beat on him for half a minute out of tiredness with the world. For Cas this became a celebration owed to old sadnesses. Kay Cee maybe had to be a bastard and he'd been a real one. This poor whelp was only putting on the style.

It was over as suddenly. Cas poured a shot of whisky on the badly bleeding palm. He half pushed and half lowered the boy into a chair. Boy, hell, he was big enough and old enough to get himself a licking. With a clean bar towel Cas tied a tight bandage around the hand. The doctor, Frazier, looked on approvingly. As Cas finished the last tie he asked the boy, "You all done? I want this to be over and ended right here and now."

The boy who had been beaten was desperately trying not to cry. He looked into Cas's eyes which made no attempt to stare him down. They went on for a long way and he could see deep inside them. They were softly clouded as though with a haze. Then this man offered him a drink. The kid took it with his good hand. The man was finished hurting him, although he was not showing any friendliness. There was no smile and no offering to shake hands like pals. This wasn't like other times, after a frolic had turned fighting mean. The man before him was asking if it was over. With the drink swallowed and his other hand pressing down on the bandage hard, the boy nodded that it was.

Cas turned back to where he'd been at the bar. Denver hadn't moved or even looked around to watch the altercation. He spoke very closely. "I rather thought you to be a man of peaceable nature. Such a man would not involve himself with this kind of a thing."

"I don't," Cas said. He was talking just as quietly. "When a little earth falls funny on your face, or maybe you hear a mine timber sigh, you tell me what you think about?"

"I see what you mean," the miner said.

Kincade had been standing quietly beside a shadowed doorway. A sheriff or marshal's job was to recognize trouble before it was happening. He hadn't moved rapidly. His attention was directed toward the young man's companions. They didn't mix in. What had happened had gone by too fast for any proper brawl to start. Just like Indians, white men had their own rituals and there had not been time to get the proper words and stances started.

As a peace officer he had the responsibility for seeing that certain things were finished, so he went over to ask if the boy was all right. The boy nodded yes. Kincade could see that he was being thoughtful. The physical part of the evening was over.

Denver raised a fresh drink in toast to Cas on his one side and then to Kincade on his other. "Here's to that boy Chalk, out of the jail, and here's to whatever this drummer has got to sell."

"I'll drink to that," Kincade said. He turned to Cas. "And you aren't selling anything. You're buying in on what's just passed in this town. I saw how glad you was to dig up that man who got shot by Chalk. I could see personal happiness in your expression and atop that there was the little extra that comes from when a man has done his job."

When the judge and jury reconvened, Kay Cee lay on a trestle at the hotel's back porch. As testimony developed it became necessary to go out into the cold and look him over. He was keeping real well. Somehow his head had gotten turned to one side and then frozen there. This position made him look somewhat uncomfortable. No matter, he wouldn't have to be there long. The short day's business was accomplished inside. Cas introduced himself as a friend of the court. In privacy he told both the judge and Kincade that he worked as an agent for Allan Pinkerton, all the way from St. Louis. In the little cabin while they'd dug down, Cas had told old Denver who he was. Certain miners can keep confidences close. No one else needed to know.

In front of the jury Cas suggested that shooting people, in general, was to be deplored. For a fact, and they knew it, it was often punishable by being killed yourself. An exception to the general rule, Cas said, was outside keeping quiet in the cold. If a man has other people's blood dripping from his fingers and is wanted for several vicious crimes if that man got shot it wasn't murder at all but merely simple civic betterment. Cas admitted that a known thief and murderer could be standing in the midst of a bank robbery with no connection to it. For comparison he said, "It's as likely as a trout in milk that's had no water added."

Later in the judge's chambers—a quiet corner of the bar—Cas explained both for Kincade and the judge. "It is the policy of my employer to make absolutely sure that we don't waste time hunting men who are already dead. There's so many alive ones who must be apprehended. I've paid for the digging out of pocket and I am satisfied . . ."

The judge gestured and the court was reconvened. "Just now, back there in my chambers, you said you were satisfied with something. Please tell the court."

"I'm satisfied that Chalk there is entitled to all the dead or alive rewards that are outstanding for the apprehension of Mr. Kay Cee Smith, who has gone by so many other names that I won't bore you with them. Here is his photograph and descriptive card. All the measurements and all the features are the same and if the court was cleared of ladies I could describe the device tattooed on his arm."

The judge decided there was no need. Only weak truths had to be over proved and if they needed it too much there was a breeding ground for lies. He told Chalk that he was free and he was glad for him to have the reward. The judge added that he'd be heavier on the congratulations if there'd been less fool luck involved.

Standing, the judge motioned to the silent man called George. "We might as well get you started on your way to jail." There was no answer. "I can appoint myself a constable of my own court. It'll save the waste of sending someone else back up here and another hire of the sled and team. It's not just the money, a man's time would be involved. And speaking of time, the sooner a convicted man starts doing his, the sooner he's finished. That's true unless he ends up doing life."

Freed with exoneration, Chalk looked back. He had in part even accepted his own death. In shooting Kay Cee he had tried to do something that appeared to him quite sensible. He hadn't held back. He hadn't waited to be so sure that the time for doing anything was passed. That immigrant boy had been a witness who had seen Kay Cee riding with the robbers as they came into the town. Kay Cee had been about to silence him, and he was going to kill that silent bastard, George, so it would appear that he'd been fighting on the side of the law. That George was really something. With a couple of words he could have testified to Chalk's innocence, but at the trial and even before he'd never even spoken one of them. Chalk had made his move and it had nearly got him hung.

This man Cas had come here just to dig up a corpse. Ann, writing one little letter that found its way through, had brought him here. With all of this behind him now, Chalk felt he'd known clearly what he had been doing when he'd shot that man down in the street. Rising from his chair a free man now, Chalk walked out of the hotel lobby to see the only man he had ever killed. The people inside let him by and no one followed.

There were men who had reputations. There were men who were great gunfighters and pistol shots. They'd killed lots of others. Chalk had only killed this one. He thought for a second, then he knew he wouldn't notch his gun. Bar fights, soldiers, drunken cowboys, and even Mexicans, the big gunfighters he'd heard of killed most every kind of person. The person Chalk had killed was a real bad one, an outlaw of importance. Something special. Doubtless he'd be the only man that Chalk would ever kill. Raw amounts didn't even come to buffalo chips. This day the world was a better place to be in and he, Chalk, could sign his name to the improvement. Without even a sip or smell he felt like he'd been drinking just perfectly.

He didn't want to forget any part of this day. His heart was lifting up. The smell of rope, the thought of it, makes a man apologetic for things he hasn't even done. All of that sadness was over now, and Chalk had bounded back.

Everybody was wondering how Chalk would take seeing the

man he'd killed and what he would say, if anything. No one guessed, because as Chalk came back though the door he said, "I want him stuffed."

The room was silent. It was like no one heard. Chalk repeated, "I shot him and I want him stuffed."

Denver turned from the bar to look. "I've heard of critters being stuffed, never people."

"Well he's got no kin here, and hell, you all planned to bury him like a dog. You've done that once already." Chalk was warming up. "He was an important man to shoot. I'd like to have the memory of having done it. There wasn't one here who seemed to want the job. Or if they wanted it, they were slow to take it up."

A dense silence filled the room. Chalk had been hangdog in that jail's cell for weeks. He wasn't hangdog any longer. He was past apologizing for every little thing. It didn't mean he wasn't willing to explain. "I'm not talking about anything out of the way or strange. I just want to keep his head as lifelike as can be managed." Chalk felt he'd told that clearly.

The judge asked, "You ever see anyone with a stuffed head around his house? Closest thing is scalps, I guess. Even Indians don't keep heads."

Chalk had him there. "Well, they move around a lot and scalps is easier to tote. That's maybe why they don't keep heads."

The judge was not open to this argument. "It's not how you feel or what you want to do. The answer to your plan has to be no." The gavel came down lightly. The judge spoke in a calm and even manner. Around the room, the audience slowly heated up. They could no longer be critical of Chalk's precipitous actions. He had been acquitted and more. That didn't mean they couldn't have their feelings. One person was heard to say, "The desecration of a corpse."

The prosecution's lawyer turned on Chalk. "For all I know,

young man, what you want to do may be illegal. It might even be
in violation of your country's constitution."

"How's that?" Chalk asked.

"A cruel and unusual punishment."

Chalk looked upward a second and then he shook his head.
"That's just nonsense. After you've shot a person you can't figure
out anything to be," Chalk paused, "whatever you said it was."

Another shout from the crowd said, "Forget the whole thing,
Chalk."

"That's easy for you to say. He was not only pretty important,
he was also hard to shoot. If he'd been easy someone else would
have done it long ago. I shot him and I want to have just a little
part of him stuffed. Just his head over to the taxidermist's. You all
want to have him thrown away." Chalk was addressing the gathering. He continued. "It seems to me that for persons with no real
interest nor claim to that body, you are all in an all fired hurry to
rebury it. Why?"

A very quiet lady spoke in the ensuing silence. She had come
to be a teacher in the town's new school. Her hands were folded in
front of her. She hunched a shoulder slightly forward as she spoke.
"I can assure you, young man, that if you succeed in pursuing this
project it will give you absolutely no satisfaction."

"You ever shoot anybody, ma'am?" Chalk asked and then he
waited.

"No . . . of course not," was her eventual reply.

"Then how do you know anything about the satisfaction to be
got from doing it?" Chalk had her caught for the length of a pause,
but he couldn't go against the whole town plus Ann.

She was looking from the corners of her eyes. Softly she said,
"Chalk, if you want to keep some stuffed heads around our house
it's going to have to wait until you start in to shooting better-
looking men."

What had seemed a sensible plan was now getting firmly blocked, and to a point where he could almost get mad at Ann. Nearly this whole damned town had been quick to have him hung. In the darkest part of being in jail, so many were against him that Chalk, himself, had started to think that maybe they were right.

Now the jail was over and he was back into his life again. But Ann was not going to let him run it, even in such a little thing as taking Kay Cee's head to the taxidermist. He was about to get mad at her all over again, until he looked over to where she sat nearby, glowing as usual, and how could he ever be mad or angry at her? As usual she was right, and maybe taxidermy had only *seemed* like a good idea. Cas held up his hand to indicate that he was a part of the conversation.

"Chalk, I am not a prissy man, and what you say may make a lot of sense. There have been, as they say in law, precedents for it."

"Well, now that you mention it," the judge pointed out, "Tom Tobin cut off Espinosa's head and then his nephew's too."

Cas affirmed. "Yes, judge, but that was just being practical. It was to qualify for a reward."

"I agree, because Tom Tobin would never cut off a man's head just for side. Even after the man was dead." The judge looked at Chalk. "And anyway that was in California and near twenty years ago."

Chalk was about half won around, so Cas continued. "Cutting off a live man's head would be something different."

"You mean like that English king that kept changing wives?" Laura asked this question. Though not married herself, she had studied the subject in detail and most particularly when men's dissatisfactions with it ended up in her establishment.

"No, not him. I'm thinking," Cas said, "about when they took Micajah or Big Harpe just after the colonial days. Now those was rough times. They'd cut his spine with a musket ball and they was waiting around for him to die. After a while they got tired of waiting and got to sawing through his neck. They wanted the head off for evidence. The last thing Big Harpe ever said was, 'You are a goddamned rough butcher, but cut on and be damned.' The man wrung off his head, just like you would a hog's if you were a man that had the knowledge how. I don't. Well, they had that head in a bag and they started for home. It happened they got lost and ran out of food. They did have a little corn, and they boiled the head in the pot to stretch it."

"The head?" Chalk asked.

"No, not the head, the corn. The head was just like having a boxed lunch along. When they finished eating they nailed the skull to a tree and I'm told it's there to this day. Those man hunters then were bad, but the Harpes was worse."

While Chalk still felt he had his rights, he was well into hearing Cas's argument. He kept silent and Cas finished up by saying, "And furthermore, Chalk, cutting off Kay Cee's head would spoil him for his appointment in Chicago. I want him to be so dead that no one has to take my word for it."

"The first part of the journey will be tough. I'll have to pack him out on a led horse. But when we get to the trains he'll be iced in style like fresh live oysters all the way from Long Island Sound."

Before leaving town, Cas, knowing something of Chalk and of his abilities for managing various responsibilities, found occasion for speaking to Ann alone. He wanted to know if he should have the three thousand dollars of reward money delivered to her. He found her at home with the new baby. Chalk was already up and gone off somewhere. This was on the morning following the decision to take Kay Cee back East all in one piece. Ann asked Cas in. She reached the coffeepot over to the front of the stove. There was morning sun in the room and even the darkest old oak furniture was glowing.

Everything that had color showed it. Cas inhaled deeply the light, the shadows, and the clean kitchen smells.

Ann's beauty wasn't the first thing that came to Cas's mind. It was her liveliness. There was enough spirit here to illuminate almost any person's face. She was so busy being alive that she never paused long enough to think of how other people saw her. Too many comely girls lived from mirror to mirror, and in each of those silvered glasses there was barely enough room for themselves.

Ann pushed air with her hand. She didn't want the money. Chalk had earned it and by rights it was his. Of course some people in the town sneered on it as blood money and made talk about those who would build a life around it. It was Chalk's claim that he'd shot the man for free. The reward money had come later. If Chalk was going to loose or squander it doing any kind of crazy thing, it would have been used according to his lights and it was his. Ann told Cas that she was with Chalk as a wife and not as his mother or his nurse. If things were ever to go smash, she wasn't going to say, "It would have been better if only."

The coffee was hot and poured. Ann's words flickered in the room. She was talking about her man now, and Cas had never heard a woman talk so lively about a man without at least a hint she owned him.

In speaking her thoughts Ann said, "If things should ever all go to smash, I want it to be because the two of us let our lives get too damn miserable." She looked over at the cradle and added, "There are three of us now, in addition to the children, and I have good hopes it will never happen. Still, the money's Chalk's and there's no question. He should have it. Another thing about Chalk that's special, Mr. Cas." He nodded. "He doesn't stand off to one side looking at me so as not to see the missing arm while making himself a dream that it's not gone."

Cas's face dimmed to thoughtfulness. That was exactly what

he had been doing. If it ever came to quieter times and Cas could have a full-time woman, he'd very much want her to be like Ann.

Except for Kincade, the street outside was empty. Cas asked about Chalk, and the marshal fell into step beside him while motioning toward a sound of hammering. A barn was being raised, and Chalk was hammering and mauling right in with the best of them. It was willing work. Chalk had helped in so many places, Kincade explained, that if books were kept he owned a fair-sized portion of the town. From those who had money Chalk took pay, but for those without it who had a need of help, for them, Chalk worked for free.

Cas asked him to come down off the scaffolding. Chalk descended, interested, open, and as usual a little afraid that this occasion, or any other, might be the one to branch him away from the life happening here. Come to think, if this man was law, there wasn't anything Chalk had done to tremble his nerves about. So far as he knew, it had been proved in court. Chalk was showing very little as he walked up to Cas. He was only showing that he'd been at work and someone had come along to stop him. This was as near as Chalk ever got to being impatient. It was a fine thing to show, and in a way it was true. It just didn't happen often. It was more usual for Chalk to stop himself, long before the thing he was doing ever got done.

Chalk knew about the reward, but was shy to ask. Too many events became disappoints to him. Their ends were so different from their beginnings. So Chalk was slow to question anything or anyone, and the last thing he ever expected to see was his own luck. He couldn't stand there silent, so he started with a shy and uncommitted, "Hi there, Mr. Cas," followed by the willingness of the question, "Is there anything I can do?"

"You've already done what you can and it's appreciated. I'm

sure you know that there's a long-standing reward been posted for Kay Cee's apprehension."

Chalk only nodded.

"Money was put up by the railroad, but it is in Chicago and it will take some time to have it credited to your name in the bank here. It could be sent out solid as gold coin but that would take some extra time. If it's all right with you, the agency would prefer dealing through the bank."

As always Chalk was easy and said, "Suits me fine."

"The total amounts to three thousand dollars."

"That suits me even finer." Chalk was proud to be getting that much money. He smiled inwardly to himself and thought he would be even prouder when it actually got to the bank.

He smiled and the two men ceremoniously shook hands. Then Chalk went back up on the scaffolding to maul a beam in place.

Sufficient morning remained so that Cas could leave. His horse was saddled, and Kay Cee was wrapped in canvas and ready for his trip. He was so well froze the packhorse didn't even look around as he got tied in place.

The miner and the barkeep both came out to watch Cas leave. They waved and he waved back.

"Imagine being buried here," Denver said, "and triple as deep as the law requires. The next thing you know you're dug up and on the way to Chicago in the cars. Today even being dead pans out to be a restless thing."

"You could not be more right," the bartender agreed.

9

As Cas rode out of town he wouldn't try to think what it would be like to lie with Ann. Some people, and Chalk's woman was one, are entitled to a bigger share of privacy than others. There were lots of things she held inside, and he was sure they were mostly good ones. Courage certainly was one and dignity was another, although she let quite some of that be seen. Most people were as obvious as a hand of cards spread on the table when the game's been played.

Sunshine in winter. There wasn't a place that Ann's presence didn't lighten. No one, Cas thought, would ever think of her as just another pretty face concerned only with the capture of thoughtless admirations. Her hand was strong, she kept it hidden, and he would never bet against it.

A deep regard for Ann's modesty didn't mean he'd had to keep out of a place like Laura's. Lying with people there was how that game was named. There was a long ride in front of him because he couldn't take the stagecoach. Stagecoach passengers always complained if there were corpses waybilled through. Cas would have to ride one horse and lead another until he got to the trains. On the trains nobody cared who or what was riding in the baggage car, so long as the freight agent knew to keep plenty of ice laid on.

That place of Laura's hadn't been half bad. Cas looked back at the led horse. He hoped that all he was taking out of town was Kay Cee tied to it. Whorehouse hours might not be the best way to spend your time, though they could sometimes be like booze and get the night quieted for sleep. Also, but not always, they made up memories that gave a man something to grin about on a long and lonely ride. The horses were walking nicely and it was soft dead grass underfoot and damn that Chalk for how much luck one man could have. If Chalk could find that girl Ann, well, with so much natural luckiness what sort of chance had there been for old Kay Cee standing in that street?

There were just so many pines to see and a sprinkling of other trees. After a while if you'd seen one you'd seen them all. An occasional animal might move between them here and there, just as you were riding by, but it was not so often as to fill the thoughts of a man's entire day. Maybe, Cas thought, he shouldn't dream. To travel and to be on good terms with old Kay Cee, he'd have to plan their trip carefully. However, riding easy and with the led horse easy too, in his mind Cas walked back through the door he had entered yesterday.

Way back there in Chalk and Ann's town in the midst of all the laid-out muddy building lots, there were a few houses scattered up along one of the streets that branched from this turnpike road he was still riding now.

He had not expected to find a palace whorehouse in a town that size. On the other hand it had not been a crib. It was a large, clapboard building painted white. The snow around it had evened up the ground. The town was too new for lawns, and he remembered the madam had met him at the door. He'd seen her before when court was held in the lobby of the hotel. There she had been far more plainly dressed. Other men were just visiting around the parlor room and one girl could almost play the piano in the corner.

Her coworkers sat or stood around. His memory was so clear that it could be happening all over again, right now as he rode.

Cas seated himself and, yes, he'd have a drink. He didn't stretch out long, and he didn't stand around nervous. He just sat as he would in any drawing room. The parlor wasn't very big but there was space enough if some couple wished to dance. This place was neat and clean inside. It was usual for whorehouse furnishings to crowd up a room. Either this establishment was very new, or there was one madam who was not the furniture salesman's fool. The girls weren't pushy and that was a pleasant change. It gave a man some time to think about what he wanted to do. Cas sipped his drink again. It was a quiet, dignified house. Men and girls moved in and out of the room, and while the girls remained the same the men changed slowly as the evening turned. Of course there was one always present. He was kind of dude-ish with the usual look of a man who likes nice clothes better than he likes to work. The madam spoke to him often. She also found time to visit with Cas. She wasn't being forward, and after all they'd practically met over at the court. She asked if there was anything she could do and there was no leer to the way she talked. Cas thought if he was here it should be for something else than sitting. He could have been doing that in the hotel lobby or the bar. There was a girl standing in a doorway. Something likeable, something very likeable, hovered about her. As Cas noticed, Laura shook her head.

"You wouldn't use a cutting horse to off-wheel a stage. This is a well-thought-through place, and just because you might at first take a fancy to a girl, well that doesn't mean she's right for you." Cas was just a little curious as to what was "right for him." Before he could think up a mannerly way to ask, Laura continued. "I wouldn't tell John W. Mackay what goldmine stock he ought to buy, but if he were ever to tell me, I'd listen close. Now, there's things I know a bit more about than most and you'd do well to hear some friendly advice." Laura shook her finger slightly at him. Cas had started to rise from his seat. "Please don't," she said. "I'll just sit here in this chair nearby."

Like Frazier, Cas was well bred enough not to waste a whore's time in talk. There were some, men mostly pretty citified, who thought it was some kind of a favor for them to talk to a whore for free. They should know that as time and the evening flowed, the girl got no work done. This was the reason Cas was shy. He said, "Talk's no help for a working girl."

Laura knew that too, but she appreciated being told. "I'm glad to hear a man mention that, but I'm not one of the regular girls, so talk is not an imposition on me."

"A what?" Cas asked.

"Conversation doesn't use up my working time."

If it was all right, Cas was just as glad to talk. He could guess what a girl would be like. He found no excitement in exploring the body boredom of another human being.

"I once knew your employer," Laura said. "During the war when he was Major Allan."

"It was nice of you to keep the meals going over to the jail when Chalk was being held," was the reply to that.

To explain, Laura said, "Well, he is Ann's husband." At the mention of Ann, Laura saw a kind of smile on Cas's face that was rare in a parlor house. Usually there was only loud laughter and loads of noise and bustle. That was most days but there were exceptions. Sometimes there was a man like Cas, whom any girl could take a good deal of pleasure in. There was also the money coming in, but Laura wasn't thinking about money now. She was thinking how at least once or twice a year, fresh off the range or from the lumber camps some wonderful kid on his way to being an excellent man came to this house and fell wholeheartedly in love with her, a grown woman he saw as a girl. This man Cas was not a kid. Still, Laura twinged with envy for that smile at the corner of his mouth.

"Hey there, if you've come here to moon over some other girl, well, I guess we're paid to help men do that too. If that's the help they want. But," and Laura was serious now, "you aren't thinking about Ann."

Cas shook his head. "No, of course not. She's married with a baby. Why the concern?"

"Oh, I guess because she stayed here with us the first year in town. She wasn't a pet. She worked her way along and not on her back. She wasn't going to grow up to be a whore. A girl who has lost her arm like that has suffered more than's needed. A lot of people'll look down on a girl that's hurt. You take and cut some pieces from a man and people see him as a hero from the war or somebody who's been injured working big out there in the world. It doesn't matter that the bastard was drunk on a train and fell between the cars. Girls are counted differently. Well, there wasn't many men to marry her. After that war they're still in short supply. Hell they'd spent four years killing each other off, and the god-damned women kept cheering them on. When I think of just one corner of any battlefield and all the young men crumpled dead . . ."

In thought she paused, holding the back of her hand to her lips. "Well, I don't think there'd be one of them—if he could be here and loved—wouldn't have traded all that foolishness and glory for a life with a woman who loved him, even if she had only one arm. Then Chalk came along and she married him. Every man with any sense in this town is half in love with her, and having that much sense they aren't even holding a smidge of jealousy at Chalk. Would you believe that?"

Cas knew what Laura was talking about. Blond corn silk hair, blue eyes, and a pretty face don't come to much unless some live-liness gets put in behind it. Cas guessed in part and could also see that Ann's liveliness glowed in many different ways. She'd survived the loss of an arm and the wagon journey that brought her here. Survived was hardly the word, because she'd brought three children and the baby to safety. Alive was what Ann's presence said, and she brought out whatever bits of liveliness those around her had.

"What I just asked you was, would you believe that?"

Cas's attention returned to the room. "Oh, I most certainly would."

"Now that's over, how do you like our town?" This was a new idea to Cas and he didn't really answer quickly. "Oh, I see what you're thinking. Me calling this town 'our.' If you don't think the whores have a seat in this game, then you just don't know a thing. When Julia Bulette was strangled, they closed down Virginia City for the whole day. Closed down everything, mills, mines, the whole works. Almost a year later they caught the man that did it. They closed the whole town down all over again merely to see him hanged. She was part of that town, and I am a part of this one. Barkeepers, farmers, everybody, they are all planning how this town is going to live. Leave it up to just a marshal and a preacher and that is not enough. You've been in a lot of towns. Now you tell me, how many was decent?"

Before Cas could answer, a commotion started at the front door. Several men had entered, somewhat drunk and talking loud. They were hunters of some kind or maybe trapline men. Well, this was the shinybackman's job and not a customer's responsibility. Cas hoped he'd had lots of rest because the quieting job at hand was looming bigger all the time. In fairness the man was up and already started across the room. However Laura got to the foyer first.

Laura wasn't shouting, but she could talk clearly and at the same time very loud. "Buffalo runners are doubtful enough to be with even after they have been double scrubbed. If you men think that you are coming into my place fresh—and I use the word advisedly—off the staked plains from a season of buffalo running, well let's all of us forget it. I'm not just talking about the contamination to the real estate. You're not here for rocking chair practice. You want to be introduced to the ladies who work here. Well, that is impossible without you being scrubbed and maybe even sheep dipped, because this place, my place, is run like a top-line outfit. I never ask one of my girls for anything I'm not up to myself. And let's face it now, unwashed buffalo runners or whatever in the hell you've been doing is a certain something I can't even bring myself to touch."

The men were silent. One of them, not for argument but to set the record straight, said, "We were only trapping beavers, lady." He was already edging toward the door.

"Same thing goes, and I never want to be so expert as to be able to sort beaver trappers from the men who hunt the buffalo."

"We just wanted to be nice," one of the men complained.

"Son, you cannot be nice to girls and smell like that." A big man and no more drunk than the rest pushed himself forward from the group.

"What the hell you talking about, being nice to girls. That's not what I'm spending my money for—"

"Well then you just hold on with the loudness, mister, because you've brought your money to the wrong place. Being whores is hard enough on these girls, and there's enough decent men that's lonely so I can at least afford to pass all the mean ones up."

"Let's rip it up." Growls and a few shouts came from this knot of men. Laura kept her eye on the big man in front of her. The gentleman friend was standing slightly to one side. Cas hadn't gotten up. He hoped like hell this wouldn't become a useless craziness. Laura still didn't shout, but her words bounced back into the room.

"There's no need to threaten me," she said. "Just figure for yourself your chances if you were to wreck the only decent whorehouse for a hundred miles around."

The front door was opened and there was a draft as the beaver trappers filed out. The piano had been silent as the player watched. As Laura went back into the room she asked the girl to give out a snappy tune. She'd walked right past her own man standing there. The girl at the piano started up her best try at liveliness. Laura walked to where Cas still sat. "Now I'm flustered," she said, "and you might join me for drinks up in my room."

Cas didn't look around to question anyone. He was smooth onto his feet and just a step behind her. Laura did know how to walk up stairs when being followed by a man, Cas thought, dignified and promising with no whorehouse wriggle, like a jackrabbit with one of its hind legs tangled in between its ears.

In her room Laura didn't leave the door discreetly open. She poured herself a real bourbon drink and handed one to Cas. "I only had time to tell those beaver trappers just a little bit. There's more to come out so you just, please, sit right down there and listen." Cas sat.

"Those bastards come in all sizes and shapes. Some are off the range from nursing cows. They'll be in town less than a week or until their money runs out, whichever happens sooner. Best chance they'll never come back even to look, let alone to settle. You know something? You most probably do. Even when they come into this place they come in not like some family man just gotten home from a long day's work. No, not like that at all. At first they come in here on a high lonesome, maybe months of cattle trailing at their backs with nothing but heifers for excitement and that turns out to be almost more than they can handle. The only thing I'm saying is, that party's soon over. Then those crazies are in a frenzy looking for a mother for their children. A wild-looking woman all spangles and net stockings, she's just talk around the campfire. Plain farm girls with freckles take all the money here. If it wasn't for a few of the older men who know exactly what they're doing, the all-in-fun girls who work for me would doubtless all just slowly starve to death."

Laura was walking back and forth as she talked and sipped. She generously refreshed her drink and then took up a small cigar. As she went to light it at the chimney of a lamp, she remembered to ask Cas if he would mind. He wouldn't. Without anything else to think about, he was noticing that Laura wasn't using corsets to hold herself together. She had the cigar lit now and she turned around.

"But those men tonight," she hadn't stopped thinking, "they do stick in my mind. I've heard the most raunchy buffalo runners, in my own saloon bar, filled up to the eyes with indignation. You guess what they were bitching about?"

Cas shook his head not knowing.

"They were complaining about the morality of Sioux Indian maidens. Well that pricked up my ears, because I'd wonder how they'd have anything harsh to say about the morality of rutting hogs that had gotten strayed, let alone people who have their own decency. Well, it came out at last. They'd been funning themselves some place up north and they were shocked to the very core of their sensitivity when they discovered those Indian maidens had anted up a wad of clear buffalo fat just before the bets were on, so as not to have their godforsaken seed growing in their bellies. I for one— and it's not often I speak with total knowingness, so listen when I say—there's damn little excitement, joy, or even down-home humanness to be had from bedding buffalo runners. Those Indian maidens weren't into it except they needed presents of the sort to keep them and their babies living through that very mean winter on the plains. La-de-da, those buffalo runners were complaining that those girls were somehow low-down and dirty not to want to take their spawn. The bastards should have kept their goddamned mouths shut, because it's a privilege for them even to touch another human being. Christ knows, if all men were like them I'd have it in my mind to do something different, if ever I could figure just what it might be."

"Girl," Cas said, "you do go on."

Laura knew that herself, but she knew when to stop. Cas was

long past useless excitement, and he never swung an axe in places where there were no trees. On the other hand he responded well when there was clear reason.

It seemed to him that Laura had been just about long enough smoking away on that cigar, so he asked, "Are you warming up to burn off your lips?"

She looked at the short butt and, snuffing it, said, "I didn't notice how rank it was getting. I'm sorry, but I guess my mind was probably somewhere else, and a girl shouldn't smell like the men's washroom on a Pullman car."

"No need to apologize. My mind was also somewhere else, and I very much hope it was in the same place as yours."

It had been.

Cas lit a cigar of his own. Good lamps in a room could color everything so warm, and Laura was a smiling kind of woman afterward.

"Laura, Laura, Laura." Cas looked toward her. "Is there any last name to it?"

"Why?"

"No reason."

"Well, if there's no reason then it is just Laura or Laura's when I talk abut my own establishment." There was no archness as she changed the conversation. "I hear you're taking our first resurrected citizen back to Chicago in the cars. Why?" She smiled as she asked, but Cas didn't want to talk about other things so soon. He stroked her forehead.

"Laura." Her name just hung in the air beside them.

"Now, don't you be too overly romantic. My name is certainly Laura. I'm not waiting for some fresh-faced Scand-a-hoovian boy needing my assistance to improve one hundred and sixty acres of the prairie that's out in the Dakotas where the winters blow to make you forget why you are alive. Here I can get out the old cribbage board. We don't play for money, so I don't have to watch my gambler friend's hands too close. It may not be the best time in the world, but after those tough wartime years it sure is a comfortable one. That counts for more than most people think. The girls do what hard work there is and, well just for remembrance, I sometimes take on one of the pleasanter jobs myself."

Cas smiled. "Just for the remembrance of what?" Modesty forbade Laura from answering directly. Cas thought how afterward some girls looked rumpled like a slept-in suit of clothes. Laura looked fine. Lovemaking had not used up all her energy.

"Just to remember. That's all. The trouble with getting old is that your memory gets weak. It needs reminding more and more." Laura's face was smiling now, and Cas wanted to know what else she was thinking of.

"Athletics," Laura said. "Athletics are fine, but there's nothing so rare about them. However, when they are there with friendliness, well then that's something a girl doesn't so often see. It is such a time-saver when a man can do this and be friendly too."

She looked at Cas, who could stand around without a need to strut when his clothes were off. "You are," she said, "the kind of a son of a bitch a girl'd want for a pet. Believe me, though, the pets girls get, damn it, just aren't in any way like you."

"I guess it will soon be time for you to watch the store."

"Duty's call? I guess, but not 'til now." Laura had gotten out of bed. Both of them were getting dressed.

Cas asked, "How much money's owed?"

Laura shook her head and Cas said further, "Oh, come on now. I haven't had that dream since I was maybe fifteen. In this real world, 'Kiss me, don't pay me' simply does not happen."

Laura laughed on top of a smile. "No, Cas, it's something else. If you hadn't come here I'd have had to wait 'til Chalk was almost hung. Then I'd have saved his life, but doing it would have been a serious embarrassment for me."

"How?"

Laura described the tattoo on the inside of Kay Cee's arm. She also said, "I'd been with that man for too long a time. It wasn't something that I'd want people to know. I couldn't want to tell it, but I would have had to. You saved me from that. I've done lots of things that was salty, but living with that bastard was the only dirty thing I have ever done against myself."

"I wouldn't know anything about that, Laura, and I wouldn't want to guess."

They were now both fully clothed. Laura was at her mirror with face powder and then lip rouge in her hands. From long practice she made her lips perfect. It seemed there was no need for her to look.

"Cas?" He turned to her. There's not much for a man to do after making love. "You are right not to know some things. There is a sort of rottenness that Kay Cee had, just knowing of it might spoil a decent person out of manhood's wholesomeness. But even what you know, I'd appreciate you'd never tell."

"I never do," Cas said.

"I mean about me and Kay Cee."

"About anything, Laura."

"Like I said, Cas. I have done salty things in my life, time and time again. Only once did I have something to be ashamed of, and it was being with that man. You just look here."

Laura walked across the room. From a hidden place beneath cushions she brought a small japanned lacquer box. She opened it to show newspaper clippings from just when the war was over and a few others that were from during. Kay Cee had been in many places, and in later years he had been suspected of being in many others. Cas read the clippings through. Many of them he already knew.

"You weren't seeing him now?" Cas asked.

Laura looked quickly across at him. Laura indicated the bour-

bon bottle. Cas poured them both a drink. She raised her glass for
a toast. "Well, thank you, Cas, and as I said before, knowing too
much about certain things can spoil a person for being a man, and
can for that matter do the same for a woman. So thanks, Cas, and
bottoms-up again. As Chalk would say, Powder River and let her
buck!"

Cas raised his glass. There was one final thing that Laura asked,
"This may sound mean," she said, "but just do me a little favor
when you get to the depot in Chicago. Buy a cup of very hot coffee,
black with lots of sugar, and then throw it in that crummy bastard's
face."

Cas looked back at the packhorse following. Even here in a shadowed pass there wasn't snow enough to block their way. The trees
to ridges went on forever. They were undisturbed and grew here
solidly. The sun shone down through branches near the place where
stars would start the night. A dead man was a small thing to be
toting through this wilderness. Cas's reins were held in his mit-
tened left hand. His right was warm in the pocket of his Mackinaw.
Cas's feet were warm too, and this was a comfortable day to ride.
There was fog from the horses' breath, and inside that long canvas
covering Kay Cee was doubtless comfortable as any dead man could
expect to be. For the train trip things would need to be a lot more
formal. Kay Cee'd have a nice pine box for his arrival in Chicago.
In the depot, he'd be unable to lift the screwed-down casket lid,
so he couldn't throw that cup of hot coffee. Cas practiced the
particular wrist flip that would be needed to accomplish it. Not
knowing all the circumstances, and even if he could get the casket
open, people in the station would be indignant and upset. Well,
it had been a harmless promise to make to a girl, and thinking it
would be keeping it enough.

10

I n the town and all around it, winter came down hard and snow grew deeper everywhere. The miners who were going to, came into town. Those who stayed in their cabins readied themselves for hibernation. The town's miners gathered in the hotel bar, as there wasn't any other place for them to socialize. Chalk became more and more exposed to talk about placer riches and fabulous hard rock discoveries. At first the strange words of this miner talk flew around his head. But through repetitious telling, he finally picked up on the vocabulary.

There was a way to make mercury that had "sickened" well. Mostly the sickness came from contamination with oil or grease, and then the mercury's ability to gather gold was gone. Sickened mercury had to be washed. Lye, weak nitric and acid, or sodium cyanide were listed as the cleansers of choice.

"Booming" was the same as "hushing" and both practices were resorted to if a miner's water supply was low. A dam needed to be built some distance upstream and an automatic gate, driven by the river's flow, released the dammed-up water in a series of sudden surges. When there was no water at all, a Mexican dry washer was used. The gold catchers, or riffles, in a long tom or sluice were pole, block, cross, or Hungarian. Each had its defenders. There were systems of common gold recovery, and there were ways to track down the mother lode. That was the El Dorado, the miner's dream, and it must exist, because didn't all this gold have to start from somewhere?

They told of the Blue Bucket Stream where innocents from a wagon train had stopped to fill a watering pail with yellow shining pebbles. The man who told the story let each word drop as though it were itself a nugget. With those weeks of miner talk, Chalk was barroom-expert enough to join in with the laughter at those poor, stupid immigrants.

In the bar, Denver greeted the men he knew, drank slowly, and seldom if ever took part in these conversations in what had become a miner's social center. There was a hard rock mine in the hills above the town. A Mr. Compton had brought it in, and it got worked all through the winter. Ore wagons freighted out the gold-laden quartz until the roads snowed over. Even then they could work underground and pile ore to be hauled out in the spring. Compton worked himself like the hammers of hell, and his men worked just as hard. When the men from the Compton mine got into town they supplied Chalk with fragments of a hard rock education.

Time passed and the winter was talked away in a thousand conversations. Virginia City, Angel's Camp, the mother lode country; gold was everywhere. Chalk did not catch on that the reality was somehow different from the telling. These miners were so quick to tell where and how great globs of gold could be found. Their eyes sparkled when they talked about fantastic fortunes and great discoveries. In the meantime they'd stand up at the bar and carefully nurse one drink for hours. They weren't poor. They were merely resting in between explorations.

Chalk found one bonanza. If you bought one of these old hard rockers a beer, the stories and the information would come pouring out like the gold locked in their wilder dreams. Chalk was very careful to heed warnings often given against mistaking fool's gold for the real thing. There were a variety of tales about misguided men who'd carried pyrites across deserts and through frozen mountain passes. Lives were risked and some were lost. The journey's end was at last achieved after endless suffering. Then it was discovered. The treasure had no value. All the miners showed one restraint. They never told long tales of their own empty searches.

At home the children's education was enhanced. The bar talk found its way into Chalk's house and it livened conversation there. Ann listened carefully while he told each new thing he'd learned. Specific gravity, for one thing, helped the children with their arithmetic. Chalk was able to explain that fool's gold only weighed a quarter as much as the real, even when the volume was the same. He even made up special problems for the children to do. "How many miner's inches would be needed to sluice ten yards of gravel fully when the sluice sloped one inch to the foot?"

The town's school was well established now and the new teacher had gotten settled in. She was the only one for all the different classes. Ann knew that getting the children across the country was fine, but her work hadn't ended there. She couldn't let them grow up in ignorance. Before the schoolmarm came, they'd schooled at home as best they could. The real school helped, yet Ann still kept at the kids. Now, Chalk was on them too, and his crazy excitement kept them eager. Jim and Maggie would solve mining problems even before Chalk could find time to make them up.

Long toms, rockers boxes, and the cradles. The mining talk went on and on until finally Chalk was ripe to be the owner of a claim. In time Chalk realized that the claim he bought was not the sort of claim that a person should buy. To begin with, there were still unclaimed stretches of stream that held about the same amount of gold. But the act of buying was important to Chalk, and in fairness the location's gentle beauty would have tugged at any person's heart.

The prospector who sold out to Chalk was not a total cheat. There was gold along that section of the creek, equal in value to what Chalk had paid, but getting it out would be the problem. The return of Chalk's capital would take an entire summer's digging.

Just before the claim changed hands, Ann suggested someone other than a seller should be spoken to. Wasn't there an old miner, name of Denver, always around the town? Chalk didn't want to trouble this man with asking. This time it wasn't only Chalk's shyness. He was making his very own kind of hopeful decision, and he didn't want to be warned away from it. He knew this himself. The talk he wanted was the talk he'd bought with beers and it had him all aglow. Even empires were possible. Sometimes in the bar they discussed how a man might freight in a stamping mill once the bedrock was reached. Often the conversation so exited Chalk that an untasted beer would flatten in his hand.

Denver knew what Chalk had bought. It was a little bit of decent gravel. With a rocker box, that summer he and Ann would doubtless recover about what she could make washing miner's shirts. As an addition, of course, they would have the children to help with the digging.

When summer finally came, the miners drifted one by one back into the hills. Some walked, leading patient burros, while other more substantial seekers rode a horse with a second led.

Spring was almost gone before Chalk had his outfit ready. On this one occasion he wasn't holding back, except so far as to be sensible. In the high mountains it would be foolish to arrive for work before the snow was gone.

As it had been so many times before, Laura's offer to look after "Babe" was gratefully accepted. Jim, Maggy, and Bill's sister was

now four years old. At that lively age she was unsuited for camp
life in the midst of a wilderness. As usual Ann made Laura promise
not to spoil Babe, knowing full well that she would. At the same
time the young lady looked eagerly toward the fond and loving
care that was in store for her. Her parents had died before they'd
found a proper name for her, so her sister and brothers had called
her Babe, and the name stuck. Jim and the other children had
decided that they would wait and let Babe find her own formal
name from some event or sign, as though she were an Indian.

Ann looked at the loaded wagon. In fairness she had to admit
to Chalk that he'd forgotten nothing they might need to get gold
from a creek. Their wagon groaned with extra boards, shovels, and
tools enough, you'd think, to build an entire house. They even had
a cast-iron cooking stove along. Most people wouldn't think to take
a stove out to the woods. Ann knew to do it. There was an oven
for baking bread. Although the crossing had been three years ago,
she still had had enough of campfires. She'd never enjoyed trying
to cook seriously over an open fire. Meat on sticks, maybe, but
forget bread. Always ended up mixed with ashes and burned black
outside with the inside still an unrisen paste of dough. In Ann's
mind a decent stove was one of the places where civilization got
its start.

They had a fly sheet tied to the wagon. That was a room where
the two girls slept. Jim bunked in the wagon, while Ann and Chalk
had the luxury of an old army wall tent that was nine by twelve.
It was nearly as roomy as a home. Another fly sheltered the stove.
Ropes were led through pulleys attached to nearby trees so that the
camp's food could be raised away from the reach of nighttime animals.

The stream trailed out from a short rock pool. They camped
on the bank. There the sod sloped from underneath the trees. It
was graze so good a horse could hardly want to wander. The cow

was there with them too. Neither Ann nor the children wanted Cow to be left behind. Besides, they'd have milk and butter fresh all summer long. On arrival Chalk had made stools and benches and also a proper table where each of them had a place. He said that they weren't going to live down on the ground like Indians.

This was not the lost Blue Bucket Stream. They could hardly have hoped for that. The gold was here all right. There were colors in every pan. Chalk had been told to concentrate on back eddies and the ends of pools. There gold could be seen without squinting. Chalk was not entirely green. He knew even bright colors in a pan could be worth less than a couple of cents. In cold water all day, twenty pounds of gravel to a pan; at the rate the gold would come to maybe fifty cents or with much luck a dollar and a half a day. In the good places they bettered colors, but anything you might call a nugget was few and far between.

There came a little bit of a flash between Chalk and Ann when he said that maybe they should move on to another place, either up the stream or down. The kids were all at the table right in the middle of dinnertime. Enough sun remained so they could sit without being chilled. Ann listened. She didn't say anything for a while. It was a bean-pot-and-bread dinner because Chalk and Jim had been panning for three straight days. No hunting had been done. Ann put down the serving spoon.

"I say we stay and rocker out or long tom what we can. There's not one of us here a prospector. What we are is mine owners. I believe we'd better mine what we've got."

Chalk had started to look somewhat sullen. "Damn it, Ann." The children at the table winced. "How many times have I told you that this isn't a mine. How many times have I told you that this is a secondary auriferous placer."

"Chalk." Ann picked up the serving spoon, but there were no more beans to ladle out, so she set it down again. "Then we are secondary auriferous placer owners and what gravel we've got we'd better get washed if we are really owners. You bought this place, but now we all own it."

"We all?" Chalk looked at the children seated around him. Each one looked back at him just as clearly.

"We all," Ann repeated, and she reached over and gently rocked the cradle board that hung from a tree beside her. Chalk took another piece of bread and spread butter across it. There were few mining camps that knew to live this good. Tomorrow he'd get the rocker boxes built. Then they'd see what they could find for themselves.

Ann was glad they'd gotten it over this quickly. If Chalk was going to be hateful about the mine or placer or whatever it was, well then he'd be hateful. Of course he'd have to do it alone. Ann wasn't washing gravel, clothes, or dishes or cooking anything in the middle of a pinch-faced meanness.

Coming across with the children in the wagon, freezing had been hateful. Sand had been hateful. It had been harsh to be burned at by the sun. As often as not they were half starved, but they hadn't ever been hateful to each other about any of that. Maybe it was because in those tight times they couldn't afford to be.

Some of Ann's old memories were tough ones, but she made the most of them. When looking back, Ann didn't dwell on her own personal sadnesses, though often she thought about how others had been roughly handled.

Those two hats as fragile headstones for the children's dead parents, whom she had in part replaced, fluttered in her memory. She often thought to find a way back along the wagon's trail to where the cholera-killed couple were buried. It would be nice to have a real carved granite stone for them, but what was more important was that, whenever she thought about those two hats facing east, she wanted to do something helpful for some person who was right here now and alive.

Chalk said nothing else. What fight there was had ended. Now they'd get on to digging gold and to the pleasures of living comfortably in the wilderness.

Much of the reward money remained, as Ann was ever careful to head off any extravagance, but she was glad that they had bought more blankets than most people could believe. One nice thing about money was you could own blankets beyond all sensible need. Not scratchy old army blankets or little nothingness cotton-sheety ones. These were Hudson's Bay four pointers. When she got into their bed at night, Ann never failed to favor herself by touching a corner of the soft wool to her cheek. It lay over her like a warming cloud, and she could remember clutching thin cotton coverings those snowfallen days before they found their way into the village of the Sioux.

Snow remained in the mountains that soared above the camp. On some of the highest it was there all summer. Ann tried to imagine broiling deserts where people and their animals might die of thirst while here was a place always covered by snow. Right from the camp, whenever it pleased her, she could look up and see it.

In these mountains when the snow melted, it melted from the valleys upward. Then there came the grass and in some places flowers in a blanket that looked as if the snow was back, if snow ever came in a million colors. The ground was bouncy underfoot, and for drinking water there was a little stream right by the camp. It flowed over rocks that were softly covered with moss. As thickly as that water fell it hardly made a sound. The water in the big stream was fine enough to drink, but the small one was a chore saver. It came right by. They'd set the camp well back from the big stream's bank just in case high water ever came from a sudden storm.

They started the rocker box in a place that panned out about the same as any other. Chalk had built the rocker in town with the carefully drawn directions Denver had given him. It was made so as to be quickly assembled beside the stream. It proved tight against leaks and this would save them wastage. With gold this thin there was the need to get the very last bit. Chalk washed his gravel carefully, shoveling through the day as lively as a Chinaman.

To help with the recovery Chalk had a flask of mercury that some called quicksilver. This heavy liquid metal had to be carefully contained because it acted as if it wanted to go everywhere at once. Chalk filled the final riffles with it, and this strange liquid acted almost like a magnet that gathered up every last particle of the gold they sought. At day's end the mercury was gathered to be distilled. This was done in a little iron pot with a boltdown top. This retort, or still, was heated over a special campfire, because while Ann said "our" to the claim, the wagon, and almost everything else, the stove was "my." It could not be touched or even approached by who-knew-what kind of a poison chemical that mercury might be. Far from "her" stove, the separated mercury was carefully saved to be reused.

It was already dark when the first day's concentrate was scraped from the pot. Inside the tent by the coal oil lamp they carefully weighed their find. The gold just slightly favored one-half ounce. All they had was wages. Chalk was hopeful that maybe the riffles weren't properly set, however, that was not the problem. Almost every evening ended in a series of one-half-ounce days.

It went on like that, as treasure poor, yet as a living, adequate. On occasion they'd hit a fifty-dollar pocket. Here, that was so rich they took it for bonanza. Ann wouldn't look at the slow days harshly. Most men who worked weren't under trees and beside a stream. When you hungered here, you could depend on more fat trout then ever you could eat. There was squirrel meat in plenty and venison was everywhere. As weeks passed, it looked like nature was an easy place.

One late afternoon, Ann had supper cooking and rising bread was in the oven. With work done, the rest were off someplace, both Chalk and all the kids. Maybe they were downstream fishing at the

long pool, or in search of wherever Cow had gotten to. She was
belled and never seemed to get too far. Or did they have the pans
out trying distant prospects in the hope of getting up above the
usual one-half ounce a day?

Head ropes snapped and mules were gone. No noise, not even
squeak nor squeal. When they had discontent they would most
usually grumble. They'd paw to tell you that the grass around was
chewed and they wanted to be moved. Now, as Ann looked up,
silent hoofs were galloping across the turf.

Whatever in the hell was that about? she asked herself. Then
from the far side of camp, opposite from where the mules had gone,
movement started. A bird or a squirrel winks its eye. If you are
looking in the right place and your eye is sharp enough you can
spot that slight movement in the full thickness of the forest. What
Ann saw was as though the hillside moved a little and then stopped.
On the edge of her awareness it was so huge as to be nearly invisible.
It was a noiseless wagonload of fur, with more bulk than a
mule. As it cleared the forest's edge, Ann could see that it was a
bear. She reached into the wagon, to get the Zouave rifle out. The
baby had been safe asleep, in his cradle board. But safe from what?
Out of the trees this animal came. Ann didn't want it to see her or
the child. Where were the others now? And if they were here what
could they do?

Jim hadn't been anywhere. After a day of shoveling he'd rested
without talk just enough away so if Ann wanted some slight camp
help he could pretend he didn't know about it. Jim didn't do this
often and was never so far away that he'd fail to be right there
should Ann be in real need. He'd seen the bear moving too. He
walked quietly to be with Ann.

A snake can be dangerous. It can kill you, but see it first and
you can whomp it with a hoe. Here was this bear revealed. With
a finger to his lips Jim took the Zouave from Ann. He motioned
for her to draw the Navy Colt holstered at his hip. The cartridge

box and the big powder flask hung within the wagon. He could reach them from here. There was no use for the cartridge box. He'd not have time to reload the rifle. One shot might kill the bear but that didn't look as if it could be true. The bear stood up and up and up and up on its hind feet to look around. He sniffed. Both Ann and Jim could see his nose at work. His attention was drawn to the nearby stove.

A two-armed person could snatched up the cradle board and keep the revolver too. Ann did get one strap of the cradle board over her shoulder askew. It hung down on her left side. Still asleep, the baby didn't make a sound. The bear walked closer without seeming to notice the people standing there. Jim had taken a single slow step forward. He poured the contents of the powder flask in a semicircle in front of them. Soundlessly he then placed the emptied flask on the ground.

In complete silence, talking with his eyes, he acted out the plan. He wanted Ann, as he fired the rifle, to ignite the powder train with a pistol shot. Then she was to hand the revolver to him. He motioned with his fingers furtively. At the very last she was to run for the trees behind the camp. He would stay here and make his fight. Ann watched the bear intently. It approached. Once more it stood until its height could not be believed. If they had a cannon, maybe. Otherwise this animal was too huge to kill. Ann was glad Chalk and the two younger children were off somewhere else. Then again, this wasn't hopeless. The bear could miss them just as if it were a lightning bolt.

Jim was looking at the various places on the standing bear. Maybe he should try to shoot it now with all its underparts exposed. As it walked toward them it seemed so huge as an oncoming train. You could wreck a locomotive with a sledgehammer if you hit it enough times, sure. If you had enough licks you could pound on vital parts until it never ran again. But stand out on the track with just one swing. As that train came down on you, you'd better think of something else. One other thing was bad. Bears don't run on tracks. It was nearer and nearer the stove. They could hear his breathing. The bear would probably have been frightened away if there had been a fire. Most animals have a fear of fire, because it is something they don't know about. But because Ann wanted a stove, the fire was inside and invisible. The bear moved forward once more. The oven's baking bread smelled so good that the bear sniffed just a little bit too close and touched his nose to the stove.

Faster than any eye, a blurred paw crashed against the offending stove, only to be burned itself. Lids, ashes, and coals were everywhere. The powder train went up. It went with a red flashing, roaring *whoomph* that vomited a cloud of coarse gray smoke. The nose-choking fumes engulfed the bear. This was a fight he didn't understand. Right here, inside one second, was all the energy and all the strength of five hundred barroom brawls, drunken battles, and stompings. As the bear made his moves they were just about as sensible. The way it moved and thought was wonderful, because it moved on by. The bear took his bulk and his injuries away. Ann hoped he would know to soak his nose and paw in a distant snowbank or a running stream. The trees he'd casually broken in his flight were thicker than a strong man's neck. What a mess that bear had made in a few flurried seconds. Ann and Jim looked at each other. The baby had slept as an avalanche of animal passed.

That poor stove. Like a small wrecked steamboat, boilers blown and stranded on a bar. Ann's compassion thought a stove should never be hurt so bad as that. Slightly later, while they were picking up spilled things, Ann saw that the bear had tipped their wagon over as he'd gone rushing by.

Jim could not stop his head from shaking back and forth. The fury was unbelievable. Just on its own and passing, what a wreckage that bear had made. He turned to Ann and said, "I hope to hell this isn't going to happen all the time. Maybe that's what," he pointed at the disaster surrounding them, "Chalk hinted when he said the man who sold it gave out vague warnings about this place."

She'd kept the question from her lips, but very soon Ann would have Chalk's answer. It was a clever bastard who had sold this mine. And damn it, if she liked she would call it just that. He'd told Chalk that there was something here to be wary of and whatever it was had been given as the reason for his willingness to sell. And dear Chalk was so busy pretending not to be afraid of anything that he'd never thought to ask about how much recoverable gold there was.

On Chalk's return he became both angry and indignant.

"How did our wagon get turned over?" he asked even before he said, "And look at the condition of our stove."

With a total disregard for Chalk's mood, which was getting close to petulance, Ann asked, "Didn't the man who sold you this . . . this claim, give you a vague warning about something?"

"He warned me fair enough."

Chalk was not going to be specific, so Ann said, "I don't rightly know what kind of a warning's fair, but probably without one you would have never bought the claim."

This got them back into a discussion of the condition of the camp and the reason for the wagon lying on its side. Chalk started to tell Ann, and for that matter Jim too, about the vital places where a bear might be shot so as to be in an instant killed.

"You could have gotten him," Chalk said. "The place to aim is—"

"Chalk, you goddamned weren't standing here," Jim said. "You even may be right. I maybe could have killed him, but that's too thick a clump of 'maybes' growing out here in the woods. As the thing's been ended, I'm glad I didn't try to move in any different way."

As Chalk started to go on, Ann interrupted. "If you had been here you could have told that bear that you were the man who'd shot down Kay Cee Smith. If he was a smart bear, just knowing your reputation he'd have stayed away. Chalk, I've made few calls on you, and this one is for always: Don't tell me how to shoot mountain bears after they've gone away." Ann burst into tears and added, "And one of them has just wrecked my very own cast iron stove."

Chalk knew to stop. He took Ann in his arms to quiet her. The next thing he did was put the parts of the stove together. He got it fixed, or sort of piled back up. He held it together with a cement of small stones and clay, which baked with the stove's own heat until, in time, it was near to being so solid as a brick.

When those mules were found they pulled at a tackle to haul the wagon right side up. Bill and Maggie kept wanting to hear about the bear, every five minutes and over and over again. They found the place in the soft ground where the bear had taken off across the little stream. For a memento they wished somehow they had a way to keep a print of that paw. The best Bill could do was mark it out on a wide piece of plank. They always wanted to re-member just how big that bear had been, even if they hadn't been right here in camp to see him. There wasn't much fancy woodwork to be done in a mining camp, yet they had the bow saw along. Bill cut the board to the outline of the foot. The imprint of the claws wasn't absolutely clear. In an attempt to exaggerate their length Bill cut them close to exactly right.

With the stove wrecked they started supper all over again, Indian style, around a campfire. They built the fire big as night settled in, and its glow lit the trees surrounding them. Where the small stream ran, the firelight danced back from its rivulets. Repairs and order had been made, and the powder flask was refilled from their magazine. Chalk kept two kegs double wrapped in rubber cloth. They were cached at a distance from the camp. Pine boughs were piled inside the wagon. They made a sweet-smelling bed, and when dry they could be burned as flares.

Chalk drew the loads from his twelve-gauge English double

gun. He recharged each barrel with a load of buck and ball, just as fearsome as they'd loaded those old-time muskets from before the war. He'd bought the shotgun as heavy as he could find. It wasn't a pleasure to carry, but charged like this it was at least as much a weapon as if he'd had one of those crazy two-shot Lindsay muskets in his hands. They also strung ropes with flutters of white rags tied to them. Cow, who had been missing since the encounter with the bear, came back that night just before full dark. They heard her bell in the distance over all the nature noises, and soon they had fresh milk with stick-roasted fish. The younger children made quite a thing of cooking on an open fire like they were Indians.

When all the children were asleep, the fire was banked down to embers and heavy logs were put in place to burn through the night. From this last chore Chalk walked with Ann around the camp. All seemed quiet as they made their way into the tent. Before coming to the pallet, Ann carefully tied the tent flap shut. She turned the lamp down very low, and for a moment Chalk thought about tying a small piece of string so as to keep away an animal who'd knocked over a loaded wagon with a slap as he'd passed by.

The blankets were warm where Chalk had already been. She never stopped from wonder over how nice they were. As she drew them up she said, "I want to ask you something."

"Sure," Chalk said, and turned to kiss her. She pulled away.

"I'm not asking that," she said. "I want some talking now."

"Does it gotta to be now?" Chalk always thought of talking as an afterward. He slid over one hand to hold Ann's head from behind her neck.

Snuggling, she could feel each one of the shovel-handle calluses. "If not now, it's never. Mornings, we are just waking up. Days we're working and nights we're loving. So there's no time right. You'll just have to tell me and tell me now."

He wanted to kiss her on the eyes. She closed them and shook her head.

"He didn't say anything about bears?" Ann asked.

"No."

"Or other critters?"

"Who was meant to have been talking about critters?"

"The man who sold you this . . . auriferous placer. When the bear was gone, Jim said that something had been told."

"Now, Ann." Chalk gently rubbed her neck just below her gathered hair. That was a thing to make his woman purr, but Ann wouldn't be misled or confused away.

"You tell me now what's come with this mine," she said, reaching back with her own hand to his. She'd not brush him away. She'd just hold up on his playfulness until they'd talked some sense.

He didn't correct her. "There's fearful times, I guess, Ann. And fearful things and men. It's not a worry though. All the man said was that there were maybe people here. Yet all the time he had the claim they never bothered him."

"Are you saying people and really meaning Indians?"

Chalk held his free hand up to indicate a pause. He was thinking about how he could say it. "The man didn't think that. There was only tracks he saw. They was of horses, and those were cleanly shod."

Chalk brought their faces together now. It was time for real kissing. Just before saying, "But you let me worry, dear," he pulled her close with his other hand going to where her back muscles turned inward at her waist. From the low lamp there was enough light so they could see each other's smiles. Just then a noise outside the tent was more horrible than fear.

"My good God, what was that?" Ann asked. As it repeated she knew without Chalk telling her. A Washoe canary was making its presence known.

"A burro, dear," Chalk said, "has caught the scent of his misfortuned relatives."

"His whats?"

"Our mules."

Chalk's pants were pulled back on and the Navy was pushed down inside his belt. It was a damn cold barrel against his bed-warmed flesh. Though he could do without a shirt, he needed his hat scrunched on even before he turned the lantern up. The damn tent tie was better at keeping him in than keeping grizzlies out. Or maybe it wasn't, because he finally pulled the knot. A lamp was only a target, so he turned it down again before stepping outside.

How that burro did go on. Along the creek he could see a flicker through the trees. A man wouldn't mean harm who'd carry a lantern in the night. The mules must have heard a shade of meaning that required replies, and Chalk turned his lantern up. Even before he could see who approached he held it high so as to guide them. Coming from the trail beside the river, he could see a burro being led and a mounted man who followed. "Hey, Chalk!" a voice called out.

Before him, with his burro was the old miner, Denver. Frazier still sat his horse. The miner raised his hat quite gallantly. Chalk turned to look back toward the tent.

"Hello there, Ann," Frazier said. Ann had dressed quickly. She stood in skirt, blouse, and cloak. Her forefinger was trigger curled, her thumb behind the hammer spur. The Zouave was pointed for the stars, the butt tucked into her hip.

From the description of this placer, overheard in the bar, Denver had closely figured its location. He had been feeling crowded in the town, so when Frazier asked if he'd ever made any prime locations of trout-type fish, the miner said that Chalk and Ann's prospect was nigh to fish like miners dreamed of pocket gold.

"We came to see the baby," Frazier said. "I mean, a doctor's job is to follow up and see if nature's running right." Frazier knew that when it didn't there was little any doctor could do. That had always been the hardest thing to tell.

"He's fine," Ann said, "and growing like the trees among them." She'd put the rifle back inside the tent.

"Besides," Frazier continued, "I've heard that this is a stream I want to fish before you miners make a mess of it." He dismounted. Denver was putting a hobble on his burro. The packsaddle and gear were already off.

"The more mess in the stream," Denver said, "the more gold's gotten out. Just this one cradle here," he'd seen its small shadow as they found the camp, "won't change the ways of God and nature in any real ways you'd notice. The doc's . . . I mean Frazier here, is right to get in early. In California there are places torn up so they'll never be the same."

Having spent the entire day and into the night getting up here from the town, the travelers were trail tired. They'd eaten further back. Now they had a place to spread their blanket rolls, and Frazier's horse was hobbled too, grazing with contentment. Only then Frazier said, "If a person had a cup and some water maybe too, I think we could have a drink." Chalk hung up his lantern and got to rummaging.

Sociability was fine, Ann thought. He loved her enough she knew, but damn he could show at least a smidgen of regret for what they'd put aside. Of course he'd come back to that, and real visitors weren't a daily thing.

"Would you take a drink, Ann?" Frazier asked.

Chalk was aghast. He looked at her as though the thought could not have happened. Ann hoped that this would not be an evening so deep as to wash away tomorrow, and she planned to make sure that was not going to happen. Ann added water to a small whisky until it suited her taste. Frazier toasted to "fat trout and gold-filled riffles." The cups all rose up.

Chalk took only the smallest sip from his. "Ann," he said, "I didn't know you drank."

"I don't," she said, tasting the whisky carefully. "I tried it once. I opened my mouth like I was a nestling baby bird. I poured it in like the momma bird was bringing my worms home to me. Well, the world became a funny place and my lost arm grew back again. I forgot all my troubles. Everything was nearly perfect until the next morning came." Ann was suddenly unsmiling.

"A person with real troubles had best not forget them. It's too damned much to lose the same arm twice. A one-armed woman by herself had a lot to think about. So, since then, I've never drunk so much as to forget exactly where I'm at."

"Good sense." Frazier raised his cup. "You'll not turn me to temperance, Ann, but I've never heard it better said."

Though Chalk seemed slightly sad to have a party over, inside the tent his spirits were quick to recover.

Hobbled animals moved quietly nearby, and smoking in their blanket rolls the two travelers wished each other good night. "Damn, damn, damn, damn," was all that Frazier said, though he said it pleasantly.

Sunshine in winter. There was never a place Ann's presence didn't lighten. He never saw her as just some pretty face only concerned with how brightly she was painted.

Ann's earth was never beaten down. Turf, sod, soil, and even the dust of wagon roads bounced right back in all those places where she walked.

Denver knocked his pipe against a tree. "I am sometimes regretful too," he said, "but not so much as once."

The first morning of visitors could start a little late. Frazier had brought fresh eggs safely nestled in his flour canister. There was a new slab of that good lean bacon where every bit cooks out to meat.

The last biscuit was eaten and the second cups of coffee steamed. Chalk looked around his camp. It was nice to have hospitality. "Denver?"

"Eh?"

"Frazier's up here to catch some fish, but you have always been a miner."

"You might say that."

"Come up here to . . ." Chalk was eager now.

"Well I don't fish, except when I'm hungered, and then only when there's no animals about. Maybe I was just getting crowded sitting around the town."

"But," Chalk looked from the hobbled burro to the heavy load carefully placed beside the miner's headboard tree, "you've brought all your traps along."

"Well of course. If I hadn't, I'd be like Frazier," the miner pointed down toward the stream where the doctor was working a fly carefully in the smooth water where it slacked behind a boulder "without his fishing rods. I wouldn't have an excuse for going any-where."

11

The rock overhang was huge, and within it six bed rolls were scattered like discarded paper flowers among the shards of fallen stone that lay in patches on sterile, age-old earth. A sparse fire glowing between two rocks was almost covered by an enameled coffeepot. One small fleck of blue showed through its smoke-blackened sides. There would be coffee soon. It was morning and three of the men were awake. They were partly dressed in gray fragments of military uniform. One man struggled into his shirt while staring down at the started fire. He went to button it across his chest and the material tore. He scratched himself thoughtfully and the shirt that had nearly rotted on his body gave way beneath his fingernails. He harrowed the feeble material back and forth, and then, in a fit of anger he tore off the remaining shreds and threw them on the ground.

"Texas, if my shirt had been that rotten," another man named Candy observed, "I think I'd scratch myself, and then I'd put it on."

"Never you mind that," the now-shirtless Texas answered him. "Look down at your own damn boots, opened up like the mouths of dogs with your own toes hanging out as tongues."

A third man, somewhat older than the rest who was nicknamed Chick on account of a partial Chickasaw Indian heritage, voiced his own discontent. "I just wish we had some soap, if only just to shave ourselves where there is the need for that."

"Well, grow a beard," Texas said, "and save your mouth to wish for some decent grub. This sure is a piss-poor way to live." He poked idly at the fire with a stick. "Not only the way, but the place isn't much to my liking either. If you promise not to drink all the coffee I'll go down and turn the horses out on graze."

Down beside the lake there was a corral made of poles and piled stones. It held a dozen horses. A small trickling stream flowed into the lake, and there must have been strong hidden springs because more water left the lake than entered. The meadow here was grown to heavy grass and flowers, now that summer had at last risen into these hills. A fourth man, Dade, was waking now. He sat right up in his nest of blankets and stretched. While looking from the smoke-blackened recesses of the overhang down to the blue lake water and then to the horses grazing, he said, "I'm giving my parole and I'll take the allegiance pledge. This rotten-assed camp don't grow no better just by being stayed in."

He got out of his bed to walk toward the fire. A canvas bag was in his hand. He made a place for a big skillet next to the blackened coffeepot. From the bag he took boiled potatoes and a small slab of bacon that was mostly fat. He cut strips of bacon into the pan with a bowie knife. He cut thoughtfully and every slice was so even it might have come from some sort of a machine. When he started to slice the potatoes, Candy, standing in his broken boots said, "Wouldn't you water-wash your hands before cutting up our food?"

"You want to do it?" Dade asked. The potato and the knife were offered.

Candy shook his head and turned away. Still crouched over the fire, Dade went back to slicing. If it had been better bacon it would have cooked with an appetizing smell. However, it did serve to fry potatoes, and even its rancid smell reminded the men of meat.

"I'm cooking. Texas, after tearing off his clothes, is looking to the horses. Two of our men are either asleep or dead. Tell me now, Chick, why don't you go out and kill some kind of critter that we can eat? Indians is meant to be able to catch all kinds of animals."

"Whitey's the hunter," was Chick's reply. "I'll get him on up. Hey, Whitey, Whitey. It's morning. Time to rustle grub. Let's get up and out and maybe shoot us a nice deer or two. I can almost see their tracks down by the lake from here."

It was Whitey's turn to stand and stretch. He'd slept fully dressed with his gun belt on, and he had only to reach nearby to find his cavalry hat. "Take a pot and you go down by the lake. Gather up those tracks and bring 'em here. Set 'em on the fire and rise 'em to a boiling heat. Then we can all have a nice filling meal of deer track stew."

He thoughtfully walked toward the fire as though he had just so many steps to use. "I do hate to kill a critter. With a dead critter you've got meat in the pot but tracks are no longer getting made. One critter will make millions of tracks, enough for all the starving peoples of the world to eat their fill of track stew. The trouble is that how to cook tracks is something few men have the knowledge of."

Each man had his own cup and a pan or some sort of mess kit. Two of them had been tinkered up from old tin cans, and one of the dishes was the bull's-eye half of an unsoldered army canteen. The cook was sampling fried potatoes with the point of his bowie knife until it seemed that the sample was exceeding his fair share. He stood aside and everyone served themselves. A smoking greasy residue remained for George, who was also called Wilkenson, and he'd doubtless had many other names as well. He was limping slowly down toward the fire, using his Winchester for a cane.

George nursed at his food for several seconds and then tipped his plate out on the ground. "I do believe that our bacon's gotten too rotten for a decent man to eat." He poured some coffee, and there was still a little sugar left. He broke off a hunk and dropped it in. He watched the bubbles rise as it dissolved and he used his little finger to rescue several dead and drowning ants. "Really, somebody should look after our supplies better. This coffee is bitter enough already, without the addition of ants."

Then, finally ready to eat, Whitey was disappointed to find all the cooked food gone. He pulled a cold potato from the canvas bag. Salting it carefully he said, "Potatoes salted ain't so bad cold." When he'd risen from his blankets it seemed that a warm steam or mist had risen with him, or maybe it had been a cloud of dust. Even though it was outdoors and the weather in these heights was cool, there was maneuvering around the fire because, rough as they were, even these men couldn't care for the full force of each other's unwashed nearness.

Whitey finished his cold potato. He wiped his hands on his shirt and Texas observed that this wasn't a very clean thing to do.

"If you had a shirt to wipe your hands on, maybe you wouldn't be so quick to warn people off from doing it on theirs. Besides it's not like we had grease to put on 'taters. It's wiping grease on clothes what gets them dirty."

It was obvious to all that they had fallen into a way of life that was far from pleasant. What was worse is that they had stayed in it, one way or the other, for the full six years since the war had come to an end.

As Texas thought about it he could see most of their time was spent waiting for people who never came. Or, when they did come, they came with long talked-up reasons for bringing nothing. No money, no food, no weapons, and no recruits. Then last year there'd been that one man who had come to join, Kay Cee Smith, a Yankee and a mean one at that. Kay Cee had talked the brothers and that youngster, Sonny, into going on a long reconnoiter. Somehow that

trip got turned into an attempted robbery. Well, Kay Cee couldn't
be blamed now because he was dead and so were most who'd gone
with him, Sonny and two of the Wilkenson brothers. The last of
the Wilkensons, whom the judge had christened George at his trial,
was the only one to make it back alive. Chalk had been exonerated,
but George had not been so lucky. There'd been a jail delivery soon
after the judge had handed him down twenty years. From the battle
outside the bank, George had been so shot up that nobody thought
he'd run. He had though, when his boys from here had brought
along some help. He'd run and ridden without a wince or whine.
He was here on the mountain now, but sickly. Had the guts to live
with so many bullets in him as to nearly rattle when he walked.
Shot so bad, it was hard for his body to get well. He wheezed with
every other breath, and sometimes his cough made you hurt all
over just listening to its rack.

For these men the war had never ended. Perhaps it never would.
They'd fought their war in Tennessee, and while U.S. Grant was
fine toward General Robert E. Lee, the Federals didn't feel the same
toward the rebel ridge-runners there. When they commenced taking people out of the hollows to hang them, the only way to run
was west. Kirby Smith gave in at the end of May in 'Sixty-five, and
these men had been pretty much on their own ever since. Mexico
was first until that Indian Juarez decided the time had come to
shoot the Frenchman emperor. Then they'd gotten back to the
States and up north to Canada. There they found the beginnings
of a fresh new war. It was only of the smallest sort and soon over.
Indians and breeds, claiming to be a real government, took it into
their heads to hang a white man. That was when the time came to
head south again. Now, they were down below that border waiting
to know what to do.

As they winced away from the beginning day, the men around
the fire heard an accustomed noise. A saber scabbard was banging
over rocks. Whitey had gone to strap on his sword. It was a damned

useless weapon, but having one was what made them all soldiers
still. Whitey's sword was his original from South Carolina and the
one he'd started with. Through travel, raids, and ambuscades all
the others were pick-ups. There were Massachusetts swords and
even one real fine one from France, gotten from some Maximilianist
whom a Mexican had killed.

"Now, that is too many people," Whitey said.

"What's too many people?" Chick asked. He was through cooking for now and had started to worry how he'd get his kit to the
lake and washed. The men just sat. There was a cloud of feasting
flies around every unwashed plate. Short clay pipes were burning.
It was a satisfaction after food and helped to keep the bugs away.

"He means down to the placer where we've been watching."
Candy spoke looking up from his toes, to realize he'd nearly forgotten the wreckage of his boots, and knocked his pipe embers out
against their nakedness.

"I maybe better watch them closer," Texas said, "because they
might have an extra shirt that a man could have. Damn, I do need
a shirt." He pulled at a shred of rag that had stayed caught beneath
his belt.

Whitey wanted the conversation back. His pipe was going well
so he didn't have to putter. He just blew smoke comfortably and
had his sword to fuss with. He held it across his knees. For a reminder he drew the blade slightly to read "Columbia, S.C." at its
base. Without looking up from the markings he said, "Well, there's
just five that you might count as guns. If a one-armed woman can
shoot, that is. There's also two younger children and a cradled
babe."

Texas had also made an earlier reconnoiter, but he hadn't told
anyone about it. It had to do mostly with the pain of his woman
hunger and how long it had been on him. Like most of his plans
it had failed. He was disappointed but didn't feel in any way badly
about the thing he'd tried to do.

"Well, damn." Candy was back from viewing his toes. "You say they have a one-armed woman in that camp?"

"And the two new men that rode in last week. Or maybe it was the week before. It isn't easy to know when things happened if a person doesn't have a calendar. They made up the five. A burro prospector and another, looks like a dude but rides a decent horse. I spotted them at sundown riding toward the camp. I just guessed they were going there because there's no other place around here to go." In recent days Whitey had scouted the most.

George flopped back on a rock. No longer needed for a cane, his Winchester was held between his knees. "So, there's a whole damned family there with little kids and all." While George most days was feeling too poorly to ride, he had enough health to form strong opinions. "Those people, I mean families with kids, they have no business out here. That's just what I am suggesting."

"Oh, they've got lots of business," Whitey said. "They go on panning and washing gravel like they was some kind of a machine."

"By now then, no doubt they've got something that's worth getting from them," Candy said. "Whatever else people are in danger of nowadays, they don't look to be hit by cavalry."

"Candy, we are just that," Whitey said, his hand still at his saber's hilt, "and we aren't here to sluice-rob some family of snipers summering on a sparse gravel bar. Virginia City's been Union from the start. If we go robbing we'll go robbing there."

George's cough interrupted. When he finally finished he spoke and his voice was scratchy. "A one-armed woman you say. There's not many of them, so that would be the wife of the man who shot down Kay Cee Smith. I half believe he should get killed himself."

Whitey asked, "I don't know how much that man Smith meant to us for us to take the trouble to revenge his death. I mean, he joined us late and wasn't with us in the war. Come to think on it he never said which side he fought for, or if he even fought at all."

"That still doesn't mean we have to let the man who killed

him live," Wilkenson suggested. "And, Texas, are you sure about that woman having but one arm? I recollect you told about it quite a little time ago."

Texas was sure. He nodded his head. He'd made his reconnoiters at night almost two weeks ago. His shirt hadn't been torn then, and he'd not worn a clanking saber. He'd walked all that way down the mountain and around. A horse might at any time whinny his presence away. He'd only thought that maybe there was a girl or woman down there. There was naught to be done at the lake so he'd just planned the night to spy her out. There'd been no reason for telling this to the others.

It was just after the time of the bear, when the stove got wrecked. This was the other bad time for Ann. Someone had grabbed her in the dark and made a fright that needed getting over. It was a one minute fear and she couldn't let that ruin the whole summer for the family. Since that night she had an underbreak seven-shot little Smith and Wesson concealed in her clothes. It was a puny excuse for a gun, yet if you put all its bullets in a man's head, he'd be dead pretty fast.

She'd been away from camp and in the dark. Their latrine was a ways off from the camp. Barefoot you could feel your way along the path. A lantern wasn't needed.

One arm grabbed Ann across the stomach. Its hand grasped her right wrist. Another hand reached across her mouth to force back her head. The hand knew to hold a person's face so as not to be bitten. Ann tried to wrestle the weight behind her away. She struggled until she was so tired the two hands held her motionless. Then she was lifted off her feet and thrown down on the thick rubble of the forest's floor. Their bodies fell with hardly a sound. A weight was over her now and a whispered voice said, "You cry out and I'll burn you down just like you was Lawrence, Kansas."

Ann didn't know exactly what that could mean, but there was anger in it. She'd never heard anyone speak about rape but she guessed if someone was raped properly it was better done without the man starting a conversation. Rape was something no one ever talked about. Ann was in a fighting rage, and it was so like her, in desperate circumstances, to be more angry than afraid. Hearing him talk she did at least know that he wasn't an Indian. She was flung over now and the hand covering her mouth slid behind her neck. The breath of this man in the darkness smelled like a can of sun-killed worms. She couldn't kick, or hit and she was damned if she'd bite. She spat toward the smell of the face. The hand behind her neck disappeared. It would hit or stab or ward away an expected blow. There was a flurry of movement. The hand was searching to grab where her missing arm should be.

The expected blow from the girl was now, it seemed, a long time in coming. Maybe it wasn't in her mind to put up a fight. A little loving might even be the thing was wanted. Then why did she pull away like hell with the arm he held? Finally in reaching he felt the rounded shoulder where an arm had been. What in the hell was that? It was a damn sorry broken thing. He let go of it fast. He was a little angry now, but he wouldn't hit her yet. Still in a whisper, Texas asked, "Why didn't you just say that you wasn't all there?" His shoulders shrugged. He was sitting up now. "What in the hell sort of man could ever want you?" he asked.

Ann couldn't see him in the dark, and she'd make no report in the morning. The man was gone and she hoped this was a person from some place very far away. There was nothing to be done and news of the event would only serve to spoil the quiet of this pleasant world that had grown around this streamside claim. There was only one other thought she had. From now on she'd carry her own little gun. Released and silent she jumped to her feet. Long strides brought her back to camp. It had almost been too sudden for fear. She hadn't thought of anything to say into that bastard's face.

But, now she considered with regret, as they'd struggled she should have tried to piss on him.

Of course Texas was sure. He stated very carefully, "Oh, I seen her all right. She's ugly-looking and in some ways coarse."

This statement puzzled Wilkenson, who had been called George at his trial alongside Chalk. That one-armed woman had been sitting there. He hadn't talked but he had noticed. Texas was either a liar or going blind. Wilkenson wondered about all those people down in the town. The marshal, Kincade, had shot one of his brothers dead. That was the job he was paid to do. That marshal certainly wasn't the dude who'd rode into the placer camp. He wondered. "Texas," he asked, "as poorly as you saw the girl, what was the dude like that came in with the miner?"

"Dude?" Texas had seen Frazier from a hidden vantage point. "Don't know if he's a dude. He's a little thick around the body, yet he's not got enough fat so as to be pudgy. Yet he is not range hard or lean. When he rides he looks around, but he isn't watchful. His head keeps turning but his eyes stay mostly in one place. And he didn't seem to have a gun, at least where you could see it."

Wilkenson was relieved to know that this addition to Chalk's camp wasn't Marshal Kincade. Nor was he Cas. It wouldn't be Cas. This group here had always taken precautions. They'd been careful to stay away from robbing either Wells Fargo or the trains.

It was a rough camp underneath the rock overhang above the lake. They had some luck with hunting and there was venison most times. Once they'd even had a fair-sized black bear to eat. They had little money between them, so about every two weeks one man or a couple would dress like everyday civilians. Then they'd ride out to bring back supplies obtained through either purchase or theft. When they robbed, it was far distant from the mountain and they never left witnesses. Bodies they'd hide or mutilate to make a person finding them believe the outrage done by Indians.

Enough time was over so no Federal troops would fight against them, even though they still wore shreds of Confederate uniforms. Yet these riders had needed to avoid the troops. To be real rebel soldiers they would have to fight any blue coats that they found.

They always dreamed and planned toward the assay offices and stamping mills of Virginia City. They regretted deeply the loss of Wilkenson's brothers. With them along they would have had enough additional punch to go most anywheres, but damn it, they, Sonny, and that Kay Cee Smith had all been wasted against a rotten small-town bank.

They also waited for that man from Canada. He'd promised to come back with riders and with money. Sure he had promised, but they never heard from him again.

It was middle August when they decided to ride out to almost anywhere. They patched what was left of their uniforms and sewed up their saddlery as best they could. Leaving, they were ragged, yet they had the look of soldiers. They wished they'd had some plunder for their led horses to carry, but all they packed was rotting blanket rolls. If Mexico was over and Canada wasn't ever going to start, they'd have to find their way back to living in the States.

By that same middle of August, Chalk and the family had been washing gold for six straight weeks. In boxes hidden in the tent they had nearly seven hundred dollars in dust and nuggets. They continued to eat well, and there would be no mean winter started for another month. The cost of the claim would be out by then and certainly they'd made improvement. Ann sometimes kept on about getting their money back. She also asked Denver about proving out the claim. If they did that the land right here could be theirs forever, just like if it had been bought and owned. They would of course have to come back each year for a time to work the claim around. It wouldn't be a hardship. Ann would look forward to it. It wasn't her plan to have them wash away their lives for wages. This was a fresh new clean place to be. On the other hand, town had their friends and what little happened in the world was going to be happening there. There wasn't any hurry. They had time enough to find out how they would plan to live.

Coming across the country in the wagon, and before when the war was on, it seemed being alive at each day's end was the outside limit of ambition. You prayed for it and hoped for it without much expectation. Now the world was easing up a little. Hopefully there was always something more to plan or do. Ann wondered if they would enlarge the house in town. Enlarge seemed so much more luxurious than merely making bigger. Or would they go and live some other place? They'd set out in the wagon. She could see them leaving now. They would go where there was ocean and wide rivers, with cities growing up along their banks. The houses would be built of brick and stone and there would be railroad trains running off to everywhere. Or maybe they'd go east to see what the peopled part of the country was like. They had near to fifteen hundred dollars in the bank and their gold would be a thousand more. At least Chalk had it, and he always shared. For now, something had cured him of laziness. Ann could see that on this placer. As each day started, Chalk moved into it handily.

During his visit Denver poked around. It wasn't long before he'd told Chalk this place was just what they'd all suspected. It would trade eating money for hard work, but don't count on it to raise a man to riches. In the stream bed he showed them a variety of important prospector's tricks. One was to crevice clean down to the bottom of every crack as it got exposed after the overlay was cleared. When Chalk was told carefully about something he'd listen, and in particular when Denver talked. It didn't make him surly now to have the dream part of the placer told away. What was coming out was coming out by passing gravel through a box. The

whole family just kept on at that. Chalk even gave up on his meanness toward the man who'd sold him the claim. They could have
found just as likely a place either up or down the stream and staked
it for themselves.

For the man selling the claim to tell them that would have
passed beyond expected human honesty, but at least they hadn't
bought a mine where one of the nuggets ever so faintly read, IN
GOD WE TRUST.

12

Frazier first sensed a presence from the camp. A vague sensation of movement was disguised by the dappled sunlight that filtered through the trees. These were mounted men in a line riding toward the creek. Seen closer their saved horses weren't sleek with sweat, and no sun was reflected from their hides. It seemed to him that the men were vaguely uniformed, and looking more closely now, Frazier saw that they were. And then there was that now strange sound from so long ago. He heard a saber's scabbard clank. These riders were colored nearly like forest branches and the trunks of trees. They still wore gray, and mixed with that was the color of faded butternut. Frazier watched them from the camp. There were either six or seven on the stream's far bank, and they were headed to where all the others were busy washing gravel. As these men emerged into patches of full sunlight Frazier saw how they were riding as if on patrol. It didn't seem that they could have missed the white canvas of the wagon and the square bulk of the tent. But they were going past camp toward the placer just like they knew it was there. They were close enough now that Frazier could see how constantly they looked around. They were the sort of men who kept glancing back to try and see all the unremembered places where they had been.

Frazier had been lazying in camp with the woodland and the water slowly turning by him. Never in his memory had he felt so much surrounding quietness. He had reached another side of laughter, and lying soft on the springiness of forest floor he'd pushed every strain of living from him as though he were a baby playing in its bath.

Then he'd seen the movement just slightly different than the sun down through the leaves. As the riders passed, these disheveled men appeared so harsh when seen against how clean their horses were. Should he arm himself and run to be of help at the placer? Frazier smiled. You don't attempt violence against the men he'd seen riding by. Sparks flying as a thick cordage in the sky above a hundred burning barns. Whole towns to the fire. The horror of destruction coming back. How carefully these men rode, and the fineness of each horse as it put shod hoofs against the ground.

Frazier closed the book he'd had open beside him. He then removed his coat. He didn't want to die because these men might think a weapon was hidden by his clothes. In his shirtsleeves Frazier walked down along the stream.

The riders—and now there were clearly six of them—had halted on the stream bank overlooking the workings. The earth sloped gently here and it would only take seconds if they decided to ride down. Two men dismounted just where the slope started, and two others walked their horses carefully to the water. Gear was carelessly spread around the placer. In the water and with all that mud and sand washing by, a man wouldn't want to bring either his good clothes or his gun. Inside its old flapped cavalry holster, Chalk's Navy was up on the bank. George slid off his horse to stand by it.

Chalk felt naked. There were six strange men above him, and his pistol belt lay on the ground. It would have been easier if somebody could bring themselves to say hello. Ann put her dipper carefully down. She then walked over to pick up the baby in its cradle board. Nothing had really happened and the baby was still asleep. As well as that was, Chalk thought, he didn't like that these silent men wore swords as though there was still a war. And what in the goddamned hell were they doing messing around in his gear? Their horses were rein-trained to stand. One of the men looked familiar. It was George who had Chalk's own Navy Colt out of its holster and in hand. There was a small scrap of board that had been cut, lying on the ground. George picked it up and threw it to where the smooth pool slid across its tail to become the start of rapids. As the board dashed down the water the pistol bucked in the man's hand. Chalk could see the board dodge and dance, each bullet kicking it sideways in the water. The man didn't click after shot five. He smiled, lifting his lips away from his teeth.

"That was heavy charged. So much so as to kick mean. Makes it hard to come back on. There's no need. Light load for shooting men. Quantrill knew to do that, and there's heaps of powder can be saved."

The shooter carelessly threw Chalk's gun back to where he'd picked it up. Chalk saw these wise bastards could be meaner than was ever needed. And that goddamned smile. Chalk knew who had picked up his gun. There was but one straight-toothed smile such as that. How long had he watched it in the courtroom and the jail. And what in the hell can you say to a man like George when he rides in with five others at his back?

There was more to jail, Chalk thought, than a judge saying that you had to go there. In addition the jail had to know how to keep a person in it, and obviously the one George had gone to didn't.

With lips drawn tight, Chalk's own neighbors had gotten thoughts of hanging him. Then that man Cas had come into the town. Cas had showed them what Kay Cee Smith had been, and

Cas wouldn't have left his pistol safe and dry up on the bank where he could not get to it. The man he'd bought this claim from had hinted everything wasn't right in the woods around it. Now what wasn't right was right here in front of him. Cas wouldn't only have known to keep his six-gun handy, he'd have scouted around and he would have found them first. Nor would he have left so clear a track to tell others where he lived. That all didn't matter because he wasn't Cas—Chalk would have to find his own way out from here.

Frazier walked over. He came with his hands showing. Obviously he had no weapon anywhere.

"I heard some shooting, Chalk," he said.

Whitney's hat was even on his head. He dismounted slowly, carefully watching the people at the rocker box. Lightly his rein dropped to the ground. Corn-husk ends of hair wisped out from underneath his hat. He spoke to Chalk.

"Mister, you have let a lot of people and many things set right around where I make my home."

Chalk was never fast to think up any sort of answer, and long before he could, Wilkenson had his say. "We was looking along the trail of two horses. One had tracks mixed in with little drops of blood, and it's just possible for it to have been packing a fresh-killed deer. Therefore, I hope we are here in good time for dinner." George drew his Winchester from its saddle scabbard. He used the rifle as a combination crutch and cane, carefully keeping the butt end down. This wasn't the most comfortable way to move, but George didn't feature getting a rifle barrel jammed with dirt.

"Jesus damn." Texas spat and then spoke as he looked around. "You all must like money more than mortal men to work for it so hard." He'd just glanced over a half summer's trailings of gravel moved and washed.

This was a sort of waiting Frazier knew. Most fearful things were vague and night-hidden and never gave a true hint of where and what they really were. Here there had been two—a bear and now these people.

Their hint wasn't hidden in any way. There was no shading to it. They said death and they meant it. These were the sort of men who could of a sudden become animals. For some it came from living woodsy too long. For others it was just natural from childhood, but most of it had been born from the war. He was glad to be a quiet presence that hopefully wouldn't start them. The man who seemed to be the leader though he was young, gave way to a frightful fit of coughing. Frazier professionally expected to see, at any moment, great glouts of blood come pouring out. Now he recognized him. It was the silent, unspeaking George who had been sent away to jail for twenty years. Obviously this was a world that didn't always work the way judges told it to. One thing to be said for hanging, hanged men didn't keep turning up afterward. That cough was very nearly like a hanging. Most men and a lot of horses couldn't have been shot so bad as that and lived. Frazier knew enough of body damages and agonies. Wanting to live, no matter how hard it's done can't get a person over them. He was hearing lungs hurt past fixing themselves. It was just a matter of time. Some people are able to keep walking for a little while after most men would be dead. Everybody waited. The coughing stopped. There was not even the particular smile now. His face had been reddened up. Now it washed white from inside pain. That cough would have hurt any mother's heart to hear, but there was no help for it.

Wilkenson looked at the diggings by the stream. These people had work clothes on, rough from wear and mud. Their faces and the faces of the kids weren't dust-covered and gray. They'd not been under the rim rock of the cave, nor had they come from the soot-blackened slush of a city he remembered from the past. This was a clean and healthy place. Even the old fellow, the miner, looked new-washed enough to live forever. He was that same old

miner who had been at the trial to testify, and for wages he'd gone
to dig up Kay Cee Smith up out from that frozen ground. As the
men had rode through they'd glanced at the camp and come by
thinking it was empty. But the doctor fellow had been there, and
he'd come down to join the rest. The camp had been spied out
many times before, and usually during the day everyone was down
at the workings.

Men hiding out by themselves did not manage camp life as
well as this. At the cave they had naught else to do, yet house-
keeping was let go to hell and they lived there like animals. That
made here a little harder to figure out. Of course there was a woman
to keep it a homier place. There was no mistaking what Wilkenson
thought as he looked at Ann.

He took his eyes from her to see the man who'd just walked
up. Imagine, a white linen shirt out here and dress pants like a
gambler's. He'd come up and all the men had turned, but there
was no danger there. What could he do against the six of them?
In fact he was another from the town. The dude, a sort of maybe
doctor fellow who'd been at the trial too.

"Well, I'd guess we haven't been asked to dinner yet." Just
after coughing Wilkenson's voice was very quiet, yet he could be
heard over the sound of the running stream. "So maybe we'll be
taking the dinner along with us. I saw a deer hanging under cloth
back there."

Chalk had to say something, even though he could see Frazier
shake his head by moving just his eyes. Chalk would not have
anybody talk for him. "What are you taking our deer for?" he asked.

"Because he's already dead," Whitey answered. "And he's something special. The deer I shoot are like everybody else's. They need
gutting out. I don't mind shooting things at all, but I do have a
laziness for cutting them up. I tire very easy."

Chalk was listening to Whitey while watching George, who

again started through the strange facial movements he used for a smile.

Jim looked around. He held a shovel in his hand and he hated. Ann stood quietly holding the baby, who was sleeping again. Bill sat by the rocker box with his toes dangling in the water. Denver had been resting easily nearby and didn't speak or move. Margaret went over to stand beside Ann.

As Candy examined the rocker box he thoughtlessly stepped into the stream. Cold water quickly filled his toeless boots. He'd already looked carefully at all the people here but, damn it, not one of them had feet even near as big as his. He moved some gravel with his hands. "If they's trapping gold, it appears to me none has yet been caught. Maybe they've cleared the dust and nuggets for the day and what they have is probably hidden somewhere right close to here."

That was phlegm in a miner's throat. "Being soldiers still is rotten enough, but sluice robbing too—"

"You shut up now, old man. Being old don't mean being safe. You talk enough and you might get a race started between me and God to see who's going to kill you first." Denver quieted. There were still a great many prospects that needed looking to.

"Now don't you worry about that." Wilkenson spoke. The miner's mention of them being sluice robbers had stung. "We are not sluice box thieves. If ever we talk of robbing, we talk Virginia City. There's money there and I've always felt that whole town was Yankee from its start."

The riders mounted, even though the trip from here to camp was short. They took Chalk's Colt with them. It was Candy who picked it up. Everyone followed at a slight distance.

Whitey grinned openly at Ann. She wondered if he could have been the one.

"That mining operation you have here," he said, "is shiftless."

"The hell it is," Chalk countered. He was looking at the calluses on his hands.

"Working at the same thing every day is just another kind of shiftlessness. Where's the adventure and the style? I mean, what do you do to bring excitement to a day or for that matter into a night?" Whitey dropped his jaw slightly to show that he had finished speaking. Chalk was staring, his eyes burning.

"Excitement," Ann said. "Oh, I've had some of that. It comes with trouble and I've had my share. When I was a girl there was a fall of shells and bombs on Vicksburg once. It was part of the war that took my arm away. Then there was a bear that three-quarters wrecked our camp, and there was even a time when this young lady here had to kill an Indian." Ann pointed to Margaret, who now held the baby. "So, I've already had about all the adventures I need."

Texas walked right up to Margaret and asked, "What's this? You killed an Indian?" Margaret stared straight ahead while keeping a simmering silence. "Maybe did you, little lady, just eye-flash that red man to his death?"

Margaret stayed silent. Ann spoke. "You look over there," she pointed to the wagon that that was back at the camp.

"What in the hell's that?" Dade wanted to know.

"Dade, you are ignorant." Whitey was quick to point out. "That's nothing but Indian pictures on the canvas of this wagon. Didn't you see them as we were riding through?"

"It tells," Ann said, of when a ten-year-old girl killed an Indian warrior chief. There wasn't even any harshness in her doing it. She just didn't want to see her brother whomped. All she could do was pull that hammer back, and everything was made right in one big smoky flash. If she could have thought out any other way, doubtless she would have. It was a little girl ten years old and all by herself.

"That girl is more than ten." Whitey was looking at Margaret, although he spoke to Ann.

"The Indian is some years dead, and the girl then is holding on to my baby now." It hadn't been Whitey and it surely hadn't been gimpy George. Ann recalled how she had been threatened, so to all of them she said, "You Reb rabble made a brag about burning down a town." Now, one of them knew and Ann thought maybe she oughtn't to have told. They looked hard and were silent, still Ann didn't stop.

"You six fellows aren't going to do anything. There are no more Lawrence, Kansases. That's a nonsense this country's gotten over. George, your friends would be alive today if they hadn't tried to hard-ass better men." Ann was talking fast and sharp. She'd called them friends but didn't know that two of the dead bank robbers had been George's brothers. She had time to think about courage being churned to foolishness, yet if the little stove could have helped it, she thought, it wouldn't have singed the grizzly's nose.

"Six men riding together and all you can think to do is burn down some people's town, set fire to people's houses. I wouldn't spit, you bastards, thinking about you. I'd be afraid that where that spit fell the grass would turn up its roots and die." Ann could see Chalk's thoughts grinding away inside. It would be much better if a woman said these things. Chalk wasn't being silent from consideration for her say. He was just slow to get words started. She hoped he'd think enough ahead to keep his own mouth shut. To give him time, she was talking on. The way to save Chalk from this would be to build a ten-fueled fire under the saddle-worn asses of these bastards. Of course she couldn't tell anyone that. And she wouldn't be able to hold off Chalk forever.

Chalk was pointing from one man to the other. "You aren't no more soldiers than I am a king. Besides you're in the wrong uniform. I mean, fellers, that war is over."

"That's what you say?" Dade answered him in a voice that was even and mean. With Chalk talking, Ann started to be apprehensive. She knew about tough situations, and fear never led you out of them. These men were like having the bear come back. Just as crazy, just as mean, and probably about only half as bright. She hoped Chalk wouldn't get into their craziness. But under the circumstance, it being his camp and claim, that would be hard to avoid.

Texas didn't have a shirt. His eyes turned from Ann now that Chalk was speaking. "That's what he says, Dade. But it don't really matter. You know who he is?" Texas cocked his right-hand fingers down on Chalk as though they were a gun. "Our comrades in arms," he went on, "and our murdered brothers was shot down like dogs in the streets of Comptonsville. One who shot our boys was married to a one-eyed woman, or could she have been one-armed?"

Ann looked at Texas. She looked back at him blue-eyed and straight until he looked away.

"There's no one-eyed woman here," she said. He was open mouthed. She could see his teeth. They were rotten, broken, black. Doubtless he was the one who had come at her in the night.

Texas turned on her. "Kay Cee Smith was the one I know about the most. They say your man shot him in the back." Turning to Chalk he added, "I mean, if you're her man then you must have murdered Kay Cee Smith. That is unless I am misinformed or . . ." He paused for emphasis. "I am a liar." It was spoken as a simple challenge and the speaker was coiled like a snake with fingers brushing nervously against the butt of his holstered gun.

"Bad things happen to everyone," Ann said. "Look where I should have an arm."

"Blame that on the Yankees, honey. It was they who was shooting up the town."

"I'm sure I don't care who's to blame, Pemberton as much as General Grant. Neither had the right to be throwing bombshells in the air. What I am saying is, the arm's gone, and thinking about it is gone too." Ann had taken the conversation back. As always she was clearly concentrated in the middle of what was happening, while the invading gray clad riders were only drifters trying to live in a time that was forever lost.

Frazier noticed that this man Texas, his attention drawn by Ann, now had seemingly forgotten all about killing Chalk.

"Lady," Wilkenson said, "you can't talk us six grown men to death about your goddamned arm and how you lost it as a kid. For now let's talk sensible. I've never wanted a person dead unless there was either need or profit."

Frazier was listening closely. This man George hopefully had these men in charge. They looked at each other.

"And you, Doc, would be a sorry thing to kill. There's bad luck in killing a doctor. It's not that they are healthier than other men. It's more like tearing a page from a printed Bible book." George talked and his men paid attention with fixed expressions on their faces.

It was all going to be very simple. The camp would be isolated and watched. If there was any attempt at leaving, everyone in it could easily die. Wilkenson talked fast and he wouldn't hear an interruption. Several times he used the term martial law, and then he directed his men to search the camp. Texas rummaged through the wagon. Ann and Chalk stood very still until Whitey, his sword's scabbard still clanking as he walked, came from the tent without the cocoa can, now so nearly filled with small nuggets and dust. When Ann had finished talking and it seemed all right, she'd taken her baby back from Margaret's arms.

Candy and Dade had the dressed deer down, and as they lashed it to Frazier's horse Dade observed, "This here's somewhat better than those rotten potatoes fried in rancid fat." Then they gathered up the mules and tied them. They had Chalk's horse too, and Chalk stood arms tight at his sides, half sick from the sweat stink of his rage.

Texas also went through Frazier's gear. It had been hurriedly thrown underneath the wagon. In the sleeping bag he found a

holstered army revolver. It was lightly oiled and nearly new. He
buckled on the belt, saying, "Inside a sleeping bag is the most
unhandy place I can think to keep a gun." The gun rig had been
wrapped in an old woolen shirt. It occurred to Texas he could use
that too. If arms were being contrabanded, whatever covered them
also was fair spoils of war.

Frazier knew better than to speak. He'd be able to get another
revolver someday. It would be identical. But there'd never be a way
to get as fond of any other shirt. It was his fishing luck, and that
would be a real loss. The mules were led over and tied quietly beside
Frazier's and Chalk's horses. It took both Dade and Chick somewhat
longer to round up Denver's burro.

Then Chick went into the tent to bring Chalk's shotgun out.
Whitey had the Zouave rifle from the wagon. He also took the
pistol from the holster beside the seat. The final weapon was
brought forth as he turned toward Ann. She'd moved. For an instant
he'd seen a single angle underneath her blouse. The gun he held
was *click, click, click*, and pointed. The brief movement seemed relaxed and casual. Chalk knew he would move on the sound of the
shot. He looked to the man nearest him. His muscles bunched.
Ann only said to Margaret, "Hold the baby, please."

"Just between two fingers, ma'am," Whitey said, "and do it
proper and slow. I mean the gun and not the baby. It would not
have been mannerly to search you with our hands."

Ann opened the bottom button of her blouse and reached beneath it. As ordered she produced the little seven-shooter, holding
it between two fingers like the body of a mouse. She dropped it on
the ground in front of her.

"We all being in this woods together," Wilkenson said, "it
might be best, as was said before, that you all stay on. Just to help
that happen, we'll look after the horses and mules, and though I
wouldn't know about riding a burro, someone might.

"This old wartime gun and the double barrel you'd better keep for hunting. You'll soon be after another deer. If it should come time to leave, we'll tell you." Wilkenson paused, watching these people. They looked tame enough to stand where told. He continued as an afterthought.

"One more thing. Don't wander up to where we are at. It's most of the time a rotten place to be, but neither corps nor army could root us out from it. So just stay put now, because we don't know when the idea might come for us to pay a visit."

The six gray-clad riders moved out, taking with them everything that could be ridden. The burro kicked a few times and then went along. George with his limp had been the last one mounted. His rifle was slid into its scabbard and he turned while the others rode away. No one else could hear him because he spoke so quietly to Chalk.

"I watched you watch Whitey as he was coming out from your tent. You had just the trace of a smile that you did your best to hide. It doesn't matter the things he hasn't found. When we want what you've panned, we'll just ask for it, and do you know what? It will be here." George pointed his finger to the ground in front of Chalk. "Right as plain in sight as where I am pointing now. As a favor to all, don't hide your gold so good you'll not be able to find it yourself."

George's yellow teeth were, as ever even. He showed them for a second. Then he brought his horse around and followed the others with an easy lope.

As soon as those men disappeared, Chalk and Jim snatched up the two remaining guns. Ann, without speaking, started to lay a fire in the stove. She'd get lunch ready now, because the day was spoiled for going back to work.

It was a silent meal that ended as large pieces of fresh bread wiped up remaining stew. Now that, Chalk thought, out in the woods, was a civilized thing to do. With his last bite finished he wished for something more than water as a drink. He wished for lots of it, and there was none. No beer, no nothing, they'd even taken Frazier's whisky bottle.

"I hope that Swede farm boy is making something of his life, because seeing that bastard George again makes me almost wish to hell I hadn't shot down Kay Cee Smith."

"Without that reward money," Jim pointed out, "we wouldn't even be here on this claim."

Chalk moved his head sadly. He hadn't thought about it quite that way.

When no one was looking, Denver scratched his stomach underneath his shirt, because it was purring from all that good food just like an ear-itched tabby cat. "I figured maybe for bears," he said. "And there be Indians and maybe others who might take your horses and your life. The craziness I didn't assay to find was a little bit of the war leftover in these hills. They sure are something different, still wearing soldier swords with all those long years gone by."

"And God damn the difference," Frazier said.

No one looked shocked. They all knew what he meant. In the long frenzy of those four years, grown men of knowledge, and women too, whom everyone dearly loved, beat that drum so hard for war. Near all had gone along. To see it over again up here in these mountains, alone and by itself, oh, sweet Jesus, did it not sicken a man. Yet what was there to be done?

Frazier had quieted himself in the new town of Comptonsville, so far from all he'd ever known. He'd have sat there 'til he died off, either from boredom or of drink, it didn't matter whichever. Then a little kid, up too late at night, pulled him out of the bar. Bill had done that by himself. Getting a person from a bar wasn't the same as knowing to tell him where to go. Lately Frazier had been warming back toward a real life. In this camp the days were starting better, and now at night it was something deeper than just mountain air that let him sleep so easily.

Frazier looked often at Chalk. There was a person who had changed through being out here in these woods, and certainly changed for the better. Just the way he stood was so much more gathered than before. In town, drinking with him, Frazier had sometimes glimpsed a shimmer of that deeper humanness. There, in that hotel bar, it had been fogged by all the fears of all the things Chalk knew he couldn't do. In this camp their friendship didn't deepen. As before they were just quietly together, and it never came about that there was very much to say or speak about.

Seeing Ann and her baby was always a joyful occasion. And there was Jim at the beginning of his manhood and the other children who were of an age to be born new with the dawn of each passing day. Both Bill and Margaret were growing fine. It might not be perfection, but this camp was a fair example of just how good the world could be.

Up from the town with Denver, Frazier'd watched him move over the land, burro behind him on a rope and not one stone nor fold of ground he didn't take a pleasure from. As they traveled, the satisfaction of discovery never failed to carry Denver eagerly along. It almost seemed that proving barren sand pleased him as much as turning the flash of bright colors in his pan. Now, here at Chalk's claim, Denver would pan various samples every day, but the placer stayed pretty much the same: just ten new dollars at sunset, no matter where your cradle rocked.

Once when they were trailing in, Denver suddenly stopped and said, "Right here, Frazier, with enough mules, men, and wagons, hydraulicers could come in poor and walk out rich. Of course the damage would be just tearing up this whole mountain side. They'd be in here with their water cannons and they'd melt the mountain down. It'll happen yet, though not for some time to come. Do you know what? When it does, I won't be the one who told."

The camp had been a great place to read and rest or only rest. Frazier had packed in several soft leather-bound volumes, and fortunately small books were something people seldom stole. Often, looking up from his reading, it had pleasured Frazier to see Chalk at work. Not that work itself was so great a thing, but here Chalk seemed to start each day with half a shuffled step as though into a dance. He was as eager toward a shovel handle as if it were the neck of a bottle filled with ice-cold beer.

Now ruination had come. There had been no way to fight them off, and in violence men like those were to be believed. They kept telling you to bend beneath their anger, and sometimes they even pleaded, because they knew best of all the sudden horrors hidden within them. Often they seemed to hate it in themselves, but hating something, Frazier knew, wasn't the same thing as being able not to do it. He said it to himself, "It would make no sense for some of us to run. The bastards would come back and doubtless kill all who stayed behind." They had promised that. With nothing to keep them occupied and busy, they could lurk day and night always watching everyone. These men were like a disease from which you sickened and died, and no one knew why, or how it had gotten to you. When he had been an active doctor Frazier remembered how it so often ended, no matter what he tried. It ended with a corpse and then the tears. Finally the liars came and said that it was the will of God. Frazier often wondered why it happened, but he knew God couldn't be the reason, particularly when small children and babies died. He, Frazier, certainly didn't know why. One thing he did know. The men in the woods around them in heart and dress were keeping that old war alive, retaining its violence as a reason for their lives. The sorry sons of bitches. Once more Frazier looked to where Ann's left arm should be.

Here beside this stream and on this mountain the old war went on, and it was one-sided because these people, Ann, Denver, Chalk, and Jim, they didn't even have weapons or the knowledge of how to make a fight. And if they did, Frazier's heart would not be with them. A part of it had broken in the war.

After four years of agony the war had bled to death. Angry battles had festered like pus-filled boils. Now the infection was ended with the skin of the land scarred over, and a few of the wounds had started to heal. As a doctor, Frazier couldn't know how bad the country had been hurt, but getting well didn't mean just staying alive. He'd looked into Ann's face and then he thought of George and his companions. Both Ann and George had been injured. George had brought it on himself with the attempt to rob the bank, and his wounds, like the nation's, might never heal.

How goddamned ugly and how stupid with their sabers and their uniforms to keep old agonies alive. These men were infused with the disease of hatefulness and would never recover, and it seemed the whole country had been like that. Then in places and with the war over, a betterness had started growing. This camp, until now, was the most of this Frazier had ever found. George and those men were spoilers and there was no plan to keep them away. Yet everything here still seemed so much the same, with children playing and Ann still at her stove. To have the vermin leave, cleaned up a place but clearly they were not gone for good.

At certain times Chalk could pretend to himself that maybe they weren't coming back, but he clearly knew they would. The following day he armed himself with a shovel and he fed the rocker gravel like it was a steamboat furnace burning dry pine knots so as to win a race. When he'd had an insult—and usually it was in his imagination—it took forever for him to let it go. He'd gnaw it over and over for a long time or until another came. More immediate than the danger from those empty-faced, long-riding bastards was a gut bitterness. It tasted like the dry old penny inside your mouth in the middle of a losing fight. Chalk tried to think about saving his camp. If killing those men was a way to do it, fine, but he couldn't shoot them all. He wasn't sure if he wanted them dead. He only wanted the inside agony of insult stopped. He wanted them gone so bad he couldn't think clearly about the camp or Ann, their baby, or the kids.

He didn't speak of this to the others, and for a long time he secretly held his hurt within. He doubted Frazier'd have a plan, and Denver wasn't useful in a situation like this. If there was a man like Cas here, he'd know what to do. Of course he would. Good goddamn it and go to hell, that was his full-time job. Chalk couldn't stop the knife that was turning inside him. He remembered when that big-assed ranch foreman had come into the bar with two of his hands along. There was a reason ranch foremen were called ramrods. Straight, unyielding, and made of either hickory or steel, they were also men who had their actions planned long before they knew exactly what they were going to do. If this was the foreman's problem he would have already thought of something, or at least he'd not have been so quickly buffaloed. But like a lot of other people, that ranch foreman wasn't here. Only goddamned Chalk was here. Maybe they would never come back. Chalk was back to that. It was a hope to dwell upon, but it had its own bitterness. They'd be gone forever and he, Chalk, would never know it. This was no comfort in the slightest. Maybe they were just passing through and the whole story was to frighten the camp so Chalk wouldn't go for Kincade and the law. How rotten-mean to do something like that. Maybe they cared so little that they could ride away and forever leave the stink of fear behind them. It was also possible that they might be watching the camp's every move. Chalk glanced furtively at the surrounding trees. Any place at all in there, he thought, spying out the camp or gone, it didn't matter much because they'd made the forest's trees around him into a rageful fear.

And supposing they were on the mountain. Chalk looked to peaks where there was still snow. But again George had said an army couldn't pry them out of their hideaway. If he took the shotgun and the Zouave? No, that was nonsense. A three-shot ambush would be a failure from the start. George had promised such a vengeance if attacked. No, there had to be a way to get each one of them and sure. Even with a big posse and everything proper, men like that weren't taken easily. If he was able to get help from the town, it might not be enough.

Chalk was thinking in circles. George's people were either gone or waiting to pounce. And even if they all left the camp successfully, could they hole up somewhere and hold off six heavily armed men? Not with a baby along and not with the children. And should they, suddenly in the middle of the night, flee to town? George and his men had horses, so there was small chance of making that escape. And even if they were able to escape with their lives, those bitter men would keep looking and maybe even years from now, they'd be standing there, George or Dade or maybe Whitey or the three others and then Chalk might be very dead. For a second he thought of practicing to be a gunman, but he knew himself much better than to believe in that.

He thought to ask Jim for his advice, but that would not be fair. The boy should be looking to Chalk for some leadership, and right now it was something that Chalk didn't have. No one spoke. Ann and the kids were working at the cradle. All talk had stopped and in the silence there was just the water flowing and the rocker bumping back and forth. Looking from face to face, Chalk could see ideas come and go like fireflies in the night. Each in turn would start to think of something and then just as quick they'd see a reason for why it wouldn't work.

Decent people didn't have the practice for thinking mean. Damn George and damn all his rotten riders. Who were they, and George in particular, to give orders as though this was a school or army camp. He wasn't a kid with a slate, nor some private soldier standing to attention with his thumbs along his seams. Those riders must know this was no bonanza claim, so maybe they wouldn't wait around to rob it. This little bit of stream was being worked just to recover the cost of buying it. As poor a thing as it was, until they had come it had been his and he'd worked it through day after day, hardly ever wanting to stop himself let alone be stopped. The summer had been great 'til now but for a smashed stove and the wagon tumbled.

Ann knew no good could come from asking Chalk for things he didn't have. Someone else might have done it, but why, she thought, do something both useless and cruel. She'd seen that look on him so many times before, and those times their lives had not been in jeopardy. It was like being back in the wagon with the kids and having her right shoulder itch with no fingers to scratch it and no place to rub. When Chalk was absent for a minute she'd ask Frazier if he could think of anything to be done.

That night, for the first time, Chalk dumped dust and the retorted button in the tin without the bother of weighing them. By now they almost always knew exactly what they had. Weighing it in was only a known and friendly way to end the working day. Chalk's mind was emptied.

He held the open retort in his hands, about to bolt it back together. Then he stopped, placing the halves on a wooden box inside the tent. Ann didn't comment. She hoped this wasn't Chalk's way of saying he was giving up the claim. He certainly had every right. For him, things often got spoiled and so easily that another person wouldn't be able to notice any reason. Working their days down in the stream would be bad enough. It wasn't joyful washing gravel for others to take the gold, yet what if they stopped only to sit and wait? Then somebody might just go a little crazy. With the children in the wagon there was always a next day for going on, and Ann knew better than to stop moving here. She winced to think of those six men crouched up in the mountains somewhere, useless to themselves and forever waiting with nothing getting done. No wonder they were all half out of their minds. And just by threats and spoiling they might make it that way here. A life of waiting didn't come to boiled beer.

Ann had the dinner going. The men hung sheepishly on the edges of activity. Margaret had been in there helping without needing to be asked. Bill had come early from the stream to see that wood was cut and piled past one meal's need. The younger ones knew the grown-ups had been twisted by those strange gray-brown soldiers who'd come into camp. Bill and Margaret looked for the ending day's contentment that had always been, but lively chores were not enough to bring it back. The grown-ups walked around each other at a distance. Even Jim was quiet, off alone by himself. When it was finally time to eat, the meal was as silent as the woods.

Chalk poked at his food. Usually he ate without hesitation. This camp wasn't here just to be a picnic ground. He'd made it and finally there was a place where he could work, not just for a day or two and because some others asked. This wasn't the ranch of words, stocked with the cows of dreams. Now he didn't give a damn if he never moved gravel in that stream out there. All Chalk could see were the horsemen. They still looked down on him from the cut bank above the stream. There hadn't been a chance of fight. Fight, hell, there hadn't even been a chance for words. Even when there was, mostly Chalk found it hard to speak. Even if they had been listeners, which they weren't, he couldn't tell them how much they'd hurt him and that they shouldn't hurt that hard unless they wished him dead. Maybe they knew to be more mean than death. That was nonsense in a way. His thoughts were wasting like gold from a leaking sluice. He'd better concentrate those thoughts like they were retorted gold. It would be easy to waste his life away just from rage, and that would also be the lives of all the others. If he was to get over those rotten men he'd have to be alive to do it, however bad it pained him.

Chalk made a picture in his mind. He'd been broken out of

jail and was on the dodge with a bunch of riders to back him up. They happened to ride into a camp of peaceful people in the woods. "So there will be no news of us, we are going to be taking your horses for a while," was how Chalk would explain it to them. He'd apologize also for taking all the guns they didn't need for hunting. Even if it wasn't true he'd have said that as an innocent man, he'd been unfairly jailed.

As further reassurance he'd say, "Your horses will be freed in a couple of days to find their own way back to here."

The people in Chalk's imagination would need stay someplace for a week or even less. He would tell them the exact amount of time he needed for his escape. He'd make staying sound like something friendly. There was no call to sound like a steel trap snapping shut. You could tell a man to wait outside without locking the door in his face. Chalk would, at the least, have done it that way, the nice and decent way. But Chalk wasn't doing it. Chalk wasn't doing anything. Hardest of all he wasn't doing anything while he was sober. He studied the hairs that grew on the back of his fingers and then bit them off one by one.

If he were drunk enough it might get him raging mad. Drunkenness was his mirror. In that glass the world got turned around 'til his helplessness looked back at him as though he could beat his way past it. Then in the vague pain of the next morning Chalk would feel at least something had been tried. But in that past he could seldom, if ever, remember what it was.

Before the placer here, there had only been that one big occasion. Now it was coming back to him. He'd shot down Kay Cee Smith, but not out of anything he thought or believed. Smith had said he was going to kill George and maybe even that Swedish immigrant kid. His hand was to his pistol butt. If Chalk had thought about it any longer Smith would have been alive and George wouldn't. Then instead of George, Smith would have gotten back to the other men hidden here. It would have been the same, except there'd have been no reward and he could never have bought this claim.

One against six. Chalk tried to remember if it ever had been done: one man capturing six and making it stick. Not these. They were men who didn't capture. They only knew how to fight, reins in teeth and a revolver in each hand. You didn't call "hands up" to them, and there was no shooting all six at once. With luck you might take one or two of them. That would be much worse than getting none, because any survivors would be sure to do you in.

Gunplay of any kind was obviously not the answer. Then Chalk thought back to what he'd been told about the war and the weapons that they'd had in it. There were torpedoes in the rivers, and now it came to him. There were hand grenades on the land. Chalk had fuse and he had the two halves of the retort. He'd full pack that retort with powder just like it was a Hanes Excelsior grenade. Chalk had heard old soldiers say that they'd been too dangerous for any sane man to use. Of a certainty that was true for men being ordered to throw one. The retort with fuse would be much safer, and Chalk was doing this thing for himself. Of course, to do it right he'd have to catch the men all together in a bunch. He'd also have to cut the fuse short. Again, he'd heard from the old soldiers that long-fused grenades had a way of getting thrown back. He started to eat something and looked over at Ann. For the first time in two days he was able to smile. He made it broader thinking about what that little mercury boiler would say. He started the smile little, as in hopes of better times, and then he grew it big and wide. Thinking of those bastards dead brought Chalk's face back to life.

Denver was chewing well with what teeth he had and he was quick to look up. "Chalk," he said, "maybe they are in, through and gone like that pesky bear, with just the wagon knocked over and the little stove all gone to smash."

Frazier shook his head. "I wish I thought so. But I'm afraid we're into a solid bad time and there's no way of knowing how or when it's going to happen."

"But it hasn't yet, and maybe it's not going to." Chalk was vehement. Normally he was slow to speak. "That goddamned bear didn't mean anything. He just came on through in his own way and left a mess behind him. A being that big tends to make a big mess when he moves, especially when something happens sudden and before he has time to think."

Denver's forehead wrinkled. "Bears think? I don't believe it. They just move along for better or for worse, and it's best to be somewheres else while they're coming through."

Chalk's idea was getting slowed. His voice was sharp as he asked, "Denver, how do you know so much about bears?"

"Not so much at all, Chalk." Denver stretched each word for emphasis. "But I've been out there with 'em for a fair piece of time." He gestured to indicate the mountains and the surrounding forest. "I'm always thoughtful about bears. When I'm poking around in the hills it's usual for me to sing a bit of a song or maybe whistle something lively. I am always careful not to be the person to give them a sudden fright. The wilds are their home, and I," he leaned over to knock with his knuckles on the wooden tabletop, "have never gotten myself between them and it."

"No more have I," Chalk said, "but those damned bushwhacking rebel bastards aren't bears. They come upon us knowingly and they have the knowledge to give fear. They aren't just bumbling around in these woods."

"Nor are those bears. They mostly have a mind for food." Denver was still eating as he talked. He was slicing up a fresh slab of meat, carefully cutting the pieces small. He had time to speak between his chews. "Let me tell you about that. For one thing, those bears can dig. I was once astride a trail and I was moving slow and careful so I wouldn't come upon a bear all too suddenly.

There was, from the tracks, one of them somewheres to the front of me. Well, from half a mile away I could see where the earth had been tore up. That bear had dug so deep when he found that marmot den, those little animals didn't even stand a chance. That hole was bigger than you need each year to validate a mining claim. Cartloads and cartloads of rock was moved. Big rocks, slabs, and boulders too, all were thrown aside. The little beds of gathered moss and grasses were showing to the sky. Those marmots had run for it when that bear came through. Come to find that hole was too steep-sided for them. They never made it to the edge. At the end of each track there was blood and the place where that bear sat down to eat. Killing the marmots wasn't much, but the amount of that digging has stayed in my mind." Denver had his meat carefully cut and he forked it up just the second he was finished talking.

"Well, damn it, we aren't marmots for those bastards to hunt."

Frazier spoke softly. "Chalk, I'm sure that wasn't what Denver was telling us. Were you, Denver?"

The miner kept on chewing and as he finished said, "I wasn't saying anything excepting the amount I have seen those bears can dig. No one else was doing any talking."

Ann watched the children eat. She was pleased to see Bill down to the cooler at the creek. He was taking more milk without either being asked or told. They ate stewed berries for dessert and to-morrow Ann would bake some pies. She didn't want to talk about all of them caught here by that gang. The summer had gone fine and she'd not wanted it to end. This was the best camp in the whole world, until they were told that they had to stay in it. And were those bastards waiting just to dig them out? For a fact there was no digging needed. "We're all right here on the top of the ground," she said.

Frazier looked over to her. "I'm afraid we are, and with most of our weapons gone George and his people have us cold."

"Bears isn't goddamned people. People are different from bears.

That's foolish talk and anyway, like Denver says, bears are ten or maybe even twenty times tougher than any living man." Chalk said only this. He wasn't about to reveal the hopes he had for his home-made grenade or the details of its construction.

Bill and Maggie wanted to stay up late to catch a jar of fireflies. Ann told them to bed in the wagon earlier than that. They'd all be back to washing gravel in the morning, and in addition she'd be wanting pints of berries for her pies.

Sometimes Chalk thought Ann should be, well, just a little bit more like other women. They'd disappear to sewing when it was time for the men to have a talk. Sometimes Ann would too, but never when the conversation was of any real importance. So while they smoked pipes and walked around to let their dinners settle, Ann took time to feed the baby. Then she returned to seat herself at the table where the men had gathered.

At first they were all silent. One and then another would pause to start a conversation, then no words came to disperse the heavy hush. Jim, in common with them all, pulled trapped thoughts back and forth. All his plans for escape lead back to the listless clearing here. Always before he'd been able to come up with something more than just the firelight reflecting from his eyes. Even as a kid he'd remembered how to fix a wagon tire. It came from having watched in the Chattanooga railroad shops while he listened to the stories of what the men there had gotten done.

If only those murdering bastards were in a train. Jim could take off the fish plates and pull up the spikes from the outside rail in a curve. He'd tie a rope or wire to it, then when they were right up to the break he'd pull like hell and be glad to watch them all get killed in the wreck. These men were dressed as rebels and that made it more natural to hate them. Jim remembered his own war-time anger. It had only been a child's, yet he would never cry like that again. Staring into the camp's fire he watched an ember flare. Sparks shot up and once again he was back there in that engine house where railroad men told the stories of their trade.

On the B & O there had been a special out from Harper's Ferry and headed west for Wheeling. It came under rifle fire at Black Oak Bottom, but they brought her right on in to Oakland, Maryland. They were taking on wood and water when the telegraph clicker told rebels was moving to cut the line further west. This must have gotten the fireman either frightened or excited because he fell from the cab and broke his arm. There was a retired engineer riding in the cars. He volunteered to ride the plate and fire. No steam was wasted spinning wheels as they inched the throttle open. Full boiler head to the drivers as they pounded up the deep gorge near Cheat River Bridge. Rounding a long curve they spied a bunch of gray-clad rebels pulling ties upon the right of way. Some others were well along to prying up a rail, and it was on the inside of the curve. There were some throttle notches left, so the engine driver jammed it to the pin. The outside rail held. The inside drivers ran just on ballast and ties until they grabbed the solid rail on the far side of the break. As they went through, the fireman volunteer threw a log he'd readied for the grate. It took about ten clustered Rebs away from thoughts of wrecking people's trains. It was a straightaway now and the engine driver climbed up to the roof of the cab. He had a flask with him, and before taking a big long pull he bowed toward his adversaries. The hurried rifle shots sent after him didn't come to anything. Well out of range yet still in sight they stopped the train. The headlight was finished and there were dents to hurt an engine's pride. Still they weren't so deep to hurt how well she ran. Of course it had to be the last train through to Wheeling. Jim had heard it all as a boy because that gallant engine driver was his friend and he'd been killed outside of Chattanooga later in the war.

Well, it probably wasn't something for telling to the others, and it didn't help directly with what was happening here. Yet, just having known a real hero made Jim feel somehow far less helpless.

Jim looked about and still no conversation had started up around the fire.

Chalk's eyes caught Jim's, and what in the hell was there to say. He couldn't tell the boy. He'd have to wait until the camp was asleep. There'd be no trailing in the dark, so he'd have to take a lantern. He'd only light it when he was a ways from camp. Then he'd get to where George was, even if he had to walk all through the night. The time to take them would be dawn, when there was the deepest sleep. That might be fine, but if they'd lived out the war he'd better be in place long before there was any dawn. What would he do if they had pickets out? He shrugged. Maybe, Chalk considered, there were men who planned for everything. Well, he sure wasn't one of them. If you planned too much you never even got started. Chalk smiled over his grenade and he pictured the full-sized hell it would make inside George's hideaway.

There wasn't many men, he thought, who could figure out how to change a simple miner's tool for cooking mercury into a deadly and fearsome weapon of war. Then he planned how he'd slip out of his blankets in the tent while Ann was still sleeping. She breathed so very easily. The baby would be sleeping too.

Ann rose to get the coffee from the stove. Frazier brought the mugs. Chalk nodded as he kept on with a small smudge fire burning in an old prospecting pan. It kept the bugs away if you kept it smokey enough. First a few pine needles and then some of last year's leaves that were just a little damp. If it died out too thin there were pine cones; their scales could be added one by one. Chalk was thoughtfully breaking up a cone. He piled the parts as a reserve, on the table in front of him.

In the first excuse for talk, Frazier, Denver, and Jim made much of their appreciation for the coffee amid loud stirrings and many smiles. Ann stood to stir her cup, and Chalk's coffee steamed in front of him. Nothing as yet was added. He went on with his pine cone and the smudge.

There could have been total silence from now until everyone got up to go to bed. Then, just before full dark, and with a startle that brought the coffee drinkers to their feet, there was that same hideous night noise. It took a moment to remember what it was. Denver's burro was back. He came right to the table and the miner held out a broken piece of sugar, which it ate. Under careful examination the animal was found fit and fine.

"I suspect," Denver said, "they have a pole corral, suitable for mules and horses. But you," he addressed his animal directly, "even in places where a horse is most content, you will dig, climb, or slither out of them. I have never tried doing it, but I believe if he was ever locked in a barn and his own time came for leaving, he'd scatter like dropped quicksilver and flow beneath the door to come up all back together on the other side."

"This is one of us," Ann said, "they couldn't make to do their ways." While spoken first by Ann it was a cheering thought for all of them. The perfection of their enemies was spoiled. For Chalk this made his grenade increase to twice its size.

"It is possible," Frazier said, "they have moved on, and the burro was abandoned."

"We can scout them up tomorrow," Jim suggested. "I'd wear moccasins and move quiet like I was an Indian."

"I'm happy to have my burro back no matter what. Yet after how those woods-crazed bastards warned us, maybe this is just a test." Denver fondly patted his animal. He scratched its ears and brought forward a second sugar lump. In the quiet it seemed the animal was a messenger. But if there was a moment of communication, it ended when Denver added, "Except I'd rather think he's gotten here without them wanting him to."

Chalk's feelings had fallen and as quickly rose again. It seemed so needful. The lowest member of this community had triumphed over all of those out there; most of all over that mule-toothed smiling bastard, George. Those weeks in jail and all the time of the trial he never once gave out one single word of help or even decency.

Had Chalk gotten any madder he would have probably forgotten to take the retort with him on his way up to the lake. For now he couldn't talk, curse, nor threaten. The people here would never agree for him to go up there to the rebel camp. To work his plan would have to stay a secret.

At last Frazier shook his head. "There's no way to run and no way to fight, and those bastards know it. If the children weren't here then we could maybe try a fight. But they are all too young to decide for war, so I guess . . ."

"You mean you know a fight to make," Chalk stood and leaned across the table, "and you're not telling us?"

"I wouldn't say that, Chalk. What I said was 'if.' But even if I did know something to do I wouldn't tell it here."

Chalk's anger and resentment against George faded momentarily. Now he was madder than hell at Frazier. Frazier was talking crazy. "You damned well better . . ."

Ann touched him. "Chalk, please don't shout so loud or you'll wake up the children."

"Without us fighting they might come to kill us all."

"We don't know they will, Chalk."

"And we don't know they won't. So, Frazier, if you have a way of stopping them you'd better tell it now."

"I don't even know how to hold them back. I was just talking ifs."

"You sure?"

Frazier nodded his head.

"Well if you think of anything, maybe you'd better tell us, because thinking is what we are meant to be doing now. We've already got all the ifs we can use. Just saying 'if' is a way of telling us that there's nothing to be done." These thoughts seemed to quiet Chalk so Frazier nodded again in agreement.

With momentary cheerfulness Chalk had another thought. "What if their threats don't prove out? What will happen then? They sure couldn't hold onto Denver's donkey."

"Shush!" Denver's finger was to his lips. With the stem of his pipe he gestured toward the animal. "Burro," Denver whispered. "It is his pride to be a burro."

"I'm saying, if they lose, it would be only fair they lose just so hard as they've threatened us."

"Sure, Chalk. It would be fair," Frazier said, "but who of us would want to do a thing like that?"

"I don't know," Chalk answered, "but maybe tomorrow I'll think of something."

Frazier was so lacking in hope he found himself half believing that Chalk would.

As Ann gathered up the empty cups, one handful at a time, she looked over at Denver with the beginnings of a smile. There was hot water on the stove in a big pot. A small brush had been carefully tied to one of its handles so that Ann could scrub each cup carefully.

"Ann," Denver said, "there you go again, washing cups. Everyone knows which one is his, so why not let cups age like they was a good old pipe and let a nice thick cake of coffee slowly build up inside?"

"These are clean, white cups. I have my pride in them and if the people who made them wanted them to look dirty, well then they would have never made them white." This was a friendly old argument and a joking one. It was useful. Something, almost anything, was needed to take thoughts away from what was happening here.

As was usual she'd sleep in the tent with Chalk. The others went to their blankets early, and it was very much like a failed party would be, Ann imagined, where all the invitations had been mistakenly sent to strangers, and of a sudden all the grounds around them and the familiar table with its seats seemed a foreign land to her.

Chalk rolled down the wick and then he raised the lantern's glass to blow it out. He lay rigidly with hands clasped behind his head. He would have to wait until everyone slept. It was luck that most nights now the baby slept through without waking. Should Ann call to him as he left, he could always come back pretending he'd just been out to piss. Then he'd start out again just so soon as she went back to sleep.

In the deep night, trailing after George, Chalk had one regret. After dogging down the top of the retort, the wrench had been left behind, and he hadn't thought to bring any other powder to reload the English double gun. It was doubtful if there'd be a chance for that, so the grenade was the thing that would have to work.

13

Ann came fully conscious, neither startled by a dream nor wakened through a fear. She knew as surely she'd not been woke in fun. Reaching with a smile she felt the pallet empty at her side.

The blankets were still warm and Chalk maybe had the need to go outside and soon he would be back. She waited, turning to snuggle deeper into the bedding's warmth, but sleep would not come again. It was time for him to be back and he was already gone too long now. With her hand she drew the smooth white wool over the stub of her missing arm. That didn't suit at all. It was time to be up and doing. There was the little lamp beside the bed. Matches had always been a problem for her, but Chalk had pasted a striking surface nearby, so now she removed the chimney in the dark and then turned the wick to where she could feel it. A match flared and as a ring of fire crept around, the chimney was replaced. She only had a flannel nightgown on and her feet were bare. It was a breathless night outside, and in the still air Ann didn't need a second hand to protect the flame. She looked around the camp and she waited. In town this would be so usual. Chalk had disappeared. Of course he wouldn't leave them to go back to find someone in Comptonsville. Then where else could he be? No, if he had left the camp it would only be to go up and find George. He couldn't fight all six. If that was in his mind he'd die. Maybe he wanted to go there and promise the money he had left in town if they would let his camp here be. They must know about that reward. It was mentioned at the trial and that man George had certainly been there. When he'd been here George had not mentioned it, yet that didn't mean those rotten bastards wouldn't find a way to steal all that money too.

Ann suspected thoughts of dealing with George were not sensible. Was she being like Chalk? When things got fearful for him he always made up a story for himself about some easy way out the other side. Now she was doing the same thing by pretending Chalk was safe. There wasn't any dealing with that George or with any of those others. They were crazy people and mean ones too. Ann caught herself hoping craziness could be bought and sold as if it was something sensible, like a pound of dry beans in a store. That for a certain could not be. Craziness was always changing and there wasn't any way to set a price on it. Those rebel-dressed-up sons of bitches didn't even know what they themselves would do.

If and when he came up on them, would they toy with Chalk until they made him crazy too? Animal crazy mad, where being mad would likely get him killed? Ann returned with the lamp to her tent. She would have to wait. They couldn't move until it came light. If she couldn't sleep what use would it be to wake the others? To fret and fuss would not be of help, so she waited quietly. Chalk doubtless had a thousand plans, and of course he hadn't told her any. He wouldn't ever win by attacking them and for a second of hope Ann looked. The Zouave rifle was still here, but the double gun was gone. That made it certain. He was headed up for George's lake. If he attacked them and it failed, that would rage those men up, and when it came to killing they would not know where to stop. She had talked this over with Frazier, and his only idea was to pray, for time and hope those rebs would go away. Hoping wouldn't make a thing come true, but it was interesting to Ann that in all these last few days they'd gone on washing gravel as though their own blissful summer world was still here beside the stream. She looked outside to watch once more for the first flush of dawn. Suddenly for Ann this lovely place of theirs reeked with the stink of oncoming death.

The grown-ups had done their best not to put fear into the younger children. Both had seen the rebels come to this camp and Bill was quick to guess what they were. He'd held nothing back when he told Margaret, but neither was afraid. They never had been, even as young ones traveling in the wagon. The amount of fear on that trip could have stayed with them forever and left them quivering for the remainder of their lives. If fear's been overcome when a person is young, then later on it has a hard time getting its hold.

Different worries came flocking as Ann waited for the dawn. The one with the sword who had been called Whitey, he'd looked on Margaret . . . Chalk hadn't seen that, thank God. Frazier had, and thank God again, he was older and knew to stay away from something that would have gotten everybody killed.

Maybe in the morning, when they all woke, Chalk would be back. Then they'd only have to figure the way out of what had happened already. After a while there was enough light so she could watch for Chalk. She stood through the dawn and when he had not returned she woke the other men.

"Chalk's gone to stop them or to hold them off somehow."

Frazier was barely awake and Denver hadn't had his coffee yet. There was need for Ann to tell them a second time. She added as a question, "If he'd told us would we have let him go?"

Frazier was on his feet misbuttoning his jacket. "Of course we wouldn't." Denver nodded in agreement. He'd slept fully clothed. Frazier paused to get the buttons right and then he asked, "For Chalk's plan to work shouldn't we have been moving through the whole night by now?"

"What plan did he tell you?" Ann asked.

"He didn't tell me anything."

"Then how do you know he had a plan?"

Frazier paused and said, "I don't." There was a silence and they all knew better than Chalk's plan working, if indeed he had one. Ann still held the Zouave rifle those men had left for hunting, and she knew one thing for sure. She and it were going up to that cave or lake. When she said it Frazier guessed he'd been along so far, there was no stopping by the wayside now. Or maybe should they run? As quickly as he thought it, he knew Ann would not run with them. Of course he could order her to. Hell, if need be, he could knock her unconscious and pack her out tied up on the burro's back, but the hell with that.

Then Ann had a fresh problem. Jim wouldn't guide the children out. He got set to come out on the mountain too. That left Denver with Margaret, Bill, and the baby. Ann didn't want to reach out for the baby. Margaret held her and Jim said the directions back to town ever so carefully word by word.

"Just take the cow and pack on out. Don't follow the stream too close and, here . . ." He drew on a flat stone with a charred stick to map the directions as he gave them. Bill kept nodding and Denver paid no attention. Of course he already knew the way.

It was Margaret who asked, "Can't we just have a day of waiting just off and down the trail?" As Jim hesitated, she added, "Oh, God." The young girl's fingers went to her lips. "Oh, I mean, Ann. We are planning as if Chalk isn't coming out." She said Chalk's name with a tear-caught voice while peering closely to find the truth from Ann.

"And hoping for the very best," Ann said, "because there is no other way to plan things sensibly. You all will go down to the meadow with Denver. Stay camped there for two days. If we don't come then, start for town. Stuff rags in the cow's bell, and don't let anybody find you unless you're sure it's us."

"Your pardon for a minute, Ann?" Denver asked. Then he spoke toward the children. "I'm hoping you've heard good. You'll be going on your own. I'm going along up to the lake and my burro too. He's come out from there once already and surely knows the way."

This made hopeful sense to Margaret and Bill. Full light saw them down the trail leading Cow. Bill had the first turn to pack the baby.

Starting now it would be at least three hours before the grown-ups and Jim got up to the lake. If for all that rising walk the rest could keep up with Ann.

14

There was light enough from the stars for Chalk to pick his way to where the trail led beneath tall standing trees. Here he could relight the lantern and then douse it when he got to what he now thought of as George Wilkenson's camp. It would be found under a rock overhang and Chalk would have to get in and then above all those sleeping men. He'd have to manage the whole thing while it was still fully dark. Just after the rotten rebels left, Chalk had taken Denver to one side. Without telling any of the others he asked about the mountain country where those men were thought to be. Denver knew the place exactly and he described it as a lake overlooked by a cave. The cave, he'd said, was more nearly just a large sheltered area beneath an expanse of over-hanging rock, and loose stones were fallen in every which way there. As he walked through the night Chalk tried to figure how he could silently pick his way through all those fallen stones.

He was deep in the woods. Things seemed to move on the edge of the lantern's light, and more than once fallen branches cracked and rocks tumbled at the side of the trail. This was not a time to fool with critters. Just the sound of one shot would boom on forever in this wilderness. Chalk kept moving forward, checking the trail wherever he could make it out. There was a fair ways to get this night and any critters around here should best look out for themselves. He hoped they would, just long enough so he could pass them by. Often the trail was so rough he almost didn't believe where these men either rode or led until he remembered the old cavalry rule. A horse and man can climb together so long as the man doesn't need to use his hands.

The glint of the lake was at last in front of him, and reflected stars winked through its ring of towering trees. Even underneath them there was sufficient light so Chalk was able to snuff the lantern out. He could still feel its warmth as he stood where the edge of the forest ended. He carefully checked but the heat was from before, and the extinguished wick didn't even glow. Emerging from the trees he could see that the lake surface was smooth. It took its light from the sky and the dawn's wind hadn't started. Chalk was here, and here in time. In time at least to retain the shelter of the night. No light got into the overhang or the cave. It was a pure black, shadowed hole. The brow of a pale cliff rose toward the heights above it.

The corral was evident and Chalk prayed that the horses wouldn't nicker at him. He was relieved. All their attention had been drawn toward some shadows or dark bushes on the far shore of the lake. He'd not waste time testing the cave's darkness with his eyes. On the inside, blackness was everywhere. The opening was like an expectant mouth, the lower lip straight, the upper bowed just slightly. Chalk climbed until he could enter at the near corner where the roofline joined the floor. He moved over the loose rocks like a snail, not for slowness, but flowing his weight down evenly so nothing might shift, grit, clatter, or bang. Just the scraping of his clothing, one material against another, sounded loud to him.

Gradually Chalk made his way to the rock shelter's highest level. He couldn't look back toward the lake. He felt the rocks around him with his eyes, and he must not have his vision glared away by light from off the water. Now at last a horse neighed loudly, yet it could no longer be for him. He froze for a second and then moved again. He must have rattled one small rock because there was a voice. It might well be George, off to his right, and thank God already down below him.

"Hey!" the voice came again, sharp. "When I call, you answer." Most people, in the vague light here, would have continued with a stupid series of questions. Wilkenson paused only slightly before he started shooting. He knew his men enough to know that drunk or sober they would answer just as quickly as he called.

Chalk went to ground and the shots splattered around him. Loose rocks rolled and bullets whined. Then it was silent for a moment and Wilkenson called again. His voice masked other sounds within the cave. He didn't hear them nor did his men, who'd been asleep in their blanket rolls. They were awakened by the shots.

A bear was in there, drawn by the delicious smells of rotting food. He'd experienced few if any humans before, so that while their smell was strange, for him it was not the smell of fear. Only his nose led him along. Bacon fat was so good its smell came through both blankets and a canvas bag. The bear moved on to get his food. He felt his food fight back. Almost on top of Wilkenson's Winchester, a revolver's bark slammed through the darkened overhang. It echoed back from everywhere and then it cracked again. The bear heard the sound and felt the pain as only one sensation.

A voice that screamed "Bear!" was drawn out long into a shriek. Wilkenson's attention was still pointed upward to where he'd heard Chalk move.

"What's that?" he asked. His speech sounded harsh and heavy.

Without thought Chalk answered, "It appears to be a bear." He certainly didn't know what to do about its presence.

"Can you see to shoot him?" Wilkenson asked.

Chalk couldn't but he wouldn't admit that. He called out, "I'm not shooting nothing. If I wasn't loaded you'd shoot me just the first second that bear was dead."

There was a musky smell as blankets were flung aside, and then there was massive movement amidst the half-wakened men. With a quality of strength that would dig up a hillside for a snack, this bear started in. There was no digging needed here, only movement and attack. Wilkenson's attention was drawn away from Chalk. Those first few shots had been pegged close, and Chalk was relieved to crouch down in a hollowed place high up in the cave.

"Kill that goddamned bear!" Again it must have been Wilkenson who shouted. The space was filled with noise, and there were grunts and shouts so that it was hard to separate the sounds of animal and man. Then there were screams and sobs that didn't come from the bear. Down below they were penned up, but none of them seemed worried yet. They were six armed men in battle with a single animal.

Again Wilkenson yelled, "Shoot him, shoot him, shoot that goddamned bear!"

A solid crash of pistol shots sounded through the cave below.

In a moment of silence Chalk heard Wilkenson's strange question. "Aren't you a human being?" It took some time for Chalk to realize that his neutrality showed that he was siding with the bear. Wilkenson was concentrating on getting a clear shot at the bear. When the bear was finished they'd have plenty of time to deal with Chalk. But then, even in the midst of the furious battle with the bear, George must have caught the sound or a sight of Chalk because a rifle shot, or at least a shot that sounded louder, splashed stinging rock dust against Chalk's face. Away from the others and below him Chalk saw the muzzle flash. He hunched back down behind the sheltering rocks. The battle went on. He could sense more than see the movement. The noise was deafening. It had no direction, and with all the echoes Chalk could hardly tell who was

shooting where. The close air high in the cave brought the smell
of powder smoke thickly mixed with the scent of freshly flowing
blood. Chalk waited for the rifleman to shoot at the bear. Then
maybe he could at least catch sight of something, but the rifleman
was waiting too, and it was George for sure even in the darkness
of this cave.

As he'd stalked in here Chalk's plan had been to find them all
together. There wasn't enough light yet for Chalk to make his play.
He crouched. He had matches, a lantern, and the retort stuffed full
of rifle powder. His hope was for a fighting chance, but he hadn't
found it yet. For a certainty that must have been what he'd heard
in the woods, that bear. But what was there now for him to do?
One man moved clearly. Chalk could see him, a shadow among
shadows, clambering up toward the back of the cave.

A running figure shouted, "Get him, Wilkenson. Gun down
that goddamned bear."

Wilkenson fired and the man turned slowly to disappear.
Shooting in the near to dark went wrong very quick, but in a second
of silence Chalk heard Wilkenson say, "Now, Clayburn, don't you
draw that killer bear to me."

Chalk still couldn't see anything in the cave. The moving
shadow had sunk into the darkness of the floor, and someone different was screaming now very softly with a bubbling sound as
though his throat was tore. Another low voice was saying, "Help
me, help me, help me, please!" over and over. The "please" came
regularly at the end of the each three "help mes" as though it were
a counted bead. Chalk could hear the horses down by the lake.
They were going crazy. Either a second bear was into them or they'd
smelled the blood and fear. Now there was movement as the neigh-
ing ceased. Hooves rumbled and the corral was burst as the horses
scattered.

Chalk sensed what he guessed to be a slight glow from a dying
fire. Together with the rising dawn it was helping him to see. In

the dark his eyes were opened fully and he knew further to use the corners to catch the smallest shreds of light. He also knew not to move. He was too far from George to throw the retort with sureness. And if he lit a match in here that might just be the end of him. Even risking the match, could he know that the fuse was still good after he'd repeatedly fallen on it in the dark? Chalk looked again with the corners of his eyes. A ghost flicker of light caught on a waving saber blade. Revolvers must be emptied now, but those men down there were not afraid to fight. In the dark and half asleep they fought the bear as best they could.

There were still live noises in the cave; moans mostly and then someone coughed long and hard over on Chalk's left. Down below him there was a new flurry of movement and it seemed a faint light was coming in from beyond the overhang. The bear was running now. Chalk heard, again to his left, a rifle cock, but there wasn't any shot. The bear had run and George was doubtless saving shots until Chalk saw fit to show his head.

It was silent in the cave. Wilkenson wondered if his first shot had been any good. There was a sweat pouring over him and he'd never seen his hands shake so before. He'd been listening so hard he didn't remember hearing certain things. He tried remembering. It was just a movement he'd sensed, nothing had been seen. Or had something else awakened him? Maybe it was the bear, or even another bear. It had been too small for that. Could it be a mother bear down there and maybe above him was her cub? It wasn't near where any of the others slept. The bear was down and hopefully dead. It lay in the meadow beyond the cave as a massive patch of darkness on the grass. Even now it occasionally seemed to move, but as any hunter knows, if you stare at anything in the half light long enough the eye can almost bring it to life. He wouldn't worry himself too much about that bear. But what was there above him, here in the cave and off to one side midst the fall of rock? If it were a stranger it had to be someone from the placer. Could it be that

old miner or the doctor who'd come up from the town? There was
the girl, but she wouldn't be the one to come here. There was an
almost-grown boy, and then he remembered looking up long after
he'd gotten ready for Smith to kill him. That was when he'd seen
that crazy Chalk up there resting on the wagon bows carefully
revolvering Kay Cee Smith to death. That started everything all
over again. Well if Chalk were here and could see to kill him now,
he would. The smell of burnt gunpowder and the stink of blood,
here underneath the rock, wasn't to be believed. So many things
came up so quick to play on the inside of his mind. He didn't have
to list all those people. It was Chalk up there. They'd both been
together in Kincade's jail. Damn it, just before the bear got started
the man had spoken to him.

The morning's cool took the hot scent of blood away, but for
sure now he could smell the bear even when it had gone. There
was nothing inside to be clearly seen, so Wilkenson listened. It was
hard to hear at first. There came the sound of a tiny mewing kitten.
Well, that was a sound he knew from the war. It came just before
the last of his blood flowed out from a man. It could be any one of
them. There was no reason for calling. The weakness out there was
gone too far. Whoever was so close to death, he could no longer
say his name. The mewing stopped and the silence grew too long.

"Whitey!" Wilkenson called. There was no answer. Whitey
slept with his saber always close. That might have been the flicker
of light that had been made at the center of the fight. Once again
George heard the sound of movement on the rocks above him. If
it was Chalk he was building the loose stones around him into a
fort. It made it so you couldn't hear. "Chalk," Wilkenson shouted.
He shouted again, but there was no answer except the sound of the
stones that were being moved.

"I can't see to shoot you now, so stop moving those stones. I
want to hear who's left alive."

Chalk stopped moving rocks. The horses were either quietly

grazing or run off into the distance. Some light was coming up by the lake. Now the rocks were thickly piled and it would be safe to talk. "Hey, George," Chalk called, "are we going to die in this cave too?"

"Now don't you talk foolish, Chalk. I'm not dying anywhere."

"You did get excited though, George. You really got a little excited there."

Dawn was up outside, but it wasn't yet enough to get full light inside the cave. Both men could see that the bear was dead in the meadow. Every minute let more light wash under the rock overhang.

Wilkenson explained. "Clayburn was running up at me just when I shot. I could not know but maybe he would bring the bear. And besides, by the look of him he was mostly dead when he got killed."

Chalk knew better than to raise his head to look. If there was light for George to see the man he'd killed, there was light to see the man he'd kill. Chalk snuggled down behind his buttress of piled stones. He'd better just lie still and listen. George might start stalking over before the light was full. Chalk had only two bear-loaded charges, one in each barrel of the double gun.

There was a chink in the rock he could look through. Bodies and bedding were scattered below him. One body moved, or was it like the bear? The bear had only seemed to move when it was outside in the dark. Then someone did move. It was Dade, the camp's cook, who whispered just one word, "Please" and then he finally died.

Time inched by in the cave. It could have been two minutes or an hour. Chalk carefully pulled the ramrod from his gun and he rose his hat up on the end of it. That worked in part because Wilkenson said, "I've never shot a hat in my life, and I don't mean to start doing it now."

He was still locatable off there in his blankets where he'd been all this time.

"If you want to go down and look to your buddies, I promise not to shoot you."

"Look at them yourself, and I'll promise I won't shoot at you."

Chalk wriggled as though getting comfortable and he slowly poked his boot, with the ramrod inside, out to where it could be seen. Wilkenson shot it through where the ankle bone should be. The bullet carried it rolling off and Wilkenson said, "Why did you want to go and ruin half of a good pair of boots?"

"Just only to see if you shot other things than hats."

Wilkenson wouldn't answer and Chalk could wait. The light was stronger now, and surely there was just the two of them. Down below there were bits of bodies mixed with blood, and how much blood there was. Chalk was getting lonely for talk. He held perfectly still and breathed as lightly as a person could. He held out the tip of his tongue and almost closed his eyes so as to listen harder. To be alone among this many dead. Maybe the war had been like this and Chalk was glad he'd never known it. Finally the quiet became too long and Chalk said, "Hey, George. You can go on down and I won't, I mean I promise I won't shoot."

"How do I know you've even got a gun?"

"You know it enough so you haven't walked over and shot me. Besides without one, I'd have run for it before there was light enough for you to shoot. But mostly, George, if I didn't have a gun, why would I have journeyed up here?"

"You shouldn't ought to have, because I'm not going to let you leave. Just now I've decided that."

"We're but two left," Chalk reasoned, "so I'm willing to be quiet and forget your rottenness."

"You really are, Chalk? That's just because you want to be alive."

"Oh, George, you come on now. Everybody wants that."

"I guess a man like you thinks so. You think that every person wants to live. Why, do you know, every day I think to shoot myself and that's why I'm not feared of any other person doing it."

"Then why in the hell don't you?" Chalk shouted back.

There was a single revolver shot. Chalk winced. Now he was the only thing alive in the midst of all this dying. It got lonelier, yet somehow he wouldn't go to look. How likely was it for a man to lie out there in the street before the bank, living through all those wounds and then so soon afterward kill himself? Even while listening for the man to move, Chalk knew he wouldn't. George would just hide and wait. Pure killers seldom took time out from the hunt.

Chalk had forgotten to bring food. He hadn't even stopped to eat before setting out. So now he was hungry, but he could think it away while waiting for his first drink of water. He had a filled canteen with him but he couldn't drink and listen too. George would hurt for water first, because a man in camp would have no reason to keep a canteen nearby. After a while it was time to piss, and lying on his back Chalk did it out over the piled rocks. This effort wasn't wasted because George had to laugh and by that Chalk knew he was still alive.

"You're laughing now, but when we starve in here together it won't be so funny." Wilkenson's laughter ended in a bout of painful coughing. Chalk listened carefully but it stayed in one place, so he could take his drink of water now, sucking it quiet like a wolf. For a few minutes there was the wished-for smell of strong tobacco smoke. George must have lit up a cigar. Then the sun got into where the bear had been. People's juices and old things that had been eaten started with their smells. This brought Chalk very near to being sick.

"If you get by me, George, where do you think to go? I mean

with that cough of yours I don't think you're well, and I'm not
even the start of a doctor. Maybe you got plans about somewheres
else?"

"Sure, Chalk, I got plans. People who fight bears, they don't
have plans. But I've got plans." With the man talking, Chalk could
tell just where he was and so without looking he hurled, overhand,
the largest rock he could throw. Disappointed he heard it hit on
other rocks and then clatter away.

George was indignant. Throwing rocks was how children
fought.

"Goddamn it, Chalk, don't you throw rocks. You can hurt a
person doing that."

Maybe, Chalk thought, he should have left a note for Ann. His
plan had been to raid this place and then go back to camp and
quietly tell them that the cause of their fear was gone. He still had
the bomb with him, but it was clear he couldn't get it lit and
thrown so far as to kill George. Instead he'd toss another rock.
Again he heard it clatter out beyond. Chalk had the edge here
because George could not throw a distance that was both far and
up above him. Chalk looked out over the lake to see the sun shine
brightly on the water. Both the horses and the mules were gone.
It was obvious where they'd all moved out, right through the poles
while that bear reeked up this place with death. Maybe the horses
and mules would find their way back to the camp. He thought of
Ann waiting there. If he'd known what to say in a note he would
have left one for her.

In his mind Chalk watched the camp come awake. The tent
flap opened and he could see the way the sun was there in the
morning underneath the trees. By now they would all be up and
searching around for him. If they'd leave right now and head back
for town, everything would be all right. This one man left up here
was trapped. Chalk had seen to that. But there was no way of telling
Ann, Frazier, Denver, and the kids that everything was gentled

down. He'd have to remember carefulness. George was right. Chalk surely wanted to be alive, and he'd have to think out the very best way for doing that.

"Chalk! Look here!"

Chalk was fast enough not to be tricked. And again he put his hat on the ramrod and Wilkenson was slow, because he threw a shot at it. A man could have all the cartridges in the world or he could have but a few. Either way, Chalk thought, when he's trying to kill you with a gun, it never hurt for you to be wasteful of his ammunition. He looked silently at the hole in his hat as he wiggled his finger through it.

"Chalk, God damn you, talk." No reply. "You bastard, are you still alive?"

Wilkenson was angry at himself for shooting the hat. After a long silence Chalk thought he might as well talk. He did it in short sentences so he could listen for any sounds of movement in between them. "I already saved you once. Mostly because I didn't know better and your life was tangled with that farm kid's. He had so much guts to whip an armed man's ass with just his iced-up knitted muffler. I couldn't let that kid get shot, and there was no way of killing Kay Cee without saving you. Well, when I needed help at the trial you kept your silence then. I'll have mine now. Good-bye, George, and don't bother to thank me for the food. You ate good in Charlie Kincade's jail." Chalk felt that was something even a rotten man might be bothered by.

"He would have had to feed me if you hadn't."

Chalk thought to tell that Charlie's cooking made prisoners look forward to their hangings. It was a silly argument anyway to have with a man who might be left here to die.

"Hey, Chalk." Long drawn out, the call came faintly from the far side of the lake. Way below and just clear of the woods, Chalk saw several figures. Wilkenson saw them too. He shaded his eyes to hope that these men were for him. No, it was a horse and mules.

Three people rode and one figure walked. One rider was obviously
a girl. The run-off stock must have found their way back to them.
Chalk heard a trigger sear clicking over hammer notches. It would
be foolish for Wilkenson to start shooting now, unless he wanted
to warn them away. Chalk could almost hear the man waiting for
the range to close.

"George, you put up that gun."

"You get me help and I'll let you leave here alive." Wilkenson's
voice was like coarse gravel slowly turning in a pan.

It wasn't so bad that he was talking crazy now, but he could
hurt Ann or maybe one of the others. George might be crazy but
he wasn't foolish. It was so far to shout and Chalk couldn't think
out what was right to say, even as they rode in closer to the shelving
rock. They paused as they reached the body of the bear. The horse
and mules weren't liking it. Ann and Frazier were dismounting.
With the sight ladder up, Wilkenson would start trying any minute now.

Chalk pointed his heavy double shotgun at the rock overhead.
A shot would serve to warn the others and with luck it might knock
down some loose rock on George. He pressed the trigger. They
heard fine. Ann and Frazier were down behind the ample body of
the bear. The horse and mules were scampering. Denver ran one
way to ground and Jim ran the other. Wilkenson's Winchester
started up. He was shooting thoughtfully, evenly and slow, but for
targets moving and already warned he was too far away. Chalk
wished he had more than one shot left. He thought to light and
throw his homemade grenade. He hesitated. The retort was a part
of the mining operation and a tool much needed. To get all six
would have been a way to spend it, but not for just one man. Then
he had the idea to light and throw the lantern. He put it aside.
Somehow there was something wrong with trying to burn a man
to death, and probably it wouldn't work anyway.

He'd give them a yell now and maybe the curve of the rock

would carry the sound. Chalk's hand cupped his mouth. "Hey, Ann, there's only one of them left in here alive."

Ann peered around the body of the bear. With the sun glare it was hard to see inside the cave. She'd seen a rifle's flash and she quickly fired back. Wilkenson crouched down behind the stones. His Winchester was a repeater but those old guns left over from the war threw a much heavier piece of lead. He didn't like how close that girl was marking him. In addition that damned fool Chalk was throwing rocks again.

Chalk was sure now that he wouldn't throw his bomb. More satisfaction could be had from throwing rocks. It was a better way to discomfort the man who'd been so silently rotten and mean.

Skin was white and blood was red against the gray fallen stone. Clothes had been ripped in every way. Chalk, with nothing else to do, peered down. He could see Whitey fine, dead beside his sword. The blade, he could see it all the way from here, was clouded with blood. Whitey had tried to slash that bear in the nearby darkness and the flash of that blade must have been the faint flicker of light that he had seen. There'd been revolvering too. Chalk shook his head. It sure hadn't been enough. From Whitey's right elbow to his wrist, there was no flesh left on the bones.

At this same time Wilkenson stared down at his friends. Texas was the puzzler. He couldn't have stayed in his blankets, until now, alive. There wasn't even a wiggle. It was as if he was still asleep.

The explanation was a simple one. In the midst of struggle and fight, while feeling for a place to stand, the bear put down one foot for steadiness. It had landed right through Texas's sleeping face. From where Wilkenson lay, this fact was not visible. Clayburn's body was nearby. He was the one who had been shot. To see the body clearly Chalk would have to stand, so he'd not dare look. Further down the slope he could safely see one man who was some-how mixed up together with himself. He no longer had a body. There were just broken scattered parts where the bear had made its biggest fight. There was only one more body. It was to the side where Candy had made his stand.

Chalk flung another rock. Wilkenson looked up to get a shot. "You damn well stop throwing those—" And if Wilkenson's attention hadn't been in part on the body of the bear, he would have failed to duck at the muzzle flash. Ann's Zouave would for sure have put him down. Its Minié ball splashed close on the rocks behind him.

Wilkenson palmed sweat from off his brow. If he'd stayed up a half second more that slug would have gone right through him.

Ann readied to shoot again. The cartridge box lay at her side. She held the rifle butt between her feet. Her mouth was turned black from tooth-tearing the paper cartridges. With the load rammed down, she had the gun beside the bear and a fresh cap on the cone. The ramrod lay handy next to her. She was waiting for another chance to see that man move among the rocks.

Jim worked his way around to where the shelf of rock closed like the corner of a mouth. While he didn't dare to look inside, he was close enough to shout, "Hey, Chalk. We brought along all the revolvers that you hid." This lie was for George's benefit.

Chalk called back. There was no need for quiet now. "Hey, Jim, you sent the kids off for the marshal like I told you yesterday?"

"Oh, yes, sure. The kids. We gave them a note and the map for Kincade to come with all the posse he can fetch."

Chalk waited for George to speak. There was silence. It must be time to chuck another rock. As he hefted it, the rock felt so smooth and natural in his hand, as though it had been held many times before. He flung it.

Cowering from Chalk's barrage of rocks, and held down by the gunfire from behind the bear, Wilkenson couldn't even relax himself long enough to piss. Worse than that he didn't have a prayer to gun down that idiot Chalk. Every time he tried to look, Ann would let loose another shot.

"Hey, George," Chalk shouted. "You threatened us and now we are threatening you. Come on out and don't try to make this whole mess worse."

"Bullshit!"

Chalk was shocked for a man to use a word like that when there was a lady present. He hoped the distance was enough so Ann might not have heard. Wilkenson continued. He talked as if each word was shod.

"If I give this in, it will only be because I don't know how to make this hell any worse. Chalk, I'd kill you if I could, just maybe for bringing on that bear."

"You can't blame him on me. George, that bear came by his self, and it was your friends who started in on him. Now, George, you come on out." Chalk lobbed another rock toward where Wilkenson was sheltered. Wilkenson then put five shots into the ceiling of the cave. The rock there was soft and uneven, so he had no real hope of them bouncing down on Chalk. It was the kind of thing a person does when there's nothing left to do.

"If I didn't think you'd shoot me, George, I'd bring you over some nice cool canteen water to drink. But you would, so all I can do is fling rocks down on you. Jim out there can fling food in to me. You going to make us wait, George, or will you give it up? The whole day is hardly started yet. It's a new one, you know, and now we have all the people and we have all the time."

It sounded like George was giving in when he said, "I don't walk so good, Chalk, so I'll need my old rifle here, to use it for a cane."

Chalk gave instructions carefully. "George, crawling down you won't need any cane. Give it in. We won't have to kill you if you'll only stop being afeared. Crawl out now, but before you start, toss down your revolver."

Chalk could hear something clatter on the rocks.

Though far off, Ann could see the gun being thrown. Then she saw a crawling figure emerge from its nest of scattered stones. It inched down over the rocks until it was directly below the hollow where Chalk crouched. Chalk could now see the man from behind. Getting to his feet he pointed his big double gun, with its remaining load, into the small of George's back.

George looked back and up, discomforted as he crawled. "Go easy on how you hold that gun with all this footing loose."

Holding very steady, Chalk replied, "I'll hold it as carefully as I can." Both hammers were thumbed back, the left one just for show. They were getting to where the bear had made most of its fight.

George stopped. "I can't crawl through that," he said. By now Jim was in from the edge of the cave and Ann and Frazier were coming up from below. Frazier brought along a pole. He even helped George climb up it and then stand. Once on his feet George looked around. "All of them?" he asked.

There were flies buzzing everywhere, and bloating would soon start. It was the fresh smell of death before the rot begins.

Ann turned away from Whitey's skeletal arm. She guessed her arm had been mauled like that, or smashed in some way much the same. Frazier had been there then. Seeing this man dead, she blessed the man who'd preserved her life.

Frazier inspected the man in the blanket roll. Long claws and the bear's full weight had wiped away a face. He was only able to recognize this man by the good shirt that had been stolen from the camp. Quickly Frazier peeled back the soggy blankets. Nothing else was wrong. With a careful washing his favorite fishing shirt would soon be as good as old.

A thick blood trail led to a corpse near Wilkenson's bed. Frazier followed the trail and Chalk held up a halting hand, "George here thought his buddy was the bear."

"And?"

"He shot him in the dark."

"By all that blood," Frazier said, "he wasn't going to live much longer anyway."

"Then there's no need for George to be feeling bad. Is there, George?"

George was silent. He'd hobbled further down the fall of rock. Ann backed down in front of him. She walked so as not to see the smashed and broken bodies. With the Zouave she kept watch on the man.

Frazier tried to imagine forces that could have left such a varied mixture of death behind. Train wrecks and shell burst were the closest things. Here too, everything was changed. Some weren't even bodies, only odd parts of them. The last dead man was more understandable. Off to one side he'd found a quiet place where he could bleed. It was the one with the broken boots. In life he had never found the time to wash his feet.

They all left the cave. There was a long pause outside and George said, "You can take the guns off me now, so no one gets killed by accident." Ann raised the muzzle of the rifle into the air. Chalk lowered both hammers carefully and then he charged the empty barrel of his gun. He took two cartridges from Ann's box, using nearly all their powder to make one of his loads. At least he'd remembered to have the proper Miniés in his pocket. As he loaded, he looked into George's eyes. "I guess, George, that every day you think about dying, but that's as far as you get with it." Chalk was talking slowly and his words dropped one by one in time to the pounding ramrod in his hand. George wouldn't even nod.

"I mean it was you who talked about killing yourself." Still silence. "Well, if you aren't happy about being alive, neither does it seem to make you sad."

Wilkenson stated a quiet matter of fact. "I'd be alive if I'd stayed in that cave, there, still game for a fight. Somebody, doubtless you, Chalk, would have risked his life to jump me in my sleep. If I'd been taken I'd be where I am now, except I would have had one more chance of shooting you." Wilkenson took a sudden deep breath to continue. This brought on the cough. It took him a long time to stop. Patiently the others waited.

Frazier thoughtfully nodded his doctor's head. "George, you might have gunned us all and maybe that mean bear might not have come. Wouldn't matter. You'd have died up here anyway. That's a bad cough you have and this is deep woods and dampness country with old snow fields near. For you that's like being in the front of an Allen's pepperbox revolver. If carelessly charged sometimes all the loads go off at once. The only person safe is the man who holds the handle, and that's if he knows to hold on hard. I'm speaking as a doctor now. Maybe you should have stayed dry and warm in the territory's jail."

"It wasn't dry and it wasn't warm and I never got that far. I was delivered from what was just a little old log-built country jail. Out of ten I'm the only one left alive. That should count for something."

"Well, George, I don't think it does. But you hold that brass ring tight, because you won't have it for long. Good God, listen to yourself cough. If I'd ever have thought you were going to kill me personally, I'd only have had to walk away to save myself, with you piping tunes through all those holes in your lungs."

Frazier waited for an answer, but there was silence now the coughing was done. The doctor's voice changed slightly. An edge came on it. "Mr. Wilkenson." The man turned. "You didn't lie in that Comptonsville street holed like a kitchen colander not wanting to live. There you told yourself to be alive through all that hurt. To my mind, lately, you're going about it wrong. Your body wants to stay alive, but you don't get on well with people."

It was in this instant Wilkenson knew, for the first time in his life, to be afraid. This was a cold quiet here in the meadow. He'd been captured by men before in the war, and he'd seen others taken. Usually there was loud talk and jokes swapped back and forth with everything opened up and much relieved by the danger of dying

gone. A captive, unless you were an Indian, was something to be
kept alive. The more you'd done to get ahold of him, the more that
added to his worth. It was like in the war and even afterward when
he'd watched men holding a blood-filled louse between their fingernails. The creature had been aboard so long they felt disloyal
when time came to kill it. There was an affection for vermin after
it was caught. Wilkenson looked to see the way Chalk held that
shotgun on him. There wasn't even the hint of a smile.

Ann and Jim were getting the extra horses saddled. It was all
business. These people weren't doing anything by way of talking,
even to each other. The boy was putting saddles on two of the best
horses. One of them was Wilkenson's very own, captured when
he'd been down in Mexico. He didn't want to lose that horse, but
damn it for his own rotten luck there was no way he could complain. It wasn't really fair for them to take his horse because there
were so many others no one would be needing.

The lawman, Kincade, hadn't come. To think on it maybe he'd
not been called. Saying he was on his way had probably been just
a bluff. They'd certainly go to bring him now so as to be shut of
their only prisoner.

The girl had to reach far across the saddle to mount. This didn't
slow her down. She was seated in a single swing. The horse was
still spooked by gunfire and the bear. He tried a few sharp jumps,
followed by some fancy steps. Wilkenson's whole body winced. He
remembered the grip of his legs and how he'd held when that horse
was under him. He longed for it, but the girl was mounted and
she finally got his horse quiet and controlled. He noticed her legs,
ending into coarse boots, and there was nothing wrong with them.
She didn't even make an attempt to smooth her dress.

Before starting down the trail Ann let the horse's head turn
once, so she could look back. The rock-shelved cave was distant
now. For a second Ann wondered which one of those scattered arms
it might have been that had grabbed her in the night. Then Jim

was mounted and dead men could be forgotten because the first thing was to find the children so they could know that everything was safe and quieted.

The two riders were quickly gone into the trees, and just the four men were here now, along with the horses, two mules, and a burro that the old miner was talking to. He was fondly patting the animal's head each time it looked up from pulling at the lakeside grass. For a burro this meadow would be a paradise because they knew to live on twigs.

Just to get a poor old shirt back, Frazier had reached into Texas's sleeping blanket. Of course he was a doctor and he'd be more used to the ways people had of getting all smashed up and killed.

Chalk was right there beside him holding a double shotgun. Both hammer ears had been drawed back. Didn't smile, didn't eye light, didn't grin. He just stood there watching Frazier fold that shirt. With the shirt stowed in his saddlebag the doctor went to inspect his newly recovered mount. He checked each hoof and looked inside the mouth. Then he said, "He's fine."

Almost in puzzlement, Wilkenson said, "We wouldn't know to hurt a horse, Mr. . . ."

Now, it was time to think about leaving and there were guns scattered every place. George could even see the one he'd thrown. If only there was time enough for waiting him out. Sometime that damn Chalk would have to put the muzzles of that shotgun off him. But this wasn't happening. The old miner, Denver, walked toward the cave. He picked up the pistol and carried it inside. There he poked around until he found several others scattered among the broken bodies. After a careful search he returned. Frazier was satisfied with his horse now and Chalk was standing as rigid as a hitching post.

"I think this is your Army Colt," Denver said.

Frazier took the holstered gun and belt. He examined his revolver carefully. It was the one that had been packed in his saddle-bag and he nodded as he replaced it. Denver also had Chalk's Navy and Ann's little underbreak.

"What about all those other pistols you picked up?" Chalk asked.

Denver just shrugged. "It's naught but that brass-framed rebel trash they made during the war. There's maybe a dozen of them piled in there, but I didn't think to bring them."

Chalk didn't bother to comment. Denver was right. Those sad rickety things were worthless. He turned the shotgun over to a dismounted Frazier. Mounting Frazier's horse, he worked to bring in the scattered herd. Finally he had gathered a dozen decent animals. They'd more than pay for the time away from the placer. Denver was carefully tying the corral poles back in place. George still stood clutching his supporting staff and Frazier sat on the dead bear with the cocked shotgun across his knees. There were no more loose horses in sight when Chalk finally dismounted. The rails were soundly tied and already the horses, with heads thrust through them, were looking for missed clumps of grass.

The world around the lake was peaceful again.

Finally Chalk climbed the fallen rock to retrieve the retort that would have been a bomb. Lifting it brought back the night. He could see a sputtering fuse and the thin arc of fire ending in a thunderous roar. His body cowered from the imagined blast and then he stood straight again. The bear had saved the need.

His position, when seen in daylight, hadn't been very promising. Chalk's bomb was figured for all six of the men to be bunched. Seeing how they'd lived it wasn't likely. Chalk guessed they'd gotten along about the way they wanted to, but it sure must have been a piss-poor way to live. What did they ever say and do, because even before the bear hit them their place was a rotten mess: bones and garbage laying everywhere. There was a harsh stink to this shelter now. George was the only one of them left alive and

he was hobbled with lead and filthy to look at. It was all wrong.
They'd lived like wild animals until one of the real ones came by
and finally did them up.

The sun was fully risen now. It would have been dinnertime if
anyone could have thought of food.

"I don't know about all of you," Wilkenson said, "but up in
my blankets there is a bottle of decent drinking whisky."

Frazier wasn't having any. "Nothing personal, Mr. Wilkenson,"
he said. "It is only that I am very particular about where I drink.
Mind you, I didn't say who with. I just said where."

Chalk looked interested and then joined the thought. It wasn't
party time right now. He'd left George's rifle behind and Frazier's
whisky bottle too. The bottle had been so emptied that there was
no use to bring it along. The four men were gathered around the
body of the bear. Denver tried to heft one paw but the body had
stiffened.

"That sure was one hell of an animal. Look at them claws and
all that dried-up blood that's over them. I wonder whose it is, or
maybe it is mixed. See them teeth, Mr. Frazier. Those is teeth."

Wilkenson looked too. "So that's the bastard that got into the
cave." He touched the body with his booted toe.

"I sure guess he did, Mr. Wilkenson. But maybe he was looking
for some scraps of food or just some pieces of garbage. He doubtless
got annoyed and frightened when you all tried to revolver him.
They are strong, you know."

Wilkenson was crazy with impatience for when they were going to leave, but that old miner kept on.

"I've seen them make a hole only to get at a pocket gopher. It
would take a man a week to dig it. It comes to my mind I came
on a crater once where one of these grizzle bears had gone after
what couldn't have been more than a snack for him. They sure are
an amazement animal to me.

"Not so many years ago in California, before the war, there was a man by the name of Adams. Mostly a hunter, but I believe he mined a little on the side. His first two names was James Capen. Like some men have burros he had one or more of these bears." Denver pointed to the huge crumpled corpse.

"That I know of, one was named Lady Washington. Another responded when Ben Franklin was called. Once a wounded grizzly tried to take Adams. Ben Franklin mixed right in. He got bit bad, yet he saved his master's life. It must be something to take so much trouble with an animal that one day your life gets saved. I think I'd like that and it might come yet because I've always been good to my burros. Now, if I could train bears like that man Adams did, I'd have them go shares with me. Then, with them doing the diggin', I wouldn't have to be so persnickety about the final location of my mine."

"I don't want to hear no more about your goddamned bears." Wilkenson spoke evenly, and as he finished he made his smile by drawing back his lips to show the evenness of his teeth.

"Well, there's no offense meant," Denver said, "but it's something to talk about for now, and what in the hell have you got for us to hear?"

Wilkenson was silent. He felt a fit of coughing coming on. It didn't look as though anyone was leaving. There was Chalk and the talkie-talk old miner and also Frazier, who was a doctor dressed as a dude. Now he was in on him too.

"Mr. Wilkenson, you came to us," Frazier said. "We didn't come to you. Now it would seem you are asking us to spend time and risk of life bringing you out of here just for you to then be put into a jail. What in the hell have you ever done for us, that we should favor you that way?"

As if in answer Wilkenson started a loud and painful fit of coughing. Frazier listened with interest.

Chalk was resting after herding the horses. He stepped over to Frazier and took the shotgun carefully from him. Those close-

together black-holed muzzles were like a figure eight sitting tensely
on its side. Holding the gun, which had never been unpointed,
Chalk said, "I was once in trouble because I didn't want to see a
Swede farmer kid and a wounded gunman killed cold-bloodedly in
the street. But you saved once doesn't mean you saved again. Frazier's right in not wanting to bother. I could leave you here with
a revolver and the making of one load. Even before that I could
break your legs so as to . . ."

Wilkenson was very quiet. He'd stopped coughing and his
hand was still at his mouth. He removed it slowly. "You can't do
that. There's certain things white men don't do."

"After Mountain Meadow and the war?" Chalk asked.

Wilkenson turned toward Frazier. "You can't let him do that.
Doctors take an oath. I can't rightly say the word," the even-toothed
smile came, "but . . ."

Frazier nodded understandingly. His smile back was pleasant.
"The old Greek's name is Hippocrates. I won't explain it further
except to say you are not my patient."

Chalk looked evenly at George. He spoke over his shoulder
toward Frazier. "I don't want to shoot him. I didn't even in particular take to shooting Kay Cee Smith."

Denver half shrugged his shoulders and Wilkenson wouldn't
try the obvious lie of an apology for silence at the trial.

"I guess the three of us," Denver said, "make a fair miner's
court. Usually it's over poking around in the sluice boxes of other
men. That amounts mostly to a hell of a whipping and then being
driven from the camp. This is not sluice-box robbery we are talking
of. For myself, I'm not questioning the humanness of leaving him
here alive, because leaving him here dead isn't all that human a
thing either. It's simply a surer way of being rid of him."

Denver's say seemed over. Frazier's suggestion was next. "That
man was in jail with you, Chalk. You shared out your food with
him. I wasn't there when he was shot trying to take the bank.

Doubtless I would have done my best to save him as old Dr. Le Roy Taylor did." Frazier paused, looking carefully into George's face. He continued when his decision came.

"However, after these last few days I don't care all that much about him. If you don't mind we'll leave it up to you." Frazier looked to the old miner while he still spoke to Chalk. "It was your camp they came to, with your woman and your baby child. The danger was to them so anything that you decide, I guess, would be just fine with us. After all, Denver and I were only visitors."

Denver nodded. "I agree, and I couldn't have said it any better myself, and now I believe we have a lot of horses and mules to lead out of here."

Frazier mounted and Denver brought several of the led ropes to him as one by one he got each halter tied. Then the old miner mounted another horse. It was an unfamiliar and discomforting climb. Following, he led the remainder of the horses and his burro. The cloud of animals disappeared into the trees at the far side of the lake.

When they were gone Wilkenson asked, "Well, Chalk?" And then more quietly, "Well, Chalk, how's it going to be?"

Chalk was thinking as he slowly scratched the dead bear's skull, whose teeth were fearsome yet. While considering the fallen bear, he could still hold the shotgun on George. He only needed one hand for that. The thought had passed long and carefully through his mind when finally Chalk said, "All right, George, I'll make you a deal. Smile just once like you were a human being and then, if you let me, I'll see you safe all the way to the territorial prison."

"What do you mean smile? What in the hell do you want me to do?"

"I've asked you once already." Chalk threw the heavy double to his shoulder.

He was trying to make fear. Wilkenson knew how to deal with that. He showed both rows of teeth evenly by pulling his lips away.

Below the lake, cool under the pines where Denver and Frazier waited, the heavy booming sound repeated, distant and reverberant as though the world's heart had beaten twice. Frazier touched his heels to his horse, and Denver tugged his burro's rope. With the herd trailing, the two men moved out, knowing that presently and if nothing else happened, Chalk would be along.